Karine

An honest individual
where help is appreciated

David M...

MilHouse Publishing

It's Only Sand

by

David Milne

First published in the United Kingdom in 2009
by MilHouse Publishing

ISBN 978-0-9559269-1-4

MilHouse Publishing
Balmedie,
AB23 8YH
UK

It was a typical late winter / early spring morning, the low winter sun was just dragging itself out of the sea to the south of where he was standing. The white frost lying on the sand all around him gave the scene that slightly unreal feel that he had come to love but the cold was starting to seep into his bones. That was what he got for being out so long in this weather, he pushed back his sleeve and looked at his watch, it was almost ten o'clock and he had been up since before five, out taking photographs by half past. He should have gone away back inside when the second of his two camera batteries had died with the cold and overuse but he had wanted to wait and see the world come to life. It was something he really enjoyed and one of the reasons he still lived here alone. That shift from being alone in the darkness of the night to watching life begin to swirl around him, from here he could see traffic on the main road as it almost all headed north to Granitburgh eleven kilometres away. Looking south along the coast he half closed his eyes and squinted to see through the wind blown sand. The lights were still on in town as it was still, almost, dark. Slowly, he turned his head outward as he looked along the length of the beach at Granitburgh and along the breakwater that sheltered the channel to the harbour used so heavily by the supply vessels for the oil rigs. Along the old stonework of the pier to the lighthouse at the end and out over the grey bleakness that was the sea. It would change soon if some people got their way, they were arguing about a wind farm in the Western Ocean bay. Thirty three, five mega watt turbines, he sighed again, a deep heartfelt sound that showed exactly what he thought about wind turbines at the moment. They were done for the right reasons but in the wrong way, he thought about that for a second, they were not always done for the right reasons. The reduction in harmful emissions was accepted within the power generation phase, but the efficiency was less than twenty per cent and the life span was usually half the energy payback period, so the current generation of wind turbines needed to be balanced with a nuclear power plant to be efficient and to function as originally planned. He smiled to himself as he heard the engineer who had explained that to him do his Michael Caine impression 'not a lot of people know that' it had been a bad impression but he had smiled anyway. He had learned a long time ago that some people were more fragile than they appeared. Add to the details of the turbine the fact that they all were built with a government subsidy that the public were ultimately paying for and it really didn't stack up. One day he would need to write a book about it; mean while he was going inside to have a shower, a cup of coffee then maybe sit down and sort out the photographs he had just taken so that there was a resource showing what this place had looked like in its wild and desolate days before it was destroyed for profit.

Bending he picked up his camera bag and slowly he dragged his feet out of the small sand drift that had built around his ankles in the few minutes he had been standing there, before turning to look inland. The place had been described as barren before now and he did not really agree with that: empty of people, yes; barren, no. He looked around at the evidence of life that lay all over this piece of landscape, what they sometimes called links land and sometimes called dune slacks, it really depended on who was speaking and it said as much about the speaker as it did about the landscape. His problem was he used both words equally and so that made him difficult to describe simply. He smiled to himself; that was normal; he had no fixed opinion and was willing to listen to most people if they were realistic and honest. It was the ones that didn't tell him the truth that annoyed him most. He was fortunate in as much as he could make things fit his view of the world a lot of the time due to who he was, maybe not a good description, but he knew what he meant. He shrugged as he walked on past the Victorian ice house that had been used to store the salmon that they had netted on the beach. Almost invisible now, buried under sand and grass; it was only because a part of the roof had fallen in years before that it was visible to most people. He had seen it due to the funny shape in the ground it just did not look natural to him. He shook his head, maybe it was not a good description of himself but to be honest he did not know how to describe himself, he just was.

He just looked around at where he was physically standing, that was the bit most people could never understand, he did actually love it here and that was why he stayed when what had happened, had happened. Most people would have gone somewhere warm and out of the way, he did as well but only for holidays, this was his home, he was happy here and maybe more importantly, comfortable. He walked on slowly past yet another dark trickle of water as it leached what colour it could out of the small amount of dark soil that overlay the sand here, the small stand of willow that was the only tree that could grow here sighed and rustled as he passed by, sometimes it was almost as though it spoke to him. That was something he did not say out loud, that was a good way to get locked up. Acres of land lay here visited only by specialists, photographers and a small spread of people who bothered themselves to come and look. It was a site of special scientific interest or SSSI as it was better known but most people did not know what for, it wasn't on their doorstep and it didn't make them a profit so they weren't interested. He was cynical he knew that, but with good reason, he kept himself to himself, also for good reason, one day someone would find out about him and things would change, until then however he just kept his head down and carried on doing what he wanted when he wanted. He glanced up at the bank where his house sat, almost a hundred feet up; it was beautiful to him but looked a little odd to most people. A flash of light reflecting from glass caught his eye from about half way along the row of houses that were his nearest neighbours. Smiling to himself he raised an arm and waved, it would only be old Jock, keeping his eye on the world as he thought he needed to. Mark kept on walking as Jock pulled back, surprised at being seen so easily and quickly, how did he do that? Mark looked up again at the houses. A row of five houses, or more accurately a row of four houses and a since converted store, that sat end on to the sea just about three hundred yards from his house which they had originally been built to service. That had been a problem for a few people as well. The houses dated from the early eighteen hundreds while the coastguard station, which was now his house, only dated from nineteen fifty four or so. It was simple, it had been a replacement station, that had made it easier to convert when he first bought it almost twenty years ago and then to extend about three years ago. He smiled as he crossed the last fence and stood on his own driveway and looked around before turning and walking slowly up to the house. He could almost feel Jocks eyes on his back as he stepped up to the front door and let himself in.

+

Jock stood in his garden and looked around him the binoculars hanging around his neck as he watched Mark cross the fence and disappear towards his house. He sighed and wondered had he really seen him or had the wave been a joke? He would never know but it was pretty obvious that Mark knew he watched the area. Jock stood there thinking about how long they had known each other. It was almost twenty years ago that the younger man had bought the old coastguard station. Jock shook his head; he had been an auxiliary coastguard in his younger days so he knew the building and he had been amazed that anyone wanted to live there. It stood a little further up the hill and caught all the weather that was going, had a decent view though, Jock had to admit. He shook his head again and wondered at the determination Mark had shown, he had moved in immediately he had bought the place even though it was borderline habitable; then he had stayed there while he did all the work himself to make it into a decent little house. Jock shook his head as he looked up at the house again, he really was not sure what to think about it now Mark had extended it again, and anyway what did he need a house that size for? He lived alone now.

Jock turned round and looked along the row, next to him was the store or as it was now known Number One Coastguard Cottages, occupied by little George and his wife and child. The child was thirteen and a right obnoxious little brat. Jock hesitated, it was possible the kid was okay really; after all, he thought all children were obnoxious; it seemed to be an occupational hazard of being a pensioner. Then it was his house, number two, that annoyed him, it had been number one since it was built until Jimmy the farmer and owner of most of the houses at that time had, had the store converted to a house and changed the numbers of them all to suit. Next was surprisingly enough, number three, that was Pete and Mary a couple with a good looking daughter, unfortunately the daughter, Phyllis was her name, had moved away to London to live and work. She and her habit of sunbathing in the garden had been the reason Jock had bought the binoculars in the first place. He shook his head as he remembered the time he had seen her sunbathing topless, he had been all set to go and speak to her when he noticed Mark had been there too, never had seen if they had followed that through or not. He just shook his head again imagining what he hadn't seen. There were another two houses in the row but to be honest they didn't matter, he would go inside and write his little note for the lassie that had asked for info and when he gave her that in the pub tonight he might get a bit more than the one hundred pounds he had been promised, if he was lucky. She was a pretty girl after all, and single.

+

Mark was sitting at the kitchen table with a mug of coffee just relaxing and warming up for a little while before he would go for a shower, his boots were sitting dripping quietly onto the sheet of newspaper by the back door and the house was other wise pretty silent. There was a faint whistle as the wind blew around the outside of the structure but compared to outside it was silent; he liked the silence. That was one of the reasons this place had appealed to him. He thought back to the day he had viewed it before buying the place, it was a Monday and the closing date for lodging an offer was the Friday. It had been a howling gale with sand blowing in the wind along with some salt sea spray and his brother and his girlfriend had come with him. They both liked the location but hated the building, he had loved the location and seen the potential in the building, add to that, the item he could not tell them was that he could buy it without a mortgage.

He looked at the clock. Mandy, his cleaner, would be here soon if she was on time. She didn't realise it but she was his best way of keeping in touch with the outside world, he didn't go out much, and as far as he could tell, she didn't stay in much. They had a good laugh together and she was good for him as well as doing a good job for her cash. He opened the laptop and

4

plugged in the card reader just as the door bell rang, he sat where he was for a moment, waiting to see what happened. "Hallo, just me." Came the cheery call from the front door, It was Mandy, just as he had expected, he just grinned but didn't get a chance to reply before she bounced into the kitchen, her presence made him smile as he looked at the bright, smiley, twenty something as she looked at him and said "Cold out there today ehh?" she walked past him and checked the kettle had enough water in it before she switched it on "But I'll bet you've been out there for hours already anyway" She glanced sideways at the boots sitting by the door, She smiled to herself, it made her life easier but she had never figured out what it was that made a man do that sort of thing by himself. She was as certain as she could be without sleeping with him that he wasn't gay so that ruled out that possibility. It wasn't that she hadn't thought about it or didn't fancy him; it was more that the chance just had not presented itself. The kettle clicked off and as she picked it up, she shrugged without thinking, it wouldn't do if she slept with all her clients suddenly she gasped as the hot water splashed over her hand. She ran it under the cold tap to make sure there was no burn while he watched, she had never heard him move, he was just suddenly there, at her shoulder and very tenderly took her hand out from under the stream of cold water after a few minutes and patted it dry with a clean towel. "My Granny always used to say you should rub butter into a burn." He just shook his head "Not a good idea" he said "all you are doing is cooking it if you do that." He raised his head and looked her in the eyes as he continued "You've already done all that you can do as first aid, but" he smiled at her and she blushed a little as she realised he was still holding her hand "you're not burned so you should be okay." He let go her hand and turned away quickly as he felt the colour start to come to his face, he was a little embarrassed as well.

+

Pete wasn't feeling too well as he sat at his desk, he wondered about what his doctor had said to him the other day when he had gone for some tests. He had told Mary there was nothing to worry about, and he was probably right but he just could not shake the feeling that there was something wrong. He had always been a grouchy git but now it was worse, maybe just as well he had an office to himself.

Meanwhile at her work, Mary was struggling to concentrate on her job; the open plan layout of her office did not help her concentration any but there was nothing she could do about it. She essentially worked alone even though she was in amongst a large crowd of people so no one around her really knew what she did or cared what she did. She really wanted to be at home in case Pete went home early again.

+

The TV in reception was tuned to the news channel and they were busy doing a story on global warming as Peter Barnard stood there waiting for his appointment, he felt a little uncomfortable in these surroundings. He should be perfectly at home he thought to himself as he looked around at the deep carpet and the quiet quality of the surroundings, that was tempered with an edge of the brashness of the 'poor boy done good' type mentality. He smiled to himself and decided to relax, it may still be the same continent but Granitburgh was far enough away from Glasgow that no one would have heard of his failure over there. He still smarted at the thought of it. It had been such a good development, that it could have failed before it got off the ground had never even crossed his mind.

"Mr Barnard" said the voice behind him. He turned around to see a short man greying hair and a six inch parting, there was an arrogance in the man that he could see from here but he was not what Barnard had been expecting, he had thought he was meeting an American, this man was local. "Yes" said Barnard as he stepped forward and almost held out his hand but at the last minute he noticed the other man had his hands behind his back. The little man smiled as he looked at Barnard and wondered what was so special about this one before he spoke again "I am Marcus Dull the owner of this establishment" Barnard smiled to himself as he thought 'well named' but snapped back to attention as Dull continued "If you follow me I'll take you to meet Mr Crawford" Barnard nodded as the little man turned away, he shrugged and followed on. He glanced over his shoulder at the TV as he walked away, he would have liked to have seen the rest of that report; it was beginning to look as if there might be some basis to this global warming thing after all.

Andrew Crawford was six foot four and lean with that plastic smile so beloved by Americans and despised by the rest of the world, Barnard winced as the bigger man crushed his hand and patted him on the shoulder. "Welcome, come on in" he said as he dragged Barnard by the hand into the room and dismissed Dull with a quick glance before continuing "I've been looking at some of your previous projects and I like what I see." Barnard glanced down at the table where Crawford had been sitting and saw the front sheet of the petition for dissolution of his company before the brown cardboard cover slapped in place over the top.

6

+

Not far from Marks house, actually only about three or maybe four hundred yards away, was where Paul Gray was standing. On the top of what they had called the escarpment when they had shoots here last year. He looked down at the flat links land and onwards to the dunes that gave his estate its name and stood between the links and the sea. He looked slowly up and down the coast; from where he was standing it was almost true that all the land he could see was his. The houses to the north weren't his although he had thought they were included when he bought the estate five, or was it six, years previously. He sighed, a deep heartfelt sigh, as he tasted the salt in the air. He did not want to leave this place but he had a feeling deep down that he would have to now. He had been showing some people around for months with a view to getting some sort of deal arranged; now it looked like he had taken his eye off the ball, or more accurately starting thinking with his balls again. He sighed again and he felt his shoulders droop as he turned away to climb into the four by four that sat behind him. It was time for him to go back to the house and meet with his wife and her lawyer as she had 'requested'. How could he have been so stupid? Oh, it had been fun, but had it been worth it? "Time will tell" he muttered as he turned the key in the ignition.

+

Trente Silver was standing on the fifty eighth floor of one of the tower blocks that carried his name on the edges of Manhattan in New York. He was standing a couple of feet back from the glass as he looked out of the solid glass wall of his boardroom, he was confident that no one knew he suffered from vertigo, his arrogance was such that no one could know of any of his faults. Unconsciously he ran his tongue over his teeth, they had never been pretty but then he only smiled with his teeth during negotiations. He grinned the wolf head grin that he had succeeded in getting into the papers often enough that it had almost become his trademark and studied his reflection in the glass, he relaxed a little and stretched running his hand over the bare skin of his head and laughed out loud as he looked up at the ceiling. There were twenty floors of apartments above him, all of which he rented out, before you got to his triplex apartment at the top of the building. Most expensive apartment in New York he thought to himself as he returned his gaze to the city spread out before him. He was not really seeing it anyway he was remembering the simulation the computer geeks had run for him based on the film taken from the helicopter a few days before. It was going to be fantastic once he got it done, it should only take a year or two, the locals were no different than anyone else, basically greedy and stupid, that would allow him to make his money and leave again before it really mattered. He sighed; he would need to wait a little before he could see if Crawford had succeeded in what he had been sent to do.

+

Jenny leant forward and stroked the neck of Balthazar as the great grey gelding shook his head grateful that they were turning inland a little bit, he knew the route by now they had been riding this way for several years now. Jenny thought of this as route number two, they started by going down from the livery to the beach, south along the beach to this point, inland for about a hundred yards, then south across the fields to wards the big house, up the drive, to their own house which was originally the lodge house that sat next the main road, then they would travel south another mile or so parallel to the main road which would eventually lead them in to the city, but long before that they would turn east again and head down past the fishing station and back onto the beach where they would turn north and head back up the beach on their way back to the livery. Balthazar just plodded on and went where he was told, he was content.

Jenny just looked around her at the landscape, it was beautiful, maybe a bit under utilised, but all the more beautiful because of that, the sand was shifting in the wind again. That was something most people really could not get their head around. It was the fact that it moved that made it rare and that was also why it was a SSSI and so at least it would remain. No one could build on it and in some ways that was a problem as well, so many of the local people had had planning applications turned down because they were close to or adjoining the area it was ridiculous, but that was what local authorities were like now. She breathed in the fresh air and relaxed in the warm sunshine until they turned back into the breeze again.

+

Wee George, as everyone knew him, was in a bad temper, most people did not think that was really unusual but it was unusual for him to realise it. For Anne, his wife, to call him at work was bad enough, but to be calling him on the office line to tell him the toilet at home was choked and it was overflowing into the house was even worse. He had to go and do something about this, now.

Mark was watching as the big red truck for the emptying of the septic tank turned up at the end of the row of cottages. He hadn't thought they were

8

due for months yet, suddenly he saw wee Georges red hair bobbing about like a demented rubber ball and he sighed as Mandy stepped up close to him. "What's happening?" she murmured as she leant against his back. He smiled to himself that felt good, but she wouldn't normally be here at this time. He had asked her to stay and chaperone him while a model turned up for some photographs he wanted to take. The model hadn't turned up and hadn't called, he had been annoyed and disappointed until Mandy offered to model for him instead, if he wanted. He had agreed and was glad he had, she was good, better than he could have hoped but he wasn't sure it was a good idea to use someone he already knew as a model. She nudged his back slightly and he replied to her question "Oh looks like wee George has called in the sewage truck for his drains, they weren't due for another few months I thought." He shrugged and turned around with his camera still in one hand and smiled at Mandy. "Anyway, not my problem, I have my own tank and I'm fairly sure Old Jock will be quite capable of finding out what's going on without my help. Mandy smiled and stepped away from him again as she heard the camera shutter click as she walked, she was enjoying this a lot more than she had expected to, that was why she was still here at this time.

Down the road Old Jock stuck his head out the door as the truck reversed past his house towards the septic tank at the end. Wee George sighed as he saw that shock of white hair pop out of the door, this was going to take longer than he had hoped. Jock looked at him "What's up Dod?" George shook his head "I've told you please don't call me that, my names George, I don't answer to Dod. The tank is obviously full it's backing up at my place. As the head of the line it will show at my end first." Jock stared at him for a minute before he replied. "Din' a be daft min. You're at the head o the line, so if the tank was fu' it would be backing up at every one else's place first, no yours." George looked at him blankly for a minute before Jock said "Mind, water flows doon hill no up. Your place is higher than a' body else's so you would be the last to flood." George sighed as he realised the old man was right, he might be a pain but he had plenty of common sense, turning away he muttered. "Now I'll get stung for this all on my own, another couple of hundred pounds I could do without spending right now. Maybe I should just sell the place and move into town after all." Jock smiled to himself as he shut the door and picked up his notebook.

+

Mike was in his element, he had really fallen on his feet when he got this job working for the charity 'Greensword' It fitted his ideals perfectly and let him spend most of his time out on the dunes or that type of place looking for rare plants and wildlife. This place was an oddity though it had taken him some time to understand it wasn't the plants and animals that made it special. It was the land itself. 'Unique in this country' he'd been told and he'd no reason to doubt it. Maybe even be able to prove it merited recognition for the plants as well. He was looking for a plant he was sure he'd seen here before but now couldn't find. He smiled as he remembered almost falling off his chair at the weekend when he was over at his mums' house in Edinburgh and he saw an article in one of the papers about a flower that only grew in two locations in Europe it said. He was sure it was wrong and he intended to prove it. Suddenly he stopped, there were other people here; that was not that rare a happening but a large area was taped off and they had vehicles down here as well, that was not supposed to happen. He would find out what was going on.

Dr Marianne Presley watched as this slightly strange looking guy wandered over to where they were setting up on the sand, this could be fun, these geeks could be a real nuisance, she smiled to herself, some people probably thought of her as a geek. He smiled that was a good start she thought, "Excuse me" he said, manners she thought, another point for the geek "What do you think you are doing?" he continued without waiting for an answer "This is a protected area you need special permits to come in here with a vehicle and don't even think about digging here" The last was said as one of her assistants set down the shovels they had brought with them Marianne smiled at him "Relax," she waved a clip board at him "We have all the permits and permission we need." She looked at him for a moment before she added "Who are you anyway? Not many people would be that concerned about an area of sand." She saw him wince as she said that and wondered if she had just said the wrong thing. He hesitated for a second and dug into a pocket of his parka before produced his small laminated ID card "I'm Mike Simmons of Greensword. We have the government licence to look after this place and your forms should have come through my office to be stamped and approved, otherwise they are not legitimate." Marianne looked at him, not quite such a geek after all, without saying a word she turned the clipboard round and showed it to him, he took it in one hand and looked down at the officially stamped form as she spoke to him "We passed these by your people, its taken us three months to get clearance for an exploratory dig here and that could lead to more work if we find what we are looking for. Please don't turn us away." He looked at her, she was pretty and her team was looking concerned as they looked at him examining their documents. They looked genuine and it was the right stamp on them, it looked like they had been signed off by his boss, he would need to find out about this. He looked at her and handed back the board "I need to speak to my office, they look right enough but I should

10

have known about his." She smiled at him as he pulled out a mobile phone and walked away a few paces, he looked round and watched as Marianne turned to her team "Get everything ready, but don't make a start until we get clearance here. It's taken long enough to get this far let's not go screw it up now." He smiled to himself as he heard his boss's voice on the phone "Hi Mike, what's up? Not like you to phone in on a Monday." Mike grunted for a second "Listen Jim, I've got a bunch of Archaeologists down here with stamped permits ready to dig and I don't know anything about it. Do you?" He could hear a deep breath being taken at the other end and the shuffling of paper. "If that's a Dr Marianne Presley then yes, I signed them off myself at the end of the week. Be kind to her, her granddad was a great musician." Mike missed the humour entirely "Why didn't you tell me? I should have known about this." Was his less than happy reply "Well," said Jim "If you did as you were told and reported to the office for the group meetings on a Thursday you would have known and you would have been the one to sign it off or other wise, but as you don't seem to appreciate that you need to show up here every now and again, I did it. Is that clear?" Jim was not pleased and Mike was a little surprised at the annoyance he had heard in his boss's voice as he closed the phone on a dead line and slipped it into his pocket before walking back to the archaeological team. He smiled at her as she looked at him expectantly "Your good to go," he said "I haven't been in the office for a day or two so it's my own fault for not knowing." She smiled at him a warm genuine smile as he had been honest and not tried to blame someone else. "Are you interested in what we are doing here?" She asked him as she waved her team on and they continued unloading the vehicles. He smiled and stepped over the tape into the area they had cordoned off and Marianne led him across the hard packed sand to the bottom of the inland dune where a small section of stone wall showed through the sand.

+

Arthur looked out of the broken door into the day light beyond, this part of the estate was a long way from anywhere and it hurt for him to walk far these days but he needed water. Picking up the bucket he struggled out into the daylight and fought past the bushes that grew over what had once been a path to his front door. The well was at the bottom corner of this small piece of land and that was where he went, slowly feeling every step as he set his foot down. He picked up the rope that lay there, old and mouldering but still strong enough for what he needed, he might need to go and get a new one soon though. The lid was old and heavy, saturated wood but it slid easily enough on the stone lip of the well and soon he dropped the bucket into the water and pulled it up, he looked into the bucket, clear, clean sweet water he thought. "Pity I don't have any whisky to go with it" he muttered under his breath as he set it down and slid the wooden lid back into place before slowly, painfully making his way back to the remains of the house he had lived in for almost seventy years.

+

Sharon wondered what was going on down there as she saw a group of people inside a taped off area down on the flats. It was still quite a long way from where she was but she might go down and ask anyway, that was why she was here in the first place. The camera lens gave her a little more information; she knew one of the girls from University so she could ask on the quiet in the pub some time soon. Maybe even get an invite to the dig and do a proper piece on local antiquities. She sighed and she could feel her spirits sag as she thought about what her boss would say. All he seemed to be interested in was tits and bums. If she could get a story about some local shagging a neighbour he would be interested, otherwise she knew he would be looking for some 'favours' to let her keep her job. She shivered; she would find work elsewhere if it came to that.

+

Mark looked at Mandy as she slowly stood up from the couch where she had been modelling for him and he held out a robe for her. She was getting shy again, this happened with first time models, they floated between shy and confident. She would be scared the next time she came back here in case he had either changed his mind or wanted to use her pictures for something other than they had agreed. She smiled at him as she turned around "I suppose I had better go and get dressed then." It was almost a question about something else. 'Tempting' he thought, 'but probably not a good idea, too close to home' he settled on saying "If you must" She grinned slowly, not quite sure what he meant and turning walked slowly from the room, knowing he was watching her every step, she turned at the door and frowned as she realised he was in fact looking the other way, packing up the lights he had been using. She flounced a little and stopped, turning back she said "Can I ask a favour?" he turned and looked at her as she continued to speak "Could I do a little washing here, just add it to the stuff I do for you? The washing machine is broken at the halls of residence and I don't want to use a laundrette." He just shrugged "Of course, no big deal" he turned back to what he was doing as he spoke "As long as you don't mind me examining it as I take it in off the line." She laughed as she walked away and under her breath she said "That's what I was hoping for"

12

It was almost an hour later that Mandy eventually sat down beside him at the table to view the pictures he had taken of her and he was ready to show her his best selection of them. She had just finished hanging out the washing and wondered if he had looked at it yet, she didn't think so and that could give her a problem if she wasn't careful. She began to realise she probably hadn't thought this through very well. He noticed she seemed uncomfortable but ignored it as she leaned closer to him. Suddenly he saw what the problem could be; he grinned to himself but decided he was not going to get into that situation, not yet anyway.

It was almost yet another hour before Mandy left to go home, she was very conscious of herself as she went out the front door; she felt her breasts move and wondered if she should nip round and get her underwear off his washing line. She glanced at the house, he was standing in the living room window watching her leave, she was stuck with her first decision, she did not have the courage to go and change it. Thankfully she was only going home.

+

Sharon saw the little old car draw away from the house as she walked towards the bank and she sighed, she had been hoping to introduce herself and maybe get a cup of coffee, she was beginning to feel the cold out here. Suddenly she realised she was falling, her foot was sliding away from her in the moss and slime that overlaid the occasional rock that hid under the low bushes that were the only thing to grow down here; throwing her self sideway she stopped herself doing the splits but rolled sideways and kept rolling, she couldn't stop herself as the ground was soft and spongy with no purchase and everything she touched was wet, cold and slimy, then suddenly she couldn't breath, she was headfirst under water and couldn't get clear. Her feet were tangled in something and she was stuck fast. Panic clouded her vision as she thrashed about, the cold made her want to gasp again but she refused to as the dark brown water was all she could see around her. Her vision was going fast as the cold seeped through her clothes. Suddenly her stomach cramped and she folded in half at her waist, it was instinct but it saved her life. As she buckled, from the intense pain in her stomach her head was pulled up out of the water and fresh air filled her lungs. She ached as she lay there gasping for air on the wet, cold mossy bank by the stream with her head and shoulders out of the water along with her feet, while everything from her chest to her knees was under that dark brown, freezing cold water, that trickled past on its way to the sea. She lay there panting for a minute as she felt her self starting to chill down; all the time realising she could not stay there for long, she looked at her feet and could see nothing holding her there so she turned round and pushing her feet into the water pushed her self back up onto the bank and slowly scrambled clear. She stopped and looked around at the world, birds singing in the blue sky, the sound of grass blowing in the wind and a helicopter somewhere overhead. It would have been a good day to die as no one would have known for a long time. She pushed herself to her feet, she might still die, it was cold enough out here and she was chilled to the bone, she stumbled towards the bank, all the houses were at the top and this would be the fastest way to get help.

Her feet were heavy and she couldn't feel them, at least her hands still hurt, that told her they were still there, she was freezing and still trying to get there, where was she going? She couldn't remember where she was going or why but at least she had stopped shivering that had to be a good sign, she couldn't be that cold any more, actually was there any point in keeping going on? She was tired and the grass and bushes around her looked so soft and comfortable, 'maybe I should just lie down and relax here for a while', suddenly she stumbled and she looked down at her feet, it was tarmac she was standing on, what had happened to the grass? She just stood there and looked around, dazed and confused, it did not make sense, it was almost as though the world was cloaked in cotton wool, she would just go to sleep here and be done with it, figure it out later. What was happening now? How was she moving so fast? It hurt too, something was up against her and it was burning her skin, it was pink and making noise, what was it? She would sleep and figure it out later; too confused to worry she passed out into the comfortable numbness of unconsciousness.

Mark had been standing at the end window to see Mandy drive away and as she had done so he had glanced down to one side and had seen Sharon wandering about down on the links area, between the bank his house was built on and the dunes on the actual shoreline. He had watched her for a minute or two, just to be sure she wasn't a poacher, and then carried on with what he was doing. He had been going back over Mandy's photographs on the computer, deepening a shadow here or removing one entirely there, just minor changes to the work to make it tidier, cleaner and more professional. He had just finished and wandered back through to the living room with a mug of coffee in one hand when he saw Sharon stumbling up to the top of the bank just south of his place, between his house and the row of cottages. There was something about the way she was moving made him look again, an attractive late twenties woman with short blonde hair stumbling around as though she was drunk. Out here she could get hurt if something went wrong. She was stumbling all over the place. He set down his coffee and watched more closely as she fell over in amongst

14

the gorse bushes, she staggered to her feet and almost fell onto his driveway, there was something seriously wrong here. He was out the front door and running down the driveway before he was actually conscious of what he planned on doing. He began to shout but she did not seem to hear him as she stood there wobbling about, ready to fall, he noticed the puddle of water forming at her feet and began to get an idea of what was wrong.

He reached her and touched her shoulder enough to turn her round to face him just as her knees gave way. Reaching out he caught her in his arms. As he looked down at her face he saw her eyes roll back in her head to leave just the whites showing. The water was running out of her clothes and her skin was freezing cold to the touch. "Hypothermia" was the one word muttered to himself under his breath. Inside he found himself in the bathroom with her in his arms, the cold was sucking the life out of his own body as he set her down in the bath and switched on the shower above, warm not hot. Running to the kitchen he switched on the kettle and picked up the phone.

Back in the bathroom he looked down at Sharon and saw her as a person for the first time rather than just a thing that needed help, he dialled the number and wedged the phone on top of the toilet with the loudspeaker on and listened to the phone ring as he put the plug in the bath to allow it to fill up. He unfastened the fleece jacket she was wearing and dragged it off her. It clung to her body like the wet rag it was until it eventually came clear and he dropped it in the wash hand basin just as the phone was answered "Drimmie Medical Centre" said the voice on the other end "This is Mark Rae down at Leyfield farm, I have someone here suffering from extreme hypothermia and need some medical advice now." He almost shouted at the phone as he heard the woman on the other end draw breath "One moment please." He heard the sound of a hand covering the mouthpiece so he set the phone down on the floor and turned back to the girl, he reached into the bath and pulled up a foot with a walking boot on it, he realised he could not unfasten it, there was a length of heavy nylon line tangled around the laces and through the eyelets as he looked closer it was around her ankle as well and being nylon line he could not break it either. He set her foot down and reaching into the bath pulled out her other boot, he unfastened it easily and dropped the boot on the floor as he pulled off her sock, he was shocked at how cold her foot was until a voice startled him, the phone had come back to life. "This is Doctor Jennifer James who is this please?" It was a commanding but caring voice that demanded his attention, so he picked up the phone. "This is Mark Rae here; I live at 'the Look Out' on Leyfield farm. I have a young woman here mid to late twenties who appears to be suffering from severe hypothermia" he paused and the woman on the other end said "Right I know where you are, that's a good start, do you know how to take a pulse?" He nodded to himself and answered the next question. "It's thin and weak, very irregular, skin colour is pale, although I don't know what this girls natural colour is" the doctor interrupted "That's good, does she feel cold to the touch and what are you doing right now?" He nodded again logical questions "She is freezing cold to the touch and I have her in the bottom of the bath with the shower running slightly cool to try and warm her up." The doctor nodded at the other end and looked around at the group of staff who were listening to this conversation and thought, this guy is obviously not an idiot "Right this is what you need to do......"

It was only about twenty minutes later that the powerful red car slid to a halt outside Marks house and he heard the voice calling out through the open front door "Doctors arrived, where are you?" "Through here" he called out pulling the door open as he leant over. He looked over and saw a woman in her thirties wearing jeans and a pale blue polo shirt The doctor stepped in past him and looked down at the woman in the bath who was just starting to come round, still confused and sluggish she was not responding to any of Marks questions. Doctor Jennifer looked down at him "Stopped at her underwear, well done but I need her naked just now, so if it bothers you go and make some coffee please, one for her sweet and white, not too hot and one for me black and strong please." He took the hint and left the room.

A few minutes later he was back and carefully set the two mugs of coffee down on the stool at the side of the bath. Doctor Jennifer smiled at him and asked "Where did you learn your first aid?" he shrugged, "Bad movies and cheap novels" it was stock answer he used when he really did not want to go into anything in depth. She smiled at him and picked up the mug as she said "No matter, I'll maybe find out from you yet. Anyway, looks like you saved her life, from what her core temperature is now if she's been under that water as long as it would appear, she must have been almost dead when you found her. Tell me what happened." Mark sat down as he glanced at the clothes lying in the washbasin and began to talk "Not really much to tell. I saw her out of the front window, wandering about down below, then lost sight of her and when I saw her again she was trying to climb up the bank. Its not an easy climb so I think she did well in getting up to the top, but she was wavering around all over the place so I went out to see what was wrong and she, basically passed out in my arms" Doctor Jennifer nodded as she spoke, "Sounds like a classic case of hypothermia and right place, right time." She looked down at the blonde girl in the bath and asked "Do you know who she is?" He shook his head "I've seen her out walking here before, but that's not unusual, never spoken to her

16

before." Turning he reached into the basin and pulled out her sodden jeans and searched in the pockets for anything that might identify her. Carefully he laid out a single car key, a yale type key that could be a front door somewhere, two ten pound notes and a credit card. The credit card had the name Sharon Grant on it. He smiled and showed it to the doctor who nodded

She turned back to the person in the bath and looked down at her "Sharon, can you hear me? Do you want to try and sit up for me please?" She had lifted the cup of coffee and had a hand behind the girls neck when Mark spoke "What if I got in behind her, in the bath and let her lean against me, that way you may be able to get her to drink some of the coffee?" Doctor Jennifer looked at him and nodded "Take your shoes and your jeans off first." He shrugged and standing up did what he was told. Jennifer stepped back and watched as he stepped into the bath and switched off the shower before he stepped over the almost prone form of Sharon and slid down the end of the bath before pushing her to a sitting position and leaning her back against him. The doctor nodded as she put the plug back into the bath and topped up the water. Mark gasped as the water level rose and Doctor Jennifer smiled at him "Comfortable?" she asked as he smiled back "Warmer than I would like, but I can see why it needs to be this hot" he said as he felt Sharon lean back against him and the heat being drawn out of his body.

Gradually Sharon came back to life, pleased to see Jennifer there and far from certain about being naked in a bath with a man sitting behind her feeding her warm coffee as the Doctor watched. Eventually Jennifer smiled at her "Do you want to try and stand up?" It wasn't as much a question as an instruction and Sharon didn't question it. Carefully she stood up and wobbled with Mark behind her helping her balance. Doctor Jennifer looked around and back at Mark, he nodded to a cupboard behind her "In there, you'll get all the towels you need." She smiled at him and pulled out a couple of towels, before beginning to help Sharon dry herself.

Shortly afterwards the two women were sitting in the living room with Sharon wrapped in more towels as Jennifer decided to try and find out a little more. "So," she said looking at Sharon as she sat close to the fire trying to get warm. "Want to tell us what happened then?" Sharon hesitated a minute then shrugged. "No reason why not." She shifted slightly and adjusted her towel looking at Mark who had just rejoined them having changed his clothes "I am a reporter for one of the local papers, the 'Evening' and I was out trying to see if there was anything happening that was worth reporting, there might be but there's nothing certain as of yet. Anyway I was wandering around with my camera when I slipped on some moss and slid into a stream down there. My feet seemed to be tangled up somehow and I couldn't move at all." She was struggling to talk as she relived the moment her life had almost ended. "I couldn't seem to move my feet to regain my balance and the next thing I knew I was head first in the stream and it was so cold. I just couldn't breathe or anything." Sharon paused and drew another breath all the while Jennifer watched her and Mark sat back and listened closely as she continued. "I lay there in the water for what seemed a long time, struggling to get my face up out of the water and eventually I took cramp and folded in half. That dragged my face out of the water and let me draw breath again." She paused and sipped at her coffee before continuing "I seem to remember eventually getting to my feet and starting to walk but I don't know where I went or how I got here." She paused and both Doctor Jennifer and Mark saw her face change as she suddenly realised something. He smiled at her as Doctor Jennifer glanced at him to gauge his reaction. "My camera," she paused and looked at them both "I had a digital SLR with me, it's the papers, I must have dropped it somewhere. I need to get it back" she stood up as she said this and Mark stood up as well but it was Doctor Jennifer that spoke first "You are going no where just yet, other than to the hospital with me if you insist on this course." Sharon looked at her a little stunned "But, I need to get it back, Grayson will fire me if I lose a camera. He's already warned all of us about that." Mark sighed and looked at them both "Okay," he said standing up "I'll go look for it, I need to get myself sorted out and that will give you time to make sure Sharon is okay" He looked at Doctor Jennifer as he said this before adding "That's assuming you have the time to stay here and do this." She just nodded and smiled "I'll wait, I have no where to go anyway." She waved her hand at him and he took the hint, turning away he left the room. A couple of minutes later he returned and dropped a small two way radio on the sofa. "This will let us keep in touch, just press the button to talk and I'll reply." The two women nodded as he turned and left the room.

He stepped out and walked slowly down his driveway until he found the damaged bushes on the seaward side and slowly began to follow the trail down the bank, looking for the missing camera. It was almost half an hour later that he found the wider bit of the stream where Sharon had fallen in, the broken branches and the moss along with the marks that almost looked like some one had been dragged, showed where she had crawled out of the water. There in the water was the camera; he looked down at it first before he touched it and he could see the power switch was on. He sighed that was not a good sign. Reaching into the water he switched the camera off and lifted it clear letting the water run from it as it dangled from the strap he held in two fingers.

"What have you got there?" The voice made him jump as he hadn't heard Mike walk up, that was unusual, very few people managed to sneak up on him. He smiled, he liked Mike "Reporter fell in the burn here and dropped her camera; I said I would come and get it while she's up at my place with the doctor." Mike turned and looked up at Marks place instinctively "Not seriously hurt is she?" Mark shook his head "Very Cold, possible touch of hypothermia, full recovery expected." He paused and looked at Mike "The new doctor is with her just now, seems to be smart enough." Mike just grinned "Yeah, I know I like doctors but I've maybe found another option." Mark just looked up at him, taking his eyes off the camera that still dangled dripping from his hand. Mike squirmed for a second before shrugging "Yeah I just met her, Doctor of Archaeology, working along there on the site they found years ago, you knew about that?" Mark nodded looking along the links at the corner of a vehicle that was showing from out behind a dune about a mile and a half away, before he spoke "Yeah they were speaking about that a few years ago. Think your lot were stopping it for environmental reasons." He shot a quick sidelong glance at Mike before turning slightly and making to head off "Anyway I need to get this back to its rightful owner," he was about to say something else but the sound of a powerful engine made them both turn towards the track that ran from the opening in the dunes, inland. Mike spoke "Its just Gray the owner of the estate, he's been doing the tour with some bald guy with bad teeth in the passenger seat, looks like he's trying to hide from everyone at the moment." Mike turned to Mark and smiled "seems like the daft bugger is about to get his second divorce. Story is his current wife caught him in a fumble with the new cleaner they've got up at the big house, so he's history and the cleaner will be looking for a new job." Mark grinned to himself as he thought of the underwear hanging on the line at home; he knew who the cleaner was. "Anyway" he said turning away. "Give my best to Marianne please. Speak to you soon." Was called over his shoulder as he walked away pulling the two way radio out of his pocket.

2

The downtown hotel was a small and discreet place for a meeting; the staff knew the rules as well as the expectations and kept their noses out of other peoples business for the most part. That did not mean they were not aware of who was around. The receptionist looked up as the door opened and the bulk of a special branch officer filled the doorway for a moment or two until he stepped in and the bellhop closed it behind him. She watched casually while he crossed the lobby silently on the dark blue, deep and rich carpet. "I believe you have a meeting room booked in the name of Andrew Crawford." She smiled at him "Yes sir we do," she checked the silver pin in his lapel that was the only public mark of Special Branch membership other than the bulge made by the handgun under his suit jacket, before she continued "It's the small library over there to one side and I believe your charge is expected here in about half an hour" She smiled at him as he nodded back at her. They knew one another. His charge, as she called him, had been here several times before. "Can I have a coffee sent over for you whilst you check the room?" he nodded his thanks and pulled a multi frequency scanner from his pocket as he turned away to check the room for bugs.

About twenty minutes later the tall American came down from his room and made his way to the small library, he was not surprised to find the security guard already there, he had been warned this was likely to happen. He didn't think it was necessary. After all he was an American and the man he was meeting was only a small local government official, called himself the President or some other stupid title. Better to remember and be polite though, these minnows tended to get upset if you told them they were nothing.

The meeting had gone quite well so far, they had been at it almost forty minutes and he seemed to understand what the project was going to entail and what they would need from him. However they had not yet broached the subject of what he wanted from them. Crawford expected that to be the next point of discussion. He was not wrong; it took another hour or so of discussion before they had some sort of agreement. The President left a few minutes later followed closely by his protection officers who had not been in the room.

Andrew Crawford leant back in his chair and thought about the deal. Basically they had agreement to do what they wanted, even though it still would have to go through the formal process, they had been promised it would be rubber stamped through. He smiled to himself that would be good, it would keep his boss happy. The fact that the project would grow a lot between what had been agreed just now and the final product was another matter, but that would just have to sit with the Presidents conscience, after all he had an audio recording of the meeting. He looked down at the small cassette that lay in his briefcase and smiled. Multi frequency scanners only worked if you were transmitting something, local recording did not register.

+

The little fat man had waddled all the way back to his desk and grinned to himself as he sat down. The expensive leather chair complained as he squirmed and shifted about until his ample frame was wedged firmly in between the arm rests and he pulled it in about the desk so his belly rested against the pale wood with the leather inlay. He would wait until he got back to his supplied apartment to let his wife know of the increase in their pension fund that would be heading their way. He would not be able to touch it while still leader of the country that much was obvious but that was not a problem, he couldn't touch any of the other funds he had 'collected' over the years either so it would all just have to wait until he retired. He stretched out and picked up the phone, he had instructions to pass on.

+

The chairman of the meeting sat there at the top table looking out at the small hall, there was about twenty people in the hall and maybe another five on the stage, a good turn out for the party. "Okay" he said raising his voice "Close the doors and lets make this a private meeting" The secretary, to his left, leant closer "I didn't think this was meant to be closed, my schedule shows another two meetings before the next closed one" All the people on the dais looked at him as he said "I know, but I've received information from wee Eckie about something coming up that we need to keep close to our chests for a while" The very prim woman on the end made a sound before she spoke very disapprovingly "Don't call him that, he uses Xander these days, surely we should show our leader the respect he deserves" The Chairman sighed and ran a hand over the top of his slicked back hair and turned to look at the woman "My brother was born Alec and will always be wee Eckie to me. It serves to remind him of his roots and where he belongs. He needs to remember that or his own arrogance will overtake him again." He turned back to the group and waited until the last man sat down at the back having closed the doors. Twenty five people in a community of about seven thousand, not really a lot of support for the political party of the government. He sighed again, the pacifism of the people around here, as well as their general affluence, bothered him but this might just help the cause. He stood up and the few voices that had been muttering away faded to silence. "Right we have a point to discuss here so lets go to that and we can deal with the usual crap at the next meeting, this is more important." He looked around the room and no one challenged him, that was the way it should be, but he had not noticed the wince a couple of the others gave when he dismissed the 'usual crap' so casually. Smiling he continued "I was speaking to Xander earlier and he has advised me that a large international developer has approached him with general plans to develop an equestrian centre in this part of the country. It would appear that they have identified the Doones estate just north of here as a prospective site and were wondering if they could count on our support to make sure this went through the planning system as quickly as is possible within the normal channels and restrictions." He had added the last bit quickly; while he spoke as he had seen at least two of the group look up fast. One was against any foreign money coming into the country at all. The other had an almost pathological fear of anyone getting a good deal or a favour, everything had to be done exactly by the book. He would need to remember that when he selected the team to work the planning with the public and the press. He had no doubt 'Xander would be working it from another angle.

+

Paul Gray was sitting opposite his wife who had a small smile on her face as if she knew she had won the argument. He grinned to himself for a second and she hesitated not sure what to make of that, after all he was the one who was being manipulated, wasn't he? She listened closely as he began to speak "Well in order to make the payout your client demanded, I have been forced to make arrangements to sell the Doones estate" He always spoke to the solicitor rather than his wife, it was simpler and she was more likely to listen to him than if he spoke direct to her. She was on her feet and screaming and shouting but somehow it just did not seem real to him. He had, after all, seen her in far more formidable form at other times just in a normal argument let alone a divorce discussion. He leant back and watched, her solicitor did the same, he had obviously seen these types of things before and now let them run their course before he would step in. "Well" he started to speak "Actually, he did have the right to sell the whole place as the business aspect of it is solely in his name, not joint. That means that you are entitled to half of the value of the house but only a small fraction of the value of the rest of the estate." She looked at him with cold venom that he did not understand as she shrugged and made a sound,

22

walking towards the door she spoke over her shoulder "Make the deal, you can send the money where I told you earlier. I will be out of here tomorrow morning and back in New York after that." She stopped in the doorway and turned to look back at the two men. "So long suckers" the door slammed behind her and the noise echoed around the room for a minute or two Paul Gray looked at the solicitor across the table from him and spoke "You know," he licked his lips and paused before he continued "If it wasn't for losing the estate and the house I would almost be glad to see the back of her." The solicitor smiled "Professional integrity forbids me from saying anything," he paused and Paul smiled "but on a personal level. I can see exactly where that comment comes from" The two men laughed and Paul stood up "Fancy a beer while I've still got some in the fridge?" The solicitor just nodded before he pulled out some paperwork for Paul to check and sign.

+

It had gone well, it was silent in the small meeting room at the Wycliffe hotel in the middle of the city, Andrew Crawford had just finished giving the latest of his presentations to local businessmen. They were silent as they digested his comments and for just a moment or two he wondered if he had pitched it wrong. The tall rangy American chewed on his unlit cigar as he waited for a response then Dull, the hotel owner, began to applaud and slowly the rest of them joined in. He may be well named but he was useful at times, this pathetic little man. Crawford looked around the room, if this was the most resistance they were going to get then this one should be easy and the boss would be happy enough to pay him his bonuses as agreed. That was rare, he began to smile and Dull obviously thought that was his doing as he seemed fit to burst with pride at his achievement. It had been his idea after all to get all the businessmen together and tell them how great an idea it was before the public knew anything about it. That way there would be no resistance worthy of consideration. He was proud of himself, not a bad days work for the bar porter who had married the bosses daughter.

He sidled over to Paul Clancy, the man generally recognised as being the leader of the cities business community, the head of at least two of the organisations that told the businessmen how to vote on what issue and what to believe, of course all information was screened for accuracy before it was released to them . He looked down on Dull, more than physically, as the odious little man began to speak "I think that went quite well don't you?" He didn't reply, pushing Dull to come to the point and let him get away from him. "Do you really think there will be as much business in this for us all as they say?" The taller man carefully pushed Dull to one side of the room before he replied "Keep your voice down when you discuss things like that. There are some people here who may have supported this to begin with but are getting suspicious now that they have had a chance to look at the figures this second meeting may have been a mistake." He glared at Dull who knew he had messed up "We have to keep this going, it has a momentum already, if we can maintain that once it goes public we will have no problems and then, you, me and a few others here will be able to retire on our cut of the short term profits." He patted Dull on the shoulder even though it made his skin crawl to touch him. Smiling Paul Clancy turned away and catching the elbow of Andrew Crawford guided him to the bar and began to speak softly so that no one else could actually hear what was being said. Dull looked on in fury at being excluded from this conversation. He would find out later, Crawford was staying here after all.

Later in the evening, Crawford didn't actually tell Dull anything at all, but it took Dull almost an hour to realise that. The conversation had meandered around a number of topics before it finally ran out of places to go and Crawford made his escape back to his room. He looked at the time and decided it would probably be safe to make the call now. He hesitated, he had been Vice President of the corporation for several years now and he still was wary about talking to the boss. He sighed and picked up the phone.

Dull did not think he was a stupid as most other people believed he was, otherwise, he would not have bugged certain rooms and made sure that those were the rooms used by the people he wanted to monitor.

The call would have bothered anyone of a civilised nature, so it obviously did not bother Dull, it went something like this.
Silver answered the phone knowing who it was that was calling.
"Morning Crawford, went well I assume?"
"Of course sir, no problems, all as expected" Crawford smiled
"Sheep" was the response from his boss, Crawford waited, he knew the way his boss spoke and an unexplained word was often explained or you were meant to know what he was talking about.
"A bunch of sheep; they believed everything you told them?" "Yes not a murmur" was the reply from Crawford. He could hear his boss chuckle on the other end of the line, it was an unnerving sound. There was a sigh and his boss continued "Used the script you were given?" "Yes, exactly, word for word" He could hear Silver nodding on the end of the line "Okay, I will pay the kid that wrote it and we can see about getting started." Before

Crawford could tell his boss this was just the start of the process he had hung up. Slowly he set the receiver down as he muttered to himself "This is going to turn into a complete dump if it goes wrong in the slightest" Dull waited a moment or two before he switched off the recorder and closed the panel in the back of the wine cellar. Picking up his glass of Beaujolais he turned and walked slowly back to reception thinking the whole time about what he thought he had heard. He did not understand the bit about the script being used, but the bit about his hotel becoming even more of a dump than it was at the moment bothered him a lot. He sat down in a corner of the bar and finished the bottle as he did most evenings, alone with his imagination.

+

Sharon drew up at the end of the building and climbed out of her car before walking slowly to the door, she was nervous, it was late afternoon and she did not know what sort of reception she was going to get here. The house looked quiet even though the car was sitting out front, well, it wasn't really a car it was an old land rover that had seen better days. The door bell echoed inside the house and she thought she would wait for a minute or two. It was beautiful out here and the silence made a nice change from the housing estate up in Drimmie where she stayed with her parents. She heard the door open and turned, surprised, she had almost given up on him being at home. The smile was broad and genuine as she spoke "Hi, you might not remember me but I'm Sharon Grant, the last time you saw me I was almost dead, cold and naked in your bath." He laughed "Well that is some introduction, but in fact the last time I saw you, you were clothed again and leaving in such a hurry I really did not think I would see you again." He paused and looked at her again, "Come on in, I'm pleased you came back." She smiled and walked past him into the house, it was warm and as welcoming as she had remembered it. It was quite amazing just what bits she could remember and what she could not, but she felt comfortable here with him, after all, he had saved her life. He looked into her blue eyes and for a moment felt uncomfortable but he shook that off quickly and did what he usually did when looking at a pretty woman, he smiled.

It was about a half hour later while they were sitting at the kitchen table drinking coffee when he made a decision. "Are you busy tonight or do you want to stay for dinner?" She felt the blush rising in her face and looked at her cup. "I would love to," she replied "but first, I have to return something to you." Rising she disappeared out to her car and came back in carrying a plastic bag. "Your clothes, that I borrowed the other day; I've washed and ironed them for you, so thank you again. I would have died without you and I don't know how to thank you for that. My parents also want to thank you but we don't know how." He looked at her and realised she was crying as she spoke. "Hey" he said "no need to cry and no need to thank me. It was my pleasure. Anyone else would have done the same as me and anyway" He reached out and lifted her chin "Anyway, how else was I going to get someone as good looking as you in my house let alone in my bath." She was bright red in the face, but starting to laugh as she stepped forward and threw her arms around his neck "I forgot for a second" she said "you've already seen me naked. I've nothing to hide from you." He laughed softly in her ear, she felt good against him. "You can hide as much as you want from me. All I'll say to that is you are beautiful."

+

It was a select group of the councillors that met at the Chamber of Commerce building that evening, Dianne looked around carefully it was quite apparent to her after a few seconds that all the councillors here were members of the planning committees, that was interesting in itself. She would wait and see what was about to be said, there was obviously something happening but it really had to be done carefully to prevent a few people getting into trouble.

The wine and canapés were freely available to all as they gathered in the foyer awaiting the start of the presentation, she was a little vague about the actual details of what was to be discussed today, she realised as she studied her invite. She jumped when John touched her arm. He was the chairman of the planning committee and although he was a member of the right wingers party, a reasonable sort of man with whom she often discussed a few things. "Do you know what this is all about?" he asked quietly, Dianne just shook her head as she looked around "Seems to be quite a group; all of the planning committee, all of the separist group, a couple of independents and the usual suspects from the Chamber." She looked around and spotted someone else standing with Paul Clancy the Chairman of the chamber and Marcus Dull, Owner of the Wycliffe hotel "Don't know him though, do you?" John watched for a minute or two "No, I don't know him but he doesn't seem to want to say much just yet; although he is waving his phone about a bit." Dianne looked over at him and asked aloud "Wonder if there's a camera in that phone?" John looked at her startled "You are a suspicious sod aren't you?" They both just smiled and looked away from the tall American. "Hmmm" was the sound Dianne made as she looked back at the tall American again, now he had put his phone away. "He looks very familiar, I wonder if this is about changes to the planning law, to speed it up." John looked at her nodding slowly "That is possible, I had forgotten about the change to the legislation that's planned." He sipped from his glass, obviously thinking through the implications "If he is who I think he may be then we should not be here." He turned and guided Dianne, off to one side a little further "I heard a rumour that the Silver Organisation is wanting something in Europe, you know the resort and hotel people? If that is the case and they are here to make a presentation then it is wrong as I am sure you are aware." Dianne was nodding to herself, horrified that anyone could be so blatant. "Lets sit at the back" she said to him "If that's what this is then we can leave as soon as it becomes apparent." John nodded and they both turned round as Dull began to speak. "Good Evening Ladies and Gentlemen" it was almost comical, as from the back of the room as all they could see of the little man was his hands waving in the air above the crowd. He carried on speaking "Thank you for coming along this evening to what I believe is a very exciting presentation that will soon benefit us all and this country we love. If you would care to lift your glasses we can move into the main hall and listen to Mr Crawford and Mr Clancy describe the benefits that will arise from this work." He stepped aside and the mass of people began to move past him into the main hall. John hung back and touched Dianne's arm "Crawford, isn't that name of the second in command of the Silver Organisation?" Dianne shrugged "I've no idea, but this whole thing does not smell right at all. I'm sitting next to the door." She nodded to one side and John looked in the direction she indicated. Another blonde woman had arrived carrying a large cardboard box and it looked as if she was being berated by Crawford being late. The crowd flowed past them almost as though they did not see the little scene being played out.

Danielle had just made it in time after putting the DVDs in the folders and getting the stuff from the printers as they shut the door. She had walked in smiling at her triumph but that was short lived "Where the hell have you been?" was the greeting from Crawford, she was surprised but replied "Well, I just got the stuff from the printers, I came here as fast as I could with it. What did you expect?" He was furious "Don't answer back, you can be replaced. You had this stuff early today you should have made sure it was here before any of these people began to arrive." She opened her mouth to respond but the look on the Americans face warned her off. She was smarting from that, she was one of the best PR consultants in the area and that was why they had hired her. To now be told she could be replaced did not sit well with her. She could just walk away from it; but no, she decided, this was too big an opportunity and she did not have the courage to just walk away because this guy was an asshole.

+

Sharon drove away from Marks place that evening happy, she was confident that he was a decent bloke and she'd been invited back at the weekend for a barbeque with some of the neighbours. She was looking forward to that, it might even be an opportunity to see if she could get her job back, she sighed a little and wondered if she should have told him she had been fired anyway, she thought back to that day and wondered about it again.

Once her camera had dried out Mark had scared her stupid and Doctor Jennifer had also watched in horror as he had taken it apart and cleaned every single little element of it before making sure it was clean and dry before putting the batteries back in and powering it back up. The two women were amazed and Sharon in particular was ecstatic as it clicked and made all the right noises before he handed it back to her fully working again.

It had been the following day that the meeting had been called at fairly short notice, considering the reporters normally filed their stories electronically so they had no real reason to visit the office. She had taken all her gear as the phone call had told her to but she had been surprised when she saw that it was all the outlying reporters that had been called in, not just her. She shrugged to herself as she drove home, it had made no difference anyway, they had basically split them into two groups and the two deputy editors had taken a group each into a room and spoken to them. Her group seemed to consist of those who had already been warned about providing stories that were not 'juicy enough' or similar and they had all been fired on the spot, no consultation., no discussion just goodbye and leave your passes at the front desk.

She smiled to herself; she was actually a good bit happier than she had been now that she had thought about it. She had not realised it but although she loved the work, she hated the pressure and the deadlines along with the leering attitudes and suggestive hints of the staff at the office. Now she was free to do what she wanted, she just had to figure out what that was.

+

Dianne had only stayed in the meeting ten minutes and she had seen enough to know this was an advertising meeting in many ways and she did not want to be part of it. John followed her out about five minutes later, the two of them looked at each other and nodded. There really was no need for any further discussion but John began to speak. "Interesting to see how many of our impartial colleagues" he smiled to himself "are still in there and show no sign of leaving the meeting yet." Dianne just nodded, she could not bring herself to speak. They were out in the car park, saying their goodbyes when another six councillors walked out to join them. They all looked a little shocked and were about to start to talk to one another when John raised a hand "Not here, not now. Let's wait until next weeks full council meeting where we can raise the matter and discuss it in full council." The group nodded and Dianne said "Yes, lets be sure to follow protocol because I have a feeling that will be used against us at some point" It was only silence that met her comments as the men just nodded and the sound of gravel crunching underfoot was the only thing breaking the stillness of the evening as they all went their separate ways. All of them were very sombre as they each, separately, looked back at the building hoping to see more councillors walk out of the large double doors.

+

Peter Barnard was uncomfortable as he sat in his office, the temperature was good and the furniture more than acceptable what made him uncomfortable was not even the fact of what he had been told to do, even though it would have made most people uncomfortable. It was the fact that he was having to do it from his office back on the east coast. Technically his business had been wound up and he had no real right to be here either but he had no place else to go that would not cost him money he did not have. What bothered him more was the fact that was a lot of unhappy people around here; unhappy with him that was. That was actually the reason he drove here at six AM and let himself in after parking his car inside the shed and locking it in so no one would know he was here. He was a fugitive from his own failure. He stopped for a minute and thought about what his sister had said to him the other day. She had warned him about working for Silver, the comment had been failure makes a man strong if it doesn't break him, but it also meant he could be gotten cheap. That had hurt, he knew what he was getting paid, it wasn't a lot; it wasn't enough but it was all he could get. He sighed and thought about it for a second, well if he did a good job he should be able to get a pay rise out of them, they said they would be generous if things went their way. Leaning forward he checked his watch and picked up the phone before starting to dial.

+

The small group gathered in her living room, quietly arriving in ones and twos so it would not be obvious there was a gathering. The cars parked in the street were a little obvious but no one would notice that, surely?

Eventually she looked around the group of eleven people there were at least another four that should have been here, they were all in her party and involved in the planning process at different levels but they could not be trusted that was why they were not here. The ones in the room were the only ones she could really trust, that was a wide phrase and not entirely accurate. Most of the people had been in the room at the Chamber of Commerce earlier in the week, but only she had had a private meeting with Andrew Crawford the previous day and a very productive meeting it had been too. She smiled to herself as she looked at the people in the room and thought about those who had not been there the other night; they were loyal to the party and that meant to her, or at least it had better mean that now or she would have to see about expelling them from the party. Suddenly she wondered about those not here, she would need to keep a diary to make sure that expulsion would be simple when it happened as it was bound to.

A quick head count to make sure every one was here that should be here then she smiled at the group and drew breath to begin her speech.

+

Wee George was the first to actually get the phone call, he was interested as well, might be just what he was looking for to let him make the moves and changes he was wanting to make. He looked at his wife they might not always get on that well but she wanted to get into town and to be honest so did he, even if it was just for their son. He turned to her "Karen, that was an interesting phone call." She looked at him and waited she could never tell whether or not he was going to be talking sense or rubbish, it varied so much day to day, but he was smiling so that was a good start. "That was a guy wanting to buy the house, said he'd had a look at the outside of the house last time he was on the estate and wants to buy a holiday home here. Would we be interested?" She smiled at him "Good timing for us. What did you say?" He laughed as he turned away "I said we might be, but he's coming round Monday night to speak to us and maybe even make an offer. Lets just wait and see what Mr Paul Brown has to say for himself" He stood there looking down the garden, this could not have come at a better time for him he thought. He was smiling as he just stood there, lost in thought.

+

Mary and Pete also got a phone call that afternoon but that did not take nearly as long to discuss. Mary just caught the end of the conversation as she walked into the room "....No, we're not interested. We've stayed here

30

almost thirty six years now and have no intention of moving so the answer is no." Mary looked at him as he put the receiver down and turned round "Who was that?" He shrugged some guy called Brown wanted to buy the house as a holiday home, been here shooting a few times and wants to buy a place in the area." He shrugged as Mary made to leave the room "He'll need to find somewhere else, he's not getting our house." He sighed at her and handed over a glass, Mary sighed but took the glass away to refill it anyway; he drank too much these days.

+

Further along the row the same little scene was played out again in Carol and Andy's house. The phone call sounded the same but it was Carol that took the call "Well I am pleased you are interested in our property but we are quite happy here at the moment." She licked her lips and let a variety of thoughts run through her head. She had seen the vehicles and had heard some of the rumours, this might actually be financially worth while but not just yet; the best thing to do was to be the last person to sell.

+

Old Jock, didn't get a call he didn't need to get one, he had met the guy Crawford one day when he'd been up at the big house helping remind John the plumber where all the main valves were in the stable block, and his 'special little deal' had been done then. He was happy with it and was sure it was a good deal, the problem was he was an old man and really did not know very much about the current value of property or how little he had really been promised. It sounded a lot to him and bought his loyalty, for just now anyway, but then he had always been easily bought. He smiled to himself as he looked around the place.

+

The councillor began to speak to the group of eleven other councillors in the room. "This is a closed meeting under the terms of our own party rules." She stopped and glared around the room, once she was sure they were all listening, closely, she continued "that means nothing discussed here can be discussed with anyone not present here today." A couple of people exchanged glances and shifted, uncomfortably, in their seats as the import of that sank in "We are here to discuss the possible development that Andrew Crawford hinted at the other evening at the Chamber of Commerce." There was silence around the room for a few moments as a definite ripple of unease passed between the councillors until Janette spoke

31

"I thought we were not meant to make any commitment to any project before a full council meeting?" Marlene smiled at her in what she hoped was a forgiving and understanding way, it actually looked like a deaths head grimace but it was the best she could do. "Well, Janette, you are new to this so the confusion is understandable" she smiled again and cleared her throat "Sometimes opportunities arise that we must grasp for the good of the communities that we represent. It is at times like these that we realise that all the rules that are put in place to prevent the 'run of the mill' applications being dealt with unfairly actually hinder the special application, like this one, the once in a lifetime opportunity that will never be repeated." She paused and leant forward for effect "This application will be one of those once it officially exists, until then we must do everything in our power to make it as attractive as possible to the other councillors who either were not at that meeting or left early." She paused and licked her lips slowly "We must prepare ourselves to neutralise their effect on the public otherwise we will lose this opportunity." The silence in the room was almost palpable for a minute or two until someone said "But some of them are members of our party." She just nodded "Hence why this meeting has been designated as closed in terms of our own rules." She glared defiance around the room and one by one they all looked down and by doing that they agreed their silence and collusion.

3

Mark had a definite feeling there was something up in the newspapers round here lately, he couldn't see it but both the Evening and the Daily, imaginative names for a paper but that was what they were called, seemed to be working towards something. He just couldn't see the target yet, he usually found it quite amusing seeing which way these two failing local papers tried to manipulate the information that was fed to the public around here. They were both owned by one organisation but seemed to fight against one another all the time. Sometimes, like today, there was the one story in both papers, today it seemed to centre on the need for a way forward after the oil had run out. Mark laughed to himself at that comment, he knew a lot of people in the industry who kept telling him there was oil in the Western Ocean for the next fifty years. This place was rapidly chasing Aberdeen which was recognised as the European energy capital and was, in reality, probably the oil capital of the world although Houston in Texas, USA seemed to be clinging to the idea that it was the oil capital of the world. He shrugged to himself, that was a detail that could be resolved by other people another day. He shrugged and wondered about the strange phone call he had received yesterday evening from someone wanting to buy the house. He had been here for a long time and intended being here for an even longer time, he had said no. There was something bothering him about the call, it had just sounded wrong somehow. He stretched and padded through to the living room and looked out down his drive way as he called it, three hundred metres of tarmac was a lot of driveway but then the coastguard people had a habit of doing things right and while it was a small country, things could be a long way apart. He was just standing there looking, not seeing when the phone rang again, he jumped and moved away from the window to answer the phone. He was less than happy when he heard the voice and approach on the other end of the line "Good Morning Mr Rae, I am calling from Skyline investments, a private banking group that has reason to believe that you may be interested in some potential future investment opportunities in your area. Would that be correct sir?" Mark almost hung up but something was intriguing him about the call "It may be of interest, can you tell me how you got my number, it is ex directory after all?" The voice on the other end hesitated and he could hear the reply was being thought about "Well sir I'm sorry about that but I cannot release my sources at this time. However if you are interested, I can have some of our specialist advisers call you back and they may be able to give you that information as they discuss the opportunity with you." Mark only thought about it for a second "Okay have them call me back today if at all possible." He could hear the relief in the voice of the salesman on the other end of the line as he said "Thank you sir, I will see to that immediately and I hope we can look forward to a long and fruitful partnership with yourself sir." Mark did not get a chance to answer as the man hung up on the other end of the line. Quickly he dialled the phone company system and listened to the electronic voice tell him that the last caller had withheld their number. He was not really surprised at that but was wondering how they had his number, he had been very careful about that over the years. Slowly the handset slithered round in his hand as he stood there, thinking about what was outside the window until the bleeping sound from the handset caught his attention and he set it back down into the cradle.

The door bell and the cheery shout told him Mandy had arrived again, he had neither seen nor heard her car as he had been looking out the other window, he smiled to himself as he turned round and called out "In here, Mandy." The door creaked a little as she looked in, slowly peeking around the door "Come on in, I'll not bite you. I just want to talk to you for a minute or two." She looked a little worried as they sat down side by side on the sofa and Mandy studied her hands as Mark began to speak. "I want to clear up some local rumours about what's happened Mandy" He looked at her and was about to continue to speak when she said "I'm sorry, I only told one of my friends about the pictures, I never thought she would tell anyone else." Her head turned and she could not see him through a veil of tears as she struggled to speak but he spoke over her "Don't worry about that, more likely to do you harm than me. I'm big enough and ugly enough to deal with that. If I wasn't then I wouldn't take pictures of girls in their under wear, or less." Mandy began to grin but said "Well," she paused "If it's not that, what is it? You're not going to fire me are you? I need the job." She was now in a panic and Mark had to put his arm around her to calm her down and as she felt him pull her in she knew she wasn't going to be fired. She could feel him draw breath and exhale as he sighed and she was astonished at how hard his body was, there was more muscle there than she had realised. Finally he spoke "I am sure you have heard that Paul Gray is in trouble again" Mandy looked down at the floor and her tears began to fall silently as Mark waited on a response of some kind, eventually Mandy spoke in a soft hushed voice. "Yes I know, and you know it was me that got caught with him I guess." She sighed and raised her head at last to look him in the face "It was embarrassing having his wife walk in like that, all we were doing was snogging and he maybe had a hand on my boobs but that was it." She stood up and walked away from him "I needed the money and it seemed simple enough, I just never thought it would be that

34

embarrassing." She stopped speaking as he looked at her and thought "Well, I'm quite happy for you to keep working here anyway. I don't actually care what you get up to anywhere else, as long as I know the truth, then I can deal with any questions that get thrown in my direction, which will happen as long as folk know you do work for me." Mark paused and thought about what else he was going to say as he drew breath "Also if you need the extra cash I'm more than happy for you to model for me again at some point if you are willing to." She smiled up at him "I would love to, that was fun. Scary but fun, not really sure I could do that for anyone else." He laughed as he looked at her red face and realised that was not what she had meant. He wondered for a second and decided to ask the question in his mind "Were you paid to sleep with Paul Gray?" Mandy looked down and he could see the tears starting to fall "I was paid to get into a compromising position with him. That's what the guy said, he didn't actually say sleep with him and that never actually happened but if it had worked out that way, then I would have done it." She looked up at him pink in the face but defiant "Five hundred euros before you ask." Was her last comment as she made to walk past the sofa towards the door, but he reached out and catching her wrist pulled her down onto his knee. "Was it worth it?" He asked as her token struggle faded away "I don't know" she said as she tried to snuggle into him. It only took a second for her to realise he wasn't after that from her. She sighed and carried on talking "It cost me my job there and him his marriage and as I didn't even get laid, I would have to say no, it wasn't worth it." He was watching her and he could see the realisation start to sink in "This will always be with me now won't it? I'll always be the girl who turned whore for a few hundred euros." He sighed, she had been acting earlier but he wasn't sure any more, at least, not right now. "Well," he started to say "I'm not going to tell anyone it was you and I'm definitely not going to tell them about the money." He looked at her "That's up to you at this time. My position might change but there's a very good chance that no one will believe me anyway. He didn't notice what she was doing, as he thought about what else he might say, so that her fingers were winding themselves into his and easing his hand further up her leg. "Any way," he said "whatever you tell people they will make up their own version, it'll last about fifteen minutes than fade away like the storm in a teacup it actually is." She looked at him as she held his hand on her thigh. "Are you sure about that? I mean that people will forget." Mark nodded, he was aware his hand was sliding further up her leg and was not sure this was a good idea "People will remember from time to time but if it doesn't directly affect them they will soon forget." He squeezed her thigh as he became aware of the heat of her body through her jeans "Just make sure and don't tell them. You know I wont tell anyone but you didn't need to tell me about it either. Especially the money bit." Mandy blushed as she pulled his hand tight up against her body and closed her legs to make it difficult for him to pull it away. He grinned at her and flexed his fingers "What are you like?" he asked as he did this and she looked at him through those long eyelashes "Fancy a fuck?" she breathed at him "I wont even think about charging you." He laughed as she kissed him and he kissed her back, hard, taking her breath away before he said "No Mandy, tempting as it may be and lovely as you are, it's been too long since I took a woman to bed." He didn't get to finish what he was saying as she pulled her tee shirt over her head and said "Who needs a bed? The floor or this sofa will do me." He pulled her close and was amazed at the softness of her skin under his hands as he held her tight to stop her squirming. Eventually she stopped and they both sat there breathing hard looking at each other, it was obvious she did not understand as he tried to explain "Mandy, I think you're a great girl with a fantastic body but right now I don't think it would do either of us any favours for me to take you to bed." He swallowed and tried to carry on talking as he slackened off his grip and she eased herself back a little so she could se him more clearly. "I am more than happy for you to keep cleaning here and if you want to model then that's good as well, but I don't want to make love to you right now." She nodded and stood up before she said anything. "I think you should tell your cock that." He shrugged "Some things I don't control" She smiled and nodded "Fair enough, okay. I'll keep doing what I've been doing and will model for you if you want me to, any level you want." He nodded, knowing exactly what she meant as she carried on. "Would you object if I do my work around the house, in either my underwear or naked or something of that sort?" He shook his head as he looked at her smiling face "You know how to make things difficult for me don't you? Okay, do as you see fit, but I'm not responsible for visitors at the door, okay." Mandy smiled at him again as she stepped back and began to unfasten her jeans.

It was the 'phone ringing that made him drag his eyes away at the critical moment and allowed him to stand up while listening to an almost naked Mandy giggle as she watched him pick up the phone. It was Skyline Investments again. This time the voice was different, older more mature and definitely not local, maybe Canadian. "Good morning sir. I am calling on behalf of Skyline Investments and must apologise for the call you received earlier. While we did mean to call you, the person who actually made the call to you did not have all the information that he was supposed to have." Mark just nodded and grunted as he watched Mandy disappear out of the room carrying her clothes and smiling from ear to ear. The voice on the other end of the phone was still speaking "We actually represent a former neighbour of yours who owned some property in the area and mentioned to his family that you might be interested in buying it if they ever wanted to sell." Mark was paying full attention now and was glad Mandy had left the room. The voice continued "We have been retained by his surviving family to sell the following property parcels on their behalf. The properties are number four Leyfield Cottages, which is a..." Mark interrupted "I know the building; I am interested in purchasing it, if your price is right. What else do you have?" The man was obviously taken aback by Marks forthright attitude but gathered himself and said "Well, we have another cottage nearby but I can't pronounce the name of it its something like Ruriadh cottage." Mark smiled "It's pronounced Rory cottage, I know it, please carry on." He could hear the smile come into the callers voice as he said "and there are two plots of land, one of forty acres and one of eighty seven acres." He paused and Mark could almost hear him lick his lips as he said "Would you like me to send you a full set of particulars for these please sir?" Mark hesitated for a second. "Can you give me a ball park figure for the package please?" Silence for a second as the man on the other end considered the question "Our package price would be three hundred and fifty thousand dollars sir as our client would like to sell quickly and a single buyer would be beneficial to that." Paul smiled to himself and made a noise, Hmmmm, before saying "US or Canadian dollars?" The man hesitated "US sir, I am Canadian and very few people pick up the difference but I am in London at the moment and my clients are in the US. I was coming to see the properties this week perhaps I can visit you with details at the same time?" Mark thought for a second "Yes you can, fly over as soon as you can. I will meet you and we can discuss the situation. Meanwhile you can email or fax me the details of the properties including the location of the land packages please."

A few minutes later Mark was heading along the corridor to the fax machine which was in his office and he stopped as he looked into the open door of the utility room and found himself looking at Mandy's clothes lying in a pile on the floor. He shook his head as the fax machine began to buzz. What was she playing at? He shook his head as he thought that, he knew exactly what she was up to, he may not be certain exactly where she was right now but he knew her game, he had seen it before and he was not playing. It had happened to friends who never seemed to learn. That was why they were on wife number three or else four, Mark had lost count and almost stopped worrying about it.

The fax machine had a pile of about twenty sheets of paper waiting for him and the phone rang again as he was reading page five, it was the same man. "Mr Rae, I just wanted to check that you had received the documents." Mark nodded and said "Yeah I got them. I'll pass them on to my lawyer and get him primed up to check the ownership and that the deeds are sound etc; while I go and examine the properties myself to see if they are of use to me. When will you be here?" The man hesitated for a second "I am on a flight this afternoon and should be able to see you tomorrow morning." Mark nodded to himself "Okay 'phone me in the morning and we'll arrange a meet." He hung up the phone without waiting for a reply and stood up again to look out of the window, suddenly it struck him he did not know what had happened to John McIntyre, the former neighbour who had owned all of this land. He had lived in number four just down at the end of his drive before he emigrated to Canada to be near his family, They had not kept in touch much more than the occasional Christmas card but they had at least tried, Mark was sorry he had gone without notice locally, he had been a character and had been missed, but obviously not for long. Mark sighed and straightened his shoulders before heading to tell Mandy he was going out.

The battered old Land Rover looked a mess but it ran perfectly and kept on going in all weathers. Mark knew there would be people looking down at him from the windows of his lawyers office in more ways than one as he ambled in, just in jeans with a battered brown envelope under his arm. The receptionist lowered her gaze to look over her glasses but the voice came from behind her as his solicitor appeared out of his office "Mark, good to see you. Come on through." He turned to his secretary "Hold my calls would you please and I'll be available when I'm available." She looked at him frostily and offered him an escape route "You have Mr Jones due in shortly" The solicitor hesitated before smiling "He can wait for a few minutes" and shut the door Mark grinned at his old friend as they shook hands and they started to talk without preamble.

"You don't come here very often, must be important." Mark nodded at his friends opening gambit. "It is Steve, maybe you never knew John McIntyre but he used to live just down the road from me?" The lawyer shook his head "Well he moved away to Canada a few years ago and I got a call this morning from some guy claiming to be from a company Skyline Investments, I think he called them" Steve, the lawyer, started to scribble quickly as Mark continued "Anyway, he told me old John had died and his family had some property they wanted to sell, would I be interested." He handed over the envelope of photocopies "I said yes and he quoted a batch price which seems reasonable to me. I'd like you to have a look and see what you think. I'm going to have a look at them and meet him tomorrow. I'm interested in buying them." The lawyer looked at the property particulars in the envelope and the notes written on the outside and nodded "I think you'd be an idiot not to be at that price. Go do what you need to do and I'll look at the deeds and see what I can find out about Skyline

Investments, maybe speak to you tomorrow?" Mark nodded as he turned away "Speak to you tomorrow" was all he said as he ambled out into the reception area and nodding to the receptionist vanished through the fancy glass doors. The lawyer sat there and watched his friends back as he sauntered away and wondered what was going on now. There was almost always a second game with Mark; that was what made it fun working with him.

+

Meanwhile back at the house Mandy stood there, naked as he had left her, looking out of the office window. This was the one room Mark had always said she was to stay out of, that was why she always came in here. Still, being naked just added to the thrill of doing what she had been told not to. The windows looked down past the row of cottages and over the bay to town. There was a flash of light from one of the cottages and she looked more closely at the cottages where it had come from but couldn't see anything other than a vehicle moving along the road that ran past them. She watched as the car moved along the track and turned up onto the end of Marks driveway to come to the house where she now stood. 'Must have been a reflection off the car' she thought as she stepped through the house, pausing at the utility room to pick up a large baggy tee shirt of Marks before heading towards the door. As she walked along the hall she saw a pretty blonde woman with short hair walk past the end window heading towards the front door.

Mandy stopped at the hall mirror and wiped a hand across her face, smudging her lipstick and mascara. Hands went up and tousled her hair quickly as the doorbell sounded through the house. It rang a second time before Mandy stumbled to the front door and opened it slowly peering around the edge for a second or two before apparently relaxing and stepping back to let Sharon see Marks tee shirt was all she was wearing as the cold, fresh, air affected her body. Sharon was surprised to see this girl there.

"Sorry," she started slowly "I was looking for Mark, is he in?" Mandy stretched and yawned before she replied, making sure her boobs bounced as she relaxed, "No sorry, he slipped out of bed early, left me sleeping. Don't know where he is. You can come in and wait if you want." Sharon looked surprised as she stepped back "No, thank you. I'll maybe call later" She turned and ran back to her car as the sound of the door slamming rang in her ears. In her car she found her hands were shaking as she fumbled for the ignition key, breathing deeply she spoke to herself as she manoeuvred the car down the driveway and past the houses barely noticing old Jock as he jumped out of the way of her car as she couldn't really see through the tears running down her face. "Calm down" she told herself "There was no agreement, no promises. Just a lot of hope on your part Sharon, you're being unfair and unrealistic" She was breathing deeply as she tried to get herself under control "No reason for him not to have a girlfriend." Suddenly she stopped "If I had been the girlfriend and a strange woman turned up asking for my boyfriend. I would not have invited her in and would have been asking for her name at least." Sharon began to think as she had been taught to do rather than react and it was a clearer headed Sharon that spotted the old Land Rover turning in off the main road and decided to wait and speak to Mark directly.

+

Old Jock had been almost physically drooling as he saw Mandy standing at the window through his binoculars, it had been a long time since he had seen anything like that at all. So pretty and so close, he had been desperate to get up to Marks place and see if she was as welcoming as she looked, he had been so desperate he had almost not heard the car and been about to step out of the door when it went past. The fact it had been another woman had made him hesitate until he had decided to go get a closer look, just in case there was something to see of course, then he'd almost got run down again as the second girl had left. Now he was back inside arguing with himself whether he should go up and knock on the door or go back upstairs and try the binoculars again. The binoculars won.

+

It was a cold morning even though it was bright and clear and Marianne stood there shivering as she watched her team work almost silently, scraping away with trowels and paint brushes to clear the dirt and earth of ages from the artefacts they were finding. This site was a treasure trove of late Neolithic / early Bronze Age stuff, almost a time capsule as she had described it to her boss the previous day. She smiled, a good find in the area could mean research grants and work for years to come. Mike wouldn't be happy with all the people that it would bring in to this protected area but that would have to be accepted for a while at least. If they worked together it might work well at securing the area against too many trampling feet or even worse, the wheels of quads or motor bikes. She shuddered at the thought as one of her team shouted and began to wave frantically at her. She began to amble over to get a closer look and see what all the fuss was about when suddenly she saw what it was and broke into a run, a rare event for an archaeologist. She bent over next to where her student was kneeling and pointing and froze in shock. "Get the camera and

40

all work slows down." She straightened up and turned away as she continued speaking "I'll phone the university and get the tents along with some specialists." As she walked away she saw Mike walking towards her, threading his way through the puddles and sand drifts. She smiled, it was good to see him; he listened and seemed to understand the passion that drove her. His was for plants and animals whilst hers was for old and dead things. She grinned to herself, better not let her boss hear her say that. He might think she was talking about him.

+

Arthur shivered as he slowly sat up in the bed, it was cold and he was feeling it now, all the way to his bones. He looked around himself, the room was clean and the house could be kept warm if he once got the fire lit again. He had let it go out yesterday and now he had to light it so he could cook on top of the stove or he would be going hungry again. Slowly he got dressed and shuffled out of the bedroom into the only other room the little house had. He smiled as he looked at the door shut securely in its place in the wall. That young man had done a good job for him and refused to take anything for it. Arthur wondered what he was after, he was sceptical enough to think no one did anything for nothing so he did wonder about it, but he was grateful as well. He shuffled into the larder in the corner and sniffed at the milk bottle before starting to make his breakfast.

+

Dr Jennifer sat up in the bed and looked at the clock and wondered what she was going to do today. She knew she should go and see if she could find somewhere to stay, the bed and breakfast was comfortable enough but as she was wanting to build a life here she needed something more permanent than a room in a B&B. Slowly she slid out from under the duvet and made her way to the bathroom.

+

Sharon had stopped crying and had wiped her face before Marks Land Rover drew up along side her little car and he slid the window back to speak. He smiled down at her and said "Good to see you; weren't looking for me were you?" She nodded still not sure she could speak as he continued "Lucky I came back just now then isn't it? Going to come back for a coffee?" She smiled and started the engine of her car "I'll follow in a minute, once I get turned." The vehicles moved off indifferent directions and the man with the camera lowered that long lens and wondered what was happening as the breeze rustled through the gorse bushes that bloomed around him.

Mandy was just heading to her car as Mark rattled to a halt in the Land Rover. She carried on and unlocked the door as he said "Everything all right?" She smiled and shook her head at him. "All fine, not even any visitors. I'll maybe even do a lap dance for you next time I'm here." He shook his head as he walked towards the house "You're not going to stop trying are you?" She laughed out loud as she opened her car door and stepped in "Always keep trying, until I succeed." He hesitated and watched her drive away, something was not right with the way she was acting. He shrugged his shoulders 'probably just stress with the situation she's found herself in'. Inside he went through to the office and picked a note off the fax machine as he half watched her drive away out the road. He noticed Sharon's car come out from the farm buildings and head this way after Mandy had passed, almost as though she was deliberately avoiding her. He put down the fax and watched as the two cars went in opposite directions and stood there wondering what was happening. He looked even more closely as he saw a figure step out of the bushes in front of Mandy's car. The car slowed and stopped as the figure stepped around to the side and got into the passenger door. He wondered some more as he remembered she always kept the doors locked in her car. She drove away and up onto the main road and out of sight as he watched and only moved a moment or two later when the door bell rang. He carefully set down the paper in his hand and went to let Sharon in. She didn't look comfortable as she stepped inside, she was smiling but it wasn't entirely convincing, he kissed her on the cheek and said "Coffee or tea? Come on through here" and led the way to the kitchen, watching Sharon over his shoulder as she looked around herself while following him. "You're girlfriends gone then?" Mark looked at her for a second "I don't have a girlfriend at the moment. Mandy who we passed on the road is my cleaner and such" He turned and looked at her more closely "Why?" Sharon shrugged. "Just got the impression she was your girlfriend when I was here earlier, unless you let her sleep here sometimes." He just looked at her and didn't say a word, her eyes dropped and she shuffled a little "I, I mean…" she stuttered "it's none of my business but when I was at the door earlier she gave the impression of having just crawled out of your bed, the way she spoke, her hair was a mess and her make up was all smudged; looked like you'd had a good night." She was looking straight at him now, challenging. He was watching but thinking about what she had said as he spoke slowly "It is entirely up to you whether you believe me or not, but I am telling you the truth when I say I do not have a girlfriend and have not slept with a woman for over five years." His eyes focused on her and she swallowed "I'm sorry it's none of

42

my business," she was blushing and stammering as she spoke "it's just, you've had me naked in your arms, in your bath and I'm being stupid. You were kind to me and I maybe hoped for more." He watched as a tear trickled down her cheek as she kept her face pointed floor wards he swallowed and thought for a moment before reaching out to her and pulled her close against him. "First, I am flattered. You're a beautiful and intelligent woman so that massages my ego. Second I have not slept with Mandy. Third I don't intend sleeping with Mandy; and fourth it is none of your business and I have no reason to justify myself so I don't know why I am saying all of this to you." She sobbed a little as her arms slipped around his chest and she pushed her face further into his shirt as he sighed and just stood there holding her close.

+

It was that night in the local pub before old Jock got to pass on his information. He had been in the bar, as he often was, when he leant back on his seat close to the fire and looked along the counter. The dim light and other people in between made it difficult for him to be sure but that looked like Danielle, the little blonde from the estate office, standing along there but he couldn't see who else she was with. It was another blonde girl, he could tell that from the back of her head, but that was all. He raised a hand and waved, she smiled and turned back urgently to her friend as he sat back. He knew some of his friends had seen that and they would automatically assume he'd had her, he was good with the women after all.

A moment later Danielle slid into the empty chair opposite him at the table "Got anything for me?" Jock looked at her "Plenty in my trousers if you want to come home with me." He leered at her she just made a noise of disgust and started to stand up "Easy, easy" he said "nae need to act lik 'at. Ah'm jist funin'." She hesitated as she interpreted his accent and sat down slowly again as he produced a notebook and slid it across the table. She let it lie there until his hand had withdrawn again. Flicking open the cover she looked down at his surprisingly neat handwriting while he began to speak "Basically Wee George in the end hoose will sell in a flash, Mary & Pete in number three winnae sell, Number four is empty but belongs to a guy in Canada, he'll sell jist to get some cash back. Number five, Carol and Andy, well Carol is a snob but will sell if the moneys richt." Danielle raised her head from where she was listening to him while reading his notes. "What about the other ones, down below and behind your place?" Jock laughed and sat back sipping his whisky before picking up the almost empty glass of stout that sat on the table. She sighed and murmured "Oh for goodness sake." Turning she caught the eye of the barmaid "Can we get another round for Jock here please?" A slightly surly nod was all the response she got as she turned back to look him in the eye. He sighed and set down the glass again "Well, Mark, up the hoose at the back, winnae sell and neither will the guy who owns the bigger bit along the end doon on the flat. It's been in his family for years, so nae chance there. The ane at the bottom o' the bank will if ye can get them drunk. Sober and ye can forget it. The wan in the middle will an aw'. They're young and want to move on. So they'll sell." Danielle looked at him. For an elderly farm hand it was a surprisingly detailed account of people and their motivations. He smiled at her "Fowk ayeways hae reasons to do things. Figure oot the reasons, fit maks 'em tick and you guess fit they'll dae in certain circumstances." She nodded and reached into her hand bag and produced an envelope, sliding it across the table she said "Well done, more than I might have hoped for. If we need anymore we'll come and speak to you" Jock swallowed the last of his drink and picked up the next glass "You can come and see me anytime, sure I cannae tempt ye?" She looked down at him before saying "Not if you were the last man on earth." Quickly she settled her bar bill and slid out of the bar and in next door, into the lounge, she got to the bar and looked around quickly before ordering two glasses of wine and disappearing off to a booth where Paul Brown was sitting, nursing a warm, empty, glass, waiting on her.

+

Arthur was listening as he stood there, the sound of his gate was unmistakable and the footsteps coming up the path scared him. There was a crunching noise as something was set down followed by the same again, then a clatter as something else was dropped, before the footsteps went down the path and the gate squeaked and clattered once more before a noisy 'clattery' engine started up and a vehicle drove away. He shuffled as quickly as he could to the door and opened it but couldn't see anything to begin with until he looked down next to the door. There, sitting against the wall were two bags of coal and a bag of kindling for his stove. The grin that spread across his face was a sight to behold as he nodded to himself, he was sure he knew who was helping him. He didn't know his name but he knew who he was.

+

In a very expensive office block 'Xander was speaking to his minions, just the close, trusted and influential minions who did exactly who they were told of course. He smiled to himself as he looked at them all hanging on his every word, or they had better be. He continued speaking "We all

44

appreciate the oil in the Western ocean has made a huge difference to the wealth of our country and will last for many years yet." He looked around the small gathering making sure he had eye contact with each and every one of them before he carried on speaking "However we also need to remember the larger picture here where one day the oil will run out, the platforms will be decommissioned and this will all just be a memory. We have a large influence in the financial sector at the moment and I see no reason for that to fail, but can we trust to just one industry or should we have an option, a second string as it were? Does this not make sense to you all?" He did not need to ask a second time as the murmurs of assent came from around the table. He smiled, this was going well. "We also have the environmental argument, we have to protect the landscape for our descendants. Make sure the country is fit for them to inherit and a safe place to live as well as enjoyable place to play." He hesitated, this was where it could become difficult "We need to develop a new industry one that does not exist here, in this country yet." He could see a little more interest in some faces as he studied them. It was Templeton, the Minister for economic development and finance that spoke "What do you have in mind?" 'Xander smiled again; if he had not known it was orchestrated he would almost have believed it was spontaneous. "Simple," he said "Golf" There was silence for a few seconds as what he had said sank in before a voice came from the far end of the table "Are you daft? There are hundreds of golf courses in this country already. It's hardly an economy saver." 'Xander looked down at Johnstone, effectively marking him for execution as he continued talking "Not just Golf courses but whole resorts, hotels, driving ranges and other sporting facilities tacked onto the side; a complete package with conference facilities, world class facilities, quite feasibly the best in the world, here in our country."

Johnstone was shaking his head "That is a waste of time. Scotland is the home of golf and is not far away. They have hundreds of courses, very few of which are profitable. The ones that are profitable are only just, and that is because of the additional development. We have several hundred golf courses in this country already and to build more means nothing; without some unique selling point it is just pointless and destructive." He sighed and moved in his seat as his colleagues sat passive and silent as he gathered his breath, he knew he was on thin ice here with 'Xander as he called himself now but then he could not buckle if he wanted to mount a leadership challenge. He continued "To give it even a hint of possibility of it happening before the next election you would need to have a deal already lined up with a developer and that would mean corruption." He paused and knew he had just gone too far before adding "I don't think anyone in this room could be quite that stupid."

It was in 'Xander's office almost an hour later that Templeton spoke, nervous and uncertain "Did he know? Do you think he knows? Does Johnston know?" 'Xander slammed the door and waddled past him to the desk. "Calm down." he almost shouted "the only person who actually knows anything is you. So stop blabbering and greetin' and pull yourself together or we will actually be in trouble." Templeton looked at him and his eyes narrowed "Yes," he said through pursed lips "You would be, wouldn't you?" 'Xander froze and his voice rose almost a whole octave as he hissed "What's wrong, a million dollars not enough for you? Remember I know where it came from and I can show where it goes. You have no evidence against me, so be careful." He paused and looked at Templeton "Remember I know where all the rest of it is as well, other wise you would never have stood down for me would you?" Templeton looked away, he could not stomach this much longer but, now, he had to stay until at least the next election. He sighed; his villa in the Maldives in another name looked even further away now. Where had he allowed himself to go so disastrously wrong?

+

It was the next morning that Steve the lawyer, was still sitting at his desk looking at the email that he had received yesterday evening while he thought through the implications of it all. He really could not fathom out what this meant and he had taken it a step further than he had been told to. He had a survey report on one cottage, the other one was hard to find and the deeds for the land were clear but the boundaries were not actually visible on the ground. At least that was what the surveyor had said in his report. He sighed and reached forward for the telephone.

Mark lifted the receiver on its second ring and was pleased to hear Steve's voice. The cheery Glaswegian had never lost any of his accent in the years he had been staying here and was almost as broad as some of the locals, but just different some how. Mark only thought about it for a second or two before Steve began to talk. "I have good news for you and some simple news, not sure if it's good or bad as well as some puzzling news. What do you want first?" Mark laughed to himself as he said "Give me them in that order, the good, the news then the puzzling." The other man shrugged though no one could see him "Okay, it goes like this Number four is empty was tenanted and valued at well over the asking price, I would snap it up and put a tenant in it, we have a list here of people looking to rent houses in the area." Mark nodded and smiled to himself as he said "Okay, that sounds good, what about Ruriadh cottage?" Steve drew breath "Slightly different,

46

very run down but appears to be occupied and no answer to the door, but again would almost certainly be worth more than the asking." Mark nodded silently keeping this mornings information to himself as Steve continued, "The land is difficult to find and is not clearly marked on the ground but again the description in the deeds is good and the title is sound to both plots." He paused and licked his lips, listening to the man, who was both his friend and his client, on the other end of the line breathing as he thought. "Okay what's the puzzling bit?" Steve sighed "Well, as far as I can tell Skyline Investments, is actually owned by John McIntyre, your ex pal and there is no record of John McIntyre's death anywhere that I can find." He heard Mark sigh before he spoke "Right Steve, go ahead with the deal, buy these through my company Paradigm Properties and add it to the portfolio, we might shift some of it later." Steve could almost see his friend running his hand down over his face as he thought before continuing speaking "I know about Ruriadh cottage so don't worry about it, buy it and view it as a life rent property. The land I have seen and located, I also have in my hand a document from Skyline, their representative was here earlier today and gave me a sheet with the GPS coordinates of the corners on it. I am happy with that, so just go ahead with the deal and tell no one about it please." Steve hesitated "legal registration?" Mark almost laughed "Of course do all of that as usual. I just see no reason for anyone to know that I control Paradigm Properties." Steve shook his head "Little chance of that, it's kept far enough away from you to be safe I would think. I'll get on to this right away." They said their goodbyes and parted each to get on with their day.

Mark sat back into his chair and looked at the documents he had in his hands, they were complicated but logical. Just like John McIntyre had been, he dropped the papers on the desk and began to think about the older man. He had been a friend and an influence; he had helped Mark through his bereavement and had made sure he didn't become a drunk. They had been friends but there were still large dark areas about John that he may never know anything about. Like his family for instance, as far as Mark knew there had been none, then out of the blue he was going to Canada to live near them and now he was dead but he wasn't. He smiled to himself; sure it would all sort itself out in time. He glanced at his watch; he had agreed to meet Sharon up in Drimmie shortly so he had better get going if he was going to make his appointment.

+

Dr Jennifer was tired, she had been house hunting for a few weeks now and had seen nothing that she liked. She walked aimlessly around the lawyer's office looking at the pictures of flats and small bungalows in housing estates built in the seventies or eighties. Not her style at all she thought as she walked to the desk and waited on the receptionist finishing her phone call before she looked up and smiled. "I know this is a long shot, but you don't have any other properties for rent do you?" She looked adown at the woman who was looking over her glasses at her as she continued "Something larger, out in the country preferably and yet not too far from Drimmie if at all possible. I would be willing to do some renovation work myself if that was necessary." The woman smiled "I know there was another one property just coming in, let me check but first how many people was it for?" Dr Jennifer felt her shoulders sag as she said "Just me, I'm on my own." The woman nodded and looked at Dr Jennifer's hands, she was too slow at covering the white mark in the skin on the third finger of her left hand and the woman just gave a little small smile before disappearing through an office door at the back. Jennifer stood there and listened to the muffled conversation that went on for a few minutes before the door opened and the receptionist reappeared followed closely by a man pulling on a suit jacket. He smiled at her and spoke in a soft Glaswegian accent "Hi, my names Steve but that's irrelevant. What does matter is we may be able to help you. I'm actually just in the process of completing the acquisition of a property that will be coming onto the rental market shortly, might be up to a month by the time we get it decorated and such but it sounds like it might be exactly what you are looking for." She was relieved and relaxed a little as he said "I'm just going out there, want to come and have a look?" Her grin spread even wider as she nodded.

She was amazed as she followed his large black saloon car slowly down the farm track towards the sea. She had been here before, recently. They parked side by side, end on to the row of cottages and she glanced up at the square flat roofed building a couple of hundred metres away and shaking her head followed the lawyer along the front of the row of houses. Past number one, number two and number three. He stopped in front of number four and pulled an old fashioned steel key out from his pocket and held it up "Now," he started "I haven't seen inside this house yet but have been told it needs work." She just grinned and shrugged her shoulders "Lets have a look; I'll soon tell you if I'm interested." Inside the house was on three floors with one room to either side, a large hall at the front and another room behind the stairs at the rear of the property. The first floor had the same layout while the top floor had coombed ceilings, skylights and was split into three rooms. She was amazed "It's a lot bigger inside than I thought possible." Steve nodded; it was a large house for one person but needed a bit of work. He looked at her and wondered if she had the money to pay the rent on a place like this. He would ask Mark when he spoke to him next; she caught him off guard as she looked out one of the skylights at the back of the house "What about the guy that lives up there? What do you know about him?" Steve hesitated "Marks been here for several years now. It must be about five years ago that his wife died from a brain haemorrhage, sudden and unexpected." He paused and Jennifer could see him thinking back before he continued "Decent bloke, never seems to work too hard but works smart instead." He caught himself and looked at her "Anyway, shouldn't gossip about my clients, but I think you'd like him." Changing the subject as he headed back toward the stair he said "What do you think of the house?"

+

The university was buzzing with the news of what had been found out at the Dunes estate; it had to be kept out of the press for as long as possible. They had to get the facts before they spread any rumours, with what had been muttered about already, this could cause all sorts of trouble. Dr Marianne was grinning as she walked along the hallway from the labs to her own office when her phone went. It was the principal 'requesting' an immediate meeting. She smiled this should be good, he liked good news and obviously would be upset that she hadn't told him immediately, that she could handle because he would be happy when he found out what they had discovered.

The Principal's PA wasn't smiling when she got there and that made Marianne wonder, but it wouldn't be serious, that much she was sure of. Marianne was still smiling as she was ushered into the office, but not for long. He didn't get up before he spoke to Marianne and he didn't offer her a seat either, he just started to speak "Marianne, I understand there have been some finds on the site out at Doones" She grinned, just as she thought he was worried about being out of touch, not knowing about the latest news so she started to tell him. "Yes, that's' right. It's very early days yet but it looks like it could be the most important Neolithic come Bronze Age site in the country, we've got mixed burials covering hundreds of years and signs of industry over almost the same period. Its fantastic, should really help our funding claims for next year." The principal sat back and looked at her, silently for a moment or two, watching her excitement as it cooled quickly as she realised that was not why she was here. He sighed as he sat forward to rest his arms on the desk "It did have the potential to be one of the best things to happen to this area but I think you've ruined it now. What with starting on the dig without the necessary licenses or even worse the permission of the landowner, you've really done a disservice to both this university and your self." Marianne just looked at him "What do you mean? Paul Gray the landowner has always been supportive of our attempts to learn from the past. I may not have gotten specific permission for this dig but he has given us *carte blanche* to go ahead and dig as necessary as long as we don't interfere with the operation of the estate." The Principal sighed as Marianne's voice faded away. "Well, Marianne, I've just had a representative of the owner in here and he has stated that no permission to dig has been given due to no permission being received from *'Greensword'* that means you are digging illegally on private land without any permission." He leant back in his chair again as he continued "That means you are bringing the university into disrepute. I cannot allow that. You will go home now, consider yourself on indefinite suspension until further notice. I will have the site closed down today. Now go there is no further discussion on this matter." Marianne left the office in a complete daze not really knowing what to do or say. In the outer office the PA did not even look up as she walked past.

Another shock awaited back at her department as she got there to find the university security personnel had already cleared her office of obvious personal effects and handed her the brown cardboard box along with her coat at the door. Her students and staff watched in horror as she walked alone between two security guards, through the building and out into the street. Looking around she realised she had nowhere to go and no one to speak to.

+

Down at the dig, Mike watched, perplexed as the students and the team covered some of the finds with sheets and began to fill in the trenches before taking down the tents and other structures they had erected on the site, no one wanted to talk to him. "Come on guys, speak to me, what's going on?" He seemed to be ignored for a while until one of the students set down the box he was carrying and turned to look at Mike "As if you don't know. Dr Presley has been suspended after the landowner complained that no specific permission had been granted and no *'Greensword'* licences had been approved, so you should know all about it." He picked up the boxes and turned back to what he was doing as Mike stood there dumbfounded.

One of the other students was looking at him, almost sympathetically. "What's wrong?" she said "Never realised the university could act so quickly? She trusted you as well as liked you, and you do this to her project." She stopped and looked at him standing there shaking his head "or did you?" He stared at her for a second or two "No, I didn't, as afar as I

50

know your licenses are still valid, so stop what you're doing and leave the gear on site." The student who had spoken to him first said "Can't, Principal has told us to close down the site and clear it. So we have to, even if your right he won't let it continue, that would mean he'd have to admit he was wrong." Another one said "That won't happen, but your proving the licences were genuine might get the Prof. her job back." Mike looked at her and nodded as he walked away pulling his phone out of his pocket. "Jim," he said into the phone "Is there any problem with the permits for the Doones estate job that I asked you about the other week?" Mike could hear his boss sit back and think before he answered "No Mike, the only problem I've seen or expected was from you when you found I had signed them in your absence. Why, what's up?" Mike sighed and turned back towards the group all of whom were standing watching him "Well Jim, these guys are packing up, they've been told that the permits aren't valid and they need to get off the land." There was silence on the other end for a moment or two. "That is stupid, it must have come from the landowner, nothing to do with us here. As far as I'm concerned the dig can carry on. You're the area representative so if you are happy for it to carry on then it can." Mike nodded "Thanks Jim, I'll go and see the landowner and see if he knows anything about it."   The students were talking amongst themselves when he walked back to join the group and the girl who had been speaking to him earlier turned to him again and said "Thank you for that, we really appreciate it, but who would do this?" Mike shrugged I don't know, but I'll go and speak to Paul Gray now, he owns the Doones estate at the moment." Paul Gray opened the door himself to Mike and looked both surprised and pleased to see him standing there. "Hi Mike, what's up?" He said stepping back and leading the way into the large and beautifully furnished house. Mike hesitated looking down at his boots and the sand that seemed to be running off them and Paul stopped and looked back "Ahhh, don't worry about that, its seen worse and will no doubt see worse again. Come in and have a coffee with me." He turned away and Mike followed slowly into the tastefully decorated interior "What brings you here anyway Mike, you have normally stayed away from the house?" Mike nodded as he wandered on behind the owner of the house "Ehhh, well, that's not deliberate, Paul. It's just been a matter of keeping busy and not getting in your way." Paul laughed to himself "Might be good if some more people got in the way a bit more. You might need more people going forward, if things pan out the way I think they will." He stopped and looked at Mike "You didn't just come here for a blether though, what brought you Mike?" They were in the kitchen now and Paul had been filling the kettle and slowly set it down on the hot plate of that big cast iron range to boil.

The kitchen was a warm and homely room, calming whilst bright and functional; not exactly new it wasn't a museum piece either, it had been designed to do a job rather than look good first. Paul waved at the table and Mike sat down a little gingerly, obviously feeling out of place in these surroundings. Paul sat down just along from him, closer to the kettle as it thought about boiling. "Come on Mike, something is bothering you and you came here for a reason. What is it?" Mike sighed and looked down at the scrubbed white wood that was the table top he was leaning on before he turned his head and looked at Paul "Okay Paul, you've always been very supportive of my work and the work of the university archaeology department." Paul was nodding as Mike continued "so can you tell me why someone claiming to be the owner of the land they are working on at the moment; turned up at the university, went to see the principal and had them thrown off the site by claiming that no permission had been given by the landowner to dig and that no 'Greensword' licences had been sought or granted." Paul stared at him for a second ignoring the kettle which has just come to the boil and was beginning to shriek. Paul eventually jumped up and lifted the kettle off closing the lid behind it as he poured the boiling water into a cafetiere before he answered "I saw they were digging, Marianne and I have spoken several times and she and her team do not need any specific permission from me as long as they work within certain limits, which they are – I don't even know her boss." He turned and looked at Mike as he set down two mugs before opening the fridge and producing a milk carton. "Greensword' licenses I would expect you to deal with and so know nothing of them, but Marianne is no fool so I don't see her working without them." Mike shook his head "She wasn't, the licenses exist and are real, my boss signed them when I was out of the office. So they are real and you haven't stopped them or changed your position." He stopped and sipped from the cup that had been pushed across the table towards him after spooning in several heaped teaspoons of sugar and concluding "So who is it then?" Paul sat back and looked at him for a second "As I see it, there are two other options. For various reasons I have sold the estate to people I can't tell you about, but they don't take over for another six months anyway so they should have nothing to do with it. However there are two plots on the estate that I don't actually own." Mike sat back and looked surprised at this information, it was a revelation to him "I never even thought about that, I just assumed that you owned everything within the boundaries." Paul nodded as he sat there cradling his mug "Most folk do, I did as well for long enough until I was looking at deed plans one day" he fell silent for a moment or two before he said "Wait there a minute I'll be right back"

The house was quiet and still with all of the buzz his wife had brought to it, now gone: he did not miss it, the political groups for the USA, not even local groups and various other 'look good' causes that had no real effect. He shook his head as he padded into the study and picked up the estate plans off the desk where he had left them. He stopped and closed the French windows to the north lawn before he returned to the kitchen where Mike waited.

Mike watched closely as Paul unrolled the plan and weighed down the corners with a salt pot, a milk jug and his coffee mug. Paul's finger jabbed at two yellow squares marked on the drawing. "These are the two spots I don't own. That one just down from Mark Rae's place is about forty acres and this one over the back here, further inland and north is about eighty five acres. Is your dig site close to either of these?" Mike looked at them and wondered "Big spots in the middle of nowhere, that's not even arable ground is it?" Paul shook his head "Sand and dunes basically, nothing there." Mike shook his head and pointed to the forty acre site "I can't be sure without a GPS unit but I think that is where they're digging." He paused as Paul looked at the map as well and wondered. Eventually Mike asked "Who does actually own them?" Paul hesitated, "Good question. They used to be owned by John McIntyre, an old, long time local, who emigrated to Canada several years ago. I don't know how he got them but he had good legal title to them both, anyway I asked about them last month only to be told yesterday that John McIntyre had died and that his holding company had sold them to another holding company, Paradigm Properties." He sighed and looked at Mike "I don't know who Paradigm Properties is or who owns it." Mike shook his head "Neither do I, but I know they own other properties in the area." Paul looked at him sharply "How do you know that?" Mike nodded at him "The cottage I rent is owned by them. I deal with their solicitor, not the company direct but they've always been fair with me so I would be surprised at this being a big issue unless there is something going on I don't know about. Which is far from impossible, after all I didn't know you were selling either." Paul shook his head "Neither did I, I let myself get lured in, I took the bait. They used to call it the honey pot trap in the old spy novels." He fell silent as he mulled over his own stupidity while Mike watched him think "Do you mean you were conned into selling this place?" Paul nodded "Sort of" was all he said as he rolled up the plan. "However, that's my problem. I am happy to go and see Marianne's boss and tell him I did not send anyone in to him and I have no problem with them carrying on. You say the licenses are valid so the only problem would be if this Paradigm Properties are causing problems." He fell silent for a moment or two "Who's this lawyer of Paradigms' that you deal with?"

Mark picked up the phone and hesitated before he spoke, he thought he had recognised the number but who ever it was had already hung up. He shrugged and dropped the receiver into the cradle, it rang again immediately, this time it was Steve the solicitor. Mark looked at his watch "Eight o'clock at night, do you charge over time?" was his immediate comment to his friend who just laughed "No, but I should do, you're obviously in good humour anyway." Without waiting for another comment he carried on. "I've got a variety of things to tell you. First your new house, number four in the row. I've got all the paperwork and the deeds transfer has already started, along with that for the plots and the other cottage. Very quick and very unusual considering I only just made the funds transfer this morning. I also have a tenant for the house if your willing to let it to a determined, divorced single female who wants to move in without decoration or anything like that and do all the basic repairs herself in return for a slightly cheaper rent. I said probably, but would need to speak to the clients representative." He paused "That's you." Mark just grunted "Sure no real issue, do we know her?" He could hear Steve rustling papers and knew it was for effect, Steve's memory was almost infallible, after a few seconds he came back on the line "It's a Doctor Jennifer James, she was asking about you." Mark shrugged to himself "I've met her, she's okay. Let her have the house at whatever you think appropriate." He could tell Steve had something else he wanted to discuss and waited for him to say something "I've also had Paul Gray and some other guy in here looking for you, except they didn't know it was you they were looking for." Mark waited and listened this might be interesting. Steve continued "It appears someone went to the university the other day and told the principal that they were the landowner and that the dig that's going on, on the dunes must stop immediately as it was happening without the owners permission or the relevant environmental permissions and licences. They wondered if it was the owner of Paradigm Properties, as it was not Paul and the other guy represented *'Greensword'* who say they have issued all the relevant licences." Steve hesitated as he listened for a comment from his friend; it took a moment as Mark thought about it first. "Well," he started "you know my position on that. They can dig where they want as far as I am concerned, all we need is to be notified of any major finds on or immediately adjacent to our lands." Steve nodded "That was what I thought so I have given them a letter to that effect on behalf of Paradigm Properties." Mark nodded to himself and the conversation turned to trivialities for a few minutes before they hung up and Steve went home.

Mark sat there in the gathering gloom wondering about the phone call – why would anyone do that and why would the university fold so easily? Questions he could not answer, so he was not going to worry about them at the moment. He set down the mug and opened the patio doors out onto the stone slabs just outside the door; it was dark but it's never truly dark in the countryside and the indigo sky was peppered with a myriad of silver spots of light. The moon was behind a cloud and the air was cool with just that slight tang of salt that comes from being so close to the sea. He shivered as bad memories came flooding back to him, memories he did not want. Angrily he pushed them aside and tried to savour the night but the moment was gone. Sighing he stepped inside and locked the door.

About a mile away, as the crow flies, Paul Gray stepped into his study and stopped, the doors out onto the north lawn were open and he was sure he had shut them earlier. He looked slowly around the room, nothing seemed to be out of place, the books were all still there and the cabinet that hid the safe was still very much shut. Quietly he walked across to the doors and hesitated before he pulled them closed. He thought he had seen something move out there in the half light, he watched and sure enough a grey figure floated across his field of view, ignoring him completely. Paul sighed and pulled the doors shut before turning the large brass key in the old hardwood doors. Thoughtfully he pulled the key from the lock and dropped it into the letter tray on his desk. Turning he looked out the window again as the figure repeated its walk across the lawn; the grey lady had reappeared. He had seen the ghost before at a time of crisis and had never thought he would see her again, now he had seen her it meant that the estate was under threat of destruction; or at least that was what the legend said. He would go and see his lawyer tomorrow, before he went to the university to sort out that other bit of trouble with the archaeologist. He never heard who hit him and the blow was a professional one. A lead filled leather cosh swung sideways into the base of his skull, not hard enough to kill, but definitely hard enough to make sure he could not cause trouble for a few hours.

+

It was three o'clock in the morning and Mark was cold, he was sitting in a bush close to one of the tracks that led from the stables out into the countryside and had the north lawn on the other side. The deer did not know he was there and the Infra Red filter and flash gun was working a treat, he had a good few photographs of them feeding contentedly on the lawn when suddenly something scared them. Mark sat still he knew it was not him as he had not moved then he saw the grey figure drifting across the lawn, roughly towards him. He smiled to himself and took a few pictures, it was unlikely they would come out but it was worth a try, then he stopped, ghosts did not usually bother deer. He stayed where he was and lifted the camera to his eye as the double glass doors into the house opened and two men stepped out, dressed similarly to himself, dark colours, no metal, hats and gloves. They did not appear to be carrying anything, but he started to take pictures, with the infra red filters the men had no reason to be aware of the flash. He listened as the two men spoke to one another softly once outside the building as they walked towards the stables. Mark sat still and waited, feeling as if he knew what was about to happen but still worried he might be too late. The sound of a heavy diesel engine starting up came to his ears followed by tyres on gravel as a four by four came from the direction of the stables and up the road at his side. He took pictures as they drove towards him and away and then he sat there and waited until it went over the top of the next hillock in the track and the glow told him they had switched on their headlights.

Mark dropped his camera bag in the middle of the bush and ran across the lawn. He looked in through the doors from a few feet away, wary to get too close until he was sure of what he was walking into. The study had been lined with book shelves and most of the books were now scattered across the floor. Two things caught Marks eye immediately, the first was a pair of feet sticking out from behind the desk, the second was a cardboard box sitting on the floor with a pile of open books scattered around it.

Mark went in through the doors and pulled Paul Gray out from under the pile of books, the smell of petrol filled his nostrils as he carried the unconscious man out onto the lawn. A quick check assured Mark he was still alive so he rolled him on his side and went back inside. The box was open topped and Mark could see straight into it. Immediately obvious was the half full plastic bottle of petrol and what could be a timer. Strapped onto the side of the bottle was a number of small polythene packets. Mark grunted to himself 'probably magnesium powder'. Delicately he picked up the box and walked slowly outside with it, a long way away from the house, and the prone figure of Paul, he set it down. After a quick phone call he went back inside and running through the house convinced himself that there were no more devices inside. He grabbed a throw from the back of a settee and went outside to make sure Paul was okay.

Twenty minutes later the sickly blue light of police beacons lit the area up as the emergency services arrived. The police were horrified to see Mark had left Paul where he was lying and was himself, bent over the bomb. The bomb squad turned up about ten minutes later and jumped out of their truck, the lead man ran over to Mark and a hushed few words were exchanged before the soldier wandered back to the group. He was shaking his head and started to speak as the police inspector stepped forward "Leave him to it, he's almost finished and we know him anyway. He can do as good a job as any of my men including myself" The inspector just stared at him as one of the bomb squad spoke "Used to be one of us?" The first man nodded "yeah and then some. He'd tell you but he'd have to kill you." The soldiers nodded and headed back to their truck to get their other tools ready as the police helped the ambulance crew carry Paul into their vehicle before taking him to hospital. Mark sighed as he disconnected the last wire on the timer and stood up, slowly stretching his legs. He glanced around and walked away from the bomb and the group, casually raising one hand above his head with the thumb extended kept walking. The bomb squad team walked over to the bomb and began to slowly pick up the individual pieces before putting them into the armoured box on the back of the wheeled trolley they had towed from the truck. As they did the police inspector began to get agitated, he realised he had lost sight of Mark in the group of men all dressed similarly. Suddenly Mark stepped out of the group and handed him a memory card from a camera.

"I was sitting in the bushes over there taking pictures of deer foraging on the lawn." He started "when I saw the grey lady cross the lawn and the deer took off. Immediately after that two men came out of the doors and walked away. There are photographs of them and their vehicle on that card. After they drove away I went down to the house, found Paul, took him outside to safety and took the device outside before I phoned you" The inspector stared at him for a second or two "Why did the deer not run away or the men see you taking their picture?" Mark smiled "Infra red filters and flashes outwith the light range visible to animals or humans – comes out on the picture though." The inspector shook his head "You've got a picture of the vehicle, you don't remember the registration mark do you?" Mark smiled again and handed him a slip of paper. The inspector smiled and opened up the note before handing it to one of the other officers "Get this out and find that vehicle. I want those men arrested before daylight." He turned back to speak to Mark and looked around "Where did he go?" The other police officers looked sheepish as it became obvious Mark had just walked away.

He turned to the officer with the bomb squad and said "You'll need to tell me who he is and how he knew enough about the bomb to take it apart." The Officer shrugged "No chance" he said "He is ex forces I know who he is but am constrained by our regulations. I will speak to my CO but I'll tell you now he's on your side." The police inspector looked at him and finally said "How do you mean, how do you know he's not involved?" One of the other soldiers laughed as the officer spoke "If he had been involved, this building would not be standing and we would not be safe to be standing here. The guy he dragged out would have vanished without a trace and you would never have heard of any of this." The Policeman looked at him and saw something in the officers eyes that told him not to ask any more. He nodded and made to turn away as the officer said finally "Prying too far into the history of these guys, and there are very few of his sort, usually ends up in some one dying. Don't cross him, he will bite back and usually the state will defend him." He nodded and said "Thank you, I will speak to your CO but I will not push, that information might not be needed for this case anyway."

+

Andrew Crawford was sitting in a corner of the lounge of the hotel hoping that Dull would not find him tucked away here. He was comfortable and mellow; he'd had almost a whole glass of wine with his dinner which had been okay but not fantastic, and was enjoying the peace. He'd found to his immense pleasure that certain areas of the hotel were blind to phone signals and this corner of the lounge was one he had begun to use more regularly.

He looked up just as Dull sat down opposite him in the deep leather armchair. Dull was at least half drunk as usual by this time of night and seemed to want to talk. Crawford sighed as he put down his newspaper and Dull asked him "Well how's the plan going, any difficulties that we can help with?" Crawford smiled and thought 'why not?' "Well," he started "The estate is now ours although it'll be a few months before we can actually take it over. We've got rid of the archaeologists and should be about finished buying the first of the houses within the boundaries so things are actually going well." He paused and could see the boring little mans eyelids drooping as he seemed to be falling asleep. Crawford continued speaking "Once we get the rest of the houses which we should be able to do fairly easily, and we have the final documents from the current land owner which I should have had by now." He paused and shook his head before continuing. "We will be in total control so the rest of the job will be easy." He stopped as a soft snore escaped from Dull. Crawford smiled and leaning forward caught the wine glass as it slipped from the hoteliers' hand.

Crawford was on his way back to the lounge when his phone vibrated in his pocket, he sighed and stepped to one side in the foyer to answer it. The voice on the other end of the line was panicked and unsettled and, initially talking rubbish. "Calm down Barnard." Crawford voice was sharp and acerbic as he spoke to the failing little man on the other end of the phone.

58

"Now, tell me what's happened" He could hear Peter Barnard gulping air as he calmed himself down before he began to speak. "He turned us down, flat." He sucked in a lungful of air and carried on without waiting on a response from Crawford "I offered him the sixty thousand as we agreed and he went ballistic, called me all sorts of things. I offered him ninety as we agreed and he went for a baseball bat." He shuddered at the thought, he could still picture Wee George as they called him, his face as red as his hair as he swung that bat at the headlights of the truck.. Crawford thought the man was crying on the other end of the phone as he listened to him breathe. Barnard finally gathered himself together and spoke clearly "Basically he turned us down flat and told me never to go back near his house again. We'll need to get the vehicle repaired as well." Crawford was silent for a few seconds before he spoke "Okay so you've failed at that. We can still try on the others over the next few days." He sighed and drew breath himself, this could be a problem. "Meanwhile did the two men we hired deliver their package today?" Barnard was silent as he thought back "No, I haven't seen your two men at all." Crawford didn't say anything as he closed his phone and put it back in his pocket. Barnard was upset but managed to get his phone in his shirt pocket on the third try. The bar in the rough local hotel he was staying in was beginning to look better all the time. No four and a half star hotel for the hired help, he thought as he drew the battered four by four into the car park.

4

Paul Gray woke up to find he was in hospital with a headache. A continuous dull ache at the base of his skull kept reminding him he was not at home in his bed. Slowly he opened his eyes to find a nurse looking down at him. The nurse smiled and him and said "Good to see you awake, there were a few people worried about you for a while there." He looked over his shoulder before leaning forward to almost whisper at Paul "The police want to speak to you as well but I have orders to let the doctors know you're awake first." Paul nodded, he was old fashioned and the stories he had heard of male nurses made him feel uncomfortable now he was being tended by one.

It was more than an hour later the police inspector arrived at the hospital to speak to Paul, he would not normally be doing this type of interview himself, this was a job normally done by a junior officer initially but there were interesting circumstances around this strange little incident. Paul just looked at him as he walked in past the doctor who was walking out. The inspector introduced himself sighed and sat down. "I expect this to actually be quite a short interview as I doubt you'll be able to tell me much, but why don't we start with you telling me what you do remember." Paul shrugged and began to speak as the inspector wrote everything down.

An hour later the inspector walked out of the hospital and checked his watch, almost exactly double the time he had expected to spend inside with Paul Gray, he shook his head and headed back to the station. The two anonymous men they had in custody might have actually said something by now.

+

It was eleven o'clock in the morning when Mike knocked on Marks door. Mark smiled at him and walked away, Mike hesitated before figuring out that he was meant to follow him inside. Slowly he stepped into the kitchen and relaxed as he saw the kettle being switched on "I take you'll accept a coffee?" Mark laughed at him. Mike nodded and hopped a little uncomfortably from foot to foot. "I've just come from the hospital" he hesitated obviously expecting a comment as Mark spooned instant coffee into two mugs but said nothing. Mike sighed and decided if he was going to find out what was happening he was going to have to ask. "Paul Gray is in

60

hospital, he was attacked at home last night and the police tell him it was you that dragged him out and defused a bomb at his house." Mark just carried on with what he was doing as Mike stared at him a little frightened of this man he had known as a friend for some time. Mark sighed "I might need to go see Paul, ask him to be more circumspect in what information he shares." He stared at Mike as he pushed the coffee mug along the worktop and sat down at the table. "Yes Mike, I was out last night taking photographs. I saw something happening at the house so went in about and realised what was going on. I pulled Paul out then took care of the device, it was pretty crude but could have been effective. Any one could have done it, but I would appreciate it if you didn't tell too many people it was me." Mike nodded silently as Mark continued "Why were you going to see Paul?" Mike looked up for a second "To do with the dig" he mumbled as he looked down into his cup again as he continued "Marianne was suspended from her job at the university because the principal received a complaint." Mark interrupted "I heard about that" Mike didn't flinch and carried on "Well Paul and I were going along with a letter from the folk who apparently own the plot of land that Marianne was digging on to get her reinstated. Principal refused to even look at it. He said the complaint had been formally correct and therefore could not be overturned with a fraudulent letter." Mark looked at him "Did he explain what he meant by fraudulent" Mike shrugged "No, didn't ask really." Mark sat back and looked at Mike as he twitched and squirmed "Relax, your safe enough, what's the problem?" Mike looked embarrassed and slurped his coffee before answering "Well I thought we were getting on well, we've been out a couple of times and now for her to believe that I am responsible for her losing her job, doesn't help my case at all." Mark nodded "Don't worry I am sure she will be working again very soon." He scribbled down a name and address on a sheet of paper before he said "Go see her, tell her to make an appointment and go and speak to this lawyer." He handed over the slip of paper "He will help with a possible answer to the problem. A bit circuitous maybe but it will work." Mike looked at him, "You use a lot of big words for an ordinary guy you know." Mark just shrugged and Mike understood he was going to get no more information out of him. Mark picked up the phone as Mike closed the door behind him on the way out.

+

Trente Silver sat back at the end of the board room table and looked along it at his minions; he loved the smell of fear that seemed to permeate the air when he did this type of thing. That deaths head grin was fixed in place on his almost skeletal face. "Well," he bellowed "next week a small group of us fly over to have a look at the site. Crawford is there already and is making the arrangements. We will be almost comfortable in the best hotel in the area and we will have a few days work and discussion before we come back here and start planning properly." He looked around the room, looking for dissent and every pair of eyes dropped in front of him as he almost laughed to himself.

+

Doctor Jennifer had just unloaded the last box out of her car and parked it along at the end of the row on the common land because the garage that came with the property looked unsafe, she was not willing to park her car inside it and risk it falling in. Closing the door she leant back against it and sighed to herself, someplace to call home again, a house where she could close the door and relax knowing it was hers and she was safe inside. She looked around and realised just how dilapidated it actually was. Nothing structural as far as she could tell and the paperwork had told her it had been re wired about three years ago. So it should be safe, she turned and locked the door before doing the same at the front and climbing the stairs to the first floor bathroom, the water was hot and she soon sank gratefully into a deep hot bath. It was early but she was home and had a few days off to sort things out, she would start tomorrow.

+

Mandy was sitting in the office off the old stable block, speaking to Danielle when Barnard came in. He was white and shaking and looked scared to death. Mandy watched with a knowing smile as Danielle jumped up and made sure the coffee machine was on and fresh coffee would be available for him in a few minutes. He sat down at his desk and fumbled around with some papers for a few minutes until Danielle took him a mug of coffee and shut the door behind her on the way out. Mandy leant forward "Well, what's he like then?" The grin on her face made it clear what she was meaning but Danielle looked blank as Mandy carried on speaking. "Oh come on, you either fancy him rotten or are shagging him. I can see it in your face, so what's he like in bed then?" Danielle blushed "No idea; never got that far. He doesn't seem to be interested." She realised what she was saying as she finished off "Anyway, I would need something in return." She looked down her nose at Mandy "I wouldn't just give myself away for fun." Mandy sat back, hurt at her friend "I don't give it away either. He gave me five hundred euros for the last one and it was just a snog with that guy at the big house." The voice behind her startled both of the girls "I would recommend that you do not make that accusation again, ever. Leave this office and do not come back. Your retainer is ended you no longer

62

work for us. Goodbye." Mandy looked up at Peter Barnard as he glowered down at her before turning on his heel and walking way, speaking over his shoulder as he went "Danielle, if she isn't out of here in five minutes you'll be looking for another job as well." The two girls stared at each other in shock as the impact of that statement sank in; Danielle was horrified and apologetic while Mandy was just shocked as she stood up blinded by the silent tears running down her face, she stumbled to the door and out into the courtyard. Danielle sat there and watched as the door banged shut behind her former friend. Barnard eased his office door open and stepped out sheepishly "Sorry that had to be so brutal but I had to get rid of her, she talks too much." Danielle had stood up and walked across the floor towards him "You knew she was cheap and a risk so why did you keep her on retainer?" Barnard shrugged and muttered "Good blow jobs" he had barely finished speaking when the sound of a slap came to his ears almost a fraction of a second before the burning, stinging sensation registered on his face along with the ripping sensation of Danielle's nails as they gouged four tracks across his cheek. By the time he managed to get his head facing front again all he could see was the door to the office still swinging in the breeze as Danielle had left it behind her.

+

Sharon was sitting in the cafe speaking to Janette an old pal from University who she had met for a coffee. "So," said Janette "That's the story, the principal fired her and shut down the whole dig on the basis of this complaint that now looks to be fraudulent, but he will not even look at letters from this Paradigm Properties supporting her because he says they are fraudulent." She sighed and looked at Sharon who seemed to be miles away, but suddenly looked up at her "What if I was to have a bit of a dig around and see what I can find out about 'Paradigm Properties' see if I can find the owner and see if he will speak to the principal in person, might make a difference." Janette shrugged "I doubt it, seems to have made his mind up and is refusing to even consider alternatives. Anyway, I don't think Paradigm Properties are a problem, they were quick enough in writing a letter of support. Probably didn't even know anything about it." Sharon shrugged "Yeah, but why from the lawyer and not the owner or principal?" Janette shrugged again "Maybe not even in the country. Anyway," She sat up brightly "tell me all about this new boyfriend." Sharon shook her head "Not really a boy friend as such. Friend yes, Mum and Dad like him." Janette interrupted "Wait a minute, you've introduced him to your parents, they like him and you've been naked in his bath yet he's not a boyfriend yet." Sharon went bright red "Keep your voice down. I was in his bath because he was saving my life and that is why Mum and

Dad like him; and he didn't flinch when I dropped them on him, he took meeting them in his stride. Dad wasn't overjoyed though. Mark is in his forties, more than ten years older than me and just over ten years younger than him." Janette laughed "Who cares, he sound nice and decent, and guys like that are rare. You've caught his eye, now wrap your legs around him and sink your claws in. Don't let go." Sharon studied the bottom of her coffee cup before she said "I'm trying and I intend succeeding" Janette grinned at her and the conversation turned back to shoes.

+

Marianne held her head up high as she walked in to her meeting with the principal. Steve, the lawyer walked at her side and she glanced at him nervously. He smiled at her and spoke in a soft Glaswegian accent, "Relax Dr Presley, this will work and they will not know how to deal with it. Either way you come out of this on the upside." She smiled as she walked in through those hallowed halls of learning, her footsteps echoing off the high ceilings and bare walls of academia. The committee room was large and meant to be intimidating, Steve smiled, it was nothing compared to what the High Court in Dublin or London had been. At one side of the table sat the department principal, the head of the school and a senior HR adviser. The department principal stood up as Steve walked in behind Marianne "Sorry this is a closed meeting," he said "No members of the public or other spectators." Steve smiled first "I am Dr Presley's legal representative in this case until her own lawyer becomes available in approximately half an hour and I have other reasons to be here that will become apparent in due course." He turned and looked at the representative from HR "I assume you would have offered Dr Presley the opportunity for representation in order for the university to comply with the relevant employment legislation?" The man nodded but looked down, afraid to open his mouth. The head of the school looked at his watch and said "Can we get on with this, I have a tight schedule?" Steve looked at him and noted the principal did the same as he spoke. "Alright we have a straight forward case of an overenthusiastic archaeologist here. Dr Presley went on to dig a site without obtaining the permission of the land owner or the relevant environmental licenses for the dig. This was brought to my attention by representatives of the landowner coming to see me to complain. In order to preserve the reputation of the university I stopped the dig immediately and put Dr Presley on suspension. No evidence has been presented to the contrary so I would move for dismissal with full loss of pension and privileges." Steve sat back shocked at the blatant lies being told here while the head of the school sat forward "Dr Presley, this is a serious charge and requires a response. In speaking to the principal outwith this meeting he

64

confirmed that you have failed to respond to telephone calls to put your side of the story. Can you defend that action?" Marianne was sitting there amazed, suddenly her mouth snapped shut and she dug in her hand bag as she said "Complete lies, I only have a mobile phone, no land line and here," she pulled the old phone out of her bag "it is with a list of received calls. A quick glance will show no calls received from the university." Steve held a hand up "I will speak for Dr Presley from this point on and let me make something clear. If you are going to come up with something like that as evidence you had better prepare yourself for a defamation action of a large magnitude, which I can promise you will lose." He paused and looked at the three shocked faces in front of him. "Now let us return to the case in hand." He pulled a sheaf of papers from his briefcase as he spoke "These are the *'Greensword'* licenses that your principal says were never applied for. All signed and formally approved, all in order. This is a copy of a letter from the actual landowner which was presented to the principal last week immediately after the event he described and he refused to even read it. He has just told you the representation that actually took place by the official representative of *Greensword* and the owner of the surrounding land did not happen. One of these gentlemen is available to speak to you, if you so wish." Steve sat back quite confident that the facts had presented themselves, and the back stop that Mark had wanted was not going to be needed. The HR rep sighed and looked at the other two men "This looks clear enough, reinstate her." The principal shook his head "I see no evidence other than hearsay and lies, dismiss her." The head of school shook his head, stroked his chin then checked his watch. "Difficult," he said "but also very clear. Dr Marianne Presley, you are hereby dismissed from the post of academic at this university with immediate effect. Any and all personal belongings still on the site will be returned to you within the month. Good bye Dr Presley, I would like to say it's been a pleasure knowing you, but it hasn't." he sat back and looked at Marianne as she sat there lips trembling and eyes filling with tears. "Lunch?" was the comment from the head of school as he made to stand up, the principal was smiling and the HR rep was looking scared as Steve's face turned dark as thunder and he reached into his briefcase again and pulled out a sealed brown envelope which he tore open as they all watched him closely. "Hold on," he said "Amateur night is over, now it gets serious." he read the cover sheet quickly "This university will now be challenged under employment legislation in the civil courts for a sum of compensation totalling five million euros for their illegal and immoral actions here today. Dr Presley has meantime secured an offer of a consultancy post for Paradigm Properties new division, known as Paradigm Archaeology, personal remuneration will be one hundred and twenty thousand euros per annum with research funding of five hundred thousand euros per annum for a minimum period of three years. A deal has been struck with an alternate university so that all students who wish to leave this university and transfer courses to the alternate will receive full credit for their studies to date. In accordance with this the artefacts taken from the dig site by the archaeology department of this university will be handed over with immediate effect." Steve swallowed and set down the sheet of paper before sliding it across the table. The head of school looked at it without touching it and said "You can't do this." Steve grinned at him "Knowing the owner of Paradigm Properties I think you'll find we already have." Standing up Steve guided Marianne out of the door and a glance silenced the questions she had until a later time. As they entered the main foyer a handful of her students appeared from the other wing "Dr Presley," one of them cried "Good to see you, great news too. Will we see you over at the other place or will we need to come to Paradigm to speak to you?" She shook her head "I don't know, there's a lot of detail to be worked through yet, but we will see you all soon." Steve nodded at her and the two of them walked out through the cheering, obviously happy mob of students.

Once they were in Steve's car Marianne turned to him and said "Is this true, this dream job?" He smiled at her "Oh its true all right, don't worry about that. So is the case against the university, I'll be filing the papers when we get back to the office." Marianne looked at him, "How much of this did you know before the meeting?" He smiled, "I knew about the court case, I think I knew about Paradigm Archaeology but the details of your job and the collection of the artefacts I did not know about." She sighed as she sunk into the leather seat and asked again "Will he actually send a truck to collect the artefacts?" Steve smiled again "Knowing him, they've already been collected." She looked across at him and asked "When do I meet my new boss?" he shook his head "I don't know, maybe never. He's very secretive about certain things, you'd never know it if you met him in the street. He's a pretty ordinary guy until you scratch the surface, then he's incredible." Shaking her head she said "You know him and like him, don't you?" Steve nodded thinking to himself "I know him well; have done so for many years and I would say I actually owe him my life, so I support him. As long as its moral and ethical I will support him" Marianne just looked at the lawyer and wondered about the missing requirement.

+

Sharon was surprised when she got the call from Steve the lawyer asking her to come into his office as a member of the press to receive an exclusive press release. She was a little hesitant as she walked into the cool and distinguished lawyers office with her new camera clutched tightly in one

66

hand and her notebook in the other. The receptionist smiled at her as she walked in and looked over her glasses before saying "Sharon Grant?" Sharon just nodded as the receptionist pushed a button on the intercom.

Steve appeared at the door of his office and smiled as Sharon hesitated a little unsure of herself. The office was large and incredibly untidy, like most lawyers offices, with piles of file folders on almost every flat surface in the room. There were probably three clear spaces, his chair, the visitors chair and a small space right in front of him on the desk, there was no one else in the room. Sharon stopped and looked at him a little confused as he started to speak "Don't worry, another client of mine, Mark Rae, gave me your name as someone who might be interested in an exclusive article as a local freelance writer." Sharon blushed at Marks name and Steve paused, surprised at the reaction. He continued "Dr Presley will be working out of these offices until such time as Paradigm Archaeology get themselves set up properly with offices." He hesitated and noted that Sharon was taking lots of notes, in shorthand as he spoke. "The owners of Paradigm Properties were horrified to learn about the miscarriage of justice that had been perpetrated allegedly in his name. That was when I, as lawyer acting on their behalf was instructed to assist Dr Marianne Presley at her hearing with the University. That hearing did not comply with several legal requirements and therefore the result was not legitimate. My client had foreseen this and had taken steps to ensure the archaeological legacy from the dig site would not be lost to this country." Steve smiled as he sat back and watched Sharon scribble on the pad for a second or two more. When she stopped and looked up at him he was surprised by the intensity in those blue eyes as they regarded him coolly over the top of her notepad. "You mention owners, plural, and owner, singular, of Paradigm Properties, which is it and who are they?" Steve hesitated "It is singular but I can tell you no more than that, at the express wish of the ultimate beneficial owner." Sharon sighed, "Judging by what I've heard about the funds allocated to Paradigm Archaeology he must be fairly wealthy." Steve smiled at her "I can tell you no more than that, at the express wish of the ultimate beneficial owner" Sharon smiled and nodded "Okay, I understand that trail ends there for just now, but I might come back to it again." Steve shrugged "Until I get direct orders from Paradigm Properties I cannot tell you any more, legal confidentiality and all that." Sharon nodded as Steve concluded "Now, I'll take you to see Dr Marianne Presley and I would suggest that the university might not be too willing to talk about this matter." Sharon grinned at him as she slid her camera over her shoulder "That, doesn't surprise me, but I have to give them the opportunity to respond." Steve nodded as he opened the door "Of course." Was all he said.

Dr Marianne Presley's office was spotless, two doors along from Steve's furnished in the same style but empty of anything other than herself and furniture, she was nervous, never having met a reporter directly before. Sharon smiled and immediately knew she liked this woman. It was almost an hour later that Sharon left the building and looked along the high street. It was a bright spring morning and she now had a purpose in her life again. There was an internet café just along the street here and she would be able to file to the news agency from there once she had it written.

+

Arthur had dropped the bar on the inside of the door to his cottage for some reason, he didn't know why but he was glad he had. The hammering on the door carried on for several minutes with no sign of letting up. The screams and shouts were almost getting louder and suddenly glass showered into the room as a rock was thrown through the window. Almost as quickly as it had started it went silent again, Arthur listened as he heard nothing, he sat and waited scared to move. In the distance he could here a diesel engine as someone was driving up from the beach direction and suddenly a shout rang out. "Hey who are you? And what are you doing there?" The reply was muffled and indistinct but Arthur would have put money on it being a swear word. He could hear an engine start and doors slam followed by a crashing sound and a 'whoosh' he did not understand until he saw the flames out side the window. He cowered back into the corner and tried to hide as he heard shouts from outside, but these were different. "Oh my god, is there anyone in there? Are you alright?" The diesel engine coming from the beach was close and getting closer, faster.

Mark sledged the old land rover to a halt and jumped out dragging the fire extinguisher from behind the seats, it was an old water extinguisher that he had recovered from somewhere sometime but it still worked. He shouldered Paul Gray out of the way and shouted "The well, get a bucket of water from the well. Over there" he nodded his head in the direction of the well as he pulled the pin on the fire extinguisher and started to douse the flames.

It was almost half an hour later before the fire was out and Paul looked at Mark and said "Thanks, but do we know who those men were?" Mark shook his head "That will become obvious in time, meanwhile let's see if Arthur is okay." Stepping forward he knocked on the door and shouted "Arthur, its Mark, are you okay?" The two men could hear the bar being lifted and the door opened a crack until the wizened old face peered round the corner of the door.

68

A huge grin replaced the look of fear on the old mans face as he shuffled back and opened the door to let Mark in, he looked at Paul and back at Mark "He with you?" Mark nodded "Yes Arthur, he's a friend of mine and I hope a friend of yours too. Are you alright?" The old man nodded as he shuffled over and put he kettle on top of the stove that was now lit with a bag of coal sitting on the concrete hearth next to it. Paul looked around "Cleaner and warmer than I had expected." He stared at the place with something akin to awe as he continued "I never even realised this place was still occupied" Mark smiled as Arthur grinned to himself Arthur spoke "Was falling down around me for long enough till Mark here reappeared, he's been doing lots of odd jobs for me making the place warm and dry." Arthur swallowed and licked his lips "Don't know what the owner will think when he finds out I'm back here." Paul look startled but Mark spoke before anyone else could "Don't worry about that Arthur, I've taken care of all that." Paul just looked at him knowing he would not be getting any explanations here and now. But beginning to wonder about the neighbour he thought he had known for many years.

Mark looked at Paul and said, "Give me a minute" and without waiting disappeared out the door. Paul just looked at Arthur as he poured boiling water into the teapot "Don't worry about him, he can look after himself easily enough and won't have gone far." With that the door swung open and Mark came back in carrying two carrier bags. One was clothes, the other "Just a few odds and ends for you Arthur, milk and the like." Mark set the bags down on the table and pulled out a bottle of whisky, which he set down heavily on the table and stood there holding onto the neck of the bottle as Arthur stared at it. Eventually the old man looked up at Mark and smiled "Don't drink it all at once or it'll be the last you get." Arthur just nodded without saying a word. Paul thought he saw a tear in the old mans eye.

+

The two men were in the Land Rover driving away before Paul turned to Mark and said "We should call the police, that was attempted murder" Mark looked across at him and nodded "Yes we should, but the two thugs who just tried to burn Arthur to a crisp will assume that's exactly what we will do that and will probably stay away for a while, which means we have no interference from either them or the police." Paul looked at him "I don't understand" Mark nodded "Okay it's like this. Those guys today are probably connected to the two the other night that tried to cremate you while you were still breathing. I don't know why that happened." He looked at Paul who shook his head and shrugged before Mark continued. "However, now we can set some cameras and the like to get warning if they come back. If the police are involved then we lose that chance," Paul shook his head wondering what was in Marks head, eventually he said "Wouldn't we need to call the police then anyway?" Mark shrugged "Maybe" was his only response. The rest of the drive to the big house was completed in silence. As he stepped out Paul turned and held the door open, looking back at Mark he said "You own Paradigm Properties don't you?" Mark nodded "Keep it to yourself. It's going to come out soon enough anyway but I would rather keep it quiet as long as I realistically can." Paul just nodded "No problem." he said as he made to slam the door "Anytime you want to come round for a drink, just give me a shout." Mark nodded "Will do" he shouted as gravel crunched under the tyres as he drove away leaving Paul standing there shouting after him "Thanks for saving my life" His voice faded away as the land rover disappeared in a cloud of dust and his shoulders sagged before he turned back towards the house. He walked all the way around the outside to make sure the doors and windows were shut before he opened the front door and walked inside slowly and cautiously.

+

The council chamber was tense as the councillors filed in and slowly chatted to one another in their little groups and eventually took their seats, one by one. A few minutes before one o'clock, almost the allotted time, the Chief Executive of the council finally called the meeting to order and looked down at the almost blank agenda sheet. There was only one item on the agenda. He thought about what was about to happen and cleared his throat before he looked into the faces of those ranked all around the room. Most were placid and calm, only two councillors were obviously different, one was Marlene, the leader of the council and also her political party. The other was Dianne, a member of the same party but very much an opponent, in the nicest possible yet political way, of Marlene. He sighed he could se trouble ahead over this issue. "Members of the council" he started "This meeting has only one item and one sub item on the agenda so it should not take too long. I also only have one motion against the item and nothing against the sub item at this time." Dianne was trying to catch his attention and eventually he relented "Yes Councillor," he sighed as he looked at her "How can there be any motions against this item when we only got the agenda, or knew about the item at all about half an hour ago as we all arrived for the meeting?" Marlene smiled her deaths head smile as she stood up and said "Perhaps I could answer that?" The almost question was aimed at the Chief executive who nodded as she carried on speaking

70

anyway "The item is on the agenda because I tabled it after a recent meeting and I put the motion on there this morning. That is how it is there and I would expect that it be passed with little opposition as it is for the long term benefit of the whole area." She grinned as she looked around the chamber. No one spoke and no one argued although a few individuals moved and squirmed a little uncomfortably in their seats. Dianne looked straight at he Chief executive who shook his head slightly and said "Whether it is passed or not will depend on whether or not the members of the council see it as a benefit or destructive. Sorry, that should have been positive or negative." He paused, licked his lips and clasped his hands together before he continued, "I suspect there will be some discussion and opposition to your motion councillor." Sighing he sat back "If there are no further comments then maybe we can begin." No one said a word as he nodded to Marlene who stayed on her feet and glowered around the chamber before reaching down for the speech that had been carefully prepared for her.

It was a very heated meeting and it took over three hours before it came to a vote. Marlene played what she thought was a trump card. "As leader of the council, and chair of the mid ground party, I hereby instruct all councillors who owe allegiance to this administrative district to vote in favour of this motion. That instruction is to be taken as a three line whip." She grinned as she sat down again, expecting that to be the end of the debate. Instead all that could be heard was the sound of laughter from almost every single councillor in the chamber; even some of her eleven disciples as she was beginning to think of them were giggling away like school children.

When the vote was taken she was furious to find that only nineteen of the councillors in the chamber had supported her motion; that left a very sizable majority against her plan to get 'significant' applications dealt with by a separate subcommittee of hand picked councillors rather than the local planning committees. She stormed out of the chamber before she had even heard the Chief Executive make his summation. He said "Councillors, it looks like democracy has spoken and the need for a separate committee, hand picked to understand the regional need for development has been deemed unproven." he looked around and drew breath before he continued. "That means that all planning applications will be dealt with by the normal local planning committees for each ward and the sub motion also tabled for discussion today will fall by the fact that no main motion exists." A movement caught his eye as two people stood up and left the public gallery, a man in a tweed jacket and a young blonde woman who looked about half his age.

+

The next day the 'Daily' had a front page exclusive article, it was difficult to be sure exactly what they were saying but it seemed to be important and succeeded in giving the impression that great things were about to happen. Paul set the paper down as Mandy walked in; he looked at her in surprise. He hesitated and did not speak for a moment or two wondering if she had something specific to say. It had probably been as embarrassing for her as it was for him to be caught in his clutches by his wife. Eventually he spoke "Didn't really expect to see you back here." She looked down and fiddled with her hair before replying "I know, I mean I know I got fired and all that but now that your wife has left I thought I might be able to help you out now and again. Maybe just doing your washing once a week or something until you leave the place." It took Paul all of five seconds to consider that offer "No, thanks but no." He looked down at his desk as he figured out how to continue the conversation. "I know I was set up and that you were part of that. I can't prove it, but I know it to be true. Don't try and get round me" the last was said as Mandy had dropped her hands and looked at him embarrassedly as she stepped towards the desk. He continued "From what I understand you were probably even paid for your part in it; makes me feel even more foolish than I was. Daft to believe a young girl like you could fancy an old man like me." He sighed, a deep heart felt sigh. "Go away Mandy, I don't want you here again. Good bye and good luck. I hope you make better choices in the future." Her face flushed with temper and she stalked away to the door of the room before she stopped and turned back. "Five hundred euros you were worth, that was all. I would have shagged you for that as well." She was walking slowly back across the room towards him as she spoke slowly, almost haughtily. "You made it easy because you were a coward. Any real man would have had me in bed for her to find but you weren't good enough or fast enough to get my knickers off. Now you never will, your wife knew, you know. She was part of it. It was actually quite fun to see you fumble around thinking you were, oh so smart." She was almost at the desk again now and practically spitting with each word. "Well I hope this helps keep you happy because it's the nearest you'll ever get to me or any other woman for months." Grabbing the hem of her tee shirt she lifted it and pulled her bra up as well, flashing her boobs at him before she turned and stalked out of the room while he sat there listening until he heard the slam of the front door as she left the building. Paul sat there laughing as he pulled the small tape recorder from the drawer and switched it off. "Note to self," he muttered laughing at the quote "Change the locks, also doesn't look like Mandy appreciates

72

rejection." He grinned and dropped the tape into the drawer before going to see if the video recording gear Mark had suggested he install had worked.

+

Mark answered the door to find a very unhappy Sharon standing there, arms folded, face downcast. She was almost crying as he stepped back to let her into the house. "You arranged the meet with Dr Presley and the lawyer guy for me for nothing." He looked at her puzzled as he followed her through to the kitchen "What do you mean for nothing?" he asked "You got the interview and you filed it with the agencies didn't you?" She nodded "Yeah and its gone to a few papers and specialist journals, but the 'Daily' was going to put it on the front page they said. What with me getting fired from the 'Evening' it would have been good to rub their faces in it with a front page article as my first free lance." He shook his head as he opened his arms to her and she stepped in for a cuddle.

Later they were sitting there together when he asked her "What's this all about anyway?" he pointed at the front page of the 'Daily' "I've read it three times and I don't actually see a story here. No facts, no quotes, no numbers, no jobs, no investment just a load of verbal about how good its all going to be, soon, once this opportunity actually appears." He snorted "They don't actually say what this opportunity is either." Sharon frowned at him "Are you sure? I mean I've not actually read it. I've been so pissed off at them I haven't actually read it." Mark smiled at her as the blonde head bent over the paper in his hands as she squirmed onto his knee.

That night Mark decided he was going to the pub, not something he did often as it usually meant a drive, it was three miles away after all, but tonight he had decided he wanted to see what the local rumour was. He walked, it was a clear night and he had plenty of time anyway, it was an easy walk along the dune heads until you got to Drimmie and then just a short stroll up through the streets to the pub. A true original local pub, something that seemed to be dying out these days to be replaced with wine bars and bistros, this country looked to be gentrifying itself almost too much.

It was busy but not crowded, heading towards the weekend there were a few folk in but not as many as Friday or Saturday would bring but quite a few all the same.
It was an old building, all stone walls, oak panelling and an open fire, if Mark had not seen it himself he would have thought it was an escapee from a film set. The polished wooden bar top and the worn brass foot rail just

finished the image perfectly thought Mark as he stood up against the counter. Andy the barman and hotel owner stepped through the door and smiled at him as he pulled a pint of dark stout without asking what he wanted. "Wondered when we'd see you in here again. Sounds like there's going to be some activity round your place soon." Mark just raised an eyebrow as he raised his glass, Andy recognised the expression and carried on speaking as Mark looked around him at the other patrons in the bar. "Aye, sounds like a golf course, small hotel and a few houses are to be built in the area, might do us some good." Mark looked at him "Golf Course? We've got almost a hundred around here anyway and most of them struggle to break even. Where are they intending building all of that" One of the other locals, 'Dump' they called him, spoke up. "Up on that bare bit of dead ground just out from your place. Nothing grows there anyway, and we all know what the option is." Andy the barman laughed "Aye we all know what that is don't we, Dump." The bar laughed softly until someone else spoke up. "What makes you think it's a golf course? I was speaking to Peter Barnard the other day and he told me it was an equestrian centre, with the end client involved it was guaranteed to be the best in the world." Mark looked into the darkness at Jenny who had spoken; she hesitated and continued, "I'm not sure I like the idea. I mean, I ride horses but this landscape is supposed to be protected isn't it?" Mark nodded and spoke up "It is supposed to be protected, but you know as well as I do that wave enough money and politicians can be," he hesitated looking for the right word "convinced" he decided on using. As he looked around he saw someone else in the dim light looking agitated so he said "Andrea, you seem nervous or uncomfortable about something" She squirmed, a shy woman who did not like speaking in public but was quite determined all the same. "Well," she started "I was also speaking to Peter Barnard this week; he told me it was going to be a tennis centre of excellence, grass courts, clay and artificial surfaces all of them both indoor and outside; Also supposed to be the best in the world due to their backer." Andy the barman sighed, "Sounds like different people get different stories. The golfers are told it's a golf course, riders are told it's an equestrian centre and the tennis players are told it's a tennis centre." He paused and pursed his lips "Interesting" was his last word as he turned away polishing a glass. Jenny stood up from the table where she had been sitting on her own and came to stand at the bar with Mark, "What do you lot think about it?" Mark looked puzzled for a second as he watched Andrea stand up and join them while Jenny continued what she had been saying. "I must say I was surprised to hear that you had all sold so easily. I thought at least one of might have resisted a bit more" Mark looked at her, the puzzled look on his face causing a few people in the bar to pay more attention. "I have not sold, and neither have most of the folk on the estate. There's only one person I know

74

who might have sold and that's wee George at the end of the row of cottages." Andrea looked at him in amazement "Well, Peter Barnard stood roughly where you are now and told most of the bar that you had all sold, he had personally negotiated every single deal." Mark looked at her. "Well," he started "I don't even know a Peter Barnard let alone have sold him anything." He stopped and took a mouthful of his beer before he said "When was this?" Jenny looked at Andrea and the two women shrugged but it was Andy the barman's voice that came up with the answer. "Friday; it was Friday night, fairly early on because it was the topic of conversation for most of the night." Andy was still polishing a glass but no one could be sure if it was the same one or not "Said he wouldn't be in this evening though, got a meeting in town proper" Andy walked away slowly as Mark thought about this as he looked at the two women. "So, this guy who I have never met is telling everyone he has bought my house?" Both of them nodded slowly as Mark drained his glass and set it down on the counter. He shook his head as Andy picked it up again and waved towards the beer pump as Mark shook his head "No. Thanks Andy but I'm going home to think this one through." He turned back and looked at the two women. "I would suggest you two compare notes. This guy has basically told each of you that what is being planned is what he thinks will appeal to each of you. Obviously looking for support from you and your groups, add to that if he can lie to you so easily about having bought the houses on the estate, what else has be lied about?" The two women just nodded as he turned and walked out into the darkness.

+

At the same time Peter Barnard was having an uncomfortable meal in a private room at the Wycliffe Hotel in the middle of town. It wasn't that the meal was not good, it was actually better than had ever been served there before, but it was the company that was the problem. He was dining with Andrew Crawford the man who had hired him and, unexpectedly Trente Silver, the New York billionaire who owned the biggest property development network in the world if you believed his own publicity machine. He had no manners and ate with his mouth open. It was all Barnard could do to eat his own meal. "So," started Silver "We own the estate and have bought or are in the process of buying all the properties within the estate boundaries, yes?" Crawford looked at Barnard and it became clear in that split second he was meant to answer, he swallowed and started to speak "Well, the deal is done for the estate but, we haven't paid for it yet and it'll be almost six months before we take ownership. As for the houses we have come up blank I'm afraid, none of them want to sell or move out and one of them has threatened violence if we ever go near his door again," He did not get to finish as Silver started to speak "Good, violence always works in our favour once the media people get hold of it." He scooped another spoonful of food into his mouth and kept talking "Are we ready for the meeting tomorrow?" Crawford looked surprised "Meeting?" Silver nodded "Yes, I want you to call a meeting tomorrow with all those who live in the estate. Tell them they have to find somewhere else to live." Barnard exchanged glances with Crawford before he said "I don't think we can do that sir. We would need to find a location and we can't just throw them out of their homes." Silver looked at him with that gaze that Crawford knew meant he was almost fired, and continued "Why not?" "Well for a start they own their own homes" Silver put down his form and sat back "What do you mean they own their own homes. I was told we owned everything within the boundaries of the estate. Anyway, even if they do we can invoke the community improvement section of the property bill and get it signed by a New York judge" Barnard was shaking his head but it was Crawford that said "We can't do that here sir, that is US legislation and cannot be applied here." Silver just looked at him "I'm a US citizen, this is US development so US law applies." Crawford shook his head "No sir, it doesn't. We can come back to that argument in a moment, but if we are to hold a meeting tomorrow we need a venue." Silver sat back "How often have I told you that details are for idiots like you to fix. I've done my part flawlessly and to perfection, fix it and don't screw it up. I want a meeting tomorrow afternoon so the evening news can have pictures of me shaking hands with grateful householders who have just sold their properties for the greater good." He pushed his chair back and stood up "Good night Peter, nice meeting you. Now, go and find a venue for tomorrow." He stood there and waited until Barnard set down his spoon and as quickly as he could folded his napkin and stood up to leave the room. He remembered Silver did not shake hands and so turned and walked slowly to the door and out into the hallway. The bodyguards standing on the door barely noticed the weak little man leave.

+

Mark was almost half way home when he thought about going to see Paul at the big house. He was close to the building but not right at the door before the automatic lights came on. He smiled to himself; Paul had been listening after all. The door bell gave no indication of working but a few moments later there was the sound of an internal door opening and the flash of light from the peep hole told Mark that someone was looking out at him. Paul opened the door quickly once he had seen who it was on the step. "Come for that drink then?" he said as he stepped back and waved Mark into the interior Mark laughed "Yeah and maybe just a bit of a chat if that's

76

alright." Paul nodded "I think I can manage that." The two men were soon settled in large arm chairs either side of a log fire, with an open bottle of whisky between them, the cork lying on the table at its side as they spoke. "So," said Mark "You've sold the estate and there's nothing you can do about that now" Paul shook his head "Not a thing, If I could I would but its tied up so tight I can't move, legally I can't even tell you who the buyer is but he's not trustworthy I can tell you that." Mark looked at him for a second "Why do you say that?" Paul shrugged and looked into the flames for a second, it seemed like an age later he turned his head back and looked Mark in the face "Do I seem like an idiot to you? A simple easily controlled idiot?" Mark shook his head as Paul started to speak. "Well, between you and me. I've been easily controlled over this whole thing. It turns out that Mandy, the girl I was caught fumbling with, for lack of a better phrase, was paid to ensnare me and worse my wife knew about it." Mark just looked at him. "Mandy I can believe, she cleans for me, amongst other things and she appears to have the morals of a feral alley cat, but your wife, I find that hard to accept." Paul sighed "Well," he paused and sipped from his glass "Mandy told me this morning and I've done some digging as well, turns out she's getting a ten per cent finders fee from the end buyer as well as her half of the value of the house." Mark looked at his friend, surprised and dismayed, but not knowing what he could say. He was saved by the telephone ringing; Mark looked into the fire and thought about what he had just been told as Paul answered the phone. It was only a few minutes later that Paul sat down opposite him again, obviously furious. "Cheeky bastard," was his first comment as he took a mouthful of the fiery spirit. Mark watched him, amused; he had rarely seen this man truly annoyed. Paul soon calmed down enough to talk "That was Peter Barnard wanting to use the hall here tomorrow for a meeting with you lot. I told him to sod off. He can use one of the tents in the garden if he must hold a meeting. I'm still living here after all." Mark looked at him for a second "Who's 'you lot' and maybe more to the point who is this Peter Barnard everyone is talking about all of a sudden? I've never met him." Paul stared at him for a second "You must have met him, he offered to buy your house." Mark looked at him "No one has offered to buy my house" His voice tailed off as he thought "Except a man calling himself Paul Brown, offered a pathetic sum for my place over the phone." He paused and sipped from his glass "Is this the same Peter Barnard who is telling different people different things down in Drimmie?" Paul nodded "Sounds like him, different names different stories for different audiences. Not trustworthy, might be worth a little investigation." Mark nodded and drained his glass "Thanks for the drink and the information. Now I just need to figure out what I can do with it."

+

Jenny and Andrea had sat down together in a corner of the pub after Mark had left to compare stories. Andrea spoke first "I'm not sure what to make of all this. He sat down with me in the clubhouse and we discussed all of this in great depth, he had drawings and everything." Jenny just looked at her friend for a second or two." He came to you, sought you out?" Andrea nodded "Specifically came looking for me. As chair of the local tennis association he thought I would automatically be on his side, but I'm not sure." Jenny nodded. "He came looking for me too, as chair of the local hacking club and Gymkhana organiser. He had drawings with him then as well." She paused for a second before she said "Can you read drawings? I mean, can you truly understand what they are telling you?" Andrea shook her head "No, if truth be told I listened to what he was saying, more than try to read the drawings. I suppose you could describe it as more of a presentation aid than as a means of giving information." Jenny was nodding slowly "So was I, I can't read drawings either and I didn't get a copy. I wonder what it was he actually showed us." Andy the barman leant over the counter "You might get a chance to ask him tonight yet. He's just come back from town, must have finished his dinner early." The two women looked at each other and ordered another drink each.

+

The next morning when Mark got up at six o'clock there was a short note through the door, a hand delivered yellow envelope with a printed letter inside. The letter, on plain yellow paper, said that he was invited to a meeting at the big house, that morning, to meet with representatives of Mr Trente Silver to discuss the future of the estate. He turned it over in his hands and set it down thoughtfully as he wondered exactly what they were going to say.

It was a bright morning and he found it strange sitting on the wall outside the estate offices where they had all been gathered, talking casually to Mary and Pete and the rest of his neighbours. They all just smiled at each other as they were ushered into a marquee in the grounds, it appeared that they would not be getting into the house itself as had been promised. Mark was not surprised

The meeting started quite quietly with Crawford Andrews introducing himself and Peter Barnard, his second in command whom they all knew as Paul Brown. Mark sat and listened distractedly, something was bothering him but he could not place it, he was looking round as Andrews blathered

78

on about the three hundred million Euro development with two golf courses and about one hundred houses. It was after all just a hobby for Mr Silver he had all the money he needed and there would be no benefit to him to destroy the area and run. Mark suddenly realised what it was that was bothering him. The speakers around the room were making a low buzzing noise and as he looked around he realised almost all of the audience was in a dazed half asleep state. He thought back to some of the crowd control techniques he had been taught all those years ago. Seven cycles per second put people into an 'alpha' state, highly suggestible and easy to convince of anything you wanted. It was said that many of the evangelist churches used it to extract 'donations' from their audience. His head snapped round as he heard Andrews say "…if you just sign these forms now we can get the sale of your homes concluded so we can clear the estate and get started once the formality of planning permission is concluded." He was smiling as he looked around the room at the soporific faces of the people who were taking the forms and pulling out pens. Suddenly his grin froze in place as one set of eyes glared back at him, they did not meet eye to eye that was something Andrews could not do, but Mark was looking at his ears, not his eyes. Peter Barnard and Crawford Anderson were both wearing ear plugs.

Mark stood up and began to speak as he waved the paper he had been handed "You expect us to just sign away our homes for a pittance so you can get on with destroying the area?" He looked at the form as some of the heads began to swivel and look at him as they were sluggishly beginning to realise there was something wrong. Mark continued "Fifty thousand for my house? I had it valued last month and it came up at three hundred and fifty thousand." He stared at Andrews who realised they had a problem "Well your valuer obviously charged on the relative value of your house. The more expensive he made it, the more money he gets. Our valuer has done a proper valuation of all your homes and he says that is the most any one of them is worth." Old Jock stood up and shouted at him "My house as well? After all I have done for you, you were going to steal my house as well?" Mark continued, he would follow up with old Jock later on that one "How can you do a proper valuation without getting into the house? Another thing, is the fact that you and Barnard over there are wearing ear plugs anything to do with the background noise these speakers are putting out?" Andrews began to look scared but before he could say anything Barnard jumped up and ran from the tent. Little George was just coming out of it with a stupefied look on his face, maybe just as well, he could have become violent otherwise. Some of the others were still disoriented and it took a few minutes for Mark to pull everyone outside, away from the background hissing noise that the speakers were still issuing quietly. There was no sign of anyone other than a couple of security guards between them and the main house; Crawford had slipped away in the press of bodies trying to get out of the tent but it was obvious they were not welcome here any more. Mark turned to go back into the tent but the security guards that had appeared out of nowhere stood between him and the evidence he wanted. He decided not to push it today; he was still feeling the effects of the hypnotic noise himself.

5

About half an hour later they had all gathered at Marks place, some still seemed a bit unclear as to what had happened and who had said what, but they were all angry. Mark looked at old Jock "Anything to say to us Jock?" He looked uncomfortable and shuffled his feet as he cradled a cup of tea; he looked up slowly before he spoke "Any chance of a whisky? I feel like I need it" Mark nodded and opened a cupboard as Jock began to speak "I guess I owe you all an apology. I didn't think it would do any harm. They promised me half a million for my house if I would keep an eye on you all and tell them who to watch out for." He looked Mark in the eye as he took the offered glass "You were the one I said was most likely to fight back "Mark sighed as he looked around "Well I guess you got that right." He was interrupted as Little George jumped off his seat and punched Old Jock on the side of the face "You sold us out, traitor!" Mark had Little George pinned to the floor a second later as Old Jock tried to speak "I did it for the kids, to leave them something worthwhile" the old man was crying now as Mark refilled his glass and set him down again on the chair he had fallen off. Little George got up off the floor and Mark pushed him back down into a seat. "We are all adults here, let us act like it. This is probably what they would want, us squabbling amongst ourselves rather than dealing with them." He looked around at a mixture of expressions and a mixture of feelings, some of them extreme. "Now we are all in this together in some ways, it affects us all in slightly different ways. Some will be for the plan as it was put forward, some will be against it. Some will be for their methods, some will be against them. That is your individual choice." He looked around the room and the faces of everyone watching him, he had no desire to become a leader but that was what looked to be happening here right now. "Personally, I don't mind the idea of a golf course but I don't like their methods at all so I am tempted to tell them to shove it as hard and as far as they can." He didn't know who it was started to clap, but the round of applause was spontaneous and genuine and he felt more than a little odd standing in his own living room receiving a standing ovation.

Eventually they all quietened down and he was able to speak again "If we are going to fight this as a group, then we have to have a common public message." It was Carol, from the end house, who spoke up "What if we don't want to part of the group but still want to fight this." Mark hesitated, that was a scenario he had not envisaged, but it was Dr Jennifer James, his new tenant who replied "Surely, that's up to the individual. Everyone has to make up their own mind. We can all have our own personal position and still agree with and support the group. Just because there is a group does not mean individuals cannot make them selves known and make comment or take action on their own behalf." Mark hesitated as he thought about what she had said, it looked like most of the people there were doing the same until he spoke "So, you mean they can be in the group and still speak for themselves as well" Jennifer nodded in agreement and Mark slowly nodded. "Okay, I can go with that. If people have other things they want to say then fine, carry on. It is up to you; after all, it's your home." Carol and Andy were sitting there whispering to each other until Andy stood up and said "Well folks, we are going to leave you now. I'm not going to say we're for this thing but I'm not going to say we're against it either. So with that in mind we will not be joining your group." Mark looked at them as Carol stood up beside her husband "Well," he said slowly "that is your decision. I'm sorry to see you go but you will be welcome here if you change your mind." Slowly the group began to break up with people making their way home in ones and twos until it was just Jennifer left as Mark turned and looked out the window towards the sea. Jennifer stood up and stepped up behind him as he stood there with his head against the glass.

"I cannot conceive of this place under manicured lawns and with little flags dotted all over the place. It's supposed to be protected by law for pities sake" She had the feeling that it might have been a stronger phrase had she not been around. He turned and looked at her as she stood there "Fancy a coffee?" he asked as he made his way to the kitchen. She followed, wondering if she was meant to or not. The house was warm and welcoming somehow that she could not describe, she had felt it the first time she had been inside this place and had found a hypothermic young woman naked in his bath. 'No' she corrected herself 'he had left her underwear on' She decided to ask "How's the young woman, Sharon I think her name was?" he smiled "She's fine, or seems to be anyway. She was quite happy the other day when I spoke to her last." As he turned he knew that had been a ploy to see if she had been in touch or not. Jennifer looked at the floor and stepped over to the window "You have a lovely home here; my place is a little basic." Mark smiled to himself before replying "I'm sure if you spoke to the lawyer about it they would make the repairs etc that you want done" Jennifer was shaking her head "I doubt it, I took it on, on the understanding I got it slightly cheaper because I was going to do the work myself." She sighed and turned back to face him "Now, I'm beginning to think I have bitten off more than I can chew. It's a lot of work and I'm not sure where to start." He grinned as he filled the kettle again and turned to her "If you want a hand, just ask. If I can help I will." Jennifer smiled at him "Thank you, but I can't pay you for anything. I'm stretching myself as it is to pay

82

the rent there." Mark shook his head "I wouldn't worry too much about that. I know your letting agent, Steve the lawyer," Jennifer nodded as he continued "And I'm sure he can help you out in lots of ways. He might agree to supply a new bathroom suite if you can get it fitted." He shrugged as he turned to face her directly and was a little surprised to find her standing so close "I can help you fit it if you want." Her grin lit up her whole face as she smiled at him. He shook his head as he thought to himself 'Don't complicate things'.

Jennifer was smiling to herself as she turned away with the mug in her hands. So he had seen Sharon again and she was a good bit younger and prettier than herself, she could not fool herself about that; but he still seemed pleasant and friendly, even just as a neighbour it would be good to have him around.

+

Back down in the end house of the row Carol and Andy had just shut the door behind them as they stepped into the living room. Carol sighed as she sat down and looked up at Andy "What do you think? I think there has to be a club house at least and that will be better than walking all the way to Drimmie and that dingy dark hole of a pub. There may even be a hotel eventually and that would be good to have all that on our doorstep. Don't you agree?" Andy looked at her for a second and shrugged "Whatever" was his comment as Carol rattled on "Good, I'm glad you see it my way. As long as they leave us alone there's no reason for us to get involved in this fight at all. We'll just stay in the middle, quiet and peaceful until it's all over and we can enjoy the benefits." She looked at her husband "Can you see a problem with that?" Andy shook his head "Whatever you say. I just don't want any trouble." Carol smiled; he knew his place and that suited her perfectly.

+

It was Sunday morning and Marlene, the council leader was not happy. After the disastrous meeting where she had felt so badly humiliated she had hidden at home for a day or two and fumed, plotting her revenge. The council voting records had been where she started; she was only looking at her own party just now, she would deal with the others later when it would be easier. She had visited all her own disciples, just a quick courtesy call as they had all voted as they had been told to, like good little mannequins do. Then she had worked her way round the rest of the party, a lot of them had been plain cheeky, assuming they had a right to do as they chose or even as their constituents in their various wards wanted them to do and not as she said. That had to be corrected before it got out of hand, the public were meant to do as they were told and, as far as she was concerned, the members of her party were little more than members of the public. She drew breath; this was going to be a more difficult visit she thought as she turned her car off the main road. The five she had still to go and see were the most difficult of the lot and had always been trouble makers; in the nicest possible way of course. Marlene looked in the mirror and drew the car into the side of the road and stopped to think. Did she need to go and see them? She had never had the confidence she made out she had. Maybe an email would do all she needed. She finally decided after about fifteen minutes sitting there wondering what to do and started the car. A quick about turn and she drove away, back home.

Mandy thought she had recognised the car from here, but could not really be sure, the angle made it difficult and the hotel window was not as clean as it could be. She sighed and tuned back to the bed where Peter Barnard still lay sleeping. He might be willing to pay for this piece of information as he seemed to be willing to pay for almost anything else. She looked at the clock, it was almost time for her to get dressed and go home. Her mum had almost given up on her but not quite. If she was much later then she would be worrying and Mandy did not want her mum to worry. It caused too much trouble at home.

+

Mark was sitting looking out of the window at the bright morning sunlight as it scattered from the wave tops on the sea in front of him. There was a long shadow next the house as the sun came up inland behind him but where it hit the Western Ocean and scattered it was bright and might even be warm. The water would still be absolutely freezing to anyone who was daft enough to want to swim, but it looked lovely. He breathed deeply and relaxed as he sat there in the open doors watching the sea sparkle as he drank deeply from his mug he wondered what would happen next in this saga of the estate. He would not have long to wonder.

Eventually he realised the phone was ringing and made his way over to pick it up. It was Sharon "Is it true, have you sold up? Have you all sold up?" She was breathless and struggling to speak as Mark struggled to understand what she was asking. "Whoa, whoa, slow down Sharon, what are you talking about? I don't understand what you are asking me about?" He could hear her draw breath as the sound of a vehicle drawing up came to him through the window as he looked out and saw Paul Gray's four by four abandoned diagonally across the driveway. Paul slid from the drivers

84

seat and Mark waved at him to come on in to the house. Sharon carried on talking as Paul came in the front door "It's all over the Sunday papers. They are saying that all the householders on the estate met with Trente Silver himself yesterday and all of them sold their properties in order to assist in the development and growth of the country. None of them wanted to stand in the way of this fantastic futuristic plan for the economic survival of the country on into the next century long after the oil has run out; unquote." Sharon stopped to gather her breath as Paul held up two of the Sunday papers to show Mark the headlines. "Well," Said Mark to both Paul and Sharon "let me tell you, it was an interesting meeting and there is a lot for us to talk about but no one sold yesterday as far as I am aware. Almost all of the householders came up here afterwards to discuss matters and the dirty tricks being played by the Silver Organisation, but no one sold." Mark could see Paul smile as he heard that and Sharon breathed a sigh of relief "Can I come and see you, now, to discuss this. I might be able to put a piece together to counter this." Mark grinned "Come on over. I have a feeling there could be a few more people here before the end of the day." They said their good byes and he hung up the phone before turning to Paul who was still standing there with the papers in his hand "I didn't think you would sell so easily somehow but I had to come and see your face to be sure." Mark nodded "Yeah, to be sure" he said half jokingly "I have no intention of selling, now or ever. So forget that one right away." The door bell rang and Paul looked at Mark as Mark looked puzzled, very few who knew him used the door bell and if they did, they didn't wait on him answering the door.

It was Jennifer who eventually came in looking concerned and puzzled "I was just listening to the radio and I heard them saying that all the householders here sold their houses yesterday." She stopped talking as she saw the paper that Paul was holding up. Slowly she took it from his fingers and began to read. Paul looked at them both and said "What are you going to do?" Mark looked at him and drew breath "Well," he glanced at Jennifer "Sharon is on her way here so we can get her to do a piece and maybe see about getting a press conference set up if we need to." He hesitated as Jennifer carried on reading the paper "Maybe see what Sharon says and take it from there, see if we can get the papers to print a retraction of this garbage." Jennifer looked at him "This was submitted by a press agency or PR firm, it's the same in both papers and is very similar to what was on the radio." She paused "Did you not hear it?" he shook his head "No, I quite often don't have TV or radio on for most of the day and Paul just brought in the papers." He sighed and walked away to the window and they could just hear him mutter under his breath "Why do I get the feeling this could just be the start of a very long process."

'Xander was sitting in his official residence looking at the papers with a smile on his face when his wife came in "What are you grinning at?" He looked up surprised as he had not heard her come in "Oh, just an article in the press that makes things a lot easier." He hesitated for a moment or two before he folded the paper and turned to her "Remember that donation we received recently?" She looked at him worriedly, this was not something they normally talked about in government buildings but he seemed comfortable and carried on talking as she nodded in response to his question. "Well, it looks like the expected resistance and the heart string 'tuggers' may not be as much of an issue as we expected. They may have been more easily convinced that anyone believed possible." He turned the news paper round and handed it to his wife who was shaking her head as she read the two pages of text that said very little.

+

Trente Silver had had breakfast in his room and was smiling to himself, a genuine smile, not the usual deaths head grimace that he used, as he set the news paper down and ran a hand across the skin of his head where the hair should have been. Crawford would be here in a minute to get his orders for the day. He could congratulate him then. Sitting back he smiled to himself again, now it was in the press, the householders could never argue effectively that no one had sold to him. There were all those witnesses and even one of their own, the old man, what was his name again? Jock! That was it; he had been there and would be very grateful for what he was to receive, if he said what he was told to. After all the press loved him and his projects as did the vast majority of the public, so there really should not be a problem. This was going better than he could ever have hoped. All he had to do now was organise the bulldozers.

+

It was the Sunday evening before the story really broke that no one had actually sold. There had been rumours starting to leak out all day and the press 'feeding frenzy' had been starting to gather but it was actually the television news on Sunday night that blew it wide open. Paul could not be seen on the TV because of his already signed and sealed deal with Silver, Mark avoided cameras at all costs and Jennifer as a tenant and new comer to the area was not what the Press wanted to see.

86

So it was that Little George appeared on the TV speaking for the residents of the area. The reporter was a blonde woman about his own height who had already been speaking to the Silver Organisation. "So, what was your immediate impression this morning when you saw the headlines in the press?" George laughed "Initially plain blind fury, especially after the meeting yesterday when an attempt was made to buy our houses; a very poor and pathetic attempt at that." The reporter looked at him and nodded "I understand you have actually been in negotiation with the Silver Organisation already, that's you and all your neighbours." George hesitated "We all received verbal offers over the telephone from someone calling himself Paul Brown. He was revealed yesterday as actually being Peter Barnard, the offers were laughable and were rejected unanimously by everyone." George hesitated for a second and licked his lips but the reporter knew there was more to come so she waited and George sweated and after another few seconds broke and said "I myself did invite them round to discuss the offer as we have been considering selling for some time. Even face to face their offers were laughable and I threw Paul Brown out of my house." George looked down and licked his lips slowly before looking up and turning slightly so he was looking straight into the lens of the camera. "However, I do still intend selling my house and it will be going on open sale tomorrow to anyone other than the Silver Organisation." The reporter smiled and turned to the camera effectively cutting George off as the cameraman took his cue from her as she said "So you heard it here, the properties were not sold despite the dirty tricks being employed by the Silver Organisation and if you want a nice country property with a potential golf course nearby, or a tennis centre of excellence, or maybe a riding centre then this one." The camera panned off her and onto the view of Georges house as her voice over continued, "will be on the open market from tomorrow."

Mark switched off the TV and turned to look at the small group in his living room, Paul, Sharon, Jennifer, Mary and Pete. He hesitated as he thought about the others not here. Old Jock, Carol and Andy and Jennifer from further out; it was a small group as he saw it and he had a feeling there could be a lot of support from a lot of the public as long as they didn't think too much about it or realise what they were losing. Sharon put it into perspective. "This is all just posturing at the moment, after all the planning application has not even been submitted yet." She paused and looked around the room "It may all come to nothing yet." Mark nodded "here's hoping" he said but Jennifer added "I doubt that I'm afraid." No one said anything else to that.

+

Silver looked at Crawford who was watching the TV with him and said "Buy it" Crawford just looked at him blankly for a second as Silver continued "I don't care how you do it but buy that house. We might even keep it quiet but I want you to buy that house. To have some little shit tell me he'll sell to anyone other than us is an insult. Now see to it before I come back next month." Crawford nodded and stepped out of the car just before it went airside into the controlled area of the airport to get Trente Silver out of the country. He looked out of the window at the little white plane with a local registration number on it and muttered to himself "If it does to get me back to civilisation, if I can call London civilised, so I can get a decent meal and my own plane back home then it'll do." The car door was opened and he stepped out looking around "Not even any press to see me off." He growled as he headed towards the plane.

+

Jock stayed inside out of the way, he knew he had made a mistake and was going to try and hide for a while, they would all forget quickly enough and life would go back to the way it had been, or so he hoped.

George was watching the recording of his TV appearance that Karen had made for him. He was disappointed, it was short and he did not feel he had succeeded in getting his personal authority across. He sighed and sat back as his son watched him with something akin to hero worship. That made it all worth while. "Dad, if we get enough for our house will we be able to move into Drimmie? I would like to live in Drimmie, get to see my pals more often, you wouldn't need to drive me here and there so much either." George just nodded as Karen watched, she was wary about her husbands reaction to their sons questions. He was not always the most reasonable or logical of men. She relaxed when he spoke. "That's basically the idea, your mum and I want the best for you and while staying here is good, you need company your own age." His son smiled and jumping up ran outside as Karen looked at him "Not telling him that you also need the money to buy your franchise?" George just shook his head "Not relevant just now." She knew better than to argue, she bruised easily.

+

Mark was sitting alone on the steps that led up to the doors out of his living room with a mug of coffee and a view of the sun setting on the Western Ocean. It was a calm night with almost no breeze and just the strong orange glow reflecting off the water as it lapped gently at the beach seven hundred

88

metres away. "Hallo" the voice called at almost the same time as he heard the crunch of gravel under a light woman's tread. It was Jennifer, as he had started to call her; she walked around the end of the house from the driveway and looked at him sitting on the step. "I thought I saw you here. I can just see the edge of the doors from the attic room at my place" He smiled to himself as he said "So you're keeping an eye on me now are you?" She shook her head and sat down beside him on the step. They just sat there for a few minutes watching the sun as it sank into the sea before she spoke. "I thought Sharon was crying when she left earlier today. She was the last one left at your place?" Mark nodded slowly and a little sadly "Yes, she stayed behind to talk to me." He took a mouthful of his coffee before setting it down again and continuing to talk "I had thought we might be friends, even though she is younger than me, but she told me that wasn't going to happen." He sighed as Jennifer picked up his mug "She said she had also thought about it but with the news story as it was developing she would need to remain as impartial as possible. She could not be seen to be in a relationship with someone who was directly involved." Jennifer watched him as she said "She said relationship, not friendship?" Mark nodded as Jennifer sipped at his coffee and then spluttered and gasped for breath "How much whisky is in that?" Mark shrugged "About a third. Anyway, yes it was Sharon who used that word, not me." Jennifer handed back his mug "Did you want a relationship with her?" Again he shrugged "I don't know, I was flattered, it's been a long time and I'm fairly sure I'm not as sociable as she would want me to be." He stood up and waved his mug at Jennifer as she stood up as well "Want a coffee?" She smiled "Yeah, why not? Just, no whisky in mine please." He nodded as they stepped inside and shut the doors.

It wasn't much later as they sat on the sofa that Jennifer said "We should see about getting a group together." He looked at her as she continued "To fight this application, if the lies continue as they have started then it could get messy." Mark nodded slowly "Yes, I take your point but as the application has not even been lodged yet then we actually have nothing to fight against, yet." Jennifer nodded "True, but we know its going to be submitted soon so there must be something we can do." Mark just looked at her and began to wonder where to start. There had to be a way to do this. It was going to be difficult but it had to be done.

+

The next evening Mark was sitting in the bar of the pub down in Drimmie with Jennifer by his side and Andrea and Jenny on the opposite side of the table. Mark was speaking "...it may seem to be early as there has been no application submitted yet but we want to be ready to react when it is dropped on us. Going by the lies that have already been told it will probably be a dirty fight that might last a long time." Andrea set down her glass "Well it is early but Peter Barnard already lied to my face about this thing and I doubt he would think twice about doing it again. So," she sighed "while I need to speak to my committee about our overall support I can promise you my personal support right now depending on what is actually applied for." Jenny, who was sitting right next to her had been nodding vigorously throughout this conversation added "Me too, for all the same reasons. He's lied and changed his story to fit the audience so cannot be trusted. You have my support when it comes to it."

Mark nodded and sat back "I don't know how we are going to get this out into the public forum without the help of the local press." Jennifer looked at him as she heard the sadness in his voice, just a hint but it was there. "We can still contact Sharon and use her as our lead into the press if needs be, just because she cannot be directly involved does not mean she won't welcome a story if it comes her way." Mark nodded as the other two women looked on wondering what all that meant. Andy the barman stood there watching, polishing a glass. Suddenly he smiled and turned as the door to the lounge opened and Peter Barnard walked in. He smiled as he stepped up to the bar and Andy spoke "Hallo Mr Barnard meeting some one again tonight are we or just on your own?" Barnard just smiled for a second "Just on my own, could I get a glass of white wine please?" Andy nodded and handed over the glass of wine as he had been asked to before he said "Think there might be some locals over there want to have a word with you" he nodded in the direction of the corner where the little group sat and he smiled as he recognised Andrea and Jenny as supporters of his. His casual slow walk came to a sudden halt when he saw the fourth person at the table was Mark. "Hallo Paul" said Mark "Nice to see you again, got a new story or name for us today? I understand you are better known in some circles as Peter Barnard, so which one are you calling yourself tonight?" He bridled at that "How dare you call me a liar in public" Mark laughed "Why not, I've called you a liar in private before as well, and you did use a false name to try and buy several houses here." Barnard turned away "That's a perfectly legitimate business strategy, which you would know if you worked for a living instead of being a worthless sponger on the state." He turned back and everyone in the bar watched as the venom in the weak little man came out while Mark sat there and laughed at him as he said "I'll have you out of that house before the end of the month. I've just bought out your landlord and the same will apply to all the rented properties on the estate. We've just bought Paradigm Properties and you'll be getting eviction notices soon." He stepped back as Mark laughed even harder at him "Fool," he said "I know the owner of Paradigm Properties and that company and its assets are not for sale. So go away or maybe you want to explain why your thugs were trying to burn an old man out of his house a few nights ago." Barnard turned on his heel and walked back through to the lounge. Mark shook his head as he sat forward and made to move. Jenny leant forward and put her hand on his arm "Do you think there is any chance of them being able to buy your landlord out?" Mark shook his head. "First, I own my own house, it's not rented." He had raised his voice slightly so everyone in the bar could hear him talk without him having to shout "Second, I know Paradigm Properties is not for sale, so there is no chance of any eviction notices being issued by them. If anything they will dig in harder and deeper." Jenny nodded as Andrea said "This is going to be a dirty fight by the look of things so he will make use of the unemployed man against the empowering and investing international corporation." Mark shook his head "I am not unemployed. I am self employed; I just don't work in the public domain. That might have to change though. Anyway, it's time for me to go home." He turned to Jennifer beside him "You coming or do you want to stay for a while yet?" She shook her head "I'll come with you." They stopped as Mark set the glasses down on the counter "Sorry about that, he might move out now and I'll have cost you the business" Andy shook his head "Don't worry about it, the bastard hasn't paid his bill yet anyway; so no great loss. I don't trust him." He nodded and the two of them turned and left the pub, just as the door was closing Mark could hear the level of conversation rise noticeably as the locals started to talk about what they had just seen and heard.

They walked in companionable silence down through the village until they reached the beach area and turned south to walk along the beach. Once on the sand Mark paused and looked out to sea. Jennifer thought she heard him sigh as they started to walk slowly along the head of the dunes. "That was a deep heartfelt sigh, anything wrong that I can help with?" He shrugged and shook his head, which was quite indistinct in the moonlight, before he spoke "No not really. Just memories of other people, friends and others in beautiful places and how often they have all said this was a stunning location. Tonight proves it and then you've got some low life like Silver and his organisation using half wits who call themselves local coming along trying to destroy it all." He stopped and looked out to sea at the moonlit path across the water "Sorry," he continued "I just get annoyed sometimes" Jennifer shook the hair out of her eyes and stepped up close before slipping her arms around his waist "It's alright, we all have to believe in something. I believed in love until my husband betrayed me. That's why I came over here; away from my home and all of our friends. I had the feeling that every time they looked at me they were thinking about what had happened." She pressed herself against his chest and he thought he could feel tears through his shirt as she carried on "And with whom and while I was probably imagining it. I felt they were all talking about it behind my back all the time, like he had been messing around behind my back, for years as it turned out." She sniffed and lifted her head "Sorry, I barely know you. You don't want to listen to all of this." He smiled at her and she saw the sparkle of moonlight reflecting off his teeth in the dark as he replied "Its okay, I'm happy to listen as long as you want to talk. I think it might do you some good." Slowly they continued to walk along the dune head in the moonlight.

Several hundred metres away the man in the dark clothing lowered his camera and wondered what that meant. He would file his report as usual but he was beginning to wonder what it was his client was looking for.

The two of them walked slowly and quietly across the links area towards the bottom of the bank on which their houses were built along with the rest of the row. At the bottom of the bank was another house. It sat end on to the sea, like the row above did. Jennifer slowed and looked at the house as it sat there in darkness. "Do you think they know we're here?" Mark shook his head "They keep themselves to themselves, as long as the dog doesn't hear us, neither will they." Jennifer shook her head as they walked on up the road towards the houses still with their arms around each other.

+

Templeton was worried, he had done as he was told, like normal, but he knew 'Xander actually hated him and, to be fair, it was mutual. He had been leader of the party until 'Xander had been thrown out of the European Parliament for condoning corruption. That wasn't the public story of course but the truth would never be allowed into the public domain and that was what had happened. As far as the public and his blind followers were concerned he had 'come home' as he called it to lead the party to victory. Unfortunately for Templeton he had been the leader at the time and would have stuck it out had it not been for a small 'honorarium' that he had taken to assist a bill though the house some time ago. The 'client' had not been as circumspect as Templeton had believed. Now he was sitting there with enough money to retire but a threat from 'Xander that he had to stay until this matter was finished. He had understood that he would only be called on if the application had to go beyond the local council for approval. As it hadn't even been submitted that had seemed a long way off, now he was looking at a statement he'd just been passed from 'Xander's parliamentary secretary, a man Templeton hated even more than his boss if that was

92

possible, a sneaky, slimy, untrustworthy little worm of a man. He was being 'asked' to issue this as a press statement today. Templeton did what he felt was right for the first time in years. He drew breath again as the shredder switched off having finished what it had been given to do. Sitting back he looked at his reflection in the glass of the window that looked down upon the city. Yes they were in power, but it was a minority government, that made it touch and go from one vote to another and if you did the maths they actually only represented sixteen per cent of the electorate. It did not take a big swing to have them out of office, but a swing could only happen if there was an election. That was not going to happen soon.

+

Marlene was a little nervous as she waited on her visitor, this was unusual but not unheard of and there was a very good reason for this. She jumped as the doorbell rang; it was who she was expecting. He turned and faced her as she studied him, His slicked back hair and that green jacket he almost always wore identified him immediately as 'Xander's brother and the leader of the separatist party locally.

+

Mark looked down the track as the battered silver four by four drove away in a cloud of dust. 'Leaving in a hurry' he thought as he picked up the dirty, torn envelope from the floor behind the front door.

He smiled as he opened it and looked at the yellow sheet of paper, it was a neighbour notification, telling him that the Silver Organisation had applied for outline planning permission for a golf resort adjoining his land, it was dated three days before and the envelope had no stamp, he turned and went through to his office. The computer started up quickly and it only took a few minutes for him to get to the local authority website. The reference number on the notice led him to the actual application; it had been lodged four days previously. He checked the date on the form in his hand that meant the application was technically invalid. Somehow he didn't think little things like facts or the law would get in the way here. The covering letter was from a local architect as was the application form but it was a different name on the drawings. Mark sat back and looked at the drawings again, this was not what they had been shown in the tent up at the big house recently. He stood up and pushed his chair back, he needed to think, he was distracted by the door bell and the cheery shout "Hi, just me again." He sighed to himself "Mandy" he muttered as he stepped out of the office and closed the door behind him as she came along the corridor smiling. She hesitated a little when she saw the look on his face but she still threw her arms around his neck and tried to kiss him. He did not respond but instead put his hands on her waist and pushed her away before turning and walking into the kitchen. She followed a little way behind and asked in a soft small voice "Have I done something wrong?" He just looked at her for a moment before he dipped into his pocket and pulled out some cash. He counted out one hundred euros and handed it to her "Take this, don't come back. I don't need your services anymore." She stared at him "Your firing me?" her voice shook as she looked at him "Why?" He snorted as he turned away before turning back "You have lied to me, you've been nosing around in my office when you were told specifically not to go in there. You've lied to my friends and presented yourself as my girlfriend when you aren't. That's enough to be going on with. Now leave and leave your key behind." She sighed "I guess I shouldn't be surprised, your new girlfriend looked a bit surprised to see me here at all, let alone having just crawled out of your bed. I hope you liked what you saw because it will be the last you'll ever see of it." her voice was more strident now, almost shouting as she tried to control herself "I hope they knock your house down with you still inside" was her parting shot as she turned and stormed out of the house, clutching to the one hundred euros he had given her. He sighed and watched from the office window as she drove away in a cloud of dust and temper; out his driveway, up the hill and into history. Mark sighed 'Sounds like I struck a chord there somewhere' he muttered to himself as he sat down again and studied the drawing on the screen.

+

Dr Jennifer James had reported to the surgery that morning as had been agreed with the practice manager at the end of her locum period a few days before. Everything had gone smoothly and everyone seemed happy to see her, they had been overstretched without a fourth doctor in the practice so she was going to be busy as she settled into her new life as a country doctor. It was at lunchtime that she saw the 'Daily' lying in the receptionist's office. Four pages of editorial, the first four pages of editorial were devoted to this new planning application that, according to the paper, would be breathing new life into the area for decades after the oil had run out in the Western Ocean. Slowly she picked it up and looked at the article when one of the reception team said "Isn't it wonderful? A development like that in this area will do wonders for us. Won't it be fantastic to have that resource here on our doorstep?" Jennifer didn't answer immediately "I'm not so sure. There have been problems with his developments across the world with all sorts of things going on. I think this could be a long story

94

before anything becomes finalised." The woman looked at her strangely "But the paper says it's going to be good. That has to be true doesn't it?" Jennifer looked at her, surprised as she set the paper down again. "No, just because it's in the paper does not automatically mean it's true. It is just the news papers opinion that is usually open to challenge." Turning she went back to her room and checked her calendar for the afternoon. A soft knock on the door made her turn round as the practice manager walked in and smiled. "How are you settling in?" he asked "Well," she said "Not much different than the locum trial last week." He nodded "Of course, of course," he spoke slowly as if trying to figure out what he wanted to say. "You don't have any appointments booked in this afternoon, so why don't you take the time to go and familiarise yourself with the area. That way when you have house calls you will have an idea where to go." She nodded "Sounds like a good idea and I might just take you up on that but I want to have a look at some of the files first so I can get an idea of who is local to where I'm staying." The practice manager nodded "Sounds like a good idea, why not start with those closest to where you live, that way you'll know your neighbours." She smiled at him, a genuine warm smile that lit up her face. He smiled back as he went through to reception; she was going to be a benefit to the practice.

A few minutes later he returned with a printed list of names and addresses and set it on the corner of her desk as she turned to look at him. Something caught her eye. "Why is this one scored out?" he hesitated and looked more closely "Oh Arthur McIntyre, simple he moved away with his nephew when he emigrated to Canada a few years ago. No one ever asked for his files, a little worrying actually." He paused and pursed his lips "I wonder if we should archive them, knowing that he's gone away." Jennifer shook her head "I would keep them on the shelf until the five year limit is up then archive them." He smiled "Of course, silly me, we have rules for that sort of thing." She smiled at him wondering if she had just been tested for some reason.

It was almost an hour later that her powerful red car drew up at the end of Marks house and she looked over to where he parked his land rover. It wasn't there, she sighed as she realised there was no reason to expect him to be home. She didn't even know what he did for a living, other than he worked for himself. She moved her car and left it so it was more parked than abandoned before she got out and kicking her shoes off walked across the soft grass that was really needing cut, to the head of the bank and standing there, looked out over the links area to the dunes beyond. She hugged herself as she thought about walking home the other night. She had not felt so safe in the company of a man in a long time and she had enjoyed his company, it was nice to have a friend to talk to again, someone who did not judge her for what her husband had done.

She looked down and her eyes misted up for a second until she heard the heavy diesel engine approaching up the driveway. Quickly she slipped on her shoes again and wiped her eyes as the Land Rover pulled up along side her own car. He was smiling as he jumped out and waved at her, turning back he opened the rear door and pulled out a long box and a carrier bag from the back seat before heading towards the door. Jennifer followed him in as he opened the door and went straight to his office. The carrier bag was dropped on the floor just inside and the long box was laid carefully on the floor as he stood up and smiled at her "Want a coffee?" was the casual question as he stooped and kissed her on the cheek as she stepped aside to let him get to the kitchen. "Yes sure, I'd love one." She looked back down the hall at the open office door before she said "What's in the box? It looks interesting" he smiled and she was almost sure he blushed a little as he said, "It's a large printer, prints on rolls of paper rather than sheets. I've wanted to get myself one for a while but could never justify it. Now I want to print out a drawing to let people see it, so I can justify it to myself." She sighed and kicked off her shoes behind the kitchen door before she said "Wouldn't be anything to do with the planning application that is worth four pages of editorial would it?" he looked at her a little surprised "I haven't seen the paper yet but by the sound of it, probably, yes."

It was about half an hour later that Mark was sitting at his desk with Jennifer sitting on the arm of his chair watching the new printer produce a large scale drawing. It was almost two feet wide and four or five feet long. Jennifer stared as the sheet began to roll up on the floor "What are all these blocks marked on the drawing?" Mark picked up the curling sheet of paper and stretched it as far as it would go across his desk. "This is us here," he said pointing at some coloured blocks on the sheet "This is my house where we are now and this is the row of houses where you stay at the moment." He looked at another coloured block on the sheet "This is a block of flats or apartments that were never mentioned at the meeting in the tent up at the house nor was this hotel" he finished pointing at yet another coloured block on the drawing. Jennifer stood up and looked out of the window "How far away are they going to be? You might never see them from here." Mark looked up at her a little sharply "About fifty metres away, not as far as that first ridge in the field." Jennifer looked out at the ploughed field just inland from the window she was looking out of "Oh," was all she said as Mark continued studying the drawing while the printer finished its job. He tore off the sheet and stood up "What bothers me almost as much," he said as he stepped around the desk "is the fact that the SSSI is not even mentioned."

96

Jennifer looked at him "Sorry, SS what?" She said "I don't even know what that is." He sighed and looked at her, realising that just because he knew something did not automatically mean everyone else did as well.

Half an hour later they were on the balcony of his bedroom with the drawing, looking around trying to place all the features that were shown on the printed sheet when the 'phone rang. It was Jenny "Have you seen the paper?" She started without any introduction Mark laughed and switched the phone onto loudspeaker so Jennifer could hear as well "No Jenny, I haven't but I've heard all about it. Where are you at the moment?" She sighed "Oh I'm still at the school, but there's a paper in the staff room and so many people seem to think it's going to be great. They don't understand what it's going to be like." Jennifer nodded "Or they don't care" she said and Mark laughed "Unfortunately I think that might be nearer it" Jenny spoke again on the other end of the phone "Can we meet tonight? I could come round to your place this evening." Mark hesitated for a second "Yeah sure, lets get a few people together. Can you get hold of Andrea and bring her along?" He could hear Jenny nodding as she said "Of course, I'll bring her along. Meanwhile I have to go back to work, speak to you later" and she broke the connection. Jennifer sighed as he looked at her and she ran her hands through her hair "You going to come along?" he asked "Don't try and stop me" she said "I just thought I might have a chance to talk to you alone but obviously not." She turned laughing to him as he turned and stepped back inside and he said over his shoulder "Well you can have me all to yourself for a while if you let me cook. You do want something to eat, don't you?" Jennifer nodded and could not trust herself to speak; it had been a long time since a man had cooked for her.

6

That evening Mark had a house full of people, he had not really expected nearly as many people as actually turned up. He looked at Jennifer who seemed to have taken over the provision of teas and coffees from his kitchen without any involvement from him; whilst he hurried about the house looking for extra chairs that could be pressed into service. When he finally got into the living room himself he found that almost all the chairs were empty as people were crowded around the large print he had taken and hung on the wall. When he walked in the room became noticeably quieter as people turned to him and made to sit down out of his way. Self consciously he stepped through the crowd until he was standing beside the plan as it hung on his wall and the room fell silent as everyone waited for him to speak. He paused and looked around at people he had known for years and maybe not known for years as well. They were all fairly local and had been invited here by people who knew him but somehow he still had the feeling there would be at least one person in the room who thought his development was a great idea and could never see his point of view. He would worry about that later.

"Evening folks and thanks for coming here tonight at such short notice. Those of you who live on or next to the estate should have received a neighbour notification that a planning application was going in. I received mine, hand delivered, today." He held up the tattered envelope "While the application is already on the website which tends to mean that the council will have received it last week at the latest." He licked his lips and took a sip from his mug of tea before he carried on "Now some of you will already have met Peter Barnard or Paul Brown as he called himself when he first tried to buy these houses. That gives me a fair indication of the type of people we are dealing with, basically dishonest." He could hear a ripple pass amongst the crowd as some of them did not like the description. Mark looked around the room and found it a little disconcerting with so many pairs of eyes all focused on him and listening to every word he said. He continued "When we met them up in the tent at the big house a few weeks ago this was described as about a hundred houses and a golf course." He stepped to one side and waved at the drawing "As you can see it is now a hotel, two golf courses, a thousand flats and almost three hundred houses. Not what could be deemed a good idea for an area that is supposed to be protected by law." He could hear a few murmurs of agreement and one voice rose above the rest "Oh come on it has to be for the common good hasn't it?" Mark laughed out loud before he could stop himself. "Sorry, but that was a question I did not expect, could you explain common good?" There was no reply from the group; it was obvious the person who asked the question did not have an answer.

Two hours later the group had dispersed and only the usual suspects were left, Jennifer, Mary and Pete and two surprise guests Dr Marianne Presley and Mike. Mark had not expected them to come along and had not actually known they were invited, he asked Mike how they had known about the meeting. But it was Marianne that replied. "One of my students is a tennis freak. Andrea told all of her club and they in turn told me." She looked around at the empty mugs and glasses and added "And, it looks like half of the town of Drimmie." Jennifer just smiled at her as she carried on picking up glasses; Marianne went to help her out as Mike pulled Mark to one side.

In the kitchen Marianne looked at Jennifer as she filled the sink with hot water and asked "I didn't know you two were an item" Jennifer flushed "We're not." She relied "at least not yet. We haven't really even gone out together." She turned and looked at Marianne "I'm just a neighbour who so happens to agree with what he's doing and saying." She shrugged as her face took on a far away expression "I'm not sure I'm ready for anything else anyway, but we'll wait and see what happens will we." Marianne nodded "I won't say anything, just keep me informed about any developments. Now where's the dishwasher?" Jennifer laughed and shook her head "There isn't one; he says it's pointless for one person." She looked levelly at the other woman "That'll change" They both giggled as they turned back to the sink.

In the living room Mike waited until Marianne had left the room and said "Thanks for that hint about the lawyer, he really put Marianne in the right direction and as for the new job. She is delighted." He paused and looked past Mark before he continued "You don't know who the owner of this Paradigm Properties is do you? Its just that it's driving Marianne crazy at the moment and she is terrified that she's being set up for something" Mark just shook his head "Tell her not to worry. I'm as certain as I can be that she's not being set up. I've known Steve, the lawyer guy, for years and years and I would trust him with my life if it came to it. So believe me she's as safe as anyone else in a job at the moment." Carefully he looked away at Mary and Pete and said "You guys okay or do you want another drink there?" Stepping to one side he took Petes glass from him before he turned back to Mike "Fancy another beer?" Mike nodded as he sat down next to the other two while Mark disappeared to the kitchen for a clean glass for his friend.

When he returned with a tray of drinks, the three of them were deep in conversation and Mark went over to stand looking out of the window at the moon on the sea and the sparkle from the few waves there were still visible out there. He sighed as he listened to the conversation going on behind him.

+

Mandy was in a mess when her mum found her, she was sitting propped up in a corner in the bar in Drimmie, asleep. Her mum sat down beside her and sighed as she did so, carefully easing the empty glass from her daughter's fingers. Andy the barman came over to speak to them as the bar was almost empty. She looked up at him with tears in her eyes as she asked "Why? Why does she do this to herself?" He shook his head. "No one can ever be really sure other than the person themselves, and sometimes even they cannot be sure of the real reasons. Sometimes its an internal problem, sometimes its external." He dug in his pocket and handed her a card "Here, leave this lying around where she can find it. Don't give it to her or suggest that she goes to a meeting. Just leave it where she can find it, eventually it'll do its job." Mandy's mum looked at the card in her hand. It read 'Alcoholics Anonymous'. She shook her head before sighing and slipped it into her pocket without a word.

+

Crawford's was smiling at the three men sitting across the table from him in the private dining room at the Wycliffe hotel "You have all been very cooperative and forward looking in your handling of this somewhat sensitive issue to date." He moistened his lips slightly almost like a snake would do with his tongue slithering out and back in quickly, silently, before he continued speaking. "As a token of our appreciation we would like to give you these." He slid three large brown envelopes across the table as he spoke "These are membership packs for our golf resort. Once we are complete here these will give you lifetime membership of the golf club along with access to the other facilities on site." Greyson, of the 'Evening' picked his up and tore it open hungrily and looked through it quickly. Jamieson, of the 'Daily' slid his off the table and turned it over in his hands, obviously thinking about it, whilst Jackson the MD of the 'Local News' group of companies left his where it lay but said "There's a long way to go before anything is confirmed. Let's go guys." Standing up he waited on his two minions doing as they were told before he said "I don't think accepting this is a good idea for me, thank you all the same. The others have to make up their own mind about how they deal with it."
100

Greyson looked up at him and shrugged, saying nothing he tucked the envelope under his arm and followed his boss out of the door. Jamieson, held his own unopened envelope between two fingertips and nodded to Crawford's before he followed his boss out of the room. Crawford's steepled his fingers and sat back to think as the door shut behind the three men. Dull knocked on the door almost immediately and walked in without waiting for an answer. "Well," he asked "Go as expected did it?" Crawford's looked at the annoyingly arrogant little man for a few moments before he nodded and spoke curtly "Grayson, grabbed it with both hands, Jameson took it but seemed to think it was a poisoned chalice" he sighed "Jackson didn't even touch the envelope" Dull grunted "'bout what I expected. Grayson has always been a greedy bastard, takes everything that comes his way. Jamieson wants to be but is too scared to just go for it and Jackson takes nothing publicly." Dull turned to leave but stopped and turned back to Crawford's "Remember, he was brought in by the new owners to clean up the papers so he won't want to be seen as taking anything in front of his staff; might work better behind closed doors with him, alone." Crawford's waited until the door had closed behind the little man before he said "Prick!! As if I need advice from that little shit about how to bribe anyone" The security guard standing silently in the corner behind the door said nothing and made a point of not moving, he did not want his boss to realise he was still there. He had a feeling this project was not going as well as had been hoped.

+

'Xander's brother smiled to himself as he took the cheque from Paul Browns hand, it was a nice addition to the parties funds and the fat brown envelope underneath it was what was actually making him smile. "Thank you very much Paul, the Party appreciates your assistance in every way and will in turn be ready to assist you in any way that we can, within the appropriate limits of course." Peter Barnard nodded "Of course, of course, we would expect no more impropriety than is absolutely necessary" The words held an obvious meaning and the smile said more than words ever could. The man with the slicked back hair stood up and shivered slightly as he walked out of the office before driving away. He shook his head at himself in the rear view mirror as he slowly manoeuvred up the driveway past the big house and on up towards the main road. He was now in a dangerous position, he had a weakness and the people who had put him there were the ones most likely to exploit that weakness. He wondered how his little brother survived with this threat level all of the time.

+

Marlene sat there looking at the brown envelope that sat on her coffee table in the middle of the room. After her recent meeting with the local leader of the separatist party she had been prepared to assist in almost any way she could, this was her way out of this place and into the big time. The brown envelope had been unexpected. She had hoped for it, but had not expected it to actually happen. She had always been warned by her old friends, who had been politicians for years that she should be careful not to get sucked into the brown envelope trap. Shrugging her shoulders she leant forward and tore it open. There were eight bank drafts made out to 'cash' and two thousand Euros in twenty Euro notes. She grinned widely, ten thousand Euros, she'd have done it for half that amount but they had not negotiated. They just accepted her first request and here was the evidence.

+

Dull wasn't particularly happy, he didn't like being called a prick, or any other profanity for that matter. He had wondered for some time what the Silver organisation really thought of him, now that they had started using the meeting room he had had specially prepared with microphones and cameras he was a lot happier and he now knew exactly where he stood with them. He sighed as turned back to the machine and lifted off the DVD, wrote on its surface, just the date and time of the meeting along with those present. He grinned slowly to himself as he clipped it into its case and added it to a growing pile on the shelf by his desk in this, his hidden office at the back of the wine cellar. He really would need to do something about the empties though.

+

Paul Clancy had been surprised to see Andrew Crawford in reception waiting on his return. While he was welcome at the chamber offices it might have been better to be a little more circumspect. Sitting out in reception was possibly not the best idea in town at the moment. As soon as he got himself settled he called the receptionist only to get a surprise "I'm sorry sir he's gone." Paul Clancy was amazed "What do you mean gone?" he almost shouted at the poor receptionist. "Well, he came in to speak to Greta, our training coordinator, she became available just as you arrived and he left just a moment ago with a folder full of information to assist him setting up a training programme." Paul Clancy just grunted, this he did not understand "Thank you." He said before hanging up the phone. He would need to find out what they were up to. They may be good for business and his overall personal image but he was not sure he liked or trusted any of them as far as he could throw them. He sat back to think in peace.

+

The man with the camera was sitting in a hotel room downtown in the middle of a nondescript hotel. He had been told quite clearly not to go to the Wycliffe; that might be just too obvious. He grinned to himself as he reviewed the photographs he had already taken and he was already beginning to realise this was becoming complex as he had known it was going to. He would need to repeat his request for more personnel and a proper functional base. Shaking his head he turned back to his photographs and the images of some of the locals along with some of the Silver Organisation people. He wondered if any of them realised how obvious it all looked from the outside, where he was standing.

+

Mark was on his way out the next morning when he saw the dirty grey pick up truck for the first time, it was to become a familiar sight around the estate as it seemed to appear in the strangest of places for a while. When he saw it first it was sitting in the mouth of the back drive to the big house where it joined the farm road that almost all of the householders on the estate used to come and go. It was far enough off the road that it was not actually in the way but it was obvious because it was not normally there. There was no one obviously around but Mark could feel himself being watched as he slowed down and took a good look at the truck so he could identify it again.

The guard with the dog on a chain watched from a few yards away, behind the gorse bushes that spread so freely and turned the country bright yellow at this time of year. The old green Land Rover slowed down and studied his truck before it carried on its way. He shook his head, he hated these types of jobs but this one would only be a few months he had been told. He shook his head once more, they had said that before as well. That job had taken two years.

+

'Xander was quietly watching a TV documentary and if it had been a public room a few people would have wondered what it was that was bothering him. As it was the TV was in his own office and no one saw him sweating and pondering and sweating some more. Just along the corridor

Templeton was watching the same programme and was wondering if 'Xander was as well. It was an early evening documentary about corruption in politics in the 'homeland' as they were now trying to call it. It all started with expenses from last year; that did not bother him, he'd stopped that almost two years ago just in case this type of thing happened. He was watching carefully but not really seeing the politician in tonight's show sitting in front of the camera and trying to explain away a fifteen thousand Euro surround sound system that he had claimed on expenses for, five years ago. 'Xander was worried, five years ago his accounts weren't that clean. Along the corridor Templeton was laughing, he may be in trouble now but he did not have the track record of 'Xander. It would almost be worth it to see the slimy little fat man go to jail. He hesitated with his hand above the receiver and thought about it, reluctantly he pulled his hand back several minutes later. There were others involved who would also be damaged by his revelations, he did not think they deserved that; yet.

The programme ended with the presenter turning to camera and saying "One more corrupt politician going down. Our files have been passed to the police already and I believe they are waiting outside for tonight's guest. Tune in again next week for another of our 'political masters' to be shown for what they really are."

Templeton and 'Xander both sat there watching the credits run, followed by the adverts, each one was thinking in very different ways, one was sweating and scared and one was giggling like a little girl.

+

In the safe house the man with the camera had also watched the same documentary along with three of his newly arrived colleagues. There was silence for a minute or two once the show ended until someone picked up the remote control and flipped the switch. They looked at each other before one of them said "Do you really think Silver would be that stupid?" The original man nodded, he had been following the Silver organisation around the world for years, unfortunately usually too late. This time it might be different, he spoke. "Yes he will be that stupid, because he believes he is untouchable." He sighed as the other two turned to look at him "He believes US law stops at the US border except when he tries to invoke it. This time he is going to be in for a shock." The blonde woman leant forward "When do we go? Do we have to wait until permissions are granted or what?" He shook his head "It'll be a while yet I'm afraid, it's not so much a case of the permissions it's a case of experience." He looked around at his friends "Silver has been at this for a lot of years and hides his tracks well. I hear that one of our internal teams is only now getting the final evidence on a Chicago job that he was involved in fifteen years ago, almost at the statute of limitations. Here, there is no statute of limitations so if we catch him, no matter when we get the info the national Police can deal with him. Basically we are looking at his contacts locally. When one of them makes a mistake then we can move in, with local assistance and access their bank records." One of his other colleagues looked at him blankly "Why do we need local assistance?" He shook his head and sighed "We have no real jurisdiction here. If we see suspicious funds going out of the states we can do something then but we need a reason and the amount of money flowing through the Silver accounts is huge. Mainly circular though, the guys over at exchange think he's been technically bankrupt for almost eight years." He drew his breath "Anyway, here we can't legally go and look at anyone's bank account without proving to the locals by other means that they have 'reasonable cause'. So that is why we need the locals for this end of the deal anyway." The nods around the room made him comfortable that his team understood the problems.

+

The dirty grey four by four coasted quietly down the big house driveway turning off before they got to the house itself and went past the stable block where Brown had his offices and he was to get his orders. He pushed the vehicle further along the road, it was obvious that vehicles had not passed this way regularly for some time but someone had started coming this way again not very long ago, the broken and cut branches on the bushes that overhung the road told him that loud and clear. Slowly he edged forwards and was surprised to find a small cottage tucked away in the trees along here. There was smoke coming from the chimney and he thought he saw a face at the window as he let the truck idle past on the narrow road. The road followed round and came back onto the track that led to Leyfield farm. Tyre marks in the gravel showed him that someone was using this route fairly regularly, and this end of it a lot more than the part that passed the estate offices. He stopped his truck, patted the dog carefully and slid out of the driving seat. From here he could see a lot of the houses that the boss wanted to buy, he could see why, they were small and ugly; the local word was traditional. He had never understood that. As far as he was concerned a bulldozer would be too good for them. He looked forward to getting the gates up and keeping the heathens out.

+

Marlene had seen the same television documentary as 'Xander had done and now she couldn't sleep, She imagined every creak of her council house cooling down in the night was the feared knock at the door. She had a deep fear that every favour and obligation she had ever done over the many years that she had been a local politician would now be laid bare for all to examine. She knew that when it happened it would not be a pretty sight. Lying there, on her own in the dark she knew without a shadow of a doubt that one day she would be found out – how could she have been so stupid?

It was the next day whilst at the council offices she met the leader of the separatist party in the canteen. Over a subsidised cup of coffee she asked him. "Did you see the documentary last night?" He looked at her sharply before nodding his head slowly as he realised there was no hidden meaning to the question. She was beginning to think that was all the answer she was going to get until eventually he said "Been just about sweating blood ever since." He looked up and around carefully to see who else was in earshot before he continued "First time I've ever done anything like this, feels like it might be the last too." She just nodded. There wasn't much she could say to that.

+

'Xander was standing in front of the mirror trying to figure out how he could get away in a hurry if things did go bad but he just could not hide who he was. He knew just how well known he was and how well loved by the people he also was. Anyway, he decided, he would never have to run away, no one could ever find out all of what he had done.

Templeton had arrived early at the parliament that morning and had scared the security guards stupid. He had been known to leave very late, even into the early hours some days but never, never, had he ever come in to work early. But then he knew 'Xander would not be in for at least another three hours.

He had to leave the office door open as that was the way 'Xander always left it unless he was actually in a private discussion with someone. The computer seemed to be making a lot of noise starting up and the chair squeaked as he sat in it. He was uncomfortable as he sat there in the little mans chair searching for private files that he knew must exist but there was nothing, nothing at all.

Templeton made his way back to his own office about two hours later and sat here looking at this own computer screen as it slowly came to life and

106

he typed in his password. Suddenly his head snapped up, of course, that was it. It was actually obvious now that he looked at it. The password he had used was an old one and so it had only shown him files up to the date of the password. To get to the newer files he would need a new password or a computer geek willing to help. He sighed and sat back, that was not it either. Even at the time he had accessed 'Xander had already been 'on the take' as he called it and so those files should have been visible to him, they weren't. That meant they were somewhere else, he would need to be smarter and look harder. He began to scroll through the in house training menu, but he doubted that computer hacking would be a course listed as available for members of the parliament to take if they wanted it.

+

The business in the council chamber was fairly routine that day until the matter of planning applications came up again. Marlene was surprised, she had already decided that she would wait until it came up at the local planning meeting. She was on that committee after all so it should not be a problem to get the right answer. She leant forward to listen as Councillor Wilt, a mushroom farmer from the inland boggy part of the region stood up to speak. He was a member of her party but some unkind soul had once said all he needed to do to put fresh compost in his sheds was stand at the door and speak. She began to understand what they had meant when it was almost ten minutes before she realised what he was actually talking about. Almost all of the other councillors in the chamber figured it out at about the same time and they obviously blamed her for asking him to resurrect the topic. It took almost an hour before it came to a vote with the same result as the last time. The motion fell quite dramatically, exactly the same as the last time it had been voted on. The chairman looked up as a man in a tweed jacket and a blonde woman about half his age left the public gallery.

+

The department principal was sitting sweating in front of the Head of School; it wasn't that he was nervous, although he was.
That wasn't the reason he was sweating. Truth was he was seriously worried; they had done as they had been asked by shutting down the dig site out at the Doones estate but instead of receiving a research grant as they had been promised. They had lost their best academic in the field to their biggest competition and most of their students had gone as well. As he sat there looking at the head of school a strange thought began to form in his mind. 'What if it had all been fabricated to allow Dr Presley to transfer without any problem?' He looked at his superior who looked almost as

unsure as he spoke "The trouble is we don't even really know who it was we had the agreement with, do we?" The principal shook his head without saying anything as he thought through the issue. He sat back and looked at his friend and colleague of many years before he spoke "What if it was that other place that was behind it all?" His boss looked at him "How do you mean?" He swallowed and thought for a second "Well, we have now lost our best academic, most of our students, all of the artefacts from the dig site and what's worse is they have all gone to our competition." He sighed as he slapped his own thighs and stood up, he thought better on his feet. "We were supposed to be getting a fee for stopping the dig so now we can't even expect that as the dig is continuing with the control of the other university. We can't even publicly accuse them of stealing our staff because if we do that, then we are admitting trying to set it up in the first place." The Head of School looked at him closely and pondered for a minute "I think this Paradigm Archaeology or Paradigm Properties or whatever they call themselves may have something to do with it as they now have the services of Dr Presley, they own the site and are claiming ownership of the artefacts." The Principal looked at him "Are they? I never heard that." Head of School shrugged "neither have I but in their position that's what I would do." The principal shook his head "I almost agreed with you there for a moment, be careful where you say that." The head of school shook his head and smiled. "We need to find out who Paradigm Archaeology actually is." The Principal did not answer.

At the other side of town Dr Marianne Presley was sitting in a new lab with all of her former students as they showed her what they found after she had left the site but she knew they were all dying to ask her questions about other things, like Paradigm Archaeology. Eventually she sighed as she carefully set down a Bronze Age sword she had been examining and peeled of her rubber gloves before she replied to a question she had actually been asked. "Okay, well in answer to your question. I have not met the owner of Paradigm Archaeology and have been told it's possible that I may never meet him, and yes it is, a 'him', apparently." The students laughed amongst themselves as she began to relax. "I have basically been told to do what I want, I have a budget to spend, a very good budget to spend in fact and if I want to spend it all on this dig then that is up to me." She looked around the students before she continued "It means that this university basically has a free research professor and I can afford to fund this dig for a few weeks yet without worrying about it." She laughed as the students cheered loud enough to attract the attention of the department head as they called them here. He walked in laughing as he saw her 'holding court' in the lab. "How are you all? Settling in well I hope." There were a few nods and smiles but no one actually said anything, they were here because of

108

Marianne after all. He knew that it would take time for them to accept him as every single one of them had actually chosen to go to the other university. That meant that this was a second choice for them all.

+

It was mid evening and Mark was feeling uncomfortable as he strolled across the dune line and onto the beach. Immediately he knew he was no longer being watched, so that meant it was someone from inland and not on the dune line, so no bird watcher. He shrugged and worked his shoulders for a second or two, he could not explain the sensation but he knew when it was working, it was exactly the same as standing at a party and staring at the back of someone else's head. They knew they were being watched but could not explain it. The sensation he had just had was exactly the same, just a little more developed. It had saved his life a few times in the bad old days as he sometimes thought of them. He shook his head and looked along the beach, it was absolutely beautiful in the setting sun as it streamed across the sea. It was calm but not flat, it was never flat here, the waves had been thinking about it too long before they hit this beach but the low angle of the sun making reflections off the water meant there was no shadow on the beach. The orange and red sparkles from the wave crests glittered almost like jewels and the air was fresh and salt laden as he squinted into the fading light.

He breathed deeply and hesitated as he turned inland to head roughly towards home. He was uncomfortable because he knew that as soon as he crested that ridge, thirty feet away from him, he would be visible to everyone who cared to be looking this way as he would be silhouetted by the setting sun behind him. He took another step and stopped on the ridge, immediately scanning as far as he could see to see who was looking at him. Two flashes of light caught his eye, probably from binoculars or such like. One was from just beyond his own house and one from further south, almost on the direct route he had been about to take to Ruriadh cottage. Sighing he adjusted the small pack he was carrying and began to walk towards the light, both reflections vanished at about the same time.

+

Paul Brown was a nervous wreck; he had seen the TV documentary a few nights before and was now convinced that the police would be coming after him very shortly. He sat in his room, in the hotel and looked at the TV, almost frightened to switch it on. He was hungry but did not want to eat in the hotel, he did not like 'good wholesome food' as they called it. Suddenly he stood up, having remembered something, across the main road about five minutes walk from here was another pub and restaurant called the 'Pig and Whistle'. Tonight would be the first time he had tried it, it had never looked worthwhile before, after all it would be bought out soon enough.

It was quiet as he stepped in through the outside door into the vestibule and stopped to look at the menu that stood there, trying to entice customers in. He wasn't really looking at the menu, he was actually looking in through the bulls eye glass in the door at the bar and beyond. He sighed to himself and pushed the door open before stepping into the warmth inside. The barman smiled at him and nodded as he walked up to the counter "Is it possible to get a table for one?" he asked as the barman finished polishing a glass. "Sure, shouldn't be a problem tonight. Normally you would need to book but tonight we seem to be quieter than normal for some reason." He paused and looked at the man standing in front of him. "Do you want to sit in the lounge until your tables ready or would the bar be okay for you?" Brown shook his head "The lounge would be perfect" He regretted that as he stepped in through the door to a largish room with a real wood stove and no one else in it, that was a saving grace but the room was cluttered with a mix of chairs, couches, sofa and all sorts of junk on every flat surface or wall space you could imagine. Things like wash boards, butter churns and toy drums cluttered the room to the point it was almost unusable, he ducked as he avoided a madly swinging bicycle that was suspended on fishing line from the potentially authentic blackened beams that were part of the ceiling, whilst the barman rubbed at his head where the bike had made contact.

Sitting down in the corner he took the menu from the barman and gave him a drinks order before looking around the room more closely. He waited until the door closed before he picked up an antique looking butter pat and turned it over. 'Made in China' the label proudly proclaimed, he set it down again and grinned to himself. There might be an opportunity here yet he thought as he opened the menu. When the barman returned with his drink Paul Brown asked him "Are you the manager here?"

+

Jenny was getting annoyed in the small office at the livery stable where the gymkhana association held their meetings. It had been lively so far and now it looked like a real argument would be next on the agenda. It was Alison, one of the other locals, who was speaking. "I'm sorry but I think it's a good idea. A full blown equestrian centre, probably one of the best in the world right on our doorstep and you won't support it?" She paused and

110

drew breath for a second before she said "I think you should stand down as chair if that's your opinion." She smiled and stood back as a hush settled over the group while Jenny breathed deeply for a minute or two to gather her thoughts before she responded. Leaning forward she tapped the drawings that lay open on the table before she spoke "As I already told you. Peter Barnard lied to me and us all. These drawings show it as a golf course and housing development. There is nothing horse related on here at all. Look" She pointed again to one of the notes at the side "Special fencing to be erected to prevent roaming deer and horses from causing damage to the grass on the course." She looked at Alison who stood there arms folded and a determined look on her face "Read it for yourself, this is what was submitted as an application to the local council just a few days ago. It is a golf course and housing development, it tells you on it." She pointed at it with a slightly broken and chipped nail while Alison was looking straight at her face and ignoring the drawing. "I saw the drawings that were to be submitted" she finally said as a silence fell on the group "This is not one of them, I'll bet you had this made up specially to do this. I don't know what you're up to but it is not for the good of the community or this group." She drew breath and unfolded her arms before she continued "I suggest you stand down as chair of the gymkhana association. You are no longer working in the best interests of the group" Jenny stared at her for a second "Alright, there is a process for this, let's have an election and see what happens." Alison smiled and in that moment Jenny knew she had been played and had fallen for it. This was what Alison had wanted all along, without a word being spoken the group split into two physical groupings. Alison had one person standing behind her whilst Jenny had four, Alison suddenly looked worried. "You can't believe her do you? I saw the drawings; Peter told me what was happening." A deep sigh came from behind Jenny and she turned around to see who it was about to speak. Mabel one of the older members of the group looked at Alison and said "This," she waved at the drawing on the table "is what has been submitted, I checked this morning myself. If Jenny had not brought this to our attention tonight I would have." She pointed at the lockers where they were on the wall behind Alison "I have another copy, not as posh as this one but still very legible, in my bag in my locker." Alison's voice was trembling as she said "I don't believe you, Peter wouldn't lie to me, why would he?" Jenny sighed as leant back against the wall. "Alison. He is untrustworthy. The folk out on the estate, know him as Paul Brown, that's what he is known as because that is what he called himself when he first spoke to them all trying to buy their houses for pennies." Alison was shaking her head as she stood there with tears starting to trickle down her face. "I don't believe you, he wouldn't lie to me. We have a future." With that the tears began to run properly and she turned and ran into the stable yard outside.

Mabel was shaking her head as the door slammed cutting out the cool breeze had been blowing into the small office.

+

Dianne was sitting in the pub, quietly close to the bar chatting to Andy the barman when the door opened and the less than subtle scent of horse sweat filled the bar as the group of five women walked in. Andy smiled at Jenny and lifted a wine glass while shook her head angrily "No, bugger the wine, give me a pint of cider" Andy just looked at her and did as he was told while Dianne pricked her ears up while the women began to talk. Eventually Dianne asked "What's up girls? Something sounds serious." Jenny looked across and smiling came over to join Dianne at the table and soon enough all the group were seated around the corner table next the bar. Jenny explained what had happened and ended by saying "What's your position? As a councillor you must an opinion." Dianne nodded "I do, but as a councillor I am not allowed to comment on that opinion until after the meeting where an application is heard. What I will tell you is that a lot of people are having doubts about this application because it seems that a lot of people are getting different stories at different times." She picked up her glass and hesitated "By the way, there has been a motion set to bring that application forward to the next council meeting, so if you have representations to make. Make them soon." The group all started to talk over one another as Dianne watched them start to work as a team.

+

Trente Silver was having some private time to himself as he stood in the washroom off his office on the fifty third floor of his office block in New York. He checked, again, that the door was locked he really did not want to get caught by anyone doing this. He felt such an idiot standing there with the bottle of fake tan and a cloth trying to make sure he didn't miss any bits on his head. He should get his wife to do this for him he thought but then he remembered he was currently on wife number three and as it was wife number four that really liked this shade, so he couldn't explain that to her. He used numbers because he couldn't pronounce names, they weren't US born so they didn't have proper names and as such were worth so much less as people. That was how it was easy for him to dispose of them when they no longer pleased him, he just traded them in, a bit like a used automobile.

He smiled at his reflection and ran his tongue over his teeth to check they were still there before he went back to his desk to see how much all of this was costing him.

112

He looked at the figures and he knew it didn't balance properly in the corporate view of things but he was not going to let this one go. He might need to do a couple of franchise deals to get the cash to make it work initially but after that it would work the same way it always had. He sat back and allowed himself to dream for a moment, he really had to understand more about the system over there, after all he did not even know what title they would give him for being so kind to them and throwing them a lifeline for after the oil ran out. He laughed to himself, as if oil was going to run out, impossible!! But if they believed it, it would suit his purpose perfectly.

+

Dull was speaking to a few of the other people at his table at the business breakfast, most of them were held at the Wycliffe hotel these days so it made it easier for him to get there without the risk of losing his licence due to the Beaujolais from the night before. He was holding court with the local hoteliers association, most of the members who mattered anyway and Paul Clancy was half watching from another table. Some one on his left who he did not know leant in a little closer and muttered "Sober so far is he?" Clancy nodded and spoke without thinking "Normally is only half drunk at this time, takes him till midday to fully sober up; means he's in a shit mood all afternoon until he starts to drink again about six." He sighed and turning round looked at the man who'd been questioning him and froze. He knew the face but had not seen him arrive. It was Michael Feltham, divisional chairman of the National bank. It wasn't that unusual to see him at these breakfast meetings. He came most times when he was in town and they had a meeting, it was the line of questioning that bothered him more. Feltham sat back a little and the conversation changed "Nice building this. Do you know what it used to be?" Clancy nodded "Yes, it was a large country house, in the middle of town." A smile flashed across Clancy's face "Rumour has it, Dull won it in a bet against the last owner." Feltham's eyes did not flicker, he was giving nothing away. Clancy watched as the mans eyes suddenly did flicker and not towards Dull but at a table at the other side of the room, one of the odd extra tables that were occasionally needed to allow for the extras that occasionally came along, most of whom were of no importance.

Paul Clancy turned round to look over his shoulder in the direction the other man was looking "See someone you know?" Feltham nodded "Important client, busy man, but not obviously so." Clancy looked around again but could see no one he knew. By the time he turned back Feltham

113

was on his feet as the formal part of the meeting was finished and he was heading towards Dull. Clancy struggled to see the table Feltham had been looking at and made a note of the table number. He would be able to get the list from the office of who had been seated there. Looking around he noted Dull and Feltham were talking animatedly to one side. He grinned that didn't look good for Dull, but then, it would be no great loss to the local business community.

He stepped outside for some air as the group began to break up and watched slightly distractedly as an old green Land Rover rattled out of the car park and down onto the main road. Somehow he had a feeling that was important but it didn't make sense to him yet. He shrugged and headed towards his own car to get back to the office.

+

Crawford's looked at Barnard and struggled to conceal his contempt at the other mans presence "Well," he asked "How's the glad handing going?" Barnard smiled "Well, really well. I've gotten to about half of the councillors and have contributed to about half of them, maybe just a little more, maybe twenty people." Crawford's interrupted him "What do you mean about twenty, don't you keep records. We need to account for every dollar and cent we dish out to our boss. Make sure we have a note of every cent you hand over and to whom." Suddenly he smiled "It might be a good idea to keep two sets of records. One genuine for our own lord and master and one that is a little," he hesitated as he looked for the right word to use before he continued "enhanced." He finally said "Did you see the programme on TV recently? If we have records we can scare these people into doing as we ask for years to come. It'll save us money in the long run." Barnard shrugged his shoulders "No problem, I'll make sure they are written up and large enough to make it fun without being too ridiculous" Crawford's nodded as Barnard licked his lips "How about some of the more influential people in the capital," Crawford's held up his hand and stopped him there before he could ask his question. "Don't you worry about that." The American said "It's all already in hand. You don't need to know the details." Barnard nodded, in many ways he was pleased not to know. It meant he couldn't drop himself in it by mistake at some point in the future.

+

Mark had just parked the Land Rover and was standing on the bank looking out at the sea again when the silver four wheel drive rolled up to the end of
114

his house. He hesitated as Paul Brown stepped down out of the vehicle and strolled across to speak to him. He stopped and looked Mark up and down quickly without recognition, a reasonable suit in an odd location and no sign of a vehicle other than the old Land Rover that didn't look like it was capable of going anywhere. The eyes bothered him though, there was an intelligence there that could not be hidden and with it came an intensity that scared him. He had only ever known a handful of people that looked at you like that. Mark looked back and saw a balding middle aged man with a growing paunch and a salesman's smile. The new wax jacket still smelled of the shop and the fashionable blue Wellingtons looked like it was the first day they were out of the box. Mark suddenly recognised him, he knew who this was and he knew he neither liked nor trusted him. Brown opened his mouth to speak "Owner not around is he?" Mark hesitated for a second and said "There's no answer at the door." Brown grunted not really noticing his question had not been answered. Suddenly he smiled "You wouldn't be a debt collector by any chance would you?" Mark smiled at him "Now you know I couldn't answer that even if I was" Brown giggled to himself as he fished in his pocket for a business card. Holding out the little yellow piece of pasteboard he said "If that does turn out to be the case and you are not succeeding in your normal negotiations than perhaps we can come to a deal." Mark did not say anything as he turned the card over between his fingers. "If the tenant of this property is in financial trouble my client would be interested in taking over the debt and I am sure a" he hesitated as he pondered how to describe the bribe "finders fee, would be available." Mark surprised himself by not hitting the weak little man who stood in front of him as he continued to study the small scrap of yellow pasteboard. Eventually he said "Thank you," he consulted the card again "Mr Barnard. I am sure we will talk again." Barnard grinned and stuck out his hand after a second or two it became obvious Mark was not going to shake it so Barnard ran it through what little hair he had left and turned away to climb into the shiny silver four by four and drive away. Mark watched Barnard manoeuvre the vehicle round clumsily and awkwardly before he drove away, watching Mark all the while in the rear view mirror. He accelerated as he passed wee Georges house and disappeared up the road in a cloud of dust. Mark shook his head and reaching into his pocket produced a key. Once inside Mark sat down at his desk and began to do a little digging to see what he could find out about Mr Barnard.

7

It was Andrea the tennis coach that saw the article first, her father was staying with her and her husband, and as he was American they had a US news channel on the satellite TV. It was there that the first real news broadcast about the development broke on the unsuspecting world. She stared in horror at a computer generated visualisation that showed scantily clad locals opening doors to a faux Georgian monstrosity that was described as being the 'hotel of the future'. She stared in horror at the gold taps and fake crystal chandeliers. Suddenly she jumped forward and pushed a new blank disc into the machine and that sat below the television and recorded the news piece.

Saturday morning, it was almost lunchtime and Mary and Pete were ambling casually up the drive towards Marks place with a newspaper clutched tightly in Pete's hand. Mark was happy to see them; it was not unusual for him to see them at some point over the weekend, they were good friends and were welcome here at any time.

Pete didn't say a word, he just thrust the news paper into Marks hands and said "Here, read that." His forefinger stabbing at the page where an article was ringed in bright red marker pen. Mark hesitated and looked at the paper in his hands. He glanced back up at them as he turned away and walked into the house talking over his shoulder. "You'd better come in, the kettles on and it's going to take me a minute or two to read this anyway."

It was a few minutes later that he raised his head from the page and looked into Pete's slightly bleary eyes as Mary made a pot of tea. Mark sighed and set the paper down. "It's only a newspaper report, we can't place too much faith in it. Even less when you have a look at the ownership of the group." Pete looked at him "What do you mean?" he asked as Mary set the mug of coffee down in front of Pete. Mark sighed again as he decided how much he could tell them just now. "Well," he had made the decision "I've been doing a little digging into various things, amongst them some info on the Silver Organisation and their holdings." He sat back and smiled at Mary as she handed him a mug of tea "It turns out they own, almost 100% of 'The Shiny Media Group' who own over 50% of 'The International Dependant'" He sighed as he lifted and dropped the paper Pete had brought him. "So he owns the paper, then? Does that mean the story is rubbish?" Mark shook his head "Yes, he does own the paper. No that does not necessarily mean the story is rubbish." Mark picked it up and looked at the picture and the story again, as much to give himself time to think as anything else. Mary started to speak slowly as she considered her words carefully "Is it possible that it is just a form of advert." Mark looked at her quizzically as she continued "He's telling us and the rest of the world what he wants us to hear through a medium he controls" Marked nodded slowly as he studied the headline again. It said 'New Silver Project to build the best in the world guaranteed permission by local government'. "It's very possibly the start of the mind games that he likes to play. Problem is, for mind games to work you have to have a mind, and they don't" He folded the paper and laid it on the table as the door bell rang at the far end of the house.

It was Andrea from the tennis club, who came slowly into the house. Unsure of her welcome the woman followed Mary through to the kitchen where Mark had already refilled the kettle and switched it on. Andrea seemed to be shy and unsure of herself at first amongst strangers but she soon relaxed as the coffee came out and they began to talk. She saw the newspaper article and picked it up "Oh my God." Was her first response to the written word. She dropped the paper on the table and dug into her bag which she had dropped on the floor. "This fits perfectly," She muttered half to herself as she rummaged through the contents of the bag and produced the shiny silver disc in a paper envelope. "This," she said brandishing the disc, "Is a news article from one of the US news channels. I recorded it last night, you need to watch this." As the group of friends trooped through the house to the living room Jennifer appeared and said hello to everyone. Mary hung back in the kitchen to make sure she got a cup of coffee like everyone else already had. As the kettle boiled Mary looked at her knowingly "I was surprised when we got here this morning not to find you already here." Jennifer shook her head and laughed softly, a bright joyous sound that almost seemed to light up the room before she replied "I might be an early riser during the week, but I like my weekends to relax a bit" Mary nodded "I understand that, I just thought you might have stayed here last night" Jennifer blushed a little as she poured water into a mug "I like him, I think he likes me, but we haven't even kissed yet so I'm not likely to get an invite to his bed." She smiled at her neighbour "Equally doesn't mean I'd refuse it if it came my way." Mary smiled as the two women made to rejoin the others. "Don't think he doesn't see you. We've known him a long time and he doesn't show his emotions very easily." Jennifer laughed softly this time before saying "Typical man then."

The living room was silent as the two women walked in. All eyes were on the TV screen which was showing an animated artists impression of the completed resort as the presenter described it. The picture broke into lines and changed to a gray screen as they watched. Mark leant forward and picked up the remote control before restarting the disc to watch the five minute clip again. They had watched the film three times before any one spoke. It was Jennifer that spoke first "That is horrible, all bling and trash and junk." Mark nodded "That's their impression of us. Wearing furs and killing rabbits for food each day. Don't forget how few of their people actually hold a passport." He sighed and stood up to look out of the window. It was Andrea who spoke next. "My Father in Law is American, that's why we were watching this last night, but they believe we are backward and immature people. He didn't even know where our country was until his son wanted to marry me." She sighed and looked away as memories bothered her.

Jennifer was watching Mark as he stood looking out of the window, obviously deep in thought about what he had seen. "Okay," he finally spoke "It looks to me like they are trying to convince their backers back home that this project is a done deal." He paused and turned round to look at his friends who sat there listening. "To me there are basically two options, there may well be more but there are at least two that I can see right away." He drew breath and licked his lips "First, they have done some back door deal and the permission has been granted at a higher level; which would mean that the current planning process is just window dressing and everything that the public consultation process is meant to do is wasted and meaningless." Again he looked around the room "Or second, this is just an advert with more than the normally acceptable amount of exaggeration by the advertiser." Jennifer looked at him surprised "Do you really think they would lie so easily to people? I mean saying that permission has been approved is a fairly serious matter." Mark nodded but it was Pete that spoke. "Yes it is but this is a US news channel. Did they expect it ever to be seen over here or is it just a case of they didn't believe the people here would ever know of it?" Mark nodded slowly as the conversation began to revolve around the group as they spoke amongst each other.

+

Paul Brown leant back in his chair and smiled to himself, he had been shown the TV footage last week, after all he did feature in it as the man on the ground and now he had a copy of 'The International Dependant' on his desk, it all pointed the right way, maybe a little more aggressive than he would have liked to have his name on, but if that was the way it was. He opened out the paper again and looked at his picture taken at the end of the driveway next to the article. The headline read 'nation ecstatic at being chosen for world class resort'. Peter Barnard smiled and set the paper down again wondering if he should have the page framed.

+

Mandy was feeling seriously ill again as she sat on the sofa in her mums house. Her mum just looked at her and shook her head, it looked like she was hung over again as well as feeling sorry for herself. Mandy slowly pushed herself to her feet and headed to the kitchen to make herself a cup of coffee. On the window ledge sat a business card, she looked at it more closely and looked away again, quickly. She didn't need or even want to stop drinking and even if she did she would do it on her own, she wouldn't need help. It was quite easy just to not drink for a while, wasn't it?

+

Paul Gray sat at his desk and fumed, he had just newly set the phone back in the cradle after hanging up on the journalist who had casually advised him that he and his team would be arriving later today to finalise the third piece for the magazine. The bit that had really annoyed Paul was the comment that as he had been so helpful already they were sure he wouldn't mind letting them stay at the house during their visit. It had been a shorter conversation than the caller had expected. He sat there and fumed for a few minutes more before he finally realised that made no difference, he now had to do something about it but he didn't know what. Slowly he stood up and let himself out of the house. Standing in the stables yard he sighed to himself thinking, for a moment, of happier times. Shaking his head he turned and walked to his four by four that sat in the corner and climbing in, drove away.

He was driving through the estate on autopilot, not really paying attention to where he was going and it was with some surprise he found himself pulling up in the field behind Marks place. He hesitated for a second when he saw a strange car parked there but then he recognised it as being local, he still didn't know who it belonged to, but it was local. He switched off the engine and slid out of the drivers seat.

Paul was taken aback when Jennifer answered the door. "I'm sorry" he smiled at her "I was looking for Mark Rae." Jennifer just smiled "You're not alone, he's inside, come on in." She guided him into the living room where a silence had fallen over the group as they waited to see who had come to join them. Mark smiled as Paul came into the room and stopped "Don't just stand there, come in and sit down." Jennifer hung back and

119

waited until Paul had sat down before she said "Tea or coffee for you? Anyone else need a top up?" A murmur of various nods and grunts passed around the group as it seemed like everyone else would like a top up of tea or coffee. Jennifer and Mary vanished towards the kitchen leaving Pete, Mark and Andrea to show Paul the TV news from the previous night, Paul turned to Mark and smiled at him "Pretty girl, who is she, one of your tenants?" Mark just nodded and said "Local, now watch this, you might find it interesting." A few minutes later Jennifer came back in with a tray with Mary following close behind. Sitting down between Paul and Mark she leant over and held out her hand "Dr Jennifer James, I now live down at number four and it's a long time since anyone called me a girl." Paul went pink before he replied "Sorry I guess I deserved that. I'm Paul Gray soon to be moving out of the area, I'm afraid."

Over on the next hillock only about two hundred metres away the grey pick up truck sat just over the crest with the dog lying sleeping in the rear cab. The driver was out of the vehicle watching the four by four abandoned in the field and the house next to it that showed no sign of life. What ever they were all doing, they kept it inside. Suddenly he made a decision and jumping up ran to the parked vehicle, a quick check showed no dog in the back, so he leant in and released the hand brake. Without waiting to see what happened he turned and ran over the hillock to his own truck and jumping in released the hand brake and allowed the vehicle to roll downhill away from the coast. Half way down the bank he slipped the vehicle into gear and dropped the clutch with a crunch and a grind the engine started and he drove off steadily and as evenly as he could. He still remembered from years ago being told that it was not so much noise that attracted attention as changing noise. So an engine revving would attract more attention than a steady beat of a diesel which is what he now had as it took him away from the house inland in amongst the trees.

Behind him the old four by four trundled slowly down the slight incline just behind Marks house and rolled through a fence before stopping up to the top of its front wheels in the pond at the bottom of the hill. It made remarkably little noise as it rolled down over the grass in the field, there was a crunch as it took out a fence post on the way through followed by a twanging sound as the wire finally gave under the two tonnes of vehicle stretching it to its limit. There wasn't even a proper splash as the wire had stretched so far before the vehicle reached the water it had almost stopped. In the house It was Pete who almost turned around in his seat "What was that?" Everyone else looked at him "What was what?" was Marks response As Pete finally managed to actually turn round "Thought I heard another vehicle drive away." Jennifer stood up and looked out the end window which looked down the drive way. "Nothing to be seen here," She turned and looked at Paul as Mark said "How did you get here?" Paul shrugged "Came over the field and climbed over the wire." Mark laughed "New owner might get upset at you doing things like that." Paul laughed "So let him sue me, right now, it's my fence and I'll do what I want with it." The group laughed as Mary went to the door into the conservatory and looked out "Exactly where did you park Paul?" He looked at her as a puzzled look crossed his face "Just out in the field, right behind this place. You should see the big red four by four just there." He was laughing as he stood up, but the puzzled look on Mary's face made him a little concerned as he walked over to beside her. "Shit," was his only comment as he realised the vehicle was not where he had left it.

The group in the room began to break up as Andrea looked at her watch "I have to go now, I'm late already." Mark smiled at her as Jennifer nodded "We understand, mind if we keep the disc for just now, maybe make a few copies?" Andrea shook her head as she headed for her car "Help yourself; I recorded it for you guys anyway, thought you might be able to use it." Jennifer nodded "Thanks again" she shouted as Andrea closed her car door and drove away. Turning round she saw Paul standing there looking shame faced as Mark and Pete began to laugh at the sight of the old red four by four nose first in the duck pond about a hundred yards away. "I was sure I had left the hand brake on, and I usually park across the bank anyway." Paul muttered to himself as Mark put his head down and muttered quietly but loud enough for the rest to hear. "We're not alone; about a click inland there's light reflecting on glass, someone is watching us." Silence fell on the group for a second until Mark said "I'll get the landy and a couple of slings, we'll have you out of there in no time." Paul just nodded as Mark turned away.

About a kilometre away on the head of the next small rise the man who had driven the grey pick up that was now parked down behind him, was disappointed. The group had shown no great upset or annoyance, he had expected screams and shouts at finding a vehicle missing but they had just quietly got on with it and in a matter of ten minutes or less the three men had towed the now wet four by four out of the pond and had it started and running again. The two women had watched and talked while this had been going on.

The other man in the combat clothing had the whole thing on film he was struggling not to chuckle at what he had seen going on. It was obvious from the body language even at this distance the man he and the rest of the team now referred to as 'thug one' was disappointed at the practical approach of these people. Somehow he thought he might get an opportunity to film more of his behaviour over the coming months.

+

Mary and Pete had strolled away just after Paul had driven the still dripping four by four across the fields, roughly towards the big house leaving Mark with Jennifer. She looked at him as she slipped an arm around his waist "So," she started "I'm one of your tenants am I?" He sighed as he turned to look at her as she almost laughed at him "Paul asked a question when I left the room. Pete overheard and told Mary and Mary told me while you lot were pulling Paul's truck out." Mark shook his head and laughed softly before he said anything "That figures, I knew it was a mistake to tell anyone anything." He sighed again and took hold of her arms, gently as he said "Yes, I own Paradigm Properties, why do you think I know what you'll get away with down at the house. Next thing you'll be screwing me for decoration and all the rest." She laughed and blushed deeply as she said "Well, you're maybe half right but I'm not worried about decoration. However, are you going to tell Marianne and Mike as well." She paused and looked at him as he wondered what she was actually talking about. Until she carried on speaking ""I assume that if you own Paradigm properties you will also own Paradigm Archaeology?" Mark nodded "Yes, I do. I guess you're now going to push me to tell her as well?" Jennifer just nodded "She does work for you and she's going to be getting a lot of hassle from people who want to know what's going on." Mark nodded "I'll tell them at some time over the weekend"

+

'Thug one' was uncomfortable, he could feel himself being watched as he slid down the banking and headed back to his vehicle. The dog whimpered instead of barking, it was eager to get out of the truck but he left in the back, until he knew more about the way things worked here he wouldn't risk losing a dog, even if it wasn't his dog. They wouldn't let him bring his 'Rhodesian Ridgeback' with him this time so he had borrowed this dog locally, it was something they called a 'Rottweiller', he didn't know the breed well at all, it wasn't viscous enough for him.

The other man in combat gear was waiting for the dog to be released as he watched this through the camera lens. As the vehicle drove away he watched closely to make sure it was actually leaving the area before he eased the safety catch back on the tranquiliser gun that lay by his side and breathed a sigh of relief. 'Thug one' was obviously a soldier with a good

122

senses, they would need to be more careful around him and his associates in future.

+

Dr Marianne Presley was down at the dig site not far away when Mark and Jennifer returned indoors at the house on the head of the bank. She and Mike had taken a drive out to the site and were carefully looking around as the students did what archaeologists do, dig holes. Marianne was looking at what they were doing while Mike was looking out at the landscape around them, studying the wildlife that ran around them that most of the dig team never even saw was there. He froze for a second and looked again at the small clump of trees just about a hundred metres away, it would be directly down in front of Marks place. Without thinking Mike looked up at the head of the bank, from here only the edge of the roof was visible so there was no way to know if there was anyone at home this morning. His eyes turned back to the copse and he noted a bush or two swayed the wrong way for the breeze to be pushing it. He smiled to himself, the deer were back.

Behind him Marianne struggled to stay on the edge of the trench and let the students do the digging, she was almost desperate to jump into the trench and get down on her hands and knees herself. It was incredible what was coming out of the ground here a whole variety of finds that showed the site had been inhabited and used for many hundreds of years from Neolithic stone age right on through the Bronze Age, things seemed to taper off after that, but that did not worry Marianne at all. She was staring as the trench nearest to her revealed a stone axe and a number of various flints being uncovered next to a skeleton.

Eventually she straightened up and found Mike at the edge of the dig site, where he was on his knees looking at tracks just outside the barriers the university team had put up. They were boot tracks, probably from an adult male, quite deep and sharp edged so fairly fresh. Maybe been left last night by some one who had come close but not actually entered the site as far as he could tell. Who ever it had been, had taken a good look over their barriers and walked away up the cut beside where the trickle of a stream came down from, and vanished inland. He straightened up, deciding not to tell Marianne just yet. She smiled at him and said "Fancy going to see if we can get a coffee from Mark?" Mike just smiled at her; he wanted to speak to Mark as well, just not about coffee.

+

Arthur stood absolutely still; where he was at the well outside his little cottage he could not be seen easily from the door but he was worried as he had left it open. He could see the front end of that grey pick up truck as it sat idling on the track just in front of his cottage. He had heard it coming just as he had started to pull up the bucket of water so he couldn't just drop it and hurry back inside. Truth be told he doubted he could make it inside quickly anyway, he couldn't make it anywhere quickly these days. He had heard the driver walk up the path and knock on the open door, of course there was no reply Arthur was standing outside, watching, waiting for something to happen. It was almost as though he could feel the other man moving around, he didn't think he had gone inside the cottage but he wasn't sure where he had gone. The woods around had gone very still as Arthur stood there listening just balancing the bucket of water on the lip of the old stone well. The only sound was of boots on the stone footpath as the man moved around, for a moment Arthur thought he saw the mans face as he looked around the corner of the cottage obviously looking for the occupant of the cottage. Arthur just stood still and maybe even held his breath until the face disappeared back round the corner and he could hear the footsteps vanish back out the path. There was the sound of a car door and the growl of a dog filled Arthur with fear as he stood there silently. "Shit," was the only word Arthur heard followed by the vehicle door slamming again, then another voice. "Can I help you, are you lost out here?" Arthur knew he should know the voice but he couldn't quite put a name to it; another voice, a stranger, possibly American sneered back at the speaker "I should be asking you what you're doing here. I'm security for the new owner." The first voice, the one Arthur should know spoke "Well in that case you can get back into your vehicle and get out of here. I am the current owner and as your lot don't take over for a few months yet you have no right to be here at all. You can tell your bosses that if I see any of you here other than at the offices in the stable block that they are renting I will be reporting you to the police. Now please leave." There was no discernable reply to the comments just a growl that obviously came form the throat of 'thug one' before he got back into his vehicle and drove away. Paul waited until the vehicle was out of sight before he turned back to the cottage and called out "Arthur, it's Paul, I was here with Mark a couple of weeks ago. Are you alright?" It was all Arthur could do not to laugh as he picked up the bucket and chuckling to himself shuffled round the corner into Paul's line of sight. "Fancy a cuppa there lad?" he asked as he smiled seeing Paul's concerned face "I'm fair glad to see your face here now Paul." Paul took the bucket from the old man and followed him into the cottage, closing the door behind him.

124

Outside the man in camouflage was confused. He did not understand where the old man fitted into the puzzle but from what he had read the actions of 'thug one' fitted the way the Silver Organisation did business.

+

Jenny from the gymkhana association was taking a long slow look over the newspapers in the local library, she was far from impressed with what she had read so far. The local papers were only apparently printing one side of the story there were even quotes with her name against them saying how fantastic it was going to be once it was all finished and she could share the spa at the new hotel with a film star or two. As a result, she was more that halfway through writing a letter of complaint to OFCOM in her head and had almost filled a notebook of comments and news stories about the Silver Organisations activities elsewhere in the world. She was going from being slightly annoyed to being extremely scared and angry very quickly and easily. She decided she had enough to be going on with and stood up to leave when a soft voice behind her made her jump slightly. The pretty blonde woman spoke with a slight accent but clearly and with a firmness that made it worth listening to what she said which was "Excuse me; I couldn't help noticing that you seem to be looking into the Silver Organisation?" It wasn't really a question but it gave the impression of needing an answer. Jenny shrugged and looked past the woman at the two men who seemed to be hovering in the background. She sighed and shrugged "Yes, I am, what of it?" The woman seemed surprised at the response and stepped back in surprise "I was wondering if we could talk about it, maybe we could buy you a coffee?" Jenny was suspicious but she was known here and she had been going for a coffee anyway so she nodded and let the woman lead the way towards the coffee shop. The two men stepped aside at the door to the library and let her past, both of them fell in behind for the short walk along the corridor to the coffee shop.

The blonde woman seemed very nervous as one of the men paid for four coffees and joined them at a table in the corner. Jenny sat with her back to the wall as she looked at the three Americans in front of her "Okay," she said "you wanted to talk to me, talk." One of the men looked around and the other two just looked uncomfortable, they obviously were unused to this type of response. Eventually the woman looked up and began to speak "I am here to find out what the general feeling locally is to the Silver Organisations proposals to turn this area into a 'world class golf resort. Where do you stand in relation to that?" Jenny smiled at her, a cold smile "Why didn't you just say you were press? It would have been much easier for you." The blonde smiled again and shrugged, Jenny saw the men relax as well but it didn't mean anything to her as she started to speak "Well I think its despicable, they sought me out specifically as I am the chair of the gymkhana association. That rat Peter Barnard told me it was going to be an equestrian centre and he told Andrea of the Tennis Association it was going to be a world class tennis centre. Seems he told everyone it was going to be what they most wanted it to be." She paused and looked at the two of them that were watching her, the other man was listening to his mobile phone, which Jenny had not heard ring, but not speaking. She carried on "At the same time as he was promising us the earth he was busy trying to buy homes on the Doones estate at cents on the dollar while calling himself Paul Brown." Jenny stopped as one of the men muttered to himself "Usual pattern, same all over." The woman nodded before she said "Is there any form of resistance being formulated at the moment? Is there like a focus group that we might be able to speak to? Or anyone you could introduce us to that might be willing to talk to us?" Jenny hesitated before she answered slowly "There might be one man who would be happy to speak to you at the moment but I need to clear it with him before you all turn up with cameras and the like." The woman nodded and pulled a yellow pad of sticky notes from her pocket. She wrote a mobile phone number on it and handed it over. "Ask your friend to call me on that number if he's prepared to speak to us. He doesn't need to go on camera if he doesn't want to." Jenny nodded as the three Americans stood up and walked out of the café. She bit her lip as she looked at the slip of paper in her hand and turned it round a few times before she made up her mind and standing up slowly left the café to go and see Mark.

+

Sharon Grant was a little surprised when she got the call from one of her former colleagues at the 'Evening' but it wasn't long before she understood what they were after. The call started innocently enough with the usual 'Hi how are you' type conversation but rapidly moved on to "Tell me, that guy you were seeing for a while. Mark Rae I think his name was, what was he like?" Sharon didn't really answer, she knew this type of call from her own time at the 'Evening' and knew it would be being recorded so Sharon was deliberately non committal. "Oh he was fine, nice guy actually." "I see" was the response, accompanied by the scribbling of a pencil on a reporters note pad "How often did you need to see the doctor when you were with him?" Sharon suddenly knew where this was going and hung up the phone as fast as she could. She sat there holding the phone in both hands, crying and trying to stop herself throwing the phone across the room. She decided she had to phone Mark and warn him, this was going to get dirty, but she didn't want to do that either. She knew now that if she heard his voice she

126

would run to him, if he would have her back. She missed him, badly. Crying still, she set the phone down and walked away from it.

+

It was mid morning one day during the week that Mark got the first phone call from the press, it caught him a little off guard to say the least. "Good morning sir," said the voice on the other end of the line without introducing itself it carried on "I'm calling about this story in the 'Evening' this afternoon can I ask you how long you beat your girlfriend for?" Mark was stunned "I beg your pardon, what are you talking about?" The voice on the other end of the phone line chuckled before saying "How long for? I mean, was it hours at a time or just a few sharp slaps each time? Did it go on for days, weeks, months or years?" There was a pause as Mark tried to get his bearings before the voice continued "The public has a right to know" Mark decided that enough was enough and hung up the phone. It rang again almost immediately with another reporter asking about the same subject but the tone was altogether different. "Mr Rae" it started "I was wondering if we could have a few words about some allegations that seem to have surfaced today." Mark sighed "Yes I would like to know what the allegations are and who you are as well please." The voice on the other end of the line laughed "Of course, I am Jonathon Diarmond of the *National Central*' newspaper, maybe you've heard of us?" Mark smiled and sat down "Yes I have heard of you, what do you want to know?"

At the end of the conversation Mark slowly hung up the phone, it rang again immediately and hurriedly he reached over and switched off the ringer. He needed to think for a few minutes before he did anything rash.

It was almost seven at night when Dr Jennifer James finally drove that red sports car of hers down the road towards her house, instead of parking in the usual spot behind the row and alongside an old wooden garage she really wasn't sure was stable, she turned the car up the hill and stopped at the end of Marks house, carefully she picked up the news paper she had taken from the reception area at the surgery and walked up to the house. She was surprised as she walked in to find Steve, the lawyer sitting there with a coffee mug in his hand, Jennifer may have been surprised but she was also pleased. She looked down at Mark and handed over the paper before she said "It looks like you probably already know about this." Mark nodded, the obvious temper on his face deepening as he read the actual article for the first time.
Eventually he spoke, his voice deeper and more measured than Jennifer had ever heard him before "I find this whole thing interesting, according to this,

and I don't believe it for an instant, Sharon went to them with this story. Whilst she may be freelancing I do not believe she is desperate enough to do this to me just to get an article printed. I doubt even further that she would have gone to the 'Evening' with anything. Also this bit here says I refused to answer questions is far from the exact truth. They harangued and accused me, so I hung up. I barely said a word so this bit about a mouthful of abuse is just lies." Steve nodded "I know you, have known you for years, so you don't need to convince me." Suddenly he smiled "Remember when that girl kissed you in the mess in Belize? I thought you were going to run a mile." Mark smiled slowly as he recalled a shared moment from years ago before Steve turned to Jennifer "I assume you are actually the doctor in this report?" Jennifer nodded "I am, and I also know that the hypothermia incident was the first time the two of them had met. I've also been discussing this with my practice manager as some of the details in here would be a breach of medical confidence if they were true and I would be in serious trouble." Steve nodded "I can see that." He sipped from the mug and Jennifer realised it was not just coffee in there, relaxing a little she sat down next to Mark as Steve began to talk again "We need to get to Sharon and see if she will give us a statement, will the fact that you two don't see each other any more be a problem?" he asked Mark who shook his head before answering "No, shouldn't be. She left me and I don't hold it against her. I just hope she's happy and safe." Jennifer nodded before she said "Maybe I should speak to her first." The two men looked at her, not understanding, she continued "She may be embarrassed to talk to you now it's in the paper," she said to Mark and turned to Steve "and she may be wary about talking to his solicitor." She finished pointing at Mark. The two men nodded, she was right.

So, it was Jennifer that picked up her phone and went out of the room to make the call. A few minutes later she came back in smiling and handed the phone to Steve before sitting down right next to Mark. As Steve stood up and went into the hall Jennifer turned to Mark and said "She wants you back," he looked at her without saying anything "She realises that she made a mistake and wants to be with you." She looked into his eyes as they sat close together "Do you want her back?" He shrugged "She's a pretty and intelligent girl, but a lot younger than me. I don't actually believe she really wants me." Jennifer sighed, one day men might start to understand women but probably not in her lifetime. She kissed him on the cheek and laughed as he looked at her in surprise.

+

128

Grayson sat and giggled like a little girl as he thought about how it had worked out. Not only had he devalued that little bitch of a 'wannabe' reporter who had not so much as even given him a flash of her tits, to the point where she would probably never work again, he had completely nullified the effect of the guy who might actually get in the way of his membership of the 'best golf course' in the world. He was still giggling as the door to his office was thrown open and Jackson strode into the room, he didn't wait for an introduction or any niceties "What the fuck have you done?" It wasn't really a question, more of an exclamation of disbelief as he threw a copy of the paper on Grayson's desk. Grayson looked up at him still grinning but not actually laughing now, slowly he turned the paper round and looked at the headlines, deliberately not saying anything, he studied the paper for a few minutes before he turned and looked up at the man who thought of himself as his boss and said "My job of course. I'm paid to sell papers. This story sells papers, the public don't like a wife beater, okay so she was just a girlfriend but its close enough." He sat back fairly confident that nothing could be proven against him now anyway, but somehow the fact that his bosses face hadn't changed bothered him and his mind flashed back to that brown envelope left lying on the desk, surely he had gone back for it later, privately hadn't he?

Jackson stood there shaking his head as he looked down at the man behind the desk, without saying a word he turned on his heel and stepped out through the open door. On his right, sitting on a chair often occupied by a failing journalist was a pile of other news papers from around the country. These were this mornings take on last nights 'Evening'. They were collectively known as the 'qualities' mainly broadsheet in size it was a big pile of paper. The headline on the top one read 'Evening Lies' in large bold type right across the top of the paper. They landed with a thud on Grayson's desk as Jackson dropped them. "When you've read them" he said stepping back "I'll see you in my office in one hour. The lawyer will be there as well." He half turned away before he turned back "We need to see if we can dig you out of this one. It's going to cost us a fortune whatever happens." Grayson barely noticed as he heard the door click shut behind his boss as he slowly and carefully picked up the first paper and began leafing through the pile. The picture he left in his bosses head was of a slack jawed, scared man sitting behind a mountain of newspapers but the feeling in his stomach was of deep sickening dread. The 'Evening' had been on thin ice for a long time, this might just be enough to finish it, completely.

It seemed a long flight of stairs and a very empty corridor that Grayson walked along to get to Jackson's office in the corporate corner of the building. It was on the top floor but there were only about three offices up here occupied, two were basically admin staff and Jackson who, technically, was in charge of all of them but they usually ignored him and got on with the job. Grayson had that sinking feeling in the pit of his stomach that told him that had maybe been a mistake.

The Corporate PA sighed at him as she looked up when he opened the door into the corporate area. He couldn't be sure but he almost thought she had shaken her head at the sight of him. There was no twitch as she walked away from him to the door of Jackson's office and disappeared inside. She was only gone for a second or two before she reappeared and pushing the door open for him, waved at him to go ahead. She had never said a word to him. He wondered how many more of the staff would be like that now. Had he really overstepped the boundaries? He had just done what his bosses had done when he was starting out; it was the way he had been taught. The way a real newspaper man behaved, wasn't it?

The office was cool and light, being on the corner it had a great view over the city with the Western Ocean visible if you looked out sideways. Grayson wondered if you could actually see the Doones estate from here, by distance it should be fairly easy but he could not get his bearings to figure out the direction. Slowly he sat down and nodded at the lawyer, he had met him a few times before. Jackson was reading yet another broadsheet, which he folded and set on his desk before turning to look at Grayson, he looked tired as he prepared to speak. Before he got the chance the PA reappeared in the room and picked up one of the TV remote controls from the desk said "Channel seven relevant and important". The three men turned to look at the screen as it came to life. Grayson groaned out loud as he recognised the faces of Mark Rae and Sharon Grant as they stood beside each other behind another man who was reading a statement. 'Probably a lawyer' he thought. It was the sharp intake of breath from the company lawyer that made him look again, he had not been listening too closely, just day dreaming, wondering if the night in the hotel room that Paul Brown had arranged for him had been worth it after all. The girl had been fun and been paid for which made it even better, but now he was really wondering if it had been worth it.

+

Dull was not in a good frame of mind, it had been a very uncomfortable discussion with the guy from the bank the other week; embarrassing as well that he had sought him out during a business breakfast. Guiltily he thought back to the pile of unopened mail that sat on the corner of his desk, his official desk, not the one at the back of the wine cellar where he was sitting just now. He stopped and looked at the tray in the recorder, the disc was upside down, that was not good. It meant he did not have the recording he was expecting from that room. It would have been good to watch, he sighed to himself as he thought once again about cutting back on his drinking. The problem was he enjoyed the flavours of the good wines so much and he had so many to choose from. Half turning in his chair he looked back through the open door into the cool of the wine cellar with its racks upon racks of gently slumbering wines slowly gathering dust. Just for a moment he wondered if the Sommelier had found the office, it probably wouldn't be hard if he actually looked. After all it had been built when the original conversion was done to give the Sommelier an office in the right place. Dull hadn't trusted them. He had thought they may have been drinking his wines so moved them to a desk in the main admin office. Most of them hated it, suddenly he wondered, 'Do I actually have a Sommelier at the moment?' he would have to check.

+

Jenny stood in the school break room and watched the TV screen with amazement as the lawyer finished reading a statement from two of her friends, she wasn't really watching because she was thinking about the yellow sticky with a phone number on it that she had to give to Mark and wondered if he would be interested or not. It was one of the teaching assistants that turned to her as they passed "That was quick, getting him in court that quick, good job too, he could have killed that girl." Jenny turned and looked at her colleague "I beg your pardon, are you talking about this story?" she said pointing at the screen. The woman stood there puzzled for a moment and nodded "Yeah that the guy in the paper isn't it? Beat his girl to a pulp a few times and then denied it. See here" She pushed over a creased and dirty copy of the 'Evening' that had obviously been through many different hands. Jenny looked at it and spoke slowly "I know this guy and the girl in question. He has never hit her and never would hit a girl unless she was trying to kill him." She paused and looked up "Do you read any other papers at all or did you watch the TV news just there?" The woman shook her head "Only usually watch the football on the TV and only need to read one paper. The 'Evening' gives us all we need." Jenny stopped herself from replying for a moment then said "The TV piece was about the two of them preparing to sue the 'Evening' for printing lies. The press Association has agreed to investigate and is offering them support and if you look at any other news paper at all you will see that they are talking about corruption in the press. Maybe you want to think about that." The woman shook her head "Nah, I'm not believing any of that. He'll be forcing her to say that. If it was in the 'Evening' it must be true, we have always read the 'Evening' always will read the 'Evening'; people like me don't need any of those other high falutin' papers. They just lie to you anyway." With that she turned and walked out of the staffroom. Jenny just sat there in disbelief at the attitude of a supposedly educated woman; she really could not believe that anyone could believe such an obviously contrived story. Slowly she stood up and dug in her bag for that yellow sticky before calling Marks number. It went straight to the answering machine, she wasn't really surprised.

+

Mark was standing in the hallway of his house with Sharon hanging on to him. She almost seemed to be more affected than he was by all of the attention, worse, she thought she was responsible for it all happening in the first place. He shook his head as he breathed deeply and caught the scent of some fresh shampoo from her blonde locks that just tickled his nose as they stood there. He didn't want to stand here but the sitting room was not an option due to the number of press people who were camped outside the windows. He sighed again. For a man who wanted to avoid the limelight he seemed to be getting plenty of it now.

+

The lawyer looked across at Grayson "Two hundred thousand!" he exclaimed "Two hundred thousand euros for defamation of character and reputational damage in a reboundable lawsuit." Jackson looked a little puzzled "What the hell is a reboundable lawsuit?" he asked as Grayson sat there quietly. The lawyer shook his head "It's new, just passed the other month but has hit the statute books so it is real. What it means is that in order for him to raise the action he lodges the money in a separate account, a bit like an escrow account but held by a judicial body. In order for us to defend the action we have to lodge the same amount in the same account. It's intended for big business to fight one another over patent claims, the idea was to make them think about it first. I don't think anyone ever thought about using it for defamation claims." He looked at the other two men "Does mean he's serious though. Did you think about that?" he asked Grayson who shook his head silently. Jackson was looking even more annoyed "What happens at the end of the case, winner takes all?" he asked. The Lawyer nodded "Yes winner takes all, plus interest and costs and if the judge is having a bad day he can award up to the same amount again to the victor." He sighed and brushed an invisible fleck of dust from his already immaculate suit "That's the only bright spot, there a limit to how much it can cost us. On a two hundred thousand law suit like this it is basically limited to about five hundred thousand in total." Jackson's jaw dropped at the figure. He turned and looked at Grayson who was just staring at the floor; he would be no use in this and maybe had out lived his usefulness at the paper entirely. Jackson wondered if the 'Evening' had outlived its usefulness entirely. That was a decision he would pass on to other people. Jackson turned back to the lawyer "What if we chose not to defend the case, what would it cost us?" The lawyer looked at him surprised "Well, you'd need to pay the two hundred thousand if the judicial body accepts the case, and that's not certain yet either, plus some costs. So not defending it could cost us up to two hundred and fifty thousand, maybe a little more." Jackson shook his head as he looked at Grayson "Anything to say?" he asked, Grayson just shook his head in response.

8

It was an early morning again that found Mark sitting on the head of the bank looking out to sea with the sun on his back and the long shadow stretching almost all the way to the waters edge from where he sat. He was day dreaming, just watching the waves as suddenly he realised he was not alone any more. Jennifer had walked up the driveway to speak to him; he was surprised as he glanced at her noting that she was in just jogging trousers and a tee shirt, not really what he expected for a doctor going to the surgery for the day. She smiled and blushed a little as she sat down next to him on the grass. "I know I'm not dressed for the office but it's early yet." She paused and looked at her watch "It's not even six o'clock yet." He laughed as she seemed to cuddle in to her side "I know what time it is, I just don't know what you're doing up here barely dressed at this time of day." She shrugged and folded her arms across her chest as the cool morning air flowed around her body. "I know, I know I shouldn't be here." She sighed as his arms slid across her shoulders "I just got up and looked out and saw you sitting here and wanted a cuddle." He smiled at the admission as she continued "So, I threw something on and came to speak to you." He laughed and kissed her face as she let herself be drawn onto his knee before she said "How is Sharon? I saw her at the surgery the other day and she seemed okay, maybe a little fragile but alright" He nodded silently and thought about that for a minute or two "She's okay. As you say maybe a little fragile, seems to spend a lot of time here during the day when she should be working, advantage of being a freelance I guess, then in the evening she goes home to see her parents." Jennifer raised her head and looked into his face "Are you expecting her here today?" he nodded "As usual, she'll arrive about ten thirty or eleven o'clock and she'll go through the mail. I think she may actually be compiling a book out of the letters and photos that I've received." Jennifer just looked at him in surprise "Yes there's still about two sack loads a day of letters coming in after the 'Evening' thing. All sorts of things, all the way from very personal offers of very personal service to insults and comments that there must be some truth in it, the 'Evening' wouldn't have printed it otherwise." Jennifer was still looking into his face as she said "It really doesn't bother you, the letters I mean?" He smiled, a slightly weak and maybe uncertain smile "The letters I can deal with, some are funny, some are just strange and some are seriously weird. It's Sharon that scares me a bit, she wants to be around me, barely lets me go to the toilet on my own let alone anything else and yet does not seem to want a full blown sexual relationship, or anything even close. Truth be known I don't know what to do. I like her but I'm frightened she's going to become dependant on me and then lose out on the rest of her life by acting as some porcelain doll at my side that no one can touch." Jennifer could barely see him through the mist of water in her eyes but she managed to say "What about you? Are you alright?" he just nodded "I'm fine. I'll always survive." Jennifer hugged him tightly to her before standing up and saying "I have to go get ready for work. Look after yourself." He glanced at his watch as she turned and began to walk back down the road. "It's still not even six yet, don't you want a coffee?" She turned and smiled at him "Not today, sometime soon you can make me a full breakfast" He smiled at her not understanding the hint "You're on. I'll hold you to that." She smiled as she walked away faster than she had been before. He was still standing on the bank almost two hours later as she drove that red car away up the farm track and into the distance.

The American in the camouflage clothing was pleased when he finally turned and walked away into the house. He had filmed bits of Mark sitting on the head of the bank and taken a lot of still photographs but he would have ideally gone home about an hour ago, but really did not want to be seen, so he had stayed where he was. His joints were stiff as he moved slowly, even when the phone in his inside pocket buzzed it seemed to take a long time for him to answer and his boss was beginning to get worried until he heard his voice. "Where are you?" the watcher replied quietly "Still watching the cottages and the old station place." The boss nodded silently "Okay we've got clearance to go speak to the guy Rac that lives there. Get back here, get some rest and we'll deal with that later today." The watcher sighed "Thank goodness for that. I'm as certain as I can be he knows we're watching and is actually watching us." The boss again nodded silently "Unlikely, but possible. Don't worry about it just get back here and get some rest." He snapped the phone shut and turned to his blonde colleague, who was sitting across the table from him "He thinks the watcher is being watched, what do you think?" She just shrugged and sipped her coffee without answering.

+

Steve the lawyer was busy trying to keep Marianne from figuring out that Mark was actually her boss. He had heard Mark mutter about having to tell her soon but that was weeks ago and now he had to prepare for the court case with the 'Evening'. They had still not confirmed if they were going to defend the case or admit defeat and just pay the money. He knew it was going to be a difficult decision for them to make, but the main point was, he thought as he glanced at the clock, it had to filed by close of business today. Maybe they were just playing brinksmanship.

Marianne appeared at the office door and knocked softly "Can I ask you a question about Mark?" Steve hesitated but slowly leant back "That depends on the question Marianne, but if I can answer it I will." She hesitated and stepped in before closing the door behind her softly, she was obviously thinking about how to phrase this. She looked down at him behind the desk and he was surprised to see the look of concern in her soft blue eyes as she finally said "I don't expect you to comment on this bit but I believe Mark is the owner of Paradigm Archaeology and as such I am obviously concerned about whether or not he can afford this court case let alone the fact that as a friend, I am worried about whether or not he can afford this court case." Steve sat back and sighed as he looked out the window, the end of his pen clicking on the desk as he thought about this question. Marianne fidgeted for a minute or two and finally said "I guess that means you're not going to tell me, does it?" He shook his head and softly said "No, it doesn't mean that. I just don't know what I can tell you." He sighed again and ran his hand across his face before he said. "I can't tell you much. Mark and I go back a long way, longer than most people realise." He turned and looked her in the face "I can tell you that he can afford this, probably quite easily but that is all I can tell you. The rest will need to come from him if he decides you should know."

+

Sharon had left Marks place at about lunchtime to go to the dentist and then just go home so he was outside again, without his camera but he did have an extra set of keys in his pocket. He stood there looking down the drive at the row of houses, wondering. This was not something he liked doing but it looked like it might be worth it just to see what the situation actually was. Slowly he walked down the drive and up to the back door of number four. The lock was a little stiff but not too bad even though it complained while the key turned. He stepped inside quickly and immediately smelt damp in the house. Slowly he walked through the house, twigs in the hearth told him there was a birds nest in the chimney and the cold in the house was seeping into his bones as he climbed the stairs. The bathroom was a nineteen sixties speciality, old, stained and chipped. Finally he was on the top floor looking out at his place and yes, you could see where he had been sitting this morning and the post that the door opened against. He smiled, that made him more comfortable as he rubbed his bare arms to keep some heat up in this old, cold house. The phone in his pocket rang and he answered it quickly as he started back down the stairs, he stopped and looked in on the first floor at the bedroom and the clothes lying neatly folded on the bed that were what Jennifer had been wearing this morning while an American voice in his ear began to talk to him. He didn't say much at first but made his way downstairs and out of the front door. He walked around the end of the cottages and smiled to himself as a net curtain twitched at Carol and Andy's. Carol was obviously at home. He was half way up the drive towards his house when the hired vehicle drove past him and parked between his Land Rover and the house. He smiled as he walked up to greet his guests, this could be a very interesting meeting. He knew if he turned round now Carol would be cleaning the inside of that window half way up her stairs that just so happened to look towards his house.

+

Karl Benson sighed as he signed the documents and dropping the pen on the desk, picked up the keys from the desk of the estate agent. A few minutes later he stepped outside and walked across the road and round the corner to the small café on the main street. Inside he carefully set the glass mug of cappuccino down on the plastic topped table and slid into the seat. The local newspaper he opened on the table next to him didn't tell him much and to be honest he wasn't really interested. To the waitress, who watched over the five or six tables that were occupied at the moment, it looked like he was talking to himself. Probably just complaining about something in the paper like everyone else did. She turned away and forgot he existed.

About ten minutes later He stood up and walked out of the café and headed to his car, he had better go and see what his house looked like empty, now he had actually bought it, even though he had never been inside it yet.

Five minutes after that Paul Brown turned around in his seat in the café and picked up the newspaper from the table behind him where Karl had left it, before he also stood up and walked out. The waitress picked up the cups and wiped the table with a dirty cloth as she looked out the window, not really caring or even interested, just looking.

+

Andrea had just come home at lunchtime, working part time was a great blessing as far as she was concerned, the post was behind the door and casually she picked up the usual half dozen items, a mix of flyers circulars and junk mail with just the one proper envelope in amongst them all. She turned it over in her hand, it was from the council. Carefully she let the kids run in to the house ahead of her as she tore open the white envelope and pulled out the single sheet of cheap copier paper that was inside.

It took a minute for her to understand exactly what it was saying, the semi legal language it was written in made it unclear but suddenly realisation dawned. There was going to be a departure hearing about the 'golf course' as they were now calling it. That meant that members of the public who wanted to comment had the right to address the hearing and give their side of the argument, directly to the councillors who would have to make the final decision. She smiled, that might be fun.

+

It was early afternoon and Mark was, yet again standing at his office window looking out. This time he was thinking about the visitors he had had this morning. An American couple with a new agency rather than a film company or TV channel like so many of the others had been so far. Mark had been cautious with them and had been very careful what he actually said to them. The bloke took notes long hand while it had been the woman who asked the questions; what had struck him as odd was that there had been no obvious attempt to record the interview. It had struck him as odd at the time, and when you added the fact that they had a set list of questions and didn't just let him speak like so many others did, he was not convinced they were from the press. He looked down at the business cards that lay on the window ledge where he had put them down; running his thumbnail down one side showed a slightly rough edge. He smiled to himself, micro perforations, he thought as he set the card down again. He had sheets like this in the drawer, they allowed him to make any number of business cards on his own printer right here at home and it looked like they had access to these as well.

The phone rang and it jolted him out of his contemplative state, he looked at the clock before he answered the phone, it was two o'clock. Jennifer was on the other end of the line "I was just about to give up on you and try your mobile." He laughed softly "Must be important, then if you need to get hold of me that desperately." He could hear her smile before she answered. "Not really but you might be able to help me here. Do you know a house called Ruriadh Cottage, anywhere on the estate?" Mark hesitated and shrugged to himself "Yes I do, its one of mine and is not available for let at the moment" Jennifer laughed again "No that's not it, but if it's not available for let, it's either falling down or is occupied. I'm willing to bet it's occupied and probably by an Arthur McIntyre, yes or no?" Mark grinned to himself "Yes that is the case. Why do you need to know?" She
138

grinned at the practice manager who was sitting at the side of her desk before she answered. "I needed to know because we have a file on him here that says he moved away about four years ago and we have no record of him going to a doctor since. I was thinking about making a house call. Would you be able to give me directions?" Mark nodded "Sure I can take you there, but I'm not sure what sort of reception Arthur will give you." Jenny grinned again and said "See you in half an hour?" They agreed she would come and pick him up before she hung up the phone and turned to the practice manager saying "Well, he is still alive and my neighbour knows him. I got the impression that Arthur's maybe not that sociable a person so taking him along for an introduction makes sense to me." The practice manager nodded "Didn't mention why he had dropped off the radar did he?" She shook her head "No, no mention of that at all." The practice manager was full of admiration for this new bright doctor that had arrived in their midst and that was why he said "Are you sure you want to go and see him? Maybe we should ask one of the male doctors to go and see him?" Jenny shook her head "I'm a fresh face and interested in this old guy, my neighbour," she pointed at the phone "knows him and can take me there without any problem. The other doctors here have had how long to go find him and haven't managed?" He nodded "Hmmm, yes okay I see what you mean." He looked down and back up "Do you trust this neighbour of yours? Do I know him?" Jenny smiled but hesitated before answering "You will know of him at least, Mark Rae, been in the papers lately, well only the 'Evening' actually." The practice manager interrupted, "That rag, wouldn't call it a paper." She nodded "Exactly, he's the guy they accused of beating up a girlfriend, Sharon Grant." He looked at her for a second "I know her parents quite well, they only live a few doors from me and they have told me quite clearly she was never touched by him. I think I may actually have met him as well at some of our fund raisers actually." He paused and Jennifer said "Well, I trust him implicitly. I have absolutely no doubts about that at all." The practice manager nodded as he stood up to leave the office "Good, I'm glad about that and to be honest now I know more about him I would as well. I think he could look after you very well." Jennifer looked down as he turned away out of the office and hoped he did not see her blush.

It was not long after that Jennifer's red car drew up at Marks place and she stepped out as he wandered over to meet her. He paused and said "Want to take my Land Rover? Arthur knows it and is less likely to be spooked." Jennifer looked at him as he glanced at the way she was dressed "Do you think that's a good idea?" he nodded "Arthur's an old man, easily scared and unfortunately he has reason to be at the moment" He did not expand on that as Jennifer obviously wanted him to. "Will I do then?" She said turning around on the spot, He laughed "Of course, what I was looking for was practicality. Flat shoes, no heels, trousers and not a short skirt; all functional and practical, what you need to go and see Arthur." He smiled at her before he finished by saying "I may like the idea of you in a short skirt and heels but today would not be the right time." She just shook her head as she lifted her bag out of her car and slid it into the back of the Land Rover alongside a carrier bag full of clothes that sat there already.

Arthur opened the door wide and smiled when he saw Mark standing there but hesitated and pulled the door back a fraction when he saw Jennifer standing behind him. Mark almost laughed "Relax Arthur, Jennifer is a friend of mine" Arthur hesitated a moment but said "Friend of yours is a friend of mine" Mark smiled "Hold that thought for a minute Arthur, Jennifer is also a doctor." The old man shrugged "Not a problem, I don't need a doctor anyway, but she's welcome as a friend." Jennifer gently pushed the door shut behind her as the three of them went inside the little cottage. She was pleased to see it was warm and dry inside as well as clean and obviously cared for. She glanced at the carrier bag Mark set down on the floor. "There's some clothes and the like for you Arthur. I've got a few pairs of socks after you mentioned a sore foot the other day." The old man sighed as Mark stepped past him and picked up the kettle to put it on the stove. He turned and looked Jennifer in the eyes "If you're with him you won't give up easily either will you?" She shook her head "First I would like to give you a quick examination just to check you're alright and see if there's anything you need from us to make your life easier." Arthur nodded as she said "Now, what's wrong with this foot of yours?" He sighed and sat down as Mark just grinned at them as Jenny opened her bag and pulled out a pair of rubber gloves.

+

Trente Silver looked across the flat shiny expanse of his desk at Andrew Crawford who was sitting there in his shirt sleeves as they spoke. "How close are they getting to us here?" Crawford shrugged "Difficult to say really, because we use locals most of the time and only perform occasional special little jobs and front end stuff it should be difficult for them to prove anything." Silver didn't seem convinced at all "For some reason I'm not actually comfortable with all of this." He smiled for a split second and that left Crawford wondering what was going through the other mans mind as he opened his mouth to speak again "One day they'll come through that door and cause me problems but up till now they can't prove anything. I'll retire soon enough and walk away from all of this and there will be nothing they can do about it." Crawford just looked at his boss he had never mentioned retirement before, at all. Silver sighed and looked at him "What's this department hearing all about?" Crawford shook his head. "First it's a departure hearing not a department hearing. It's because our application is a departure from the policies and guideline that the council have adopted and agreed to follow." Silver interrupted "So, what's that got to do with us? It's their departure not ours, this is the way we do business." Crawford sighed, sometime he wondered if this was done just to try his patience but he carried on as he had to anyway. "We have to defend our case make it obvious the benefits that would be the outcome of adopting our scheme and the opposition, if there is any, get a chance to air their opinion and try to convince the relevant councillors to reject the idea." Silver just looked at him again before asking "What are our chances?" Crawford shrugged again. "Better than most we've got more than half of this committee on our side anyway and the majority of the rest should be easily convincible and under the control of the various political groups that we've already bought, I mean convinced of the value of our position." He sighed and leant back again before concluding "Whatever happens we have another hearing to go through at what they call the Infrastructure Services Committee meeting where they decide whether or not the local authority can afford to supply the infrastructure we would need. That bit has been dealt with because even if it fails there, we have the agreement of the little fat man that the local government will support it at that point." Silver just grinned at that "So we have a time delay, but it's a delay rather than anything else?" Crawford shrugged yet again and said "If it is anything it'll be a delay, but I don't think that will even happen." Silver nodded and leant back waving his hand at Crawford who knew the sign and stood up to leave the room. He was almost at the door when he heard his boss say "It'll be beautiful, the best in the world." Crawford just shook his head as he closed the door behind him; he had heard that phrase before.

+

Karl looked around the small house, he had seen it before obviously, but this was the first time he had a chance to look at it truly accepting he would have to be living here for a while. It was smaller than he was used to but that came with the job, not always what he wanted. The small garden had a decent garage and a barbeque pit, he could have some fun while he was here, it should only be a few months anyway before he could get out of this place. The van with what they were calling his stuff would be here tomorrow to at least make the place look lived in and make it reasonable for him, give him something to sleep on if nothing else. He finished the bottle of beer and set the empty down on the floor just inside the door. He drove away in a cloud of dust and old Jock watched from upstairs as the white sports car vanished up the road. "Flash git" he muttered to himself "Might at least have been a woman so I could have had some company." He thought back about the other new occupant in the row at number four just two doors away on the other side, then he shook his head, she was too good for him and he knew it. He hadn't even tried to get close to her.

+

Meanwhile back at Ruriadh cottage Jennifer was climbing into the Land Rover with Mark having just said good bye to Arthur. The engine clattered into life and Mark eased the old machine into gear before jerkily starting off along the track past what had been the stable block. Jennifer looked across at him "Thank you for that," he glanced across at her as she continued "I don't think I would have gotten in over the door if you hadn't been there." Mark shook his head "Well, you got in and I think he likes you." She laughed softly "I certainly hope so, he's a nice old guy who just needs a little help every now and again." Mark nodded "That's my take on him as well, he just needs a little help." Jennifer nodded "Yeah, but you wouldn't cut his toe nails for him would you?" Mark grinned "I didn't know what was wrong, did I?" his voice dropped to almost a whisper "Anyway I would have been frightened to hurt him." Jennifer shook her head again "What if I treat you to tea? I would just about kill for a chip supper and it's the least I owe you for your help this afternoon." Mark shrugged "Okay, why not? We can get a take away and go back to my place." Jennifer nodded as she thought about Marks warm and comfortable house.

They were sitting at the kitchen table later drinking tea as Mark rolled up the chip wrappers and put them in the bin while Jennifer watched him closely, she felt there was something else he wanted to say as he poured them both another mug of tea. He set down the teapot heavily, and looked her in the face. "I took what might be called a landlords liberty earlier today and had a look around the house you're currently living in." She sat forward not sure where this was going as he carried on "I know it was cheeky and I'm sorry, but I'm glad I did it. I never realised the house was in such a poor state. It's damp, it's cold, the bathroom needs replaced and the kitchen is effectively non existent." He stopped and drew breath as Jennifer sat looking at him intently "I can't argue with any of that, but that is why I got the place at the rent I did." "Hmmm" he said "That's as may be but that place is barely habitable at all, so I have a suggestion for you." Jennifer just looked at him not at all sure what he was about to say as he continued, not really looking at her directly at this point. "I have plenty of spare rooms here and I want you to move in here until such time as I get the

142

repairs done down the road. If I had known how bad that place was I would never have let anyone move in there." Jennifer was stunned, it was pretty close to what she had dreamt about, maybe as close as she was going to get. She sighed and he looked at her, worried he had gone too far, "When do you want me to move in?" she laughed "Tonight too soon?" was his reply.

+

Jennifer was standing looking down the drive later, after she and Mark had collected some of her belongings from her house. She knew some of the neighbours would be making assumptions and she hoped this would not hurt Marks reputation locally. She had changed into soft cotton trousers and a tee shirt and Mark couldn't help himself but watch her shapely form as she stood against the window, he turned and quietly went into his office without disturbing her. It was nice to have a woman in the house again.

She had felt him watch her and had been comfortable with that, she hugged herself tightly, thinking about early this morning when she had come up to speak to him in what passed for her night clothes. She didn't think he had realised that at the time and she was glad of that. She was actually looking forward to a night in a warm bed when she didn't wake up with the cold. Anything else could wait. Suddenly a movement caught her eye; she had thought she could see a corner of the rear end of a car at the end of the row of cottages and now there was clearly someone there lifting a bag out of the rear of the car and vanishing inside. She shrugged and sat down on the settee and hesitated before switching on the TV.

Mark finished what he was doing in the office and went through to the living room. He surprised himself by finding he wanted to spend some time with Jennifer. She smiled as he walked in and then almost as quickly looked uncertain. "Is it okay for me to be here? I know you suggested I stay here for a while but that may just have been an offer of a room, not the use of the rest of the house." He shook his head "Relax," he said "You're welcome, I might veto a TV programme some time but other wise feel free to make yourself at home." He said as he sat down at the other end of the settee. She smiled as she stretched and he tried not to look as her tee shirt flattened her breasts slightly. She looked at him as he looked at the TV and she knew why he had looked away. That was a good sign in many ways, he wasn't embarrassed just didn't want to embarrass her, at least that was what she thought, he was thinking.

"Oh" she said as she remembered something "I see our new neighbour has turned up." He looked at her as she waved an arm towards the end of the house "Down at the cottages, I thought I saw someone unloading a car into the house earlier." He stood up and looked out of the window as she carried on talking "I'm surprised Paradigm Properties didn't try and buy that one as well." He didn't turn round as he looked down the road at the lights that shone out of the windows in the end house. "So am I," he said "We offered well above asking but some one offered even more." He chewed his lip as Jennifer stood up close behind him and looked round him to also look down the road. "I would like to know who" he finished as he put his hands on top of hers on his waist and she giggled slightly "I never even asked you what my rent would be for staying up here, instead of down in my own cold place." He laughed "Your company is all I ask for. I would not have been happy if you had hidden in your room." He looked at her over his shoulder "I like having a woman in the house, an attractive and intelligent one like you is even better, and some one who dresses like you do is a bonus" She went slightly pink as he said this and mumbled "Sorry, I didn't mean to offend you, it's just so warm up here compared to my own place." He laughed out loud "No, don't interpret what I say, listen to my words. I like the way you dress. I would be even happier if you chose to run around naked, just don't expect me to keep my hands off you in that case." She blushed properly before saying "I can take that as a compliment then?" he nodded and suddenly her expression changed as she looked past him and down the drive "Look" she said. Turning round Mark saw what she was meaning, the lights at the end had gone out and had come on in old Jocks place. Mark made a thoughtful noise "I wonder what that means now" he said as he moved away from the window and sat down again next to Jennifer on the settee.

The next morning Jennifer had left for the surgery at her usual time but only just. Mark had considered knocking on her room door but had decided it was none of his business. He had smiled however when a grateful Jennifer had rushed up the stairs to find coffee ready to drink waiting on her and had kissed him on the cheek before dashing out the door only making one comment about his house being way too comfortable for her time keeping. He stood there bemused, as the red car had driven off, carefully, down the driveway.

It was that morning that a letter from the council arrived telling him that the departure hearing would be in two weeks time and if he wanted to speak at the hearing he would need to inform the local authority no less than four days before the meeting. He checked the dates and found it was right. It had come by the postal service so there was no unexplained loss of a few days. He looked down the drive automatically, not really seeing anything until a movement caught his eye. It was old Jock out the back of his house cutting

144

the grass on the head of the bank. Mark smiled to himself, now might be a good time to go and speak to him.

So it was just a few minutes later he strolled down to speak to Jock, it was a pleasant, bright morning and only a light breeze was blowing. "Morning Jock" He called over the noise of the lawn mower as Jock finished the last little bit he had to do. Mark tried not to laugh as he looked at the bleary slightly unfocused eyes of his neighbour. "Morning," grunted Jock, his voice sounded hoarse as well, probably burnt with the whisky he had been drinking the night before "Wasn't sure if you would speak to me again after what I did" Mark just shook his head "I don't hold it against you Jock. You're as entitled to your opinion as I am to mine." He shrugged and looked around before continuing "That's one of the reasons I'm here this morning, we haven't spoken for a while, not since I had everyone up at my house, in fact. I wanted to make sure we could still speak and get that out of the way." Jock nodded, he had known Mark for a lot of years now and trusted the younger man to tell him the truth. "Well I'm pleased about that," he said nodding his head slowly "I need all the friends I can get these days. That's why I was happy to see Karl move in yesterday." He smirked slightly to himself as he saw the flicker in Marks eyes, there was little Jock liked better than having information that no one else had "Karl?" was all Mark said but Jock smiled "Karl Benson, moved in next door" he pointed over his shoulder at the end house "late last night. Came round to see me and brought a bottle of vodka with him." Mark smiled "I didn't think whisky would have done that to you. You've had too much practice for that." Jock smiled at what he took as a compliment and said "Aye, well there's that, but you'll meet him soon enough. He said he was going to be going round a'body, just to introduce himself, like." Mark nodded to himself, something did not sound right here at all.

It was almost two hours later that Mark finally got away from Jock and headed back up to his own house. An hour later he sat back, none of the details he had picked up from Jock about this new neighbour, Karl Benson, checked out at all, it sounded to Mark as though this was a false name for some reason, and he had a suspicion as to why.

It was almost six o'clock before Jennifer got back to the house that night, she was tired and at the same time pleased that she was coming back to this warm dry and comfortable house and not to the cold and draughty one she had actually rented. Stepping inside the door, she kicked off her shoes and wrinkled her nose as the smell of roasting chicken drifting to her from the kitchen made her mouth water. Carefully she walked down the hallway and pushed open the door and was surprised to see Mark at the cooker looking into the oven. He turned at the sound and smiled at her "Hope you like Chicken" was his only comment as she stared at him "I didn't even think about food being included" Suddenly he looked crestfallen "I'm sorry I never even thought about it. You've eaten already haven't you?" "No" was her almost shouted reply "I just never even thought about it. It's a nice surprise, how long until its ready?" He shrugged "About twenty minutes, maybe half an hour or so." He replied standing up as she finally came into the room "Plenty of time for you to get changed if you want or grab a glass of wine, even." She smiled at him and kissed him quickly on the cheek before stepping back "If I'm really quick I might just manage both" she smiled as he turned away back to the cooker "Better hurry them, but on you go." She darted off to her room and quickly stripped off to the skin and pulled on the same type of soft cotton trousers and a clean tee shirt as she had been wearing the previous evening. Mark smiled as she reappeared very quickly but just in time as he drained the potatoes.

Later they were both sitting there on the settee with a glass of wine each when Jennifer summed up her courage and turned to Mark "Can I ask you something?" He looked back at her with that smile of his "Of course, you can ask anything you like, just don't bet on always getting an answer." At that the doorbell rang, they both sighed as they both had the impression a moment had gone and an opportunity was lost. Mark pushed himself off the settee where they both had been sitting close together and went to the front door. He knew who it was as soon as he opened the door, the stranger was almost inside before Mark could say anything "Hi," boomed the strange looking little man "I'm Karl, your new neighbour from the end there," he pointed backwards over his shoulder "and I thought I'd come and introduce myself to you all." He waved a bottle of Russian vodka in Marks face so close the drops of condensation landed on Marks shirt as he pushed past him and into the house. "I thought we could empty this before it comes up to room temperature." He was inside and Mark sighed as he swung the door shut behind him. Karl was in the living room and made a bee line for the settee beside Jennifer before anyone said anything, bending down he leered at her as his gold chain swung, glinting in the light. "Hi honey," he exhaled in her face "I'm Karl, new neighbour, he's been keeping you a secret, everyone told me he was alone." he pointed at Mark as he kissed her quickly on the lips and swivelled around to let himself fall into the seat. Jennifer pulled back into the corner as Karl looked up at Mark "Got any glasses for this?" Mark disappeared to the kitchen and was surprised when he returned to find Karl alone, where they had left him in the living room. Jennifer returned a few seconds later with a cardigan over the top of her tee shirt.

It took them a couple of hours before the half litre bottle of vodka was finished and Karl looked at him "Got any more of this stuff?" Mark shook his head "Sorry, not really a vodka drinker" Karl looked surprised "Not even local stuff?" Mark shook his head "Need to change that if I'm going to stay around and I intend to stay around if all the women round here look like you," he leered at Jennifer again where she now sat beside Mark on the arm of the chair with her cardigan pulled tight around her. Karl hiccupped and sighed squinting at his watch "Anyway," he said "I need to move on." Carefully he pulled his mobile phone out of his pocket and dialled a taxi company. He stood up slowly and unsteadily "Want to come with me? We could go into town get a couple of escorts and go to the casino maybe? Could be fun." Mark smiled at him and for a minute Jennifer thought he was going to go, then he glanced at her openly, and said "Nah, I don't think so; maybe another time?" Karl nodded and let himself be guided out as he said "Yeah, I understand, not easy to get out for extras when it's on tap in the house." Mark didn't reply as he closed the door and watched his new neighbour wander away down the driveway towards his own house as a taxi was coming down the hill.

Back in the living room Jennifer looked at him as he came back into the room, "Is he gone?" Mark nodded "Weaving his way down the drive as I speak" Jennifer sighed as she leant forward and took her cardigan off again "Good," she said "I was melting with that on, but the way he leered at me, I did not like at all." She looked at Mark and carried on "Several times I've been around you without my bra on and yes you've looked at me but not the way he looked at me." She paused as she realised what she had just told him but finished it anyway "He scared me." Mark sighed and sat down next to her on the settee. He was shaking his head as he leant forward to pick up the glasses only to find Jennifer had hold of them already, along with the two wine glasses from earlier. Standing up she looked at him "Want another glass of wine? I don't think you really drank much of his vodka, I know I didn't" Mark smiled up at her "No, I didn't drink much of that stuff so, yes, I'll have another glass of wine." He looked at her as she paused "You know where the box is in the fridge?" She nodded "I'll find it" as she turned and walked away. He picked up her light cardigan and folding it dropped it over the back of the settee lost in his own thoughts.

In the kitchen Jennifer set the vodka glasses down next to the sink before opening the fridge. She stopped and stared, there in the fridge, on the shelf below the wine box was a small bottle rack and on it, amongst the wine and cordial bottles sat an unopened half litre bottle of Russian premium vodka. She smiled to herself and poured the wine quickly before the cold got to her.

+

It was just over two weeks later that Drimmie school hall saw the most people that it had seen for many years. They were early but it was already half full when Mark and Jennifer arrived together. Mark in a suit and Jennifer straight from the surgery. They looked around the room and saw a few familiar and friendly faces and a few unfriendly ones as well. There was Alison from the gymkhana association who seemed to be trailing Peter Barnard around as he floated about talking to all of the Councillors he could get to before the formal proceedings started. Jenny was sitting with a few others of the gymkhana association and next to then was Andrea from the tennis club. Mark looked around looking for some of his neighbours, Carol and Andy were there from the opposite end of the row to Karl who appeared with old Jock and seemed to go and sit down next to the Silver Organisation Representatives. Andrew Crawford sat there waiting, scowling and checking his watch regularly, obviously hating every minute of sitting here waiting for the process to begin.

Eventually, almost exactly on the start time, Marlene stood up and spoke, quickly she sat down again and pressed the button on the microphone that sat on the desk in front of her "Can you hear me now?" came over loud and clear. The press and public sniggered softly to themselves, it epitomised the lack of skill that most people expected from a local authority. "Right," she continued, trying to just bluster her way out of it. "We are ready to start and the proceedings should be quite straight forwards." She turned and looked along the row of councillors that sat facing the audience. "The Press are entitled to remain in the hearing but all recording devices will require to be switched off once the chair of the meeting takes over and calls the meeting to order. The councillors will then introduce themselves individually and the chair will describe the planning application to the meeting." She drew breath and looked around the hall before she continued. The applicants representatives will then present their case and the rest of those who wish to speak will be called in turn to allow them to present their arguments. Individual councillors can then make any representations they wish before the vote is called. There has been an informal agreement between the councillors present here tonight that no one will call for a vote until each councillor has spoken. That is to allow each councillor to discuss their position before the summation which will be from each councillor and is limited to five minutes each. Is that clear to everyone?" She looked around the hall carefully avoiding many pairs of eyes but giving the overall impression of checking understanding. "Okay," she said "Then with no more delay I call upon the chairman to bring the meeting to order." The old

148

man in the middle of the table leant forward and thumbed the microphone button. "Good evening" his voice boomed around the hall and a few people winced "Sorry folks" he smiled at the crowd "I am used to working without a microphone so I need to tone that down a bit more." He explained before he launched into his speech proper. "I am Padruig McCarthy, chair of this committee and thereby call this meeting to order." He turned a page over and looked at what it said there.

It was more than four hours later the hall emptied out with the Silver Organisation having triumphed and been granted their permission subject to the result of a meeting of the Infrastructure and Services Committee in two weeks time. Some Councillors stormed out in fury at the result and others were busy having their hands shaken by the Silver Organisation people all the way out to the TV cameras that began to turn on their lights. That was when the politicians vanished into the darkness. Jennifer watched as Mark stood there and fumed as Crawford paraded up and down in front of the cameras as he allegedly spoke to his boss, Trente Silver, on the phone to pass on the good news. Mark pulled out a notebook and began to make some notes about what had gone on after the meeting, adding to those he had made during the meeting. Jennifer took hold of his arm and led him away, he pulled back a little and said "Wrong way my Land Rover is over there." He said pointing to the other side of the car park. Jennifer shook her head "Leave it, we'll get Johns taxi, we are going to the pub." Mark sighed, shrugged his shoulders and put the notebook back into his pocket before letting Jennifer lead him to the pub. It was about half full in the bar as they made their way to the counter. Andy the barman appeared behind the counter still with his coat on and said to them "Give me a minute and I'll serve you two, once I get my jacket off." Mark nodded and watched as the big man started a pint of dark stout pouring and came over to see what Jennifer wanted. Mark had his money in his hand as she said "A glass of white wine please" Andy smiled and looked at Mark "Put that away, you don't need it here tonight." Mark looked at him in surprise while he went away and finished pouring the beer before bringing it and a glass of wine over for Jennifer "You gave a good show there tonight and stood up for the area, unlike some of the others around here. You have my vote anytime you need it." Mark shrugged "Thanks for that, if ever I can help you, let me know." Andy nodded and headed off down the bar only to be stopped by Alison from the gymkhana society who said "Why did you say that? He and his little band of followers are trying to destroy this place, stopping it growing and if this wasn't to go ahead, what would we do when the oil runs out?" Andy just looked at her "This development will kill this area. They will destroy a unique Site of Special Scientific Interest that brings tourists into the area and acts as the lungs of the city. The only opportunity this brings is an opportunity to destroy ourselves." Mark and Jennifer watched from where they sat off to one side as Alison and her lone companion turned back to him "Why do you think that? This development brings in high value tourists, film stars and the like; people with real money to spend who will spend it in the likes of this place. They are building a spa and the local people will have access to it so we might end up sharing it with some of the special people of this world." The bar erupted in laughter at that and Andy finally, once he stopped laughing, said "The only special people you will see here are the staff of that place all Eastern Europeans earning less than the minimum wage for one pint of beer a month if they are lucky. The gates and the guards will stop the rest of them getting out and you from getting in. The film stars you are talking about, if they do ever come here will never come out of the gates and so they will be of no benefit to me or any other business holder in the area." Alison straightened up and looked down her nose at him "You are a fool, I will never drink here again." Andy just shrugged "Your loss not mine, the doors over there" He nodded with his head as the woman red faced and obviously embarrassed turned and flounced out, followed closely by her lone associate.

Mark pulled out his notebook and set it on the table just as Jenny pulled up a stool and sat down next to them, she looked annoyed. Turning to them she smiled, a little almost self conscious smile, and said "Well done, I was watching and have just been discussing it with some of the others who, I think, are all on their way down here. Want to compare notes? There were some strange voting patterns there that we need to figure out." Mark hesitated and looked at her more closely "You okay?" She shrugged, "Yeah, I guess so; just a little unhappy. Ran into Alison out there, I've known her for years, been friends for years and she's out there shouting about how this place should be closed down because Andy there refused her a drink." She turned and looked at him "Did you?" He shook his head and just carried on with what ever it was he was doing. Jenny turned back and looked at the other two "I thought I knew her, we were friends and now she's busy shouting about the 'Luddites' here trying to stop this great development. What's gotten into her?" she asked no one in particular. Jennifer set her glass down delicately and said "Probably a man." Most of the people in the bar turned to look at her as she continued. "The only time I've seen such a massive change in a woman's attitude there has been a man involved somewhere." The others nodded and Mark looked around the group that seemed to be expanding around the table as more and more of the objectors drifted into the bar to commiserate each other and see if they could plan a way forward.

150

It was Andrea who finally said "Can we think about this please, as I saw it the final vote was five votes to four. One councillor spoke against the development and yet voted for it and one actually seconded the motion to put forward an amendment and yet voted against that when it came to it at five to four as well." They were all nodding until Mark spoke "We also need to bear in mind the fact that Marlene said they had an agreement to let each of them speak before calling for a vote to make sure the subject was properly explored. Then as second speaker, she herself called for a vote, effectively shutting up the rest of the councillors and stifling the debate." A strident voice said "Exactly, well spotted Mark. I was wondering if anyone had noticed that little piece of gamesmanship." It was Dianne one of the councillors who seemed to be obviously against this development. She made her way through the group and they made space for her on the bench seat beside Jennifer. Mark turned to Dianne and asked "Was that a manipulated little show or not?" Dianne was nodding as she said "Definitely and I'll tell you another thing, that speech that Marlene gave was not hers. Some one wrote that for her, it was logical and made sense it even had a flow to it. Hers do not. I'd love to know who wrote that for her." Mark just nodded and looked up as another tray of drinks was brought to the table by Andy. The conversation carried on and on for a few hours yet until a clear picture of what had actually happened seemed to have been developed and suddenly Jennifer looked up and noticed that the bar was thinning out as people drifted away home. She stood and stretched feeling Marks eyes on her as she did so. She smiled to herself that was alright, he could look. John poked his head around the door at that point and Mark sighed, he didn't know how John did it but he always seemed to appear just as he was needed. He smiled when he saw the two of them standing up and exchanged a 'thumbs up' with Andy who nodded "Goodnight" to them as they followed John out to his taxi.

It was a short ride home as they sat in almost silence all the way there. Mark stayed behind to pay John as Jennifer went to open the door. "Look after her," said John as he took the money from Mark "She seems like a nice one." Mark looked over at Jennifer as she stood on the step waiting on him with the door standing open, he was about to turn back to John and say they were just friends when something made him stop; he shrugged and smiled at John as he wound up the window and drove away into the still and peaceful night.

The next day was a Saturday and they were slow to get moving in the morning. Mark was initially surprised and had to stop and think for a minute or two when he woke up and found Jennifer lying beside him in his bed. The tee shirt and knickers she was wearing made him relax a little and he just lay there listening to her breathing as he recalled last night's conversation. She hadn't wanted to be alone and, to be honest, neither had he, they were friends and they trusted one another so was there a problem? He thought not and smiled to himself as he looked at her just lying there sleeping. It was a long time since he had been this lucky and he savoured the moments as eventually she began to stir and wake slowly next to him. Asking for a cuddle and giving a kiss unbidden she nuzzled close to him and it just felt right as they lay there together, enjoying the company. The warmth of her body through the thin cotton of that tee shirt made him realise that life goes on. Everywhere all of the time and the best things can come out of the worst of times. Jennifer looked at him through half closed eyes "Thank you" she said He pulled back slightly and looked her in the face "What for?" he asked and she smiled again "The fact you need to ask is good as well; for not taking advantage of the situation." He smiled and grinned at her "Don't think I haven't thought about it" he said and she smiled back at him "You're a man, you're bound to, but no matter if you thought about it or not, you didn't do anything." he shrugged slightly and settled back not wanting to say anything more. Knowing whatever he said would spoil the mood of the morning.

9

It was half past eight that morning before they were both in the kitchen and Mark was trying to make scrambled eggs as Jennifer prepared coffee with the radio playing in the background when the news came on. Mark hesitated as he heard the Silver Organisation development being mentioned and there was actually a sound bite from the 'great man himself' as the presenter put it. The voice said "I'm really proud that such an overwhelming majority of the local people want me to come and help them out in this way. I am touched and promise to do my best to make this the best golf development in the world." Jennifer reached out to turn the radio off as Mark said "No leave it just now, not yet" She lowered her hand as the presenter went on to say "Unsurprisingly, after such a crushing defeat in the council and such a poor representation form the objectors last night. None of the objectors groups were willing to speak to us this morning." He paused for a split second before he continued "In other news…" there was a click as Jennifer turned off the radio and turned to look at Mark. His face may be pointed towards the floor but she knew he was not just looking at her legs where they showed beneath the tee shirt she was wearing. That was his normal pose when he was thinking. He raised his head to look at her and she saw his eyes focus before he suddenly turned and stirred the eggs in the pan before they stuck. He turned back to her but before he could say anything the phone began to ring. Jennifer shook her head "You get the phone, I'll finish cooking breakfast." He nodded and went to answer the ringing bell that was shouting for someone's attention.

It was Jenny of the gymkhana association who started talking immediately he picked up the phone. "Did you hear the radio news this morning? Did they actually bother to try and get in touch with you or did they not bother? I am so annoyed at the way they're presenting this as if we didn't give a good show last night." Mark finally got a word in edgewise "Jenny, we agree with you why don't we try and get together maybe later today, this afternoon perhaps? To discuss this and see where we go from here." Jenny seemed to think about that "Okay, sounds like a good idea, will I get Andrea to come along from the Tennis club, she's already been on the phone to me this morning, oh goodness, I didn't wake you did I?" Mark laughed "No Jenny, you didn't wake me at all, I promise you that much. I'm usually up early so don't worry about that. Maybe see you later?" He looked up as Jennifer appeared at the office door and waited for a second obviously judging if he was going to be coming back to the kitchen or not.

He smiled at her as he listened to Jenny on the phone who finally hung up. He sighed as he set the receiver in its cradle and sat back just looking at Jennifer as she stood there, still in a tee shirt, he was about to say something when the phone rang again. Jennifer turned as she spoke "I'll bring your breakfast to you." He nodded as he picked up the receiver and found himself speaking to the local radio station, live on air. "Good morning Mr Rae we're just wondering if you could tell the public why after making such a noise prior to the meeting your people had no effect last night and were unavailable for comment this morning." Mark was a little taken aback at the tone of the interviewer but responded all the same. "Well let me tackle your numerous points in order. First we did not make a noise as you put it, we merely exercised our rights to object to a misrepresented planning application, in a peaceful and democratic manner. The various objectors to the case last night put forward reasoned and accurate positions and opinions relative to the facts of the case whereas the supporters relied on nothing more than the fact they thought it was a good idea with no substantiation what so ever." The reporter jumped in "Well that's a position based on opinion, how about the fact that none of your people were prepared to speak to any of the press this morning and that includes yourself? This is the third attempt we have made to speak to you this morning." Mark laughed "Perhaps you should check the numbers you are using. You are the first press organisation that has made any attempt at contact this morning so I would refute that allegation completely." He could hear the reporter check some notes before he asked "Finally Mr Rae, what about the financial argument, even you must agree this sort of investment in the country has to be a benefit to the population as a whole." Mark laughed out loud before he said "I'm sorry this investment is an imaginary figure our own economists and accountants show a more realistic figure is the order of three hundred million Euros and not the one billion Euros being bandied about by some of the less responsible elements of the media and as for the annual return to the local area, it is a joke, even using their own figure of sixty million Euros a year, while we believe to be nearer ten or maybe fifteen million Euros a year, but using the fifty million Euros figure you are looking at around 0.1% of the Gross Domestic Product, this is clearly a long way from a project of national significance." There was silence on the other end of the line for a moment until, finally the reporter said "Thank you for that Mr Rae" and the line cut to silence. Mark almost set the phone down when another voice came on and spoke quickly but quietly. "Mr Rae, I'm one of the producers here at 'Local FM' you can't prove this but I know they never tried to contact you earlier but they will again and so will some of the other news agencies. Make sure your mobile is on and if you can divert your land line I would do so. Thank you" and before he could say anything the line went dead. He hung up the

154

phone thoughtfully as he suddenly became aware of Jennifer standing in the door again, she smiled at him. "I would suggest you get dressed while I make you a fresh breakfast, you might need it by the sound of things." He nodded as he stood up and walked towards her, she didn't move and they hugged for a moment or two before she let him go. "Now go and get ready for your public." He deliberately didn't see her wipe a single tear from the corner of her eye as he walked along the hallway.

It was almost six hours, three camera crews, four radio reporters and almost a dozen newspaper reporters later that Mark got back inside the house. The door shut behind him as the last TV 'uplink' van disappeared down the driveway, manoeuvring its way past the parked cars of those who had come to speak to him over the course of the day. Jennifer stuck her head round the corner just to check who it was that had come in. Looking past him she said "They all gone?" as she stepped close and slipped her arms around his neck as he replied "Yeah, for just now at least. Have you been fielding the phone calls?" He could feel her nod as she slowly pulled back and he looked at her properly, she obviously hadn't had a chance to get properly dressed as she was still wearing the same tee shirt but now had a shirt over the top and a pair of jeans on as well. He sighed as he let his arms relax around her "Thank you," she nodded as he straightened himself up and continued "Now, lets see what our supporters have to say" He sighed as he walked into the living room and was faced with a picture of himself on the TV reciting the same position and opinions to yet another reporter.

It was Andrea of the Tennis club that spoke first "Well done, you've raised the profile and got it onto almost all the TV channels. That has to be good." She stood up and kissed him "Thank you" he said and noted the bright smile and the sparkling eyes while thinking 'be aware of potential complications'. He stepped past her and sat down next to Jennifer who slid a little closer to him. Jenny began to speak as the doorbell went and the front door opened, Mary and Pete called through from next door "Hallo, saw you on the telly, several times, thought we should come up and say well done." They came into the room and stopped, surprised to see so many faces. It was Pete who said "Sorry are we interrupting?" Jennifer shook her head, "Not at all, come on in, the more the merrier, coffee?" she slid out of her seat and went to put the kettle on as Andrea moved across into her seat next to Mark. Jenny carried on speaking "Anyway, what I was saying was that the only channel we can see here that you haven't been on is, TTFN which is actually owned by Silver through an intermediary." She paused as she looked at the screen which had moved onto another news item. Suddenly she spoke up "I am fairly sure that 'Local FM' the radio station that interviewed you this morning was bought by his intermediaries earlier this year. Let me go and check on that." Standing up she stepped in close and bending down, kissed Mark before saying "Well done, keep it up and I'll be in touch" He shook his head as she left he room and conversation continued.

+

"Sue that bastard" was the shout echoing around the fifty third floor of the tower block in New York. Silvers lawyer looked at him and sighed, this was going to be difficult. They had just finished watching a feed from one of the European news satellites that had showed some protestor at the Doones estate saying what a mess he was going to make of their lovely country side. Silver was as close to physically jumping up and down as the lawyer had ever seen him. He waited a moment or two to see if the heat passed as it sometimes did then said "How? He didn't say anything defamatory, as far as I can tell it was all opinion." Trente Silver just looked at him in blind fury before he began screaming again "I don't care, he's disagreeing with me and he's getting the publicity. You must stop him. I don't care how, just stop him." He looked at the lawyer and growled again "Or I will use other means." The lawyer just looked at the bald man glaring at him across the desk. He knew exactly what that meant and it was something he wanted nothing to do with. "All right," he said "All right, I'll look into it and get started on something." As he stood up and headed for the door Silver shouted after him "Don't look into it, just do it."

+

Andrew Crawford was not happy at all, he was standing there in the office at the stables block screaming at the idiot Peter Barnard and Danielle the PR girl. "How could you let that happen?" he turned away, paced towards the window and back again "How could you? We had it in place the permission was granted and they should have just faded away, like the rubbish they are." He paced again "Instead the press go looking for them and you let them find them. Why didn't you give them a false address or something? You didn't need to tell them where to get hold of him. He's been on every channel on TV and radio all bloody day." Barnard just stood there and looked at him; Danielle was getting annoyed "What difference does it make?" She shouted "You got your permission; you can go ahead; what difference does it make if they get a little air time to vent their spleen?" Crawford's eyes narrowed as he looked at her, daring to shout at him as she continued. "The more they talk the smaller they seem, that's normal and anyway isn't it true that there's no such thing as bad publicity?" Crawford's voice had dropped an octave or two and actually did sound threatening as he said "First, I don't care what they say, I just don't want to hear them at all. Second, some of what this guy in particular is saying is actually fact and we can't let too many people hear that. Third, the fact they are being seen is publicity for them, good publicity. Fourth the boss will not like it and that makes it uncomfortable for me so I need you to do something about it." he held up his hand as Danielle started to complain "Shut up, now fix it or leave. The choice is yours." She looked at him tears building in her eyes as she tried not to cry in front of him, determined not to cry in front of him but at the same time knowing he could see the tears in her eyes as he turned away and walked out the door. Next thing she knew Peter Barnard had his arms around her and she was crying into his jacket, it smelt of smoke and stale after shave, even though it was new. He smiled to himself, it was a pity he didn't actually like women.

+

Marlene had only really come to the surface about mid afternoon on the Saturday. She had switched her phone off and slept late, aided by a good half bottle of gin. She had been celebrating in a small wine bar in Drimmie rather than the normal pub when 'Xander's brother had arrived and the two of them had sat down and had a few drinks. They had gradually been joined by the supporters over the evening and not many other people had come near them, they had been loud and obnoxious and had even pushed closing time back an hour. Well the barman couldn't complain, his license was due to be reviewed in a month or so and almost all of the people in his bar were on the licensing committee. She was pleased she was alone when she woke up, she couldn't remember getting home and while she didn't mind doing business with some of these people, sleeping with them would be a different matter. She switched on the TV to see what the mood of the country was like and found herself looking at Mark Rae's face. She changed channel quickly and eventually switched it off. Suddenly she ran to the bathroom to be sick.

+

Templeton was sitting there watching TV in his office as the news stories started to come through, he sat back to watch and smiled as Mark spoke of the handling of the process and the unusual voting patterns that had taken place the night before. He smiled to himself and thought 'This guy can speak well and clearly, he's going to give them trouble going forward from here I think.' Turning to one side he pulled a copy of a piece of draft legislation from the shelves next to him and began to read.

157

+

'Xander was in a strange state as he watched the news, both happy that the plans had been passed, that meant he was due to get his second round of payments but he was also furious at the fact his guy was getting a lot of air time. He paced up and down wondering what he could do to stop it, something in the back of his head was telling him to leave it, let it go. Getting involved at this stage would only cause trouble; he was only supposed to get involved once it got past the local council level. He sighed, that meant not now then. He sat down and fidgeted some more.

+

Crawford was scared, as far as he was concerned and as far as his boss as concerned, this was a failure. He should have filled the airwaves and the TV screens of the country, and now with satellite communications, of the world with pictures of what this place would look like and how good it was going to be. Instead it was the objectors face and voice that was making it out across the world and that included the bits about voting patterns and errors made. The one thing that seemed to getting out as well was the visuals of the site being so poor. He snorted and turned away, he would deal with that one later, as long as they did not realise why they were so poor it would be alright. He waited, and waited on the phone call that did not come, which was even worse as far as he was concerned.

+

The team in the house in town were sitting around the table having a discussion about what had happened the night before, The original watcher was speaking "...still find it amazing that even here the press can misrepresent what actually happened so easily" His blonde colleague disagreed "You have to remember that a lot of these organisations are owned by US groups. Silver in particular so they kind of have to do what they're told." He shrugged "There is also the point that once one leads the rest tend to follow. We all know what the media are like, they tend to hunt in a pack. No one wants to be outside of the pack." The group fell silent for a few minutes until one of the other men spoke "This guy on the TV earlier seems to be making a decent argument and sounds reasonable, people will listen to him." The group nodded "Yeah," it was the blonde again "If he gets air time and I'm sure it will drop off quickly" The leader sat back "It might be possible that he could help us." The blonde looked at him "How?" she asked "We already spoke to him remember, I don't particularly want to go and speak to him again and tell him we lied to him last time" The leader
158

shook his head "I agree, but I am fairly certain he had us made as not being press the last time." One of the other men leant forward "So if you think he can help us, what are you going to ask him?" The leader shrugged and looked at the blonde who shrugged her shoulders as the group fell into silence.

+

'Xanders brother was a little worried, not scared you understand, just a little worried. Some of the other board members of the local party had called a meeting and his actions were the subject of the meeting. This was not the way it was meant to happen, he was in charge, they should just shut up and do as they were told. That was what he had always believed what he had always been told and what it appeared that Marlene believed as well, 'Interesting woman' he thought as he straightened his tie in the mirror before heading out of the small house to attend the meeting in the back rooms of the local village hall.

The meeting was not what he wanted to hear at all. It was only the senior committee that was present so there were only four of them. He knew he was in trouble as soon as he walked in and saw a single chair in front of the table with the four other already occupied seats facing him. He turned around just as the secretary closed the door behind him and he felt his heart sink as the door clicked into place behind him.

It was two hours later he was standing at the bar in the pub just down the road smiling to himself. They hadn't even touched on the money side of it; they were more concerned about his involvement with the political opposition. He grinned again, it was probably a case of they didn't want to know.

+

Peter Barnard was struggling with the scent of stale cigarettes and the alcohol that seemed to be oozing out of the very pores of this mans skin as he sat opposite him at the desk, he hadn't touched the coffee that Danielle had brought him. He had just leered at her and stared at her bum as she left the office. If it hadn't been for the stench and the fact he was obviously a ladies man he might have actually been quite attractive. Slowly the eyes focused and the face turned to look at him "Got any vodka?" was the question, Barnard flinched at he waft of bad breath that came his way and didn't answer. Looking back he was surprised to see bright eyes and a sharper awareness in the man opposite. He looked at the door and obviously decided it was safe before he looked back at Barnard and spoke "Right, I've got the immediate neighbour, 'Old Jock' on our side straight away, easy enough. I haven't even got the next ones at home yet. The guy up the back, Mark Rae is a non starter, he has an opinion of you lot and its fairly low I think, I can't change his mind. The ones down the bottom aren't interested, just want to be left alone, but are unsure so can probably be convinced without too much trouble. Scare them with the law rather than muscle though and it should be easy enough for you." Barnard had been scribbling notes rapidly and seriously as this man opposite him spoke. He finished speaking and winked at Barnard and as he watched the bleary eyes returned along with the disinterested half drunk attitude, it was almost like a cloak that he pulled around himself before he stood up and slowly weaved his way through the outer office and on to his car which had been abandoned at the door earlier.

Danielle watched as the dirty 'once white' car sped off in a cloud of dust along the estate road as she sat there shaking her head.

+

The planning officer was also sitting there shaking her head, but she was almost in tears as she looked at the article in the 'Planning' magazine. The shock announcement of the planning decision had been met with ridicule in the industry and she was feeling bad about it. If the truth be told she was feeling very bad about it. Her boss was standing at the door to her office shaking his head, he was convinced she didn't have the strength to carry this through. That meant she would have to go, soon; before she began to break. Unfortunately no other local authority in the country would hire her after what her name was attached to here, that was unfortunate, he shrugged to himself as he walked away, 'better her than me' was his only thought as he considered the new car he would now be able to afford.

She was shaking her head, she knew she was finished in local authority work and the private sector had never been of any interest to her, it was too much like working for a living. She knew the reports had been changed and her original recommendations to refuse permission had been over ridden. The claims that the economic benefits would override the environmental damage were completely manufactured and unsupportable. She stopped and thought about a few of the things she had been asked to do lately and began to smile to herself as she dug in her hand bag. Standing up she knew she was finished here anyway and might as well do something about it one way or another.

160

Her boss watched her leave the building and wondered what she was smiling at as she left. It was early and she shouldn't be away from her desk but he knew she was finished with the authority as soon as the final permission was issued whether she did or not. Until then they needed her as a scapegoat in case anything went wrong, he shrugged, he didn't think she was that bright anyway so it shouldn't be a problem. He would just need to give her some more applications to look after, keep her busy until such time as he could unload her from his staff.

She was sitting in her car in the middle of Drimmie looking at the memory stick in her hand. Now she had the evidence what did she do with it? Who could she trust with it? She shook her head at herself, the answer was no one at the moment she decided, as she dropped the memory stick into the bottom of her hand bag again.

+

The New York lawyer was hoping Silver had forgotten his threat as he met with him again a week after the last time, he hadn't.
"Well," the bald man bellowed "Have you found a way to deal with him?" The lawyer hesitated for a second as he wondered if there was a way to lie to this man. He decided against it at last. "No," he said "Everything he said was either opinion, stated as such, or verifiable fact. We have nothing on him or any of that group with which to sue them." Silver just grunted at the news before he pulled out a mobile phone and tapped at the screen. He finished and looked up at the lawyer before he dropped the phone on the desk at his side. "I'll do it my way now. He will make no more speeches about this." He waved at the phone lying on the desk as it buzzed. Silver picked it up again and smiled to himself before turning it round so the lawyer could see the screen. It said "Consider it done" from an unknown number. The lawyer was shaking with fury "Do you know what you've just done?" He didn't wait for an answer "You've made me an accessory to murder, before the fact." He stared at his client, 'former client' he thought "That means in the eyes of the law I'm as guilty as you." Silver just shook his head, he could maybe see more use for the professional he had just hired than for the lawyer.

+

The team in town was sitting around the table having another meeting about Mark Rae. The team leader was speaking "I feel we can trust him and I think he may be able to help us quite a bit." One of the others responded with "But that would mean telling him who we are and risking

161

compromising our operation here." The blonde sat there and shrugged her shoulders. They all seemed to heave a collective sigh and one of the others spoke for the first time "We're never going to come to an agreement here are we? I suggest you, as team leader do as you see fit and get on with it. You have the most experience of chasing this guy so you will know how he operates." Everyone around the table nodded in silence and looked at the wood grain in the surface.

+

Jennifer had just returned to what she was now calling home, for the evening and sighed as she kicked off her shoes inside the front door "Mark" she called out looking for him "Up here" was the call that led her to the small door that took her to the stupid awkward stair that finally led them out onto the lookout balcony that the coastguards had used when the building was initially designed and built. She could see he wasn't happy as he sat on the window sill and looked out at the large area of sand that was the site of special scientific interest. She didn't say anything as she stepped in close and touched his arm, he looked at her and smiled "Sorry," he said "I was just trying to picture this place as the plans show it being, and I can't. It's a horrible thought, five thousand years of evolution and natural development swept away to make room for one mans ego." Jennifer sighed deeply, he was taking this personally as she leant close to him and kissed him on the cheek "Come on inside, there's still a long way to go, we haven't lost yet and if we all believe even half as strongly as you do, we won't" He smiled and let himself be led back inside.

The man in camouflage gear on the dune line lowered the rifle and snapped the cover back into place on the eyepiece of the sight. He just lay there, watching, as some one else in sand camouflage slithered from a dune head fifty metres to his right and walked casually across in front of him, completely oblivious to his presence. He raised the rifle and took a closer look at the second man, no weapons. He grinned and lowered the rifle again waiting for a half hour before he slithered away down the seaward side of the dunes and disappeared.

+

Sharon Grant watched the TV news with interest, she knew she should have told Mark where she was going but hadn't wanted to bother him or build up his expectations of her. She was terrified of letting him down again. The programme was good and showed him in a good light, he was a handsome man after all, she just wished she had had more courage when

162

she was there, she might have still been there rather than thinking of going home to her parents for the weekend. She smiled, she would be able to go and see him at some point over the weekend. Sighing she thought about her last conversation with her mum, she had told Sharon that she should have told him she was leaving. He had been worried when she vanished after going to the 'dentist'. Sharon pressed her knees together, he had been asking for her, asking if she was okay and was she well. That made her feel good, soon she would see if he meant that personally. Slowly she turned down the bed and crawled under the covers in her little bed-sit in the capital. She smiled in the darkness, she was a national reporter now and she was where she wanted to be.

+

Jennifer lay there looking at the ceiling in the darkness, listening to Mark sleeping next to her. This strange platonic relationship was fun but she worried that she might offend him soon if he didn't make a move on her. The sharing of a bed had started as a function of her not wanting to be alone the night of the meeting and had just become a habit. She liked lying here and just hoped that one day they would be more than just close friends. She closed her eyes and tried to tell herself to just go to sleep.

+

Outside in the darkness 'thug one' looked at the house through those red view binoculars of his. He was uncomfortable, he could feel eyes on him, his instincts were screaming at him that he was being watched but he could still not see anyone, no matter how closely he looked. He shrugged his shoulders and turned away from the house, it should be an easy enough job but something about this bloke and this house made him wonder. Something was just not right.

About a kilometre away the man in dark camouflage watched through his large night scope, the green image gave everything a strange glow as he watched 'thug one' climb into his truck and drive away a reasonable distance before putting on his lights. He lowered the rifle, this was going to take a bit longer than he had hoped, the target was careful and he had orders not to compromise the other watchers, some of them were good and could get in the way because they were good, but they just were not as good as he was.

+

Next morning Mark was standing outside with a mug of coffee, half expecting Jennifer to come and join him but seeing no sign of her at the kitchen door. He half turned as he heard a vehicle coming up the drive, it was Sharon's little old blue car and it looked like Paul's red four by four was heading this way as well. He sighed and looked across at the house as he saw Jennifer in the kitchen "Better put the kettle on again." he called "Looks like we have more visitors on the way." Jennifer shook her head and did as she was asked.

It was only a few minutes later, as Paul was just turning into the end of the driveway and looking up at the house that he saw it happen. Jennifer was smiling as she stepped out of the back door and waved at Sharon as Mark hugged her close and tight, a warm welcome for a good friend. The first Mark knew about what happened was the searing, burning pain in his left ear lobe, to begin with he thought Sharon had bitten him for some reason but actually it was the passing of a high velocity bullet that tore through his earlobe as he hugged Sharon to him. The bullet passed straight through his ear, leaving a messy and painful wound but no real damage, the same could not be said for Sharon. The only saving grace was that she could never have felt a thing as the steel jacketed high velocity round entered her face between her top lip and her nose, passing through her skull and into her brain stem where it shredded the central cortex that connected it to her spinal column. Jennifer would never forget seeing the reddish, grey plume explode from the back of Sharon's head spreading pieces of skull, brain tissue and hair all over the side of Marks Land Rover.

Paul stared for a second as he brought his vehicle to a crunching halt in the gravel half way up the drive before he grabbed his mobile phone and was dialling 112 before the echoes of the gunshot had finished dying away.

'Thug one' quickly climbed back into his truck outside Ruriadh cottage where he had just climbed out of his vehicle. Arthur watched him drive away as he listened to the echoes and wondered what he was hearing. Thug one knew the sound of a high velocity rifle shot and he felt his stomach churn as he realised what he thought had just happened.

+

Steve was watching the news flash on the television with horror when he saw his friend coming out of the Accident and Emergency wing of the hospital flanked by Jennifer and Paul Gray, all of them being besieged by reporters. Mark looked pale, very unusual for him, and was covered in blood. Steve dressed quickly and left for the house at the beach as fast as he could.

They wouldn't even let him turn up the driveway as the whole place was taped off as a crime scene. He looked from the bottom of the driveway as the police officer told him "They're not here anyway. He's been taken to someplace safe for the meantime and no I can't tell you where because I don't know. His friends were going to be looking after him." Steve just looked at him and smiled, "Okay, thank you, I think I know where he is." The police man just looked at him "Then do him a favour, don't tell too many people." Steve nodded "Don't worry, I may be his lawyer but I'm also a friend." He said as he climbed back into his car.

Paul's four by four was sitting on the gravel outside the big house as Steve's car drew up alongside. Jennifer opened the door before he got there and he smiled as he saw her standing there. "How is he?" he asked Jennifer shrugged "Calm, a lot calmer than I would have been after being shot at and having some one die in my arms." Steve just nodded "Not the first time that's happened to him, that's why he acts differently to most men. I hope he doesn't decide to deal with it his own way." Jennifer looked at him and for some reason he hesitated, he wanted to tell her and he knew that Mark would not mind in this case, it was just difficult to go against so many years of enforced secrecy. He shook his head as he walked past her and she knew there was something there she needed to know.

It was quiet in the study as Mark sat close to the fireplace, across from Paul who wasn't saying anything much as he waited on Mark to speak. He looked up as Steve and Jennifer came into the room. Steve looked down at his friend as Jennifer slid onto the couch beside him and slid an arm, protectively, around his shoulders, he hesitated before saying "You alright? Told you about those cheap ear rings didn't I?" he smiled as he waved at the white medical tape on Marks ear that was the only outward sign of what had happened, Mark grinned a little and he could feel Jennifer relax next to him as he said "Yeah, I know, I should stay away from Nickel and Brass." He paused and looked up at his friend as the room stayed quiet and they listened to the clock in the hall tick away the day. "Do me a favour please Steve, get in touch with the boys and see if anyone is on the loose, anyone from the past." Mark drew breath before continuing "I hope not, if this is because of my past I will struggle to look Sharon's parents in the face again. If it's new, with this Silver thing they had better look out." Paul just looked at him across the fire; he could see a harder edge starting to show than he had ever seen in his friend before. Jennifer just hugged him tighter; she didn't want to let him go.

165

It was about that same time that Silver got a text message on his very private mobile phone, it just said "Done". He smiled and put the phone down again, on the desk at his side. Looking across the desk at the empty chair that sat there, he just wondered, just for a second what it had actually felt like to squeeze that trigger and remove all of someone's problems in an instant. He sighed and turned back to the drawings on his desk, picking up a pencil he scored out the building marked as sitting on the head of the bank.

In the airport the unidentified man strolled through the departure lounge heading towards his gate, he was relaxed, this was not his first and almost certainly would not be his last job for this client. He might even be back here before too long if he read the facts correctly.

+

'Thug one' was screaming into a radio with Peter Barnard on the other end. "How dare you bring in a contractor. If that needed doing I could have done it for you or arranged it professionally. Now we've got another party involved that's even more chance of a leak somewhere." He was almost physically shouting, but it was either this or go and see the man and that would have resulted in him assaulting Barnard, this was better for both of them. Barnard shrugged and set the radio on the desk, he knew nothing about it, so, as far as he was concerned, there was no point in getting worried about it. He turned away and got on with reading today's news paper. At the moment that was the hardest work he did on a daily basis.

Danielle was standing very still in the outer office listening to the voice screaming on the radio wondering what she had gotten herself into.

+

Andrew Crawford was still sitting in his hotel room in the capital, perched on the end of the bed where he had been watching the morning news when the first reports of a shooting at the Doones estate had begun to filter out. He was scared, Silver had threatened this type of thing before but had never actually done it, at least, not as far as he knew. If this was in anyway linked to them it would be a problem for them all. Maybe now would be the time to take up the option he had on a job based in the Bahamas.

+

In the safe house there was a lot of frantic activity as all the screens in the house were reviewed along with all the notebooks being checked for any detail they had missed or had not realised what it meant. The team leader was pacing back and forth in the lounge wondering what was going on, the problem was they didn't even really know if it was related to what they were doing here at all.

The door bell made him jump as he looked around and listened the only sound he could hear was the click of volume controls being turned down all over the house as everyone went into silent mode. He looked around and headed for the front door, the blonde got there before him and froze. She stood there holding the door half open as he arrived and looked out at the two men in grey suits who were standing there holding out identification; they were federal agents. He sighed and stepped back, opening the door to let his boss into the safe house.

The four of them stood in the living room and watched the TV as the news programme re ran the pictures of Mark leaving hospital with Jennifer and Paul. Once it was over the most senior of the two new arrivals turned to face him and asked "Well, has this anything to do with what you are here for?" the original shook his head "Not as far as we can tell at the moment. We had no sign of anything like this coming our way. We have some footage of one of the security people watching this guy and some of his friends, including the two who were with him there." He pointed at the TV "but we had no reason to believe this was possible let alone likely." The boss sighed and rubbed a hand down over his face as he looked around the bland and characterless room "Okay," he said "You will need to speak to the local police and let them know what we've got and act as an intermediary for these guys" He was speaking to the other suit that had arrived with him at the door. "I don't want them compromised, so you will take any film and pictures, copies only of course, to the local police. That way their identities and the like can be protected so they can carry on with their job here. We've been after him for long enough I don't want to let this one fall for any reason. A murder might just be enough to do it though." He shook his head and looked at the two field agents sitting there close to him. "Good work you two and the rest of your team. Keep your heads down and stay safe." They nodded and with that the two newest arrivals stood up and left, the junior of the two hesitating before he went out the door "Can you have the copies all ready for me by tomorrow?" The original just nodded "Of course" was all he said as he closed the door and turned back to the blonde who stood there looking worried.

The police officer who came to see Mark at the big house seemed uncomfortable as he began to ask questions, he finally had to say "Okay, I think I've got most of what I need from you at this time." He was very conscious of Steve standing there as well, listening to every word he said "However, we might have to come back to you at some time. I would also say that I'm afraid you won't be getting back into your house until tomorrow morning at the earliest; unless the SOCO's decide to let you in the back door by going around the house." Paul shook his head "Not an issue, they can stay here tonight if they want." Mark said nothing and Jennifer looked a little embarrassed, more than anything else. The officer nodded "That is probably the best answer of them all," he hesitated "Or is it? I seem to remember you having a security problem here already." Paul smiled "Yes, that's true. Some one tried to kill me here in my own home not long ago." He raised a hand and pointed at Mark "However you also need to remember this is the man that saved my life." The police officer hesitated "Do you think these two incidents are connected?" Mark shrugged "No way of knowing at the moment. Why don't you ask the two guys who you arrested that night?" the police officer nodded his head "That would be a good idea but I think they're in Glasgow at the moment. They are definitely on remand somewhere and will stay in custody simply because they haven't said a word yet. We don't even know their names, we will, but just not yet." Paul just nodded as Mark and Steve exchanged a glance but said nothing. Jennifer saw it but didn't comment, she had a feeling she would learn more about it later.

The police officer left shortly after that, saying they would be well advised to just lock the doors and stay inside over night. Paul sighed and agreed as he swung the heavy oak door closed behind him as he left. Jennifer waited until he came back to the lounge before she spoke "Okay you two, I saw you exchanging glances earlier, do you want to tell us what's going on and maybe you can let me know this bit about saving someone's life." She dug Mark in the ribs, gently, at this last bit and he sighed, Steve shrugged "Why not?" Mark nodded and slowly told the story of the night he pulled Paul out of the building.

The next morning the press were camped at the end of the driveway and Paul fended them off carefully until Steve arrived to issue a press release. The police telephoned at about ten o'clock to say that the house was being cleared if they wanted to go home. Mark nodded as Paul told him "That's good, we'll get out of your hair and leave you in peace." Jennifer nodded as she stood there just behind Mark. Paul smiled to himself; he was beginning to think she would be there for a long time to come.

Steve drove them out of the back gate of the big house and round to Marks place, it would only have taken them a half hour to walk but neither Jennifer nor Mark were in the mood to walk anywhere. Steve came in for a coffee just to make sure the two of them were functioning well enough together before he left them alone. Steve stood behind Mark as he looked out the window at the ocean view while he reran the moment of the shooting in his head. He had known a second or so after he had felt the bullet pass through his ear, when he had felt Sharon jump in his arms, it had been more of a spasm than anything else as the muscles tensed in response to a confused and garbled signal coming down the nerves from the ruined brain stem. He could still see that plume of blood and brain matter when he closed his eyes. He sighed, just another name to add to his list, a long list of people who he had seen die. Jennifer walked silently into the room in bare feet with yet another tray of coffee cups for everyone.

+

Dianne, was sitting in her house, alone, wondering what would happen next, she had heard about Sharon and felt hollow inside, she had met the young girl just a month or so before when all of this started to kick off and had thought then she was pretty, lively young girl full of life and hope for her future, now snuffed out like a damaged candle, broken and casually tossed aside. She had no doubt that Mark had been the actual target.

+

Grayson was sitting in Jackson's office on the top floor again. Jackson himself wasn't there which surprised him, he had been summoned and then the man wasn't there. Grayson was getting annoyed but knew he couldn't afford to show it. The door opened, Jackson walked in and Grayson's heart sank as he saw the company lawyer follow his boss into the office. The meeting was short and to the point, it was only the first stage in a formal process and all those involved knew exactly where it was heading.

Sitting in his car half an hour later he was playing with his mobile phone wondering if this was a wise move or not. Eventually he shrugged his shoulders before flicking the phone open. "Barnard," he called "yeah good to speak to you too. Do you have some time in your diary to see me today, at your office?"

169

Dr Marianne Presley was making herself a cup of coffee in the kitchen when Steve walked in from his office, shaking his head "What's bothering you now?" She laughed as she saw the look on his face and continued "Okay, sorry, I should know better by now shouldn't I? You can't tell me due to client confidentiality." Steve looked at and nodded slowly but with a smile on his face as one of his other partners came into the kitchen. "Yeah, Marianne, technically that's correct but there are times and there are things we can discuss and this I need to talk to some one about and you know the background as well as anyone here." He turned and looked at his colleague who shrugged and carried on doing what he was doing. "That was the lawyer for the newspaper group on the phone. You know that one who Mark and Sharon were suing? Well today is the last day for them to file a defence so they just called me to ask if we would still be pursuing the case after Sharon had died at Marks house in his arms. Their take on the situation is that the public might see some more truth in the case when it is presented that way." Marianne had stopped and was staring at him in disbelief as the other man spluttered on his coffee "I suppose they are conveniently forgetting about the high velocity bullet that was involved as well?" Steve just nodded as he looked at his colleague who continued "I take you told them to stuff it?" Steve shook his head "No actually, I sad we were doubling our claim to allow us to set up a fund in memorial of Sharon to support sexually harassed journalists." The other two laughed until Marianne finally said "Seriously, what did you say?" Steve looked at her "Seriously, that is what I said, I will be looking to double the case fund but I don't know what Mark will do with the money." Marianne looked at him "Can Mark afford that sort of money?" Steve nodded "Yes, he can, but I really should have asked him first. Even if he can't I'll add it myself just to make sure those bastards pay." He picked up his mug and went back to his office as Marianne looked at the other man who shrugged again "Don't ask me. Mark's not my client. I don't know any more than Steve has told us and it sounds like you maybe know this Mark guy as well as any of the rest of us." Marianne nodded and went back to her own desk.

Trente Silver was physically jumping up and down in fury. He had been watching a satellite channel on one of the seven television sets in his office when it reported the death of a reporter on the site of his newest and best ever development. The report had been a voiceover on a clip showing Mark Ray and two others leaving hospital, he was covered in blood, but he was

170

alive. Silver calmed himself almost immediately; he drew that temper down and tempered it with cold so it burned almost hotter in his belly as he thought about what he would do when things started to go right for him.

Across town his ex solicitor was sitting laughing at the same news item. After a few minutes he stopped chortling to himself and leant forward and pressed the button on his intercom "Jonny," he called into the microphone "How far on are we with boxing up the Silver documents and closing the open cases we have with them?" there was a pause before the eager young man on the other end replied "Almost complete sir. The last boxes are being packed as we speak and will be ready for shipping before close of business today." "Good" the old man smiled as he heard this and leant back in his chair, knowing this might not be a wise move.

+

The Homeland department was quite happy to have a visit from the federal agent with his bag of photographs and tape, they always liked film on a member of their society. The federal agent sat down and looked across the desk at cool gentleman in a pale grey suit and wondered 'How did this guy get into this line of work?' The thought did not last long as he began to speak "We were wondering when your lot were going to speak to us, to be honest we've been tempted to pull them in for a few days now and if you hadn't come in today we might have been making a call tomorrow." The American smiled at himself as he heard this, he had been warned these people were cleverer than they might appear to be. "Be that as it may," the federal agent said "I would rather our people are permitted to continue their work uninterrupted and left in place. That way we may be able to gather more information that is of more long term use to us both." The man in the grey suit nodded slowly as he sipped from his cup of earl grey tea and set the cup down again before he spoke. "You mean catch Silver and his team at something seriously illegal." The federal agent stared at him and eventually said "Yes, that is correct, but how did you know?" he smiled but the expression did not reach the cold blue eyes "We have a number of sources of information that feed us bits from time to time and some of our people have incredible instincts."

The meeting lasted for just over an hour before the Federal agent was ushered from the non descript office building in the middle of the capital city and he walked away slowly, stunned by the realisation that all their work to get the team in to the country undetected had been for nothing. Now however they were safe and would be allowed to get on with their own work knowing that they themselves were being watched but from a distance. Did they need to know that fact? He shook his head again, No, he decided, that information might just distract them, they did not need to know.

Up stairs in the office the man in a suit watched on the monitor as the Federal Agent walked away along the street as another man dressed in jeans and a tee shirt came into the office and flopped down in a chair opposite the desk "Well," the new arrival asked "did we know who they were or what they were doing?" The suit shook his head "No, but there's no need to let them know that. They are pretty well irrelevant, it seems to be all low level stuff they are up to anyway." He stopped and looked at another screen where a red box was now flashing to attract his attention." The visitor waited, he knew if it was relevant he would find out what had caused the suit to stop talking. The suit glanced at him and back to his screen and the visitor leant forward before the man spoke. "This is more interesting" he said, as the man in jeans walked around the desk to look at the screen "He's one of yours." He pointed at the screen as the other man leant closer. The suit felt his skin crawl, he didn't admit it but these people scared him. The fact that his boss wore jeans to the office and no one would argue had worried him initially until one night he had seen him in a dinner jacket, he had never asked any more questions. The visitor smiled as he spoke "Remember, you work for me too, just the same as him. He's before my time though and I don't know the name." The suit tapped the screen to point out a box and his visitor squinted before saying "Oh, shit, I had better talk to upstairs and see exactly who he is. That is some clearance to still be carrying after all these years away from the game." The visitor straightened up and without another word left the office, walking silently over the carpet and through the door as if he had never been there. The suit squirmed and adjusted his jacket and with one last look at the flag flashing on his screen, clicked on another button to check his email.

10

Andy was leaning on the bar counter listening to the conversation of the two old men who were his regular customers at this time on a Friday afternoon. He didn't mind listening to them as they put the world to rights with their opinions on anything and everything. After all he would be old himself one day, he stood up and was polishing a glass at the back of the bar when he heard them mention the Doones estate so he wandered a little closer to make it easier to hear what they were saying.

"......seems to be a great place they're planning what with that and all the facilities for the guests being available for the residents as well." One of the old men was saying as the other just nodded sagely. He was almost seventy and allegedly starting to suffer from dementia now as well so that was often all he did. Andy stepped in about and before he got a chance to ask the old man turned to him and carried on "So what do you think of that then Andy? All you and your friends going on about how it'll destroy the area and they're planning to put in an old folks home for the local wrinklies. Won't get a place unless you live within five miles I hear, free to be, as well; to take the load off the local council. What do you think of that then lad?" Andy shook his head "I think you're being played old timer. Exactly the same way they told Andrea it was going to be a tennis centre and Jenny that it was to be an equestrian centre. Yet when it was submitted it was a golf place tacked onto the side of a housing development. I saw the drawings at the meeting and I saw nothing about any old folks home in there." The old man just looked at him and pushed the empty glass across the counter. "So, you think they're taking the Mick out of all us old timers?" Andy nodded "Not just the old timers, everyone who they think they can get on their side. They tell them just about anything to get their support. You lot are just the latest on the list."

+

Down at the office of the livery stable there was an awkward silence as Alison was putting her handbag into the locker at one side while Jenny was doing the same at the other. Jenny just closed the door as she heard Alison sigh behind her. "Sorry," was the word that made her turn around and look at the woman who was standing in front of her, fiddling with her fingernails and looking at her feet. "I made a mistake and allowed my self to be used." She raised her head and looked at the other woman. "I thought he really cared for me and we might even be getting married at some point." Jenny didn't know what to say, so she said nothing and just shook her head; it was just as well as the other woman carried on talking. "I made a fool of myself and effectively prostituted myself to him, he wasn't even much good in bed but he had my mind so I didn't care what he did as long as it was with me. I'm not so sure that was a good idea any more" Jenny could see tears in the other woman's eyes as she struggled to find something to say. Instead she just stepped forward and opened her arms to hug her.

+

Marlene, the council leader was buying a news paper in the small shop just down at the end of her street in Drimmie. It had been saved by a special council order the year before just as Marlene had moved into the area. That had meant that the new school which had been planned was now not going to happen but, Marlene shrugged, someone had to make a sacrifice and it wasn't going to be her.

The woman behind the counter smiled at her as she handed over her morning newspaper as she did almost every day. "Do ye think it'll be a long time afore that Silver Organisation start building work?" the woman asked. Marlene shook her head "I think as soon as the paperwork is passed they will be in there getting on with the job of turning this part of the country into one of the best golf resorts in the world. After all they are planning on holding the Golf Open here in about two years time." The woman frowned slightly as she handed over Marlene's change but said nothing and just stood at the counter until the little bell tinkled when the door shut behind Marlene. She continued looking at the door for a second until she heard the beaded curtain behind her that separated the store room from the shop move as her husband stuck his head out. "Did I just hear her say that they wanted to hold the Open in about two years time?" The woman nodded as she turned round "I thought you might have something to say about that. She looked at the golf magazine dangling from one hand "What does that say about it?" she nodded at the magazine as he smiled "I was just reading about that type of thing in here." He waved the magazine slightly and looked down at it casually, remembering what it said, not actually reading. "Well first they say it takes about two years to really get a course playable and then another two years to develop and understand the actual quality of the course as it is in the real world and not in the designers mind." He looked at his wife who was frowning even more deeply now as he carried on. "It's only about then that they can start to consider a course for inclusion on the list. From there it'll usually take a couple of years to be

174

sure it can get on the list and even then," he waved the magazine again and turning the page pointed to the article. "This is a table of the next five courses that will be hosting the Open." He drew breath as his wife looked at him and said "So, you are telling me that the magazine you are holding which is a recognised international authority on the golf open, is basically saying that it will take a new golf course about ten or eleven years before it has even the slimmest of chances of hosting the Open." He nodded as she chewed her lip before concluding "yet, she is saying that they should be holding it in two years time." He nodded as she continued "Your magazine, the experts on this subject, are saying that they might have just about have finished the building work by then." he nodded again as his wife sighed as she turned back to look at the empty shop. "Well she has a nice new car in her driveway and she's been seen out drinking with that guy from the nationalist party." Sighing she looked at her husband again "maybe you're right and she is on the take." The sound of the bead curtain was all she heard as her husband went back to reading his magazine, out of sight in the store room.

+

Paul Clancy was sitting there in his office looking at the wall. He was listening to Dull making an almost gentle pitch for the job of the next Chairman of the Chamber. There was a general consensus that he would have to resign the post after this Silver thing was completed, he was not yet convinced but it did not do any harm to listen to these guys, Dull was the third to look for his direct support so far; there would be more.

Dull, actually had a reasonably good case but had no chance what so ever of getting the post. He was too well known as a drunk and being far too likely to embarrass the region at a formal dinner of some kind by falling over drunk or insulting some one. Paul just smiled at him, he did not have to make that decision, he would do what he always did and leave the difficult ones to some one else. The selection committee could make it when it sat.

Dull sat back when there was a soft knock on the door, it was the planning specialist they had been waiting on and the real reason that Dull was there.

The conversation did not take too long but left Dull and Paul Clancy in what was almost a state of shock as they sat there looking at each other. It was Dull that finally spoke first "I thought this was all agreed before hand and it should be a straight forward rubber stamp at this next stage." Clancy nodded "So did I, to be honest." He leant forward on the desk and brought his hands up to his face as he breathed out heavily, it was almost a sigh but not quite. "That means we will need to be more careful going forward from here. Don't forget, I have heard that there is support for this project from a higher authority so lets not panic let's just wait and see if anyone else picks up on this and the chance of it being not only turned down but thrown out as being an incompetent application. I bet that would cause all sorts of ripples in the system." Dull didn't say anything to that comment, he was beginning to look worried.

+

Andrea was sitting in the house with her father in law discussing what was happening locally, he was supposed to be going home in the next day or two so it may be the last chance she would have to talk to him about it. Luckily he was happy to talk. "Yeah I know about the Silver Organisation. Some people think of them as being like our royalty and can do no wrong others think he's a disgrace to our country the way he goes around the world ripping people off and leaving nothing behind of any lasting value." Andrea stared at him "You mean he's done this before? And no one has done anything about it?" He nodded at his daughter in law and smiled as he leant back to tell his tale "When you were over last time did you ever meet Jonny Jones? A big guy, used to be in construction." Andrea shook her head as he carried on talking "No, well Silver and his henchmen are the reason why Jonny *used to be* in construction." Andrea looked at him, eyes wide, and leaned closer as he carried on his story. "Jonny's company got the lead hand job on a project for the Silver Organisation. They were to pay all the sub contractors then Silver would pay them. Well that was the original agreement but it's not what happened." Andrea watched as he drank from his coffee mug before carrying on "When it came time to settle up Jonny's bill was four hundred thousand dollars. Silvers man sat down and opened his cheque book and offered him two hundred thousand dollars, take it or leave it." Andrea's eyes bulged as she thought about that "How did they get away with that?" He shook his head "Easily, it's take it or leave it. You leave it you have to sue them to get the money and by the time you get past his legal team to get to court you're bankrupt and the company is history so there is no case to answer. If you take the money you no longer have a debt and it is assumed that you are in negotiation to get the rest of the money so the courts won't touch you" Andrea stared at him in disbelief, she was worried, this sounded like a long term tactic.

+

176

Andy sighed later that day as he walked into the bar at the golf club after a bad round, he had not played well at all and was trying to listen to the conversation rather than join in too much here. It was the captain speaking as he focused on what was being discussed. "Well I think it is obviously the best thing to happen to this area in years. We need something for after oil has gone and this is it." The sigh came from Mark a regular golfer who worked as a recruiting agent "Oh come on, please at least be realistic, this place is currently advertising about twelve hundred jobs, the oil industry at the moment employs almost forty five thousand people. How does one compare with the other?" Jamie spoke up next, he was an 'executive', or that's what he called himself anyway with Point Energy limited, an oil company "Add to that," he said "We are looking at about fifty years before the oil runs out, that I am aware of in our reserves alone. The hotel and the rest of those buildings will probably have to be replaced before then" A couple of them looked around at each other, that was an angle they had not thought about. The captain was beginning to feel himself out numbered as he turned to Andy "What about you Andy, any of the golfers that stay at your place talk about Silvers resorts in the states?" Andy sighed again he had suspected that might be coming up at some point. "Well I have actually asked them that question and almost to a man, they have all said they would not come here to a Silver resort. In the States they are all the same, plastic and artificial. They come here for the authentic links golf experience, if all they're going to get is the same artificial stuff as they get at home they don't see the point in coming here at all." He looked at the captain who looked mortified. He knew he was losing this argument, the longer it went on the less the facts were stacking up on his side. He sighed deeply and said, almost to himself, "Maybe I need to do some more research on this, rather than take the public statements for granted." Andy laughed softly "The public pronouncements you are talking about are more propaganda than anything else. Tell me, "He leant forward as he said this "In the last listing of golf course rankings, where did this place come?" The captain looked at him and hesitated before he finally said "Well, we are actually thirty fifth" Andy sat back smiling "Right, this course is number thirty five in the world and I am fairly sure we have another two in this area in the top fifty if not above. Internationally recognised world class courses," He looked around the group and could see them all nodding "So what makes you think, someone who already has several courses, I think it's seven, in his home country and has not succeeded in getting any of them into the top one hundred, is suddenly going to build one here and it'll be the best in the world?" He paused and looked around the group, who were all still nodding as the logic was inescapable. Andy turned back to the captain "What were those three elements you said were essential in anyone who wanted to build a golf course?" The captain hesitated before saying

"Oh, simple, track record, history and experience." His face changed as he said it and Andy smiled "Right, he has a track record of failure and huge environmental cost and damage. The history of the site is rare and unique and as such should not be trampled upon as he intends to do; and third his experience is all bad, although not as bad as that of those who have gone along with him and not been paid." The captain nodded and stood up "Nice to talk but I have to go and get on with things here. See you again next week" Andy nodded and the other two just said their goodbyes before turning to Andy and just sitting there. It was Mark who spoke "Get the impression he didn't like to hear what other people had to say." Andy nodded as Jamie carried on "Not if it disagrees with what he's been told to believe." He leant forward and set his glass down "Unfortunately for you lot, there could be a lot of them who are doing just what they believe they should be rather than looking at the facts and making up their own minds." Andy looked at him "What do you mean, you lot?" Jamie grinned "Public opposition to this. There will be more of you than public support but most people will keep their head down and try and stay out of line of sight. You will find the next step will be some of the press trying to make you lot, the opposition, out as fringe weirdo's with no support and values that no, and the phrase will be 'reasonable person' can be seen to associate with." He looked closely at Andy "Be careful, they will fight dirty." Andy just nodded, he had been worried that this might be possible, it was good in some ways to find that others were thinking along the same lines.

+

The nationalist party meeting was going pretty well as planned, 'Xander's brother was smiling to himself as he watched the group accept the lead and then vote the way they had been told to. The next item on the agenda was the one that might cause one or two ruffled feathers. He cleared his throat and looked down at his copy of the agenda sheet; he didn't see the sharp faced woman at the end of the row nod slowly as she looked out into the group of twenty or so people in the hall. She had seen him do this several times before and had realised this was a sign that he was uncomfortable with the next item, 'and well he should be too' she thought as she read it and knew it was going to be difficult to force it through. She looked away as he raised his head and prepared to speak.

"Okay," he paused as he looked out onto the floor of the hall, this should be easy enough they had done everything they were asked to that night and there was no reason they should do anything other now, he continued "Next item is to request our elected representatives to give all permitted support to the Silver Organisations plans to develop a world class resort in the region

178

for the benefit of the community." He looked up and felt his heart sink as at least half of the crowd were looking straight at him; that meant they were thinking for themselves, they were not meant to be able to do that. He frowned "I see no reason for discussion on this matter it's quite clearly a position we must support to allow this area to go forward in to the future as a strong and confident region. Let us just go to a vote." He looked up and a couple of the crowd seemed agitated until Lydia, on the end spoke, "I think not" she said looking along the row "We need to know why this is being rushed through in this manner, and a young girl has died as well." 'Xander's brother held his hand up and she stopped speaking as he interrupted "There has already been a special committee into this and it came out in favour." He raised his head and looked at her alone, as she sat right on the end of the row, 'could almost have called it on the fringes' he thought as he carried on talking "The death of the young woman is tragic but we have no reason to believe it was related to this matter at all, and to say so is to risk legal proceedings for defamation from the Silver Organisation. Who, as everyone knows, are very happy to spend money on lawyers for just this type of thing." He paused again and looked at the crowd "To go into repeat discussion after the main committee has already approved it and 'Xander himself is in support of this development is almost a case of disloyalty and the repercussions of that should be considered closely by those considering such actions." He stopped talking and listened to the silence in the hall before he continued "Now, can we just get on with the vote please."

It was with difficulty he controlled his temper on the way to the pub. He was standing at the bar and was half way down his first pint with one mouthful before he said anything to the three minions who followed him almost everywhere. "How could Lydia pull a stunt like that? She knows that is unacceptable, she's been part of this party even longer than I have and still she tries to destroy everything we stand for." Minion one had the temerity to speak "We still won the vote so we can go ahead and do what needs to be done anyway, can't we?" The man with the slicked back hair growled at him "No we can't. It should never be that close. Fifteen votes to fourteen is unacceptable on a matter this important." He swallowed the rest of his pint and slammed the glass down on the bar so hard other glasses bounced further along "We need a seventy five per cent vote on directions to elected members to make them valid so technically we lost the vote dimwit!!" He looked at minion one who looked back reminding him of a rabbit caught in car headlights. Minion two stepped closer and almost whispered "We know that, you know that but do all the elected members know that?" The gaze shifted from minion one to minion two slowly as his head swivelled on his shoulders while his body stood stock still. "What do

179

you mean? What are you suggesting?" Minion two simpered a little as his hero paid attention to him. "Well," he began "we can send them a note telling them the voting outcome of the meeting along with the wording of the motion and just state something along the lines of requiring them to act in the best interest of the community with guidance from their own conscience or some such and just never say we want you to vote this way; or you must or anything like that and then if picked up on it later we can claim that we expected all elected members to know the rules themselves. That way we cannot be legitimately blamed for giving them a voting direction which anyway is illegal in a planning application situation." He swallowed a little as his boss stared at him with those cold flat expressionless eyes for a little while longer before he spoke "Well done lad, that makes sense and might just about work. You can see to starting that tomorrow morning." He turned back to the bar looking for Andy and only got Magda. The new highly capable Eastern European barmaid who was on a summer placement from University, he didn't trust graduates but she was in charge of the beer. Grudgingly he gave her his order and the group went away to sit in one of the booths down the far side of the room, away from the bar counter.

+

Templeton was grinning to himself, he was happy for once. He knew that what he was considering doing would probably destroy him as well but it would be worth it to see the smile wiped off 'Xander's face when he realised all his deepest secrets were in the public domain. Templeton looked down at the slim black object in his hands, that course on IT awareness at the parliament had been very useful after all. If it hadn't been for that course he would never have known what a portable hard drive was, but the course had taught him that, and he now had this one in his hand. What was not so obvious from the outside was the fact that this was a mirror image of 'Xander's own personal drive. A full copy in other words, with all the data that was on 'Xander's drive copied on this one as well, and the other spare one that was locked in the safe back in his apartment, he smiled again. It may be the end of his career in some ways but it might just be the start of him in other ways. He sighed to himself, 'time will tell' he thought as he turned the sleek black plastic block over and over again in his hands.

+

Dull shrugged as he looked at Paul Clancy, they were still sitting where they had been earlier, nothing more had been said as they thought about the
180

implications of what they had been told. Dull spoke first. "I don't think it really matters. First the information has to get out, then it has to be pushed to make sure something actually happens about it." he paused as he sat back and Paul Clancy could see Dulls mind beginning to work as it quite clearly had not done for years while he carried on talking. "I really doubt that it will get out to the public domain. Second, if it does very few people will realise exactly what it means in any real sense. Third, the council would have to admit it's a mistake and that they need to do something about it before it becomes a problem. Fourth, I am sure there will be a way that the local authority can formally accept and yet ignore such a minor administrative error as this in order to allow the process to run its course." Clancy looked at him wondering if there was any substance in what Dull had just said or was it pure optimism? He did not know but it felt better that at least some one else could see a way through this mess.

Neither of them would have been so happy had they seen what was happening in the mail room of the audit office over in the capital as they sat and spoke. There was quite a formal process for anything coming into the investigations department. Firstly it was separated from all the other mail and after that was not touched by a bare hand again. The small padded envelope was given more than normal attention because 'in these days of the terrorist threat' one could not be too careful and the padded envelope was a recognised problem. A printed label, so no hand writing and no return address made it even more suspect a package.

The security guard turned it over carefully in his gloved hands inside the bomb proof examination cabinet. No oil stains, all the stamps were the right way up and all that showed when they had run it through the scanner was a memory stick, slowly he picked up the craft knife and slit the envelope on the opposite side to the flap. The scanner had lied; there was a sheet of paper along with the memory stick. He unfolded it and looked at the single paragraph in black ink on the white paper. "Of interest to the ethics committee and maybe also the pension's tribunal...." it began. He did not read any further, it was no longer his problem and as such was of no interest to him. He pushed it out of the side of the box and into the 'onpass' box to go to the internal legal department, he sighed. He wished he would hear a bit more about what some of these things were. He might just get his wish with this one, maybe more than he wanted.

+

Marlene had called her little group together once more, at her home again, this time with less attempt at hiding and with a little less subtlety than some

181

of the other political parties would have done it. She looked at them with a mixture of contempt and hope as she realised this motley band were her best hope of getting out of the area and into national politics. She smiled at them recognising it didn't matter what she actually thought of them, nor even if they shared her own beliefs or not, they were her only way out of here and so, she had to make some allowances in her own mind and just get on with them at this time. She could say whatever she liked in private later.

+

Dr Marianne Presley was sitting in the office at the university wondering what this man was talking about. Then it all became clear as he said "We basically want you to tone down your criticism of the Silver Organisation, they are potentially large supporters of research work here at the university and your proclamations the other week of them trampling all over your dig at night do us no good purely because you are currently associated with the university." He looked up at her face of astonishment as he finished off "Is that clear?" Marianne gathered her wits before replying "No it's not clear, why don't you try putting it in words of one syllable or less please?" She was clearly annoyed as she looked at him, but he had been buried in academia for so long he did not understand how to read the expressions of another person, least of all an attractive woman. So, he tried to explain again. He sighed as he leant forward and put his elbows on the desk and clasped his hands "Well, it's quite simple." He looked her in the face "If you don't stop criticising the Silver Organisation the university will have to withdraw your funding and that might well mean that there is no money to pay your salary and the students you brought over with you will end up with no course to attend and will never get their degrees. So in addition to everything else you will be responsible for ruining their lives." He smiled and leant back and suddenly felt a rush of panic as he realised she was smiling.

Marianne nodded and pulled the digital Dictaphone out of her bag which had been on her knee as she said "Well you obviously don't know very much do you?" She shifted in her seat as she showed him the Dictaphone in her hand "First I am not employed by the university. I am employed by Paradigm Archaeology and I pay the university for the use of their facilities until we get ours built. Secondly as for the students we have applied for a University license which is due to be granted, we have already received the basic note of intent and are just waiting on the formal issue so your threat has no authority." She stood up as she said "What you have done is ensure that the university will lose the generous funding that is currently coming from Paradigm Archaeology and the services of the best Archaeologist in

182

the country." She smiled and stopped at the door as she said "I hope you have had a satisfying and productive day. Goodbye" He sat there and stared at the door as it vibrated slightly from the slamming sound it had made as it settled in the frame. He sat there for several minutes, just sitting still looking at the door watching, as it still vibrated, trying to decide whether he should speak to his boss first or the man he had been doing a favour for. Slowly he stretched for the telephone on his desk, he would let chance decide and just see whose number he dialled first.

+

'Xander had been having a good day, the debate, such as it was, had gone his way and the public seemed to like him, at least the ones that were allowed to speak to him did anyway. His heart fell a little as he heard his secretary in the outer office talking to the chief planner on the phone. 'This could be trouble' he thought as the secretary put the phone on hold and knocked on the door frame to attract his attention. "That is the Chief Planner on the phone" 'Xander just looked at him, waiting on him to continue. "He says he needs to see you, quite urgently about a planning matter that has arisen at the Doones estate." The look on his face showed that the name did not mean anything to him, 'Xander was pleased about that but the call worried him. He looked at the young man standing there waiting on an answer, eventually he shook his head slowly "Okay, if he's sure its important, make it this afternoon." He looked at his watch as the look of surprise registered on the other mans face "That means now." The young man scurried away and picked up the phone.

The chief planner looked like a civil servant which was good because that was exactly what he was. The bald head with just a band of hair round the sides, small round glasses and an ill fitting cheap grey suit all belied a sharp intelligence and a salary of over one hundred and fifty thousand Euros per year. He had been 'leant on' by 'Xander before in relation to a planning application that he wanted passed through quickly and remembered it clearly. He did not intend to let it happen again, that was why he brought his own secretary with him to take minutes of the meeting. 'Xander frowned when he saw the secretary, this was not a good sign for him even if it did show that the man was learning. He sat back and folded his hands across his ample belly so he could physically look down his nose at the man. 'Xander hated people he thought of as being less intelligent than himself. That meant all civil servants, anyone who worked for a living and all politicians who did not agree with his opinions. It saved him a lot of time in deciding if he liked some one or not. His complacent attitude was shattered almost immediately the 'little man' as he thought of him, began to speak.

+

Padruig McCarthy was standing, stirring his coffee, in the councillor's lounge looking around at the mixture of people. He loved people watching and he surprised himself by admitting that. He was an old man now who had come to politics late in his life, too late really to have a substantive career and, to be honest, had only stood for election because he could see no one he wanted to vote for in the rest of the politicians in the area. None of them seemed to be interested in the area or its people; they were all more interested in either their own political advancement or that of the party they claimed to be representing today. He sighed; the local authority was struggling as it stood at the moment. He knew several of the councillors had been paid to vote specific ways at the local committee and some had been struggling with their conscience even then, that was his explanation for the strange voting patterns he had seen there. He really was wondering what was going to be the outcome at the ISC meeting in a week or twos time, he was supposed to be chairing it as well, which was an unusual situation. He was worried it could become a major sticking point for the authority, this could really damage the reputation of the area if the councillors all acted like a bunch of spoiled children as they seemed likely to.

He sat down at an empty table and waited for the first approach to come, it wouldn't take long.

+

Grayson was giggling again, he had been getting used to it and the stuff that seemed to be coming from Barnard and his new side kick Benson, seemed to be high quality even if it did make his nose itch or was that what it was meant to do? He had lost track again of how much of this stuff he had taken but he didn't care any more. The girl was lying on the bed next to him, she had been fun but looked like she was comatose now just lying there, naked and covered in chocolate, yes she had been fun. He would find out soon if he had to find another job yet or not and if he was going to worry it would be later, not now.

Back in the offices in the corner of the newspaper building, it was Jamieson's turn to be scared as he sat in Jackson's office in the seat Grayson had occupied. He knew enough to be scared, he had done his
184

research since the incident with Silvers man at the hotel and he knew he was on thin ice because he had taken the envelope; at least he had not been as blatant as Grayson. The lawyer was sitting there at the end of the desk showing he was more on the side of his boss than on his side. Jamieson wasn't sure if that was a good sign or not, but he did not have long to wait until Jackson appeared back from talking to the PA outside his office door.

Jackson sat down and looked across the desk at another editor who truly disgusted him; it must have shown on his face as suddenly Jamieson looked ill. Jackson just looked at him for a few minutes longer to stretch the tension before he said "Your colleague, Grayson, has cost this company a lot of money by printing what are basically just lies about some of the people involved in this Silver Organisation argument." He paused and licked his lips "We have decided to defend the case but have no expectation of even coming close to winning, so as a minimum its going to cost us well over half a million Euros. Grayson himself is currently on suspension but will, almost certainly" he nodded at the solicitor at this point "be dismissed after a disciplinary hearing, after the case." He stopped and looked at Jamieson who was just sitting listening, he had heard bits of this through the rumour mill but had no idea that Grayson had already been suspended. He snapped his attention back to what was being said. It was the lawyer that was actually speaking "You realise we will need to prepare a case for dismissal very carefully and in order to make it possible we are going to ask you to look into his communications and any other information you can find that is relevant to the situation." Jamieson looked at him for a second or two before he said "I'm not sure I can find the time to do that as well as my own job. Would it not be better to just hire an investigator to do that?" Jackson smiled and Jamieson was now scared as his boss said "Well that won't be necessary. You will be moving over to the 'Evening' for a while until we get all of this sorted out and we have also hired an investigator to help you out." Jamieson just looked back at him "What about the 'Daily' how will it run without an editor?" Jackson smiled back at him, "It won't, we've brought in a temporary replacement for you to see how things work out."

Jamieson knew at that moment his career here was finished, he could probably stay at the 'Evening' for a few months, maybe even a year, but his career had probably actually ended the moment he picked up that brown envelope all those weeks ago. He sighed and stood up to leave the room. All the way across that empty carpet he was looking for some smart words to finish with, instead, he just turned gave a sickly smile and nodded before closing the door behind him on the way out.

185

The lawyer looked at Jackson "Will that be the end of the purges here?" Jackson looked back at him and said nothing for a second or two, obviously thinking before replying "I doubt that very much, but lets wait and see what our investigators produce." The lawyer nodded and picked up his tea cup.

+

Dull was sitting in his formal office in the hotel speaking to Andrew Crawford who was sipping on a mug of coffee. "Of course the Infrastructure Services Committee will approve your application, it should not really be a problem, the biggest single hurdle is now over and the press are on our side." He paused and looked at Andrews as he stared back over the rim of his coffee mug. "The only problem we have at the moment is this shooting of the young reporter. That has the potential to be messy and problematic especially if it is traced back to you or any of your people." He paused as Crawford sipped on his coffee "I would like you to assure me that neither you, your organisation nor any of your people was involved in this murderous act in any way shape or form" Crawford just kept on sipping at his coffee and looking over the rim of the cup at Dull as the little man began to get more and more uncomfortable. Eventually he spoke "I can assure you," he sipped from his cup "that to the best of my knowledge" *sip* "we have had no involvement in this type of thing at all." *sip* He sighed and set the cup down on the desk "You see, we have had no need to; the deal is basically agreed, at the level it needs to be agreed at, and the rest of it is merely window dressing to keep your electorate happy. People who actually believe in democracy are generally fools, the rest of us just get on and do the job and they never see the way the work really gets done." He sighed softly and looked out of the window to his side obviously thinking about what he had just said, before turning back to face the little, wrinkled grey haired man who now sat in front of him. "Some people struggle all their lives in an attempt to become great but they will never make it. Others are just born to be great and Trente Silver is one of those, no one can stand in his way and he will not allow infantile failure or excuses to get in his way. He has decreed this will happen, that means that this will happen. Whether your weak and ineffectual political system allows it or not, we will make this happen. This is a classic of what he does, your local authority is destroyed and in tatters and will never be a cohesive body again until most of the existing members are replaced and that will be by people who do as they are told. Told by us that is." He paused and obviously came to a decision, smiling at Dull he carefully stood up and walked out of the office. Dull just watched him walk away and wondered if he had joined the right side at that first meeting so long ago. He felt trapped as he realised it

186

was too late to even think about that now, he did not have the courage to change his mind.

+

'Thug one' was out for a walk with his dog, just a casual stroll around the edges of a field on the estate. The fact that the other side of the fence was the row of cottages just along from Mark Rae's place was a pure coincidence as was the fact his dog had not been fed and was feeling particularly aggressive as it tugged and strained at the leash. He was impressed, he had to admit he was struggling to hold onto the dog, it was a lot more viscous and easily angered than he had been led to believe, he might actually be able to make some real use of the animal.

Pete was looking out of the front window of their home and saw the man being dragged around the field, for the second time, by his dog. At first glance he laughed then slowly he calmed down and looked a little more closely as he began a third circuit of the field. Mary spoke behind him and he jumped "That looks like a viscous dog. I wonder why he's exercising it in this field." Pete snorted "Simple, he's just warning us that we're not welcome in his field. The fact he doesn't own it yet doesn't seem to bother his people." He sighed and Mary slipped her arms around him "Are we going to have to leave our home." She whispered in his ear. He could hear the tears behind her voice as she shivered against him and he stood there, just thinking and not replying for a moment. "Maybe he does actually own it now, the date for transfer must be just about up and I haven't seen Paul Gray around in the last couple of weeks." Mary hugged him and said "Maybe we should ask Mark, he would know." Pete just grunted.

+

Mark was sitting at the back of the café off the library reading a news paper when he heard a woman's voice he knew he should recognise but couldn't quite place. It sounded a fraction louder than normal as though it was supposed to be heard by as many people as possible. He sat there and tried to ignore it at first but the voice ate its way into his consciousness as it prattled on and he became aware of what they were saying.

".....of course its going to be brilliant. As I understand it it's going to have two separate price lists; one for resort residents and one for local people with discounts for everything, even the golf." Mark lowered his paper and looked across the room at the back of a blonde head that was holding court with one of the local woman's groups, she was obviously giving a presentation of the proposed development. He shook his head and opened his mouth as at least one of the women smiled at him as they recognised him

"Danielle," he said loudly enough to interrupt her pre prepared speech "have you made it clear to the women that you are employed by the Silver Organisation and that this is a sales talk?" She turned round sharply and ran a hand through her hair quickly as spoke "Mark, so good to see you again, I didn't think such trivialities would interest the ladies." He sighed "Well Danielle, as I understand it you are doing the PR work for them so you should have access to the facts and not just be in a position of saying 'I believe' or I hope' or anything like that." Danielle frowned at him "Well that may be true but there are certain things that are not confirmed yet and I am sure you understand that commercial confidentiality makes it impossible for me to divulge certain information." Mark shook his head "So that will be why you don't mention that fact that one of Silvers courses in the States only got its permit by being described as a public course. That means it is supposedly open to be played by the public, what wasn't mentioned, until after it was actually open, is that it's only open to the public one day a year with a green fee of thirty five dollars. To play the rest of the year costs a joining fee of over three hundred thousand dollars and an annual membership of three hundred thousand dollars." One of the other women in the group looked past Danielle and said "Okay that sounds a bit rough only getting access one day a year but surely that is better than nothing?" Mark shook his head "You've missed the fact that the particular day it is open to the public is limited to either the first or last day of the season, and that the green keeper has the ability to say whether or not the course is playable that day." He paused and looked at the group one by one. "So far in the seven years that course has been open, no member of the public has been able to play for their thirty five dollars." The room was silent as Danielle had no answer to his comment so he continued. "What about the one on the other coast where he gained building permission with the clause written in that they had to maintain the coastal path that went down the side of the course. It fell into the sea two years after he bought the course and had done absolutely nothing about maintaining it. The local authority then issued a notice requiring him to comply with the planning conditions, his reply was to say he could not maintain what did not exist and then he erected fences to prevent people who were using the path from walking down the coastal edge of his course." Mark paused and looked at the room where everyone was watching him "Last I heard," he continued "was he was suing the council for harassment even though they have him in court for failing to comply with planning conditions. I fully expect the same to happen here, almost every council that has bent the knee to him has wound up being sued by him for some minor issue later on." Even the staff

188

had been listening to him he realised, that would be a nice change, they had been supporters of the development until now. The woman who had spoken already spoke again, slowly, more hesitantly "Would you have any problem with me doing my own research on this type of thing?" Mark shook his head "Of course not, the more people look into this matter and this organisation, the more they will find. Some will find things in support of them, I don't believe any one can be 100% bad so they will exist as well, but most will find issues that make them uncomfortable. This is an organisation that has a very murky past with a lot of unusual happenings in their history. So please feel free to do your own research, find out as much as you can and share it with as many people as you can." He paused and looked at Danielle "Danielle, do you have any objections to that or any comment to make on what they may find?" She looked flustered as she looked around the group and knew she had lost this one "I would just advise everyone to be careful of what they say and what the press say on their behalf. The Silver Organisation has not been treated well by the media over the years and a number of lawsuits are outstanding on that basis. So just be careful what you publicise" Mark looked at her, levelly as she stood up. "Is that a threat?" he asked before she reached the door "No, just a hint." She smiled a thin lipped smile and the bell tinkled as she pulled the door closed behind her.

Mark sighed and folded his paper "Sorry ladies. I did not mean to interrupt your coffee. I just find it nearly impossible to stand back and listen to blatant lies and deliberate inaccuracies being distributed as fact." There was a murmur from the group but no one said anything directly to him until one of the staff spoke up. "I can't speak for the ladies here but for my own part I am grateful to hear the other side of the story and hear the lies being pointed out. Up 'till now we only seem to be getting one, carefully edited, version of the facts." She looked around "Anyone disagree?" there was a shaking of heads across the room.

+

'Xander was in his element, he was on an official trade visit to the States and had just so happened to be able to fit in a visit, only an extra three days, as a guest of the Silver Organisation at one of their landmark hotels in New York. Coincidentally in the block next to 'the great mans' own office block. It was the evening of his arrival in town and he was looking forward to some fun at some one else's expense.

He had been invited to a private dinner and so was ready at seven o'clock when a knock came on the door. The heavily built security guard and his two associates ushered him out of the room and down in the elevator to a waiting limousine. A few flash bulbs went off as he crossed the pavement (or sidewalk as they called it here) but that was to be expected, he was the President after all. The two well dressed women in the limousine were a bit of a surprise but he liked company.

The next morning he was not so happy, he had a serious hangover and struggled to prise his gummy lips apart before he could lift a glass of water to try and rinse out the metallic taste from his mouth. He felt sluggish, lethargic and disinterested as he looked in the mirror and tried to remember where he had been and what happened. He stopped when he stepped out of the bathroom and looked around. His suit was in the wardrobe and his shoes had been put away, that meant only one thing, someone had undressed him, he never put his clothes away at night. A short time later there was a knock at the door, but when he answered it there was no one there, there was however, an envelope sitting on the floor at his feet. His hand shook slightly as he opened the envelope having first shut the door, and tipped it up. A memory stick fell out into his hand, no note, no information, nothing else. His heart sank as he looked at it, he knew what this meant; it meant he was screwed.

+

Padruig McCarthy stood there looking down the length of his garden without really seeing what he was looking at, he was trying to see into the future to understand the risks and opportunities something like this presented to the region. He was not sure where it lay, obviously there were both positive and negative sides to this thing. The only thing he could be sure of was the fact that he was not sure about it. He sighed and turning away from the window, sat down at the desk again in order to read some more of the information that had been submitted for assessment as part of the application.

His hand hovered over the phone as he considered calling a colleague and asking for advice but he decided against it. He was the man in the seat after all and as such, had to make the decision, it was up to him. Add to that the rules of confidentiality made it difficult to ask for advice and yet still sit in the chair, or even at the table. If he told anyone before the meeting how he intended voting that would be seen as pre existing bias and would exclude him from taking part in the vote. He sighed and turned back to the piles of paper that littered his desk.

+

190

Dianne was also in the middle of a discussion on the same subject. She had been part of the initial planning meeting but was not part of the Infrastructure and Services Committee and so had no vote but she just might be there to listen to what happened if she could find the time. She had just said as much to one of her local council constituents and had just received a verbal barrage. She stood there with her mouth open as the woman ranted on "How could you vote against such a wonderful development. It is clearly in our benefit, tidying up some barren waste ground and giving people much needed jobs; the very type of jobs that this area will need in two or three years time when the oil runs out." Dianne stared at her in disbelief as the woman seemed to get more and more agitated the more she spoke, looking round for help she noticed the library staff were watching closely and one of them was on the phone. Dianne hoped it was to the police.

Another woman, a staff member, walked up slowly and began to speak "Please, calm down there's no need to shout about it. The councillor is only doing what she's meant to do and that's represent the general opinion and within the guideline of the law and formal guidance." The woman never got a chance to finish what she was saying as the first woman pulled out a knitting needle and drove it at the second woman screaming "How dare you interrupt a private conversation." Her voice had reached a falsetto pitch and the needle was waving towards the second woman's face as Dianne struggled to get out of her reach as she saw her attacker turn towards the staff member with a manic gleam in her eye. Her arm lunged towards the staff member and missed, the knitting needle tangled in the fleece jacket she was wearing and her own arm came down over the top, trapping the needle in place as the first woman stepped back and stared at her empty hand in amazement for a few seconds before she started screaming again "Give me that back," She was stepping forwards as she screamed "That is mine and I want it back now." She was so busy screaming she did not see the two police officers come running into the library building and run at her.

The scuffle was short and the woman was led away still complaining she wanted her knitting needle back from the staff member who was being attended to by yet another police officer as Dianne stood there not sure what to do. Another police officer stood there and sighed "Why do I feel this whole thing is getting out of hand?" she asked herself before turning to Dianne "Get a little heated did it?" Dianne shook her head "Not really, it all started as a fairly straightforward conversation with some one who disagrees with my position of this Silver development thing." Dianne sat

191

down heavily as she thought about the whole incident "It's almost surreal," she said to the officer who looked concerned for a moment as Dianne had sat down heavily "One moment it was logical but obviously passionate and the next it flared up out of nowhere." The officer nodded "I've seen the like before, she's probably on medication of some kind and may not have taken what she's supposed to." She shrugged "but I'm not a doctor, we'll need to wait until we get her properly assessed before we know what has actually happened." She sighed again and smiled down at Dianne who returned her smile rather weakly.

11

The hall was crowded and noisy as people filled up the seats arranged in rows across the hall. The press were there in force at the back, watching everyone as they arrived. Andrew Crawford towed Peter Barnard in like a lap dog who followed dutifully behind. Karl Benson guided old Jock in to his seat close behind the Silver Organisation delegation which numbered almost twenty people when you included all the lawyers, personal assistants and other minions. Even 'thug one' and two of his henchmen were there to act as bodyguards, trying to look threatening in cheap, ill fitting suits.

At the other side of the hall two rows back from the front, sat Mark, along with Dr Jennifer Jones who was struggling to prevent herself from grabbing his hand, Jenny and Andrea sat close by along with a few mixed representatives of other affected groups. At the last minute Marianne rushed in dragging Mike of *'Greensword'* along by the hand. He had put on a tie and it just did not look right somehow and he was obviously not comfortable. Ten minutes before the meeting started and the hall was full, council officials were now trying to close the doors and guide the extra members of the public into an adjoining hall where they could watch the proceedings on a large monitor hurriedly mounted on the wall.

Slowly the nine councillors filed into the room in front of the packed audience and took their seats facing the crowded gallery as the support staff filed in behind them. They seemed strangely quiet as though they were actors in some strange drama, all waiting for the action to start so they could play their own role before leaving the stage. The doors were shut and the crowds of people in the room were all in place, there was no longer any chance for anyone to leave the stage.

Mark could feel the eyes of the media on the back of his head as he leant towards Jennifer to murmur "Seems like a mixed bunch here, this could go any way." She nodded quickly and deftly. Over at the other side of the hall Benson leant forward to Peter Barnard who was sitting almost directly in front of him and said "How well placed are we? Is this going to be an argument or is it going to be straight forward?" Barnard shook his head "We've got at least three, probably a fourth so it should be fairly straight forward and be on our side." Benson smiled and sat back, slowly glancing around the room. Towards the back of the room Marianne frowned and squeezed Mikes hand "That guy over there," she nodded in the direction she was looking "Who is he? The guy next to 'old Jock'" Mike looked in the direction she was looking and squinted for a second or two "Oh," he exclaimed "That's Karl Benson, recently moved in next to Jock." He paused and thought for a moment "Seems to be a bit of a wide boy, very friendly, talking to everyone. Offering them all drink and escort girls along with a good chat to find out what they think about the plans" Marianne was nodding slowly "Would the term 'flash git' come close to describing him?" Mike looked at her surprised "Yes, it would actually. How did you know that?" She was still staring as Karl turned slowly and she looked down before he could lock eyes with her. Mike looked at him as the eyes travelled past on their way round the room. Marianne slowly straightened up and pulled Mike closer so she could whisper in his ear "I know him, he was at my cousins wedding about two months ago, as a partner of another guest, but he wasn't called Karl Benson then." Mike looked at her and looked quickly down the hall at Karl where he sat with the Silver organisation. "Are you sure?" he paused and before she could answer carried on saying "Of course you're sure, your memory for faces is incredible. Can you remember what he was calling himself?" Marianne nodded slowly "I think so," she said "but I want to speak to my cousin before I say anymore. Just let Mark know he is far from trustworthy if I am right." Mike nodded "I don't think we need to tell him that. I think he's working in cautious mode as it is." Marianne nodded and they turned to watch the chair man stand up to try and call the meeting to order.

At the back of the hall the media all turned to their equipment and there was a clicking and whirring of cameras and tape recorders as Padruig McCarthy introduced the councillors sitting there ranked either side of him looking out at the sea of faces that stared back. Padruig swallowed and opened his mouth to talk again "With no further ado, I would like to call this meeting to order. There is a very simple agenda with only one item on it and no allowance for delay of decision. The item is the Silver Organisations housing development and golf resort at the Doones estate just out of town." He waved his hand vaguely in the direction of the estate and sighed to himself as he sat down. "The subject matter is the effect of such a development on the infrastructure and services of the area and its ability, or lack thereof to support such a development." He looked around the room and slowly along the row of councillors trying to read faces that might give away their intentions, he decided a few were already decided and others still had a lot to learn about the project, he carried on wondering how this would look to so many others. "We have four hours to discuss this application and its merits so while that sounds like a long time, I think we may struggle so with that in mind lets get started." He turned back to the room and looked at the press congregated at the back of the room "In a few moments I will formally call this meeting to order. At that time all recording equipment must be switched off and not be used again until the meeting is formally concluded. That includes all video recording, all audio recording and all cameras of any type. The only way you are permitted to record the meeting is by the use of pen and paper as our minute takers here do." He indicated two women sitting against the wall to one side of the hall as he said this. "After the meeting is concluded, that is once the final vote has been counted and announced, you may turn your recording gear back on again. I intend having a comfort break at about half way, if the media need to file a report at that point it must be done from outside of the hall. The break is not an excuse to switch on your equipment again. Is that clear?" He looked at the gathered masses at the back and got a few nods from the ones he knew already by sight and decided that was probably about as much as he could expect from them at all. He nodded again to himself and straightening his back said "If no one has any objection or comment on any of that then I will call the meeting to order." He looked around the councillors and seeing a few shakes of heads and nothing more he tapped the desk in front of him with the small auctioneers hammer he used for this job. "Then I call this meeting to order and let's begin." In the crowd Mark sighed and settled down to listen, there was 'nothing else he could do here anyway' he thought as he listed to Padruig talk. Jennifer finally gave in and reached across to take hold of his hand, he smiled at her as she gave his hand a squeeze. What he didn't realise was that it was her that was needing the support as much as he was. Over at the other side Dull was sitting there complaining as loudly as he could to as many people as would listen. "Why do they bother with this rubbish? It's obvious it should be passed without question; if they do need anything it should just be a case of yes or no from each of them. There's no need for a speech from each and every pathetic one of them." Crawford half turned in his seat and spoke to Dull. "Shut up," he said his eyes were cold as they regarded the odious little man who was obviously drunk "This is your legal system, if you don't like it. Change it. Meantime sit there and shut up, or leave. The choice is yours." He turned back and began to pay attention to the discussion going on a few feet away from him. He regretted asking for support from the Chamber and some of its people, he should have known some of them would come along anyway and others would stay away no matter what was asked. Dull was someone who he would not have chosen to be on his side in any technical or complex discussion of any type.

The comfort break came and Marianne stepped out to the hallway leaving Mike to speak to Mark as the crowd moved about stretching muscles and limbs that had been cramped on uncomfortable plastic chairs for too long.

Mark looked around for Jennifer with no luck as Mike strolled up to him "What do you think?" Mark shook his head, "Too close to call at the moment. I get the feeling even some of the councillors haven't made up their mind yet." Mike nodded slowly "Marianne might have an interesting bit of news for you, she's checking something out right now so I'll wait until she comes back before I say anything else." Mark nodded, he could wait, there was nothing he could do with it right now anyway.

Marianne had stopped in the main hallway and was checking her phone when Karl Benson lurched out of the doorway and generally in her direction. "Excuse me mate," he breathed on one of the security guards who stepped back under the onslaught of stale tobacco and alcohol fumes, he didn't seem to notice the clicking noise her phone made as she took his photograph and turned away. The guard just pointed towards the gents and Benson nodded, mumbled his thanks and lurched off in that direction, apparently unsteady. Marianne was facing the door as she made her phone call so she didn't see the suddenly sober, calculating look he shot in her direction before pushing the door to the gents open and stepping inside.

Jennifer saw the agitated look on Marianne's face as she walked out of the ladies smoothing her skirt. "Are you okay?" was the obvious question as she looked at her friend who nodded her head vigorously "Oh, yes and I've just found out something that might be worth you being aware of as well. I'll text you the details." She said as she pushed buttons on her phone, easing the door to the ladies open but standing there waiting until her phone told her the message was on its way. "I'll see you back inside, but I have to go." She pointed inside as she stepped through the door way and vanished from sight. Jennifer shrugged as she turned and went back to the hall, knowing she would find out what was bothering her friend soon enough.

Benson supported himself on the wall with one hand as he did what he was there to do while he sighed deeply, he was getting tired of this game; if he was not careful he would turn into the 'flash git' drunk he was pretending to be. One day he would retire from all of this and go away somewhere quiet, with a garden and maybe a woman who wasn't paid for by the hour might be nice too. He rolled his head on his shoulders, listening to his neck crack as he closed his eyes and let himself dream for a minute or two. He knew he had the money, so far it had always been deposited at the end of each job as had been promised, but still there was a niggling doubt at the back of his mind. Could he really walk away without any repercussions?

In the hall Mike was asking Marks advice "I mean you've got experience of this, what do you think?" Mark shook his head, grinning broadly as he

196

thought about his reply "My experience of that was a long time ago but more importantly you have to make up your own mind. Not do it because some one else thinks it's a good idea for you." he looked his friend in the eyes "Think about it, alone. You need to make up your own mind, if you're not convinced it won't work and that is worse than anything." Mike was nodding in agreement but still rocking from foot to foot as he heard Mark sigh before he said "For what it's worth, if I was you. I would. Just remember it's your decision. Now here comes Jennifer so no more on this, okay?" Mike nodded, grinning as Jennifer strolled up to them and putting a hand out leant on Marks shoulder as she eased her foot out of her shoe "That's better, I'll be glad to get home and out of these shoes." Then she looked at the two of them as they stood there looking at her, puzzled. "What's the use, I'm talking to two typical men." and shook her head.

The crowd began to move and head back to their seats so Mark and Jennifer made their way back down towards where they had been sitting at the front of the hall, leaving Mike to wait on Marianne. It took almost five minutes for the crowd to settle down and it had just happened when Jennifer's phone buzzed silently in her jacket pocket. She bit her lip to stop herself from gasping out loud as she read the message and nudged Mark so heavily he jumped as her elbow dug into his ribs. His frown changed to a look of amazement as he read the message on the phone. It had come through with another photo of a man who was unmistakably Karl Benson, it just so happened that the name was different. The story that went with it matched the image that Mark had built up in his head as well. He shook his head as he handed back the phone, not quite sure what to make of the news but intending to do something with it. Right at this moment the best he could do, was to file it away for use later. Mark looked back to the group at the front of the room and noticed it was Councillor Wilt that was talking, that man could talk but it would take a lot of listening before he was sure what it was he was actually saying.

At the back of the hall Mike was grinning as Marianne sat down next to him and he grabbed her hand. She looked at him startled, he wasn't really very good at all of this emotional stuff but he was getting better. She had high hopes for him becoming a real long term fixture in her life but right now she had something more important to deal with. Without looking too closely at him she flipped open her phone and handed it to him, he was confused as he looked down at it. A moment later once he had read the message and looked at the photograph his head snapped back up as he looked around the hall. Leaning in close he whispered "Does Mark know yet?" Marianne shrugged "I don't know, I sent it to Jennifer so I wouldn't be surprised." Mike nodded slowly and handed the phone back as he looked around, looking for Benson, he wasn't in the hall.

Mark, like many people there, had stopped listening to Councillor Wilt. It was clear he was reading word for word from a prepared script lying on the desk that had been written in a text size, or two, too small so every now and again he had to pause and lean forward to read what the next word was. As Mark looked around he was playing with the medical tape on his ear thinking about Sharon and the time they had spent together, she had been fun and with a real future ahead of her and he snapped back to the current situation as a phrase struck home like a needle to a balloon. "….no one will get hurt and no long term damage can be done. After all the area is nothing but sand, just sand, sand and more sand." Mark felt his eyes fill with tears at the words as his ear suddenly hurt and he could feel the hot sticky sensation of Sharon's blood all over him again. His breath quickened and he could feel all his muscles tense as the adrenalin flowed through his body. There was a slight murmur of voices and the scrape of chairs became obvious but it was not loud enough to upset Councillor Wilt as Mark stood up and pushed his way to the end of the row followed closely by Jennifer who looked worried and concerned as she chased him out of the hall her heels making a clicking sound on the polished wooden floor until the local authorities guard closed the door behind her as she stepped into the hallway after Mark. Two of the press contingent saw what had happened and followed the two figures out to the fresh air.

Mark was standing on the steps breathing deeply, being watched, from a distance, by some of the supporters and objectors who could not get into the hall. Jennifer was standing with her arm around his shoulders and she could feel the tension in his body, hear the deep breathing as he fought to control what was obviously a serious temper and she thought as she realised what had caused it, a justified temper. "Are you okay? Can we help in any way?" Mark drew another breath before he straightened himself up and turned around to face the American journalist and the junior from one of the local papers who were standing there looking at him. The American stepped back as she saw the look in his eyes and noted how quickly it was contained and capped. When he spoke a few seconds later Marks voice was calm and level again but he still had tears running down his face. "I am extremely disappointed in Councillor Wilt and his lack of knowledge of the current situation. He has just said that no one would be getting hurt and the landscape was only sand. Well, in case he did not know a young woman was recently murdered at the estate and there is a good likelihood it is in some way related to this housing development that is currently being debated in the council chamber. The environmental ignorance of the man

198

who can make such a sweeping statement about a SSSI that is unique in this country alone is incredible and on a human level he now owes the family of Sharon Grant, at the very least an absolute personal apology which should be given face to face." Mark drew breath and thought for a second and spoke again before either of the journalists could ask a question. "I now call upon Councillor Wilt to go and see Sharon Grants parents this evening and make that apology in person, preferably before his pathetic and unacceptable comments make it onto the evening news. If he chooses not to make this apology then he should consider resigning his ward with immediate effect." The reporters said nothing, just standing there nodding as they scribbled on the notepads they each held. Jennifer squeezed his arm and gave a minute nod back in towards the door where the security guard who had followed them out stood. Mark nodded slowly and making his excuses to the reporters, walked back into the building. The guard smiled at them and led them back to the chamber. He hesitated before he opened the door and muttered quietly so they both had to strain to hear him. "I never said this, but well done, he's been paid to support this one, so good luck. He shouldn't be a councillor." Mark nodded, a single curt nod, as Jennifer stared for a second as the guard looked past them both as the two reporters put away their phones and came running down the hallway to get back into the council chamber.

The meeting was still going on as they crept back into the hall and there was no problem in getting to their seats. Councillor Wilt had just sat down again and had a smug self satisfied look on his face as he casually looked around the hall. His eyes met with Marks just as Mark made to sit down and suddenly Councillors Wilts expression changed to one of pure fear as he saw something in Marks eyes that he did not like. Some of the Silver contingent were looking around the hall as this happened and Mark became aware of a pair of eyes focused on him from that group. He looked back and found an almost sober Karl Benson looking at him with an expression he knew. Mark just nodded to him and the two men looked away from each other.

Danielle was sitting just along from Karl Benson, one row in front and was looking between his face and the back of Peter Barnard's head at Mark and Jennifer, she sighed as she turned back to the front, she was even less sure now that she could go through with this job, she had picked the wrong side and gone for money rather than value. She shook her head slightly and turned her attention back to the front of the hall.

Benson had been watching her out of the corner of his eye and he had waited until she turned away before he turned back and looked at the back of her head. He had wondered about her the other day at the office in the stables; he had felt that she was not happy with her role in everything that was happening, now he was sure. He caught himself wondering if she could bring herself to jump ship and if so what would he be asked to do about it. He realised with a start that he was beginning to dislike what he did for a living. He sighed and straightened quickly as he saw old Jock next to him look round, he had let his guard slip. He glanced at Jock and saw the old man shake his head to himself, not sure what he had seen, if anything, but still uncomfortable here. The old man slipped a finger into the collar of his shirt and loosened it against his neck slightly; he wasn't used to wearing a tie.

Padruig McCarthy looked around the room, it seemed quite tense but at the same time controlled and well mannered. There had been a point when that fool Wilt had been talking there was a disturbance in the crowd, it had taken Padruig a second or two to recognise the man involved, it had actually been the flash of white tape on his ear that told him who he was. McCarthy shook his head, Wilt was a fool and worse a gullible fool who would be found out soon enough; Padruig just hoped he didn't take the rest of the council down with him when he finally went. He sighed as he listened to Wilt who was still droning on, a limit of fifteen minutes had been set for each speaker and Wilt would use every last second of it as well as the allowances that were always made in these things. It could get seriously monotonous when they got to the debate stage which would hopefully be soon.

Old Jock forced himself to stop playing with his collar, it was tight and distracting him from the action here. Having said that he could barely hear what was being said anyway, he was too proud to wear a hearing aid but he wouldn't admit that either, that was just his way. He had actually been daydreaming and had hoped Danielle might have been looking at him when she was looking backwards, he knew she hadn't been though. If anything she would have been looking at Karl, he seemed to be quite a guy, had been everywhere and done most things if you believed his stories. Jock was beginning to realise that his days of being the one that the young girls looked at was long gone. It was a painful admission but might give him some peace he thought as he focused his eyes on the group at the front just as Councillor Wilt finally sat down again. It had been twenty five minutes he had been on his feet, not bad for a fifteen minute slot.

+

200

Paul Gray was sitting on a hotel balcony looking out at the blue, blue water that surrounded the island and he knew he could not stay here. He had the money, he had been paid, which he had been beginning to doubt, after the research he had done on their financial position. He had paid off his wife, or ex wife as her lawyer told him it technically was now since she had gained a quickie divorce in some US state or other, he couldn't remember where and it really didn't matter any longer. What mattered was she was gone and out of his life, he would worry about what the future held in that direction at some other time.

The sea was beautiful and the landscape was lush and green, exactly as he remembered it, but still he knew he could not live here. He looked down at the beach less than one hundred metres away, beautiful white sand shining in the sun with the waves lapping gently upon the shore, it was idyllic. He thought back to his home to the Doones estate he had so mistakenly sold for a less than market valuation. That was where his friends were and where his life was and he knew in that instant he was going home. He had slipped away without saying anything to anyone, almost ashamed that he was running away and leaving them to it. He stood up and went inside to the telephone. It was his lawyer he phoned. "Jonathon, good to hear your voice." his lawyer was surprised to hear from him "Paul, great to hear from you, how are you? Or should that be where are you?" The conversation circled around banalities for several minutes before the lawyer finally said "Okay Paul, you didn't call to ask about my health, what do you want?" Paul sighed "My estate back is the short answer," he carried on talking as he heard the intake of breath on the other end of the line "but I accept that is unlikely to say the least. Truth be told, I made a mistake and I want to go back and live amongst my friends and neighbours. If the Doones estate or anything similar comes up of course I'm interested but more likely would be a house with some land." He paused and listened to his lawyer breathe again "Okay," he finally said "How local to your estate does it have to be?" Paul shrugged before he remembered it was a phone conversation and said "As close as I can get. Tell you what, call the lawyers office in Drimmie, Steve is the name of the senior partner, ask him what's available and if Paradigm Properties have anything available. Tell him it's for me, he might be able to help." The lawyer grunted as he made notes on the yellow pad on his desk "Okay, I'll do that. Who is this Paradigm Properties anyway?" Paul just laughed "That's a long story and one I am not 100% clear on myself yet; one day I may tell you, but not just yet." Jonathon the lawyer nodded as he set the phone down, he had no idea what his client was up to but it was probably going to cause him some trouble. Slowly he opened his desk drawer and rummaged around for a moment or two before pulling out a yellow piece of pasteboard. He looked at it, turning it over in his hands so that the Silver coloured print flashed in the light from the window before he paused absolutely stock still, thinking about what he should do before he dropped the business card back into the drawer and slammed it shut. He was ashamed of himself for not having the courage to feed the card into the shredder.

+

Arthur had wanted to come but hadn't thought to speak to Mark about it so he was sitting at home hoping some one would come and tell him what happened sooner rather than later. He knew he could maybe have walked up to the road and caught a bus now that he could walk almost without pain, but he also knew he was old and needed a bit of help every now and again. The old radio crackled a little but he had warned Mark not to buy him a new one. This was an old favourite that his nephew had bought him, what seemed like a lifetime ago, he wondered when he would see him again. Arthur had been grateful when Mark had turned up that day, even more grateful when he had found out Mark was in fact his landlord and was happy to fix up the old cottage again. It was almost news time again so he turned round and switched on the radio once more.

+

Back in the council chamber the debate was now in full flow and the time allocated for the meeting was beginning to look like it wasn't enough. The crowd was getting restless as the debate dragged on and on with some councillors unwilling to recognise that their points had already been dealt with the previous time they had spoken but eventually, almost a half hour after the scheduled finishing time of the meeting they called it to a vote. There was silence in the hall as Padruig McCarthy sipped at his water before commencing the final process of the vote.

The glass 'clinked' slightly on the metal coaster as he set it down on the desk. "Right ladies and gentlemen, now that we have finally reached the concluding part of the proceedings," he paused and looked pointedly at Councillor Wilt before carrying on. "this should not actually take too long before we conclude today's protracted meeting. I will go round each councillor in turn, starting at my extreme left asking for their vote. When it reaches the councillor on my immediate left I shall then go to my extreme right and again come back to the centre leaving myself as the chair, with the casting vote if necessary. This is not an opportunity for further debate. I am only looking for a single word from each councillor either 'Approve' or 'Reject'." He paused and looked around the room before turning his gaze

202

back to the councillors "Is that clear?" All the councillors nodded their understanding before he turned and looked forward again, almost as if he was challenging the press corp. assembled at the back of the room to object or even say something. No one moved, or even said a word so he looked down at the desk for a second before he looked up and to his left "Then we begin, councillor can I have your vote please?" All eyes moved to the end of the row as the councillor looked up and smiled "Approve", all eyes moved one space "Reject" was the next councillor "Approve" and "Approve" concluded that side of the room. As Padruig McCarthy moved his head across to look to his right Mark looked across at the other side of the hall, specifically the front two rows where the Silver Organisations personnel sat. Peter Barnard was grinning from ear to ear and was already patting Crawford Andrews on the back. Karl Benson was looking at the floor which seemed a little strange to Mark, while Danielle was just looking along the row.

The councillor on the far left of the hall took the nod from Padruig as an instruction to vote and said "Reject", the next one was "Approve" followed by "Reject" and "Reject". Mark sat there for a second as did everyone else before a murmur ran around the room as people suddenly realised it had come down to a tied vote. Mark looked back at the Silver Organisations team at the other side of the hall. Andrew Crawford had not moved, Peter Barnard's face had fallen and he looked like he was terrified to touch his boss again. Karl Benson was looking at the floor with his teeth clenched and fists bunched while old Jock was casting around for someone to tell him what had just been said, Danielle was now looking at Karl Benson with a strange almost far away look in her eyes.

Mark dragged his eyes away; he would worry about what was going on there later, what was about to happen at the front of the hall was much more important right now. From where he sat in the second row he could hear Padruig McCarthy sigh as he leant on his elbows and looked up. His eyes cast around the room slowly, taking in the hard stares from the front row on his right that was where the applicant's team were usually seated. On his left were a totally different bunch of people, mainly locals and some he knew were supporters while some were objectors, he wondered how this would go down. He leant back and said "In accordance with standard procedures and protocols for chairing a meeting as the chairman I have an obligation, when a casting vote is required as it is now, to vote for the status quo. That means my vote is to reject this application." There was silence in the hall for a second or two until the realisation sank in as to what that actually meant. The scrape of chairs that broke the silence was from the press corp. at the back of the hall and not, as Mark had expected, from the Silver Organisation at the other side of the hall. They seemed stunned, as if they could not believe what had just happened then Crawford Andrew stood up followed a spilt second by the rest of the Silver organisation team. Mark smiled, it had been the sudden blaze of light from the TV cameras that had just been switched on that made him move, nothing else; he swivelled in his seat to watch the herd of reporters rush down the aisle between the seats towards Crawford Andrews before he could escape from the room. He didn't wait to be asked for his opinion "This ridiculous decision merely shows that this part of the country is not ready for any real commercial enterprise at all." He turned and made to walk out through the crowd until a single shout rose above the babble of voices "Not rushing to call your boss tonight then?" Before he could stop himself he turned and looked for the source of the voice while the rest of the room laughed. Mark stood there and watched as Andrews turned back and tried to stride through the crowd trailed by an ashen faced Peter Barnard and the rest of the team. Old Jock turned to Karl Benson and said "Well, I guess that's that then." Benson shot him a look that made Jocks blood run cold for a second before the usual, slightly lop sided smile broke through again "Don't bet on it" he slurred "They'll have some form of recovery strategy in place. I would almost bet on it." He stood up and looked around at the crowd that almost seemed to be hanging around even as the council security guards were trying to clear the hall. Meanwhile he was wondering 'what the hell just happened, I thought all of this was dealt with a long time ago.'

Mark was standing on the steps to the Council offices at one side trying to stay out of the way of the crowds and cameras. That was where Marianne and Mike found the two of them as they watched Crawford Andrews and his team disappear into two vehicles and drive away. Mike was almost breathless as he grabbed Marks arm "Did Jennifer tell you? Did you see the picture?" Mark nodded, slowly "Yes I did see the picture. Unfortunately it fits with the image I was building of him anyway." Suddenly Mikes face sharpened and his back straightened. Mark reached out and grabbed his friends arm, fingers clamping deep into the relatively soft muscle. "Don't tackle him, leave him to me and anyhow here and now is not the right time or place." Mike looked back suddenly at his friend and decided he would not argue.

The press were swarming around looking for someone to speak to, but almost all of the local press were avoiding Dull who was swaying gently as he walked slowly down the steps. He paused as he came level with the small group of friends and turned to face them with a sneer on his face. "Think you've won do you? With your pathetic peasant mentality arguments you may have succeeded here but we will just move on to a bigger playing field and crush you in passing." He swayed down a couple of steps more before turning back to shout at the doors of the council

204

offices "Peasants and fools, the lot of you. I'll see to it that you all lose your seats at the next election." He turned back and swore at the TV camera that was in his way before stumbling off in the direction of the car park. A few moments later his car left the car park. Mark glanced around and saw Karl Benson, standing with Danielle at the top of the steps, speaking on his phone to someone.

+

In New York Trente Silver was beside himself with rage when he heard the news from Crawford Andrews an hour or two later after the other man had gathered his courage. They weren't staying at the estate, they had decided that the Wycliffe hotel had more facilities and looked better in the photographs than the house did, they were about to regret that decision.

Silver had put the phone down before Crawford had finished speaking. Crawford was used to that and in itself it did not bother him at all, it was what would happen next that bothered him. He turned and looked at them all as most of his team gathered around him, Danielle was missing as was Benson, Crawford decided he would deal with them later. He sighed as they all settled into the seats around the room that had become their command centre "Right folks, listen up. As of now we close down our public face until we are sure what we want to do and need to do. No press releases, no discussions with the media in any way, especially off the record and basically we need to be silent and composed. We need to make it look as if we were expecting this and are just stepping up to the plate for our next move." He paused and looked around the room "Now go to your rooms, use the gym, do whatever you want to do, just give me some space but don't go away from the hotel. I need to be able to contact you if I need to when we finally get some information about what our next step is to be." There was a shuffling of feet and a couple of people stood up but no one seemed to be rushing to leave until Crawford himself stood up "For pities sake. Go, now, give me some space to be alone in." Suddenly when he turned round the room was empty, even Barnard had gone. He sighed, he normally hated being alone but right now it felt good. That was why the knock on the door made him sigh as he turned round and came face to face with an under manager of the hotel, who looked nervous, he was holding a telephone handset "Sorry to disturb you sir but I have Mr Dull on the telephone, he is insisting to speak to you." Crawford didn't say anything, just held out his hand as the young man handed over the phone to him. Crawford turned and walked towards the window as the under manager walked back to the door.

"Yes Dull, what do you want?" the reply made him stop and listen a lot more closely "I'm in a prison cell, they say I have been drink driving and I need to signed out by a responsible person." Crawford just listened "I don't want to use any of my people for obvious reasons, could you send some one along. There will need to be two of them, some one will need to drive my car back to the hotel." Crawford shook his head "Okay, okay, I'll bail you out and get your car back here, don't worry." He broke the connection and turned around knowing the manager was still standing by the door. The slight smile on his face told him he had heard as Crawford had intended. "Could you find Peter Barnard and send him to me please?" The young man did not say anything just nodded and took the phone before leaving the room. Crawford dipped into his pocket and pulling out his cell phone switched it off before dropping it on one of the tables and stretching out on the sofa next the window to try and get some sleep.

+

Danielle had realised Benson was not nearly as drunk as he seemed most of the time but was still trying to figure out why. She smiled at him and accepted the offer of a lift back to the site after all the rest of the team had driven off and left her there on her own, well almost on her own. She had slipped into the back seat of Karl's two door, 'had once been white' sports car and suddenly realised it might be a mistake as old Jock had stepped forward but Karl had dropped the seat back into place forcing the old man into the front seat. Jock had glowered but shrugged and sighed as he pulled the door closed behind him.
It wasn't long before they drew up at the end of the row of houses and Karl gave Jock a nudge to wake him. "Come on old fella, you're home. Get yourself inside and put the kettle on. I'll get the bottle out when I get back shortly." He glanced over his shoulder at Danielle as he spoke "I have to take Danielle back to her place first." Jock just nodded and rolled himself out of the car before ambling off towards the door to his own home. Danielle leant forward onto the seat back in front of her and smiled at Karl "You don't need to do this you know" he nodded and smiled back at her in the mirror as he said "I know, but if I don't no one will." Danielle hesitated; his voice was different and sounded softer somehow. He carried on talking "I know, it doesn't fit the image, but to be honest there is a lot that is just that, an image." He sighed "The image is my job, my job is the image. Sometimes it's difficult to remember who I actually am compared to which image and name I am using at the time." He looked round at her as he drove slowly through the estate towards the offices "Remind me sometime after all this is over and I'll tell you some stories." He grinned and looked forward again as she laughed softly close by, he liked that

206

sound. "Drop me at the offices please. I have one of the apartments upstairs at the moment." She looked down and bit her lip for a second before saying "I can make you a coffee if you want, but coffee is all that's on offer." He nodded, "I understand, that would be nice. It would actually be nice to have a friend I didn't need to lie to as well." She smiled again "Well, let's just see what happens on that will we?" he nodded as the car drew up alongside the old stone building.

+

The under manager was beginning to think this Silver Organisation bunch were more hassle than they were worth, when he got a call from the chambermaids office. "You'd better come and see this, room four twenty seven and be ready to call the police." He hesitated as the phone was hung up, he would not normally have bothered going to look at a messy room. That would be the job of the head housekeeper but she was the one who had called, he shrugged, he would find out soon enough.

When he stepped out of the lift he saw the room door was unlocked immediately, with the head chambermaid standing in front of it with an arm around one of the younger chambermaids who was sobbing softly. The head chambermaid eased to one side and nodded inside "Don't touch anything." was all she said as he stepped past her and pushed on the door with his knuckle. The bathroom was just inside the door and the door to it was open as well, he glanced in and froze. The naked mans body was on its knees in front of the toilet looking as if he was trying to be sick but the bulging eyes and pale blue colour of the skin told a different story. The under manager struggled not to be sick himself as he stepped back into the room and looked again. It took him a moment to realise the brown figure on the bed was a naked female form, she wasn't moving either.

He stepped back into the hall and pulled the door closed behind him and looked at the head housekeeper as she was still comforting the young girl who had found the bodies. "Take her to your office and wait there until the police arrive." He looked down at the girl and smiled "The police will need to speak to you about what you saw and what you touched." She just nodded and let herself be led away as he pulled the telephone handset out of his pocket and called the police.

+

Trente Silver was sitting looking at his list of phone numbers and right at the top was the assassin's number, he was tempted but even in his temper he knew that was probably not a good answer. After all there would be more than one to be targeted and he did not know who they would be. He sighed as he realised the guy had missed the last time anyway and had taken out a journalist rather than the guy he was meant to shoot, didn't even look like it had scared him away either so that had been a waste of money.

Suddenly he smiled as his eyes landed on a number on the list, this might be a way to call in an investment. He glanced at the clock on the wall and figured out the time difference before he lifted the receiver.

+

The bar at the local hotel was crowded as most of the locals celebrated their victory at the council chambers that day. It was a noisy and happy crowd generally, with good humour and fun being the most important thing to most people. Mark sat fairly quiet in a corner, watching everyone having fun as they laughed at how close it had been. It was Marianne who was sitting opposite him and had actually known him the longest that asked him the question "Are you alright? You seem to be very quiet after the vote today. You must take some pleasure out of that?" he smiled at her and said "Yes I do take pleasure out of that, and the company of good long term friends." Marianne blushed slightly and glanced quickly sideways at Mike as Mark carried on talking "but I am wary of what the Silver Organisation will do now. They were far from happy at getting rejected there today. It could be a case of acting like the spoilt children they actually are and the toys will come out of the pram." Jennifer giggled as she sat there next to him, she'd probably had too much wine already but it felt good sitting here with friends. Mark looked sideways at her and grinned as he saw the more than normally relaxed smile on her face. "They might go to ground for a day or two, but I would expect them to come back out fighting. Trouble is I don't know what they can do." Marianne stretched a little as she thought about it "Can they get their pals in the Capital to call it in?" Mark shook his head "I don't know, I don't think so. I've never heard of an application being called in after it was refused. I thought the legislation only allowed for it to be called in if it was approved where it shouldn't be." He shrugged "Technically the application is dead, as I understand it anyway, and to go on with it they will need to resubmit a new application." He shrugged again "We'll need to wait and see what happens." Suddenly he smiled as he saw Mikes head nod. "Why don't we get Johns taxi to take us all to my place and you two can stay overnight. I have the space and its only five minutes up the road instead of thirty minutes into town." Marianne looked at Mike who was struggling to keep his eyes open as Mark continued "Anyway, none of you are fit to drive." Marianne just grinned at him and nodded "Okay then; whenever you're ready."

+

Dull was not happy when he arrived back at the Wycliffe hotel to find a large number of police vehicles parked in front of the building so that Peter Barnard, who was giving him a lift, could not get to the front door to drop him off. Suddenly his heart sank, this would not look good no matter what it was, the only saving grace was that it might not make the news because of what had happened in town today. He was wrong.

+

Old Jock stood in his garden and looked around, sighing softly, in many ways he was quite pleased the place would stay looking the same as it always had done. After all it had looked like this for almost all of the fifty years he had stayed there. Okay the sand shifted but that was what it was meant to do wasn't it? He made to turn and go inside when Carol called across from her own garden "Hallo Jock how are you?" he sighed he knew it would be the best part of an hour before he got away from her now. "I'm well Carol, I'm well, how are you?" She smiled at him and prattled on for a few minutes about a problem she'd been having with a tile fixer who couldn't measure. He smiled and nodded and was about to claim to be tired when she asked "How did it go today? Did they get their permission?" Jock looked at her surprised she didn't know the result but smiled "No, they didn't get it. The council threw it out." Carol stared at him, in disbelief "That can't be, they were meant to get it so the value of our house would go up. That just can't be." Without another word she turned and ran back to her own house at the end of the row. Jock smiled and looked at his watch, that must have been the shortest conversation they had ever had in the fourteen or fifteen years she had lived there. He turned and pushed open the door to his own house.

+

Mark had Johns taxi take them down the big house driveway and out past the stables so he could stop and see if Arthur was okay. He had the car drive past then stop before he jumped out and went back to have a look. The little cottage was in darkness but as he opened the gate the door opened and Arthur looked out at him in the dim evening light. "I hoped you'd come in past at least." Mark smiled at the old man "Well, we won today. We'll have to see how long it lasts or what other tricks they pull out of the hat but so far we're ahead." Arthur smiled at him and looked past him towards the car that sat a little way off "You'd better go back to your friends, they're waiting on you." Mark smiled again "Okay but I'll come and see you tomorrow at some point." Arthur just nodded as Mark continued "See you tomorrow and make sure and shut the door." Mark waited until he heard the bar drop into place before he turned back to the taxi and went home.

+

The councillor's lounge had a bar that was not always open, but it was tonight and Padruig McCarthy was grateful of that fact as he stood there glass in hand. A few of his colleagues had congratulated him on his courage which was a phrase he didn't understand. He sighed as he heard a movement and knew what to expect when he turned around and there was Marlene, the leader of the council, she didn't believe in polite conversation. "How could you be so stupid?" was her opening comment followed rapidly by "Everyone knows just how good a development this is for this area. It must go ahead, I want you to apologise to all your colleagues immediately and you should consider resigning your seat as soon as you can." Padruig shook his head "If anyone here needs to resign, it's you, Have you never heard of ethics?" She stared at him almost as if he had slapped her across the face and turning away stormed out of the room. It was almost as if no one breathed until the door closed behind her. Padruig shrugged and turned back towards the bar, he noticed there was a difference in the room as the councillors split into two obvious groups those who were afraid of Marlene and those who were not. He smiled as he looked at the group opposite, there was another similarity, those who were afraid of Marlene were the ones most people thought took 'honorariums' and any other fancy word you could choose to describe a bung or a bribe. That said more to him than any threat did.

12

The next morning Mark was up and making coffee when he heard the sound of bare feet coming down the stairs, he turned and was surprised to see Marianne in a robe smiling at him from the door to the kitchen. "What are you doing up so early?" he asked and she laughed softly "Some welcome that, I thought you might remember I was always an early riser and welcome a little company." He smiled as she walked across the floor towards him and draped her arms around his neck "Mike is fast asleep and if we leave him it'll be ten before he wakes, especially when it's Saturday." Mark nodded and kissed her before saying "Jennifer is pretty much the same, so," he glanced at his watch "that gives us four hours before we have company" Marianne giggled softly "You don't improve, still as naughty as ever." He smiled back as he hugged her close "You and Mike are getting on well." She nodded and whispered in his ear "Yeah, he's a great guy, just not you and I don't think he's the marrying kind. So I'm grateful for what I have with him and can but hope that he wants to marry me some day." She sighed and leant back away from him so she could look into his face "If he doesn't then maybe things might change and we might be able to make a go of it again?" Mark just sighed "It's always possible, but I'm with Jennifer just now and I'm not going to change that no matter what else is around." He was openly looking at Marianne's body under that robe as he spoke and she was not trying to hide. She shook her head "I know, you're a gentleman with eyes. That was always the trouble, would never harm anyone or do anything to hurt them, but you did enjoy looking." He just nodded as she spoke and they stepped apart as she said "At least we understand each other." As she stepped away from him she reached out and switched on the radio that sat on the top of the old dresser where it always had done as far as she could remember. He grinned as she turned and walked away to sit down at the table, tightening the sash on her robe.

Suddenly he froze as the reporter said "After yesterdays defeat the Silver Organisation appears to have withdrawn all public contact. It is believed that none of the media organisations have been able to get a response at all from the telephone numbers or email address used by the organisation in this country and as such we have no comment from them at all. Their opponents on the other hand have been quite vociferous when the opportunity arose." The next voice was Marks from an interview he had given about four days before and Marianne looked at him puzzled as she listened. The reporter moved on to another subject as she swivelled her blonde head to look at Mark "I don't remember you giving an interview last night" Mark shook his head "No, that's because I didn't. That one was given almost a week ago and that is only part of it;" he paused "a carefully selected part of it." Marianne looked at him, thinking about what was going to happen with all of this. He sighed and poured himself a coffee as the machine had just finished, and waved a mug in Marianne's direction. She nodded and stood up to follow him outside as he opened the door.

It was a cool and fresh morning with a hint of coolness that made them shiver in the thin robes that was all either of them were wearing. The scent of a still morning by the seaside filled the air, the tang of salt and clean sand along with something indefinable, that might have been hope, or then again might have been wet earth steaming in the heat of a newly risen sun, the wisps of steam were rising from the ground and forming low level fog in the hollows between the sea and the bank upon which this house sat. He sat down on the cool slightly damp grass and squirmed a little, he hadn't realised just how cold it would be as Marianne looked down at him disapprovingly, "I'm not sitting in the ground." He smiled up at her "Then sit on my knee." She shrugged and did as he suggested. For a few minutes they sat there and watched as the deer ran from one clump of trees through the mist to another clump of trees down below them in the hollow. Then Marianne squirmed in his lap and said "Don't take this the wrong way, its almost perfect just sitting her with you like this but, it would be better for me if it was Mike." Mark nodded "I understand and it's the same for me. Jennifer means a lot and I wish she was here now rather than asleep inside, but I don't mind being with a friend either." Marianne just grinned and cuddled in against him for a few moments, before they both stood up and went back inside the house.

Once inside Marianne giggled as she looked at the back of his robe and the dirty patch on his back side where he had been sitting on the ground. Mark shrugged and she shook her head at him as they poured more coffee and went through to watch the morning news on the television in the living room. It was there the first of the real news broke.

The presenter on the morning show was shaking her head as she said "I don't really know what to make of this, it would appear that a high court injunction has been raised against the local authority in Drimmie to prevent them issuing a notice of refusal to the Silver organisation regarding their failed planning application for a housing development and golf course." She paused and put a hand up to her ear "Sorry, I've just been advised that we are required to call it a 'golf resort' at all times, but no one is telling me who is making that requirement" She looked up at the screen and continued

212

talking generally about the events of yesterday as Marianne turned to look at Mark "What does that mean?" Mark shook his head "I don't know," Mark shook his head "I don't know what that is all about. I don't know what that means at all." He chewed his lip and Marianne sighed and stood up "I'm going to get dressed, back in a minute or two." Mark nodded as he watched her leave the room, remembering they used to have fun together a few years ago. He was pleased to see Mike and her were getting on well together, he needed the company and she would be good for him.

The picture caught his eye and he turned back to the screen to watch as a picture of the front of the Wycliffe hotel surrounded by police cars appeared. He listened as the presenters voice said two people had been found dead at the Wycliffe hotel and the deaths were being treated as suspicious at this time. He was watching the screen and was sure that was Peter Barnard's car driving across the shot with Marcus Dull in the passenger's seat. The story didn't say much more but left him wondering about what had happened and who the victims were.

It was almost half an hour later when he was sitting in the kitchen laughing with Marianne again when the door bell went. She looked at him puzzled as he frowned and stood up "Still only strangers that use the door bell?" She said as he headed towards the front door "Yeah, everyone else usually knocks and walks in"

Mark knew before he got there it was the police. The same Police Inspector who had met him at the big house when Paul had been hurt, stared at him as he opened the door. "How did I guess that you would be involved in this?" Mark just shrugged "Could just be lucky I guess. Either way you'd better come in." Without waiting for an answer Mark had turned and walked away to his office

Marianne followed the two of them into the office before Mark could shut the door and smiled at the inspector as she set down a tray with cups and milk on it. She smiled at him "Tea or Coffee?" He was taken aback as he looked at her "Eh, tea please" he said, thrown off guard a little. Mark just smiled as he sat down behind the desk and looked across at the inspector who had that face of delivering bad news but needing to ask a lot of questions at the same time. He sighed and decided to launch straight into it "How well did you know Mandy Johansson?" Mark shrugged and sighed, he knew what this was about "Fairly well I guess, she used to clean and model for me" The inspector looked at him more closely "Model for you?" Mark shrugged and switched on the computer on the desk. The two men spoke freely for a while before the inspector walked round the desk and looked at some of the pictures on the computer screen that Mark was showing him, nodding as he looked at them "You couldn't spare me a couple of decent portrait prints could you? One for our enquiry and one for her mother, she doesn't seem to have a lot of recent photos of her daughter." Mark just nodded and did as he was asked while he said "I feel sorry for Mandy for what it's worth. She was basically a good kid, trying to get by. She obviously got into bad company with the Silver Organisation and everything that went down there." He paused and the inspector could see he was thinking so he stayed quiet. "Grayson, was a waste of skin I wouldn't have pissed on if he was on fire, Mandy just needed a bit more guidance I think." The inspector sighed "I can't comment on Grayson for professional reasons but for what's its worth, it sounds like Mandy died happy, she was covered in chocolate body paint and had enough drugs in her system to anaesthetise half of Drimmie." Mark nodded as the inspector spoke. It was another half hour or so before Mark closed the door behind the police inspector who went away with a lot more information than when he had arrived.

+

'Xander was screaming at the little man in the grey suit "I don't care what you fucking think. Just do as you're told." Templeton watched from his seat against the wall as the civil servant stood up and polished his glasses obviously wondering if it was worth his while replying to a man so blatantly ignorant. Deciding it wasn't worth the effort he turned and walked from the room, shaking his head as he did so.

Templeton looked at 'Xander and the veins standing out on his neck and drew breath before he spoke. "Are you sure that's wise?" 'Xander's head swivelled round to look at him. "I mean he is the head planner and he knows the law. Why not take his advice?" 'Xander studied Templeton closely, the man had changed in recent weeks, almost as if he wasn't scared of him any more, that wasn't good. He had enough on Templeton to cause him problems, maybe even end his career, but it would almost certainly be the end of him as well. He shook himself, that couldn't happen; he was President after all. He stared at Templeton and instead of squirming the man smiled back at him. 'Xander began to shout "When I need your advice, I'll ask for it. Meanwhile go do your job which is make sure this happens." Templeton sat there and looked at him "I don't think this is legal, there is definitely no precedent for it and it could bring a lot of scrutiny down on you if you push this as far as that." 'Xander stared at him for a second. When he spoke his voice was cold and lower in tone, almost growling. This was his last warning before he got physical "I've already
214

told you what to do with your opinion now go and do your job. Get out of my office." Templeton shrugged and ambled casually out of the room with 'Xander staring after him, unhappy and uncomfortable at the other mans casual attitude to being threatened.

+

Peter Barnard had been horrified last night when he returned to the hotel and found out what had happened. Now he had time to think about it he was physically terrified. He had been the one who had booked the room through Dull for the Silver Organisation for 'entertainment purposes', he had been the one who had told Benson to help out with girls and drugs. The fact it had been Mandy was just the way these things happened sometimes, but now he was genuinely scared. Too many things looked to be stacking up here. How could Benson have been so stupid as to give Grayson as much as he could kill himself in one session. That man had been just another self serving idiot who may now have cost a lot of people a lot of time and effort.

+

Steve the lawyer was shrugging his shoulders as he spoke to Mark later that same day "The case will probably go uncontested now that Grayson is dead but instead of starting tomorrow it will now be at least another week until they figure out of there are any other implications." Mark sighed "Well I must admit I would have liked to get it over and done with. The delay is technically neither here nor there as far as I am concerned. I just want it finished, especially now Sharon is dead. Steve agreed and the two men spoke for a few minutes more before they broke the connection and Mark turned to Jennifer who was still running around in a robe, even though Mike and Marianne had left almost half an hour previously. "What do you think?" Jennifer looked at him "About what?" "This planning thing," he replied "do you think Silver and his mob will walk away or will they try and do something else instead?" Jennifer sat back and looked at him "I'm not sure. I've done a little bit of background digging but not as much as you. To be honest I think they will have some other dirty trick up their sleeve. That's more their style than anything else." Mark nodded "I'm afraid I agree with you," he turned and looked at the table in front of him "I will be surprised if they know when they've lost." Jennifer nodded and looked down at him "Anyway, I need to put some clothes on and go and get some more clothes." Mark looked up at her "No what you need to do is go and put some clothes on and go and get all of your stuff so you can move in here properly" Jennifer looked him in the eyes and sat down again

"No," she said "That's not going to happen just yet." She put her hand on top of his as she looked at his face "I'm not ready for that. I think I love you and I definitely love being with you and your friends, who have become my friends; but I'm not sure yet. I still don't think I'm ready in myself after my divorce and my betrayal by my husband." She sighed as she saw the surprise in his eyes "I enjoy sleeping beside you and making love to you but I still feel the need to have my own independence. My own place to run to if I need it, can you let me have that for a while at least? Let me come to you in my own time." Mark nodded "If that's what you want I'm not going to stop you." He sighed as he leant back in the chair "When you're ready just let me know and you can move the rest of your stuff in. I want you here, with me, but that is up to you. It takes two of us to make that choice." Jennifer didn't say anything to that, she just got up and went back upstairs to get dressed.

Mark eventually stood up and walked over to the kitchen window and stood there looking out at the sand and the sea not really seeing much, just lost in thoughts and memories.

+

Marcus Dull was ready for his press conference at the hotel as he stood there in front of the mirror in his own apartment, confident he was cutting a dashing figure, until he turned sideways that is. He shook his head and turned back to study himself in the mirror, he was nervous, but sober and that scared him in itself. He realised he had not been fully sober for some years, being stopped in his car the previous day had been enough to scare it out of him; for just now anyway. He drew breath and walked downstairs, through reception and into the conference room where he was holding the press conference. He stopped for a second at the side door when he saw almost fifty journalists in the room with TV cameras, that was double what he had expected and they looked quite different when he was sober.
 He drew himself up to his full height and still no one noticed him until he walked up to the lectern and stepped onto the polished wooden step behind it. "Good day Ladies and Gentlemen," he started slightly as the lights came on and the room fell silent almost immediately, he liked the feel of this, it might be something to get used to. He looked out into the room and began to speak "As a respected member of the local business community I'd like to put forward the opinion of the majority of the local business regarding the disgraceful behaviour of Councillor McCarthy yesterday in deliberately going against council policy and practice in his voting pattern." The silence from the room was almost palpable but he could see the reporters all shuffling their feet and looking bored until one of them shouted out "Your

216

wasting our time. What about the murder?" Dull went gray, that was the last thing he wanted to talk about "I'm sorry I can't say anything about that while there is a live police investigation on going" The voice came from behind the lights again as he began to sweat "Can you confirm it was Grayson from the *Evening*' and a young girl that were found dead?" Dull was obviously sweating now as he replied "I'm sorry I can't comment on that" The press pushed him again by saying "We've been told that it was you who booked the room for the Silver organisation, is that true?" He was almost running from the room as he said "I'm sorry, I cannot comment on the unfortunate deaths that have no connection whatsoever with the Wycliffe hotel" The voice came back "You mean no connection other than they occurred here in a room booked by you for an out of town organisation that is based here at the moment and one of the dead people was a newspaper editor who you have been seen entertaining routinely for weeks." Dull stepped away from the lectern "I'm sorry that is the end of the news conference I will put my information out by written press release instead."

Turning, the little man left the room by the side door and leant on it as it clicked shut behind him. He closed his eyes and looked down at himself; he was scared and shaking never having had to face the barrage of the press in such a manner before. He looked up and felt his shoulders slump even further as he realised he was looking at the furious face of Andrew Crawford who did not look as if he wanted to buy him the drink he felt he so badly needed.

+

Marlene had called a meeting of her party members to see if there really was enough support to do what it was she wanted to do. She knew most of them were afraid of her one way or another which was usually quite useful but had to be dealt with carefully; there was not a lot of difference between being feared and being despised. She could get away with being feared, that seemed to be what almost all of the best leaders had been while being despised might actually cost her votes next time round. She had to handle this carefully.

Slowly she looked around the meeting room, noting with satisfaction her acolytes were spread around the room fairly evenly, mixed in with the untrustworthy ones, except at the left hand side of the room. There was a cluster of what she referred to as renegades all sitting together and each and every one of them hated her. Right in the middle of the group sat Padruig

McCarthy, that was a problem, he was not meant to even be aware of this meeting.

She sighed inwardly before opening her mouth to speak. "I've called this meeting of the party to see what we can recover from the mess Padruig has dropped us in." She paused, just for a second, not really long enough for anyone to interject before adding "I take it we all accept that this is a mess and we should never have gotten into this place." Dianne stood up and spoke, not waiting to be pointed out by Marlene who was surprised at the way she started to speak. "Yes I think almost everyone in this hall accepts that we should not be in this position, because this unacceptable scheme should have been turned down at the local committee stage. There was no need for it to get as far as the Infrastructure and Services Committee; it should have been sent back to the applicant for reconsideration at a far earlier stage." It wasn't that she stopped speaking, that no one heard what she said next; it was due to the volume of noise being generated by her Acolytes and one or two other weak individuals in the mass of councillors who began shouting and swearing at her, and an almost equal number who began shouting in response and in her defence.

Padruig McCarthy sat there silently in the midst of what looked like a scene from a bad movie about a madhouse, all it really needed to complete the picture was for them to start throwing chairs at one another. Slowly he stood up and walked out of the hall shaking his head.

It was nearly midnight before the meeting broke up and the members of the party began to spill out into the corridors to go home. The press that were still waiting for them were glad to see them start to appear. The council chambers were a boring place to wait at the best of times, let alone at night when almost everyone had gone home already.

Marlene strode forward and addressed the press as a whole. "The party has nothing to say about tonight's internal meeting. The subject matter and outcome of which is private to the party and should be subject to political privilege." The press just looked at her, and then looked past her at the rest of the councillors as they left the building and scattered in all directions.

The next day's paper did not say much about it.

+

Mark was surprised the next morning when he received a call from Steve, his solicitor, very short and to the point. "Can you come into my office,

218

now, please? There's something here you need to see, bring a laptop. A clean one if you still have such a thing." Mark didn't hesitate when his friend asked for him to come immediately, there was a reason. Jennifer had already left for work so it was less than ten minutes later before Mark was on his way into town.

The receptionist still gave him a frosty look but led him straight through to Marianne's office where both she and Steve were waiting on him. Neither of them said anything at first, Steve just nudged the brown padded envelope on the desk towards him. Mark looked down at it and read the address; it didn't have a name as such on it. It was addressed to the owner of Paradigm Archaeology, care of Steve's legal practice. Mark said "Hmmm," as he turned it over with the end of a pen, not really touching the envelope "No return address either. Have to say it smells okay and there's no oil stains, might be okay, but definitely strange." Steve nodded "My thoughts exactly, probably okay but I thought you might like a look at it as well before we open it." Mark looked at him and nodded "Marianne, go hang around in the kitchen for five minutes please." She looked upset and annoyed but calmed quickly when Mark turned to her, smiled at her and continued "Don't know exactly what's in this but we need to open it, less people around to get hurt if it is nasty, the better," he smiled again "and you're too pretty to get hurt." She relented even though her curiosity was such that she really did not want to go.

Marianne had just finished making three mugs of coffee when Steve slid into the door way, "It's safe come back through." and vanished again, Marianne shook her head and did as she was told.
When she walked back in Mark was sitting at her desk with Steve standing behind him looking over his shoulder. Marianne eased herself round behind her desk and looked down at the screen on the laptop. Mark smiled up at her as she set the mugs of coffee on the desk "There was a memory stick in the envelope, no note and nothing else. Steve obviously had had a good old fondle of the envelope before he called me and knew what was inside." He looked up at his friend who shrugged "I wouldn't say I knew, but I had a fair suspicion." Mark looked up at Marianne who still looked puzzled "That's why I needed the laptop. This one is what we call clean, nothing of value on it and a very strong anti virus programme so we can plug anything into it with a fair amount of confidence it won't come to any harm. This," he nodded at the screen "is a word document with track changes switched on." Marianne was still puzzled "What does that mean, I'm sorry I don't understand the significance of this" Steve stepped back and to one side as he picked up a mug from the desk. "I'm sorry Mark. I'm in the same place. I don't understand either." Mark smiled "That's okay, you lot haven't read

this or some of the back ground to it. This is the final report to the planning committee for the Silver Organisation development. With all the changes tracked and made visible. This shows who wrote what initially and who changed what and when. It is solid evidence that the report that went to council has been massaged extensively to give the result some one wanted. On the disk is also a text file, which might tell us who the author of all this is and an email archive which could be even more revealing." He leant back and pushed a fey keys and the machine began to hum. Steve suddenly looked worried "What are you doing, Mark?" He shrugged "I'm getting ready to unplug the drive so you can hand it to the police, or at least put it somewhere safe until some one comes looking for it, like maybe the police." Marianne looked at him "What makes you think the police will be looking for it?" Mark shrugged, "Not sure" he said "just a hunch really. Someone thought this was important enough to send to us anonymously, so that usually means that someone else will be trying to stop us getting this information or will at least be trying to find out where it went." He shrugged again "I just want to be ready for it so it doesn't come as a complete surprise." Steve and Marianne were both nodding as Mark pressed his knuckles around the pen drive and pulled it from the computer before dropping it back into the envelope. Marianne noticed he was holding it between his knuckles again; she frowned but did not ask any questions. She was realising these guys knew what they were doing here and it was something that she knew nothing about, she wasn't even sure what it was they were actually doing.

Steve took the envelope from his friend and smiled at Marianne as he said "My fingerprints are already on the envelope so there's no need to try and hide them but no one needs to know Mark touched this or has seen the contents" Marianne suddenly realised why the knuckles had been used. "What were you two guys, thieves?" Mark shook his head as Steve laughed "Soldiers, a long time ago, given us a slightly different outlook on life." The two men fell silent as they both thought about that comment for a second. Mark shut the laptop with a click and turned to Marianne.

"How is Paradigm Archaeology getting on, ready to move into your new offices yet?" Marianne smiled as he stood up and gave her back her seat "Almost" was her reply "They are almost ready to take over, should be ready by the end of the week then we have to paint and furnish and move our stuff out of storage or the university." Suddenly she paused "Oh, did I tell you they had threatened me?" Mark and Steve both looked at her in surprise as she recounted her version of events with the university.

+

It was almost a week later that the news broke in the general media, although it had been whispered locally for a while. The '*Evening*' said absolutely nothing about it and the '*Daily*' said only fractionally more. What it did say was a small internal headline that read 'Changes in committee makeup afoot?' It was a very subtle and understated way of not telling everyone what was happening. Mark looked at the paper and frowned, it was one of those headlines that basically told him they were not telling him what was happening. Standing up he went through to his computer and began to read the national newspapers on line. He shook his head, it was always amazing to him when a local newspaper could actually carry less detail than a national. Eventually he sat back and thought for a moment before picking up the phone, he had to get a few people together and get some information out to the public.

It was almost another week later that the meeting of the full council was gathering with the majority of the councillors being present. They appeared to be horrified when they suddenly realised the public gallery was going to be full to overflowing as the press began to appear as well as members of the general public. Even after hasty arrangements to get as many people as possible into the hall and in the adjoining ante room with a CCTV screen made available to them; there were still people standing outside showing support for Padruig McCarthy. It turned out that the already unpopular Councillor Wilt had been stupid enough to allow himself to be used again. He had filed a motion to council that Padruig McCarthy had brought the council into disrepute by voting against the planning application. There were others who would be against the motion.

The Chief Executive of the council looked tired as he stood up and called the meeting to order "ladies and gentlemen, this meeting has been called with a single specific purpose in hand. That is the motion, filed by Councillor Wilt, to de select Councillor McCarthy from the chair of the Infrastructure Services Committee. With no more ado I will hand over to the leader of the council to begin the debate." He shook his head and sat down again, obviously uncomfortable with the situation.

Marlene stood up and cleared her throat before smiling at every councillor in the room; that scared most of them worse than any threat could have done. "Fellow councillors" she began as her eyes ran across the public gallery and she froze for a second as her eyes met those of Mark as he sat watching the proceedings. The pause was barely noticeable as she carried on speaking "We are here today to try and correct a major error in protocol and a wilful ignoring of the will of the council and of those that they represent. The cause of that error was that Councillor McCarthy the chair of the committee, chose to do his own thing rather than follow the advice of the councils professional advisers and that of his fellow councillors. The motion, kindly filed by Councillor Wilt, states that the damage to the councils reputation is such that the only way to make amends and attempt to correct the situation is to remove Councillor McCarthy from his position of chair of the relevant committee. I personally agree with the motion and believe that this development would benefit the whole area for many years to come, especially after the oil runs out in less than five years time." She paused again and looked around the near silent chamber, Mark saw a little schoolgirl smirk cross her face before she continued "I therefore call upon councillor Wilt to put the motion before council." She stepped back and sat down again looking around the room getting nods from a mixture of councillor's as well as a few scowls and completely blank looks form others. Everyone stopped listening when Councillor Wilt stood up to speak and it was almost two hours later that he sat down with no one really having the faintest clue about exactly what he had said. The meeting dragged on and on with the audience becoming uncomfortable and eventually it came to the last stage where the Chief executive stood up and said "ladies and gentlemen we have come to the final stage of this meeting, but before you vote on the matter there is one person who still has the right to speak and has not yet done so. I now call upon Councillor McCarthy to speak if he wishes to do so." The Chief Executive sat down and a rather bemused looking Padruig slowly rose to his feet looking around the large and strangely silent chamber. "Well ladies and gentlemen, a strange place you have brought us to Marlene. This is meant to be one of the cornerstones of democracy, at the grass roots level as it is generally known. This is where it is meant to be right, for the people who make up this country not where things are manipulated for the benefit of a handful of self serving politicians and fraudsters." He paused and looked around the room. "There has been a lot of inaccurate rubbish spoken here today about the protocols and procedures that should be followed in order to allow democracy to happen. All you need to know is the simple fact that I followed the legal and moral protocols that should control this authority to the letter. If you do not agree with what I did, you do not agree with democracy. You have to make up your mind on the facts, not the opinions that have been stated here today and on that note I have said all I am going to say, you must now allow your own conscience to make up your own mind and vote accordingly." Padruig sat down to a smattering of applause from the crowd, both councillors and public.

Slowly the Chief Executive stood up and looked down at his aide by his side who sat ready with a pen and carefully marked out note pad. Drawing breath he said "Okay ladies and gentlemen you all know the process by now. It is simple, I will call out each Councillors name, in alphabetical order, and as a reply I require you to say 'Motion' to support Councillor Wilts motion to oust Councillor McCarthy; 'Amend' to support the amendment which is to commend Councillor McCarthy for his courage in doing what is right or finally 'Abstain'." He paused and looked around the room, his eyes lingering on the press and the public in the gallery, almost every one of them taking copious notes. He turned back and faced the chamber "With no further ado let us commence."

There were seventy two councillors in the chamber that day, almost a full turn out and it took an hour or slightly more for the voting process to be completed and another half hour for the votes to be checked and double checked.

The Chief executives voice wavered as he said "The results of the vote are as follows. There were eighteen votes to amend. Nineteen votes support the motion and thirty five abstentions" The hall was silent as was the public gallery as he continued "The motion is therefore carried by one vote. I call this meeting to a close and finish of business for today." The noise as his hammer came down was one of people talking all amazed at the outcome.
The press caught Mark as he stepped out of the door and hesitated at the top step. "Can you tell us your position on the vote recently announced in chamber to oust Councillor McCarthy from his role as chair of the Infrastructure and Services Committee?" Mark hesitated before he replied "I have to say I have never seen such a misuse of authority by a group of so called adults. This was a personal spite vote organised by the leader of the council to oust some one who had dared to do what was right rather than what he was told. Those who did not vote are almost worse than those who voted to oust Councillor McCarthy. In the position of a councillor if you are not willing to express your opinion you should not be a councillor." He drew breath and looked around at the cameras and microphones that seemed to be gathering rapidly around him. "An abstention is only an option in a very few extreme situations, not a 'cop out' as it was here today."

+

The police Inspector sighed as he pushed open the door to the house, it was an unremarkable little flat in one of the housing estates in Drimmie. The woman who lived here had the upstairs flat and her door opened straight onto the stair which led right into the living room; it was the balustrade at the top of the stairs that she had used to hang herself from. He could see her feet from here as the scene of crimes staff were busy taking photographs.

He looked at the doctor who had just confirmed death "Suicide?" The doctor shook his head "Don't think so" he replied "I mean, that's your end of the business but there's lot of what I would call defensive marks on her arms and the place has been turned over. Could be wrong but it looks suspicious to me." The inspector sighed and said "Thanks doc. Always appreciate your interpretation." The sergeant next to him looked pale "First local murder?" The sergeant nodded "I knew her, not well but knew who she was. Planner with the local council, been a civil servant all her life, quieter more peaceful person you couldn't hope to meet. Well balanced and reasonably happy until recently as well." The inspector frowned so the sergeant shrugged "Probably not relevant but she was involved with this Silver application that there's been so much fuss about lately; She was getting quite upset about it. She said something about reports being changed and all that type of thing." The sergeant went quiet "I didn't take it seriously, should I have?" The inspector shrugged "Maybe, seems to be a lot being spoken about with regard to this planning application. Maybe need to look more closely at that, even if it is just to rule it out." he turned back to look at the stair case "Who found her?" The sergeant looked down at his notebook "Her mother, worried about not hearing from her, came round and opened the door; called the police immediately." He looked up at the inspector "Want to speak to her?" The inspector shook his head "Not yet, maybe later" The sergeant looked around before he said "She wants to speak to you, said she had something that might be important to whoever was leading the investigation." The inspector turned and looked back at him but said nothing. He hated 'things that might be important' from family members. They usually turned out to be complete garbage and of no relevance to man nor dog. He was going to be wrong this time.

The woman, the dead woman's mother, was already sitting in the station talking to a liaison officer, but she wouldn't let the envelope out of her hands. It was a cheap brown envelope, the type local authorities use by the thousand, sealed and on the front of it, written in blue felt tip pen was the note. 'To the police if anything happens to me, Love Myra' The inspector came and sat down at the opposite side of the table, his eyes on the envelope as it was turned round and round and round and over and over in the older woman's hands. She looked at him blankly for a few seconds as the liaison officer introduced him as leading the case before she smiled at last and held out the envelope. "She left this with me last week. I laughed at her, I told her she was a planner, not a spy no one would want to hurt her." She paused and her voice went quiet as her face looked down at the desk in front of her "I was wrong wasn't I? Some one did kill her didn't they?" He hesitated as he took the envelope with a paper tissue and dropped it into a clear plastic bag. She watched and muttered "Just like on the telly, here,"

224

she said dropping a larger brown envelope on the table "it was in this as a protection so no one could see what it said on the front of the envelope" she watched as he again, took it with a tissue and dropped it into another clear polythene bag. He was beginning to feel sick.

+

'Xander was also feeling sick, he had just received the phone call he had been dreading from the states. It had been some unidentified 'security company' as they called themselves. The individual had access to the relevant terms and phone numbers that meant he could speak directly to the President himself and did so. 'Xander sat back and stared at the telephone as if it was some poisonous creature that might bite him if he moved at all. He was too late, it already had.

There had been no threat made as such, just a comment that the memory stick and its information was now in this country, would he care to discuss a means of obtaining the original files? It was common blackmail, nothing else, but it was implied, not stated and he knew he had to do as he was told or he really was finished in more ways than one. He sighed and leant forward he would need to go over to Drimmie the next day.

Dull was standing just to one side in the reception area as the official car drove in and straight under the portico. 'Xander was out of the car as fast as the bodyguard was, and was halfway to the front door before most anyone realised he had moved. Dull stepped around the desk and across the carpet, they nodded to one another and 'Xander allowed himself to be led without a word, along to the room the Silver Organisation was using as an operational headquarters.

Andrew Crawford was waiting as he was ushered in and Dull turned away to make sure the right refreshments were supplied. Crawford barely stood up to welcome his guest as Peter Barnard and the architect arrived downstairs and made their way to the same room. 'Xander's bodyguard watched from the doorway with disinterest, he couldn't hear from here anyway.

Andrews waited until the waiting staff had left and the body guards had checked the doors before he spoke. "It's payback time now. What can you do to rescue our operation here?" 'Xander hesitated and decided he could try and bluff it out. "Why should I? All you need to do is what everyone else would be required to do in the same situation. Take your drawings away, make some minor modifications and resubmit them as a new

225

application, then I would expect them to be approved." Andrews stood up and walked casually across the room to another desk; speaking as he walked. "That's what you said last time. We are running out of patience and so are our financiers. If this isn't resolved soon, they may pull out and the project will fold. If that is the case any fees paid will require to be repaid." He had, by now, walked all the way back to the table where 'Xander sat and he placed a slightly glossy piece of card, face down on the table in front of 'Xander before walking back to his seat. 'Xander stared at the piece of card, it was about ten inches long by eight wide and he did not want to touch it but there was a desperation building in him to know what it showed. He resisted as he let his eyes linger on Andrews for a second longer. The other two just sat there and watched, sitting off to one side like a private audience to some small drama being played out. They said nothing.

'Xander shifted "What do you want me to do?" Andrews grinned, he had always known the man was weak. "Reinstate the application, simple. Oh, and approve it as well." 'Xander shook his head "No, that I cannot do." He sighed knowing there was nothing he could do "Let me speak to some one, see what our options are" Andrews nodded as 'Xander pulled out his phone and dialled a number. "Chief Planner" was all he said before the conversation started. The others sat there and watched as he walked around the large room obviously talking about technicalities.

He came back and sat down again having closed the phone. "Well," he said "It might be possible to get it called in. That would mean a full Public Local Inquiry which is exactly what one of the campaign groups has been asking for, so it might shut them up as well." He paused and looked at Andrews "Would that help?" Andrews shrugged "Only if you can guarantee that it is approved at that stage." 'Xander shrugged "I can't promise that, but I can give you a far better than average chance of getting away with it." At that point his phone buzzed in his inside pocket. He smiled as he saw the number displayed on it, he stood up and walked away to answer it. Andrew's stood up and followed him a few steps behind until he took the phone out of 'Xander's hand and said "Don't argue just do it." 'Xander was holding up his hand to ward off the body guard who had his gun half way out of it's holster, "Give me the phone back." Andrews sneered at him and threw him the phone "Your little fuck just hung up the phone on me. You'd better fire him. Now get out of here and do what you've been told to." 'Xander shook his head slowly before turning towards the door, knowing he really had very little choice. He waved at the body guard to follow him.

The door had barely clicked into place when Barnard was on his feet and turned over the photograph that lay on the table. He stared at the blank piece of paper as Andrews laughed at him. "Sometimes the threat is more important that the fact. Sometimes the fact does not even need to exist." He shook his head and left the room to go back to his own suite.

Dull watched as the President drove away; he was unhappy at being excluded from the room but maybe a little relieved, he had the impression that it had not gone as well as some people might have wanted it to.

+

Back over in the Capital the chief planner looked at his secretary and breathed deeply. The secretary had only been in this job for a few months but he could recognise that this quiet and serious man was in fact in an extreme temper, and from what he had heard on the phone he could see why. The senior planner jabbed at the button on the recording device and stopped the machine. The secretary said nothing as his boss sat back and looked at him. "That odious little man will get his own way on this one. I have to make the 'call in', first thing tomorrow morning but I still have my doubts about the legality of this whole thing." The secretary shook his head but knew better than to voice an opinion just yet. He was better to wait until asked if he wanted to do that. The older man sighed "Do yourself a favour at the moment. Forget you ever heard that conversation. The less people that know you were here today the better for you." He raised his head and leant back in his chair; I will take the disc and make use of it at the appropriate time." The younger man nodded as he stood up and left the room. He drew breath once he was outside the door, he really did not want to know too much about the outcome.

+

Templeton had heard about the call to the head planner long before 'Xander got back to the Capital and it had been all he could do to stop himself laughing out loud. He was back in comfort mode, sitting in his chair behind his desk looking out over the skyline of the capital turning that shiny black plastic block over and over in his hands, time and time again.

+

'Thug one' was in the estate office sitting in front of Peter Barnard's desk. Peter Barnard may have been sitting behind the desk but it was Andrew Crawford who was talking, although shouting was a better description.

"Tell me again," he was saying "What do you mean you didn't think to look for the information before you killed her." He was pacing back and forth, making a point of staying out of this mans reach, he knew what he could do and had in fact seen the outcome several times. He did not want to become another statistic to him. "I would have expected you to get the data first then do what you had to." The man shrugged "It was an accident, obviously I wanted the info first but she struggled too much and when I found her neck was broken it was the easiest way to do it was hang her from the stair and search the place." Andrews sighed "Okay, Okay, it's too late now for any recriminations anyway. We're going to get what we want; we've already got that agreement. Unfortunately there's going to be a delay due to other things so it shouldn't be too important but it could be embarrassing if the information surfaces in the wrong place. Let's just hope that doesn't happen." He sighed again and looked around "Where's Danielle? the less people that know about this the better." Peter Barnard shook his head. "I sent her home, don't worry about her. It may only be upstairs but the floor is concrete so it's as good as soundproof down here." Andrews nodded slowly "Good, good. Let's keep it that way."

Upstairs Danielle was sitting there shivering, frightened to move. The little toy she had bought off the internet, that was really little more than an electronic stethoscope, had worked better than she could have hoped. Now she was scared that she knew too much and might slip up later so that they had to 'tidy up'.

Almost half a kilometre away the watching team had the same thought. The two men looked at one another, this was old technology and it had meant they had to get close to the building one night to paint the window with tin oxide. Once that was done all they had to do was bounce a beam off microwaves off the glass and it acted like a loudspeaker in their head phones. Now they knew that at least one person had been killed by this lot and they would not hesitate to silence another young woman if they had to. This was turning out to be more than a financial investigation, they waited until Andrews and 'thug one' had both left the building and gone their respective ways before they even thought of moving.

+

Back at the police station the inspector was in a towering rage, although it did not look like it at first glance "Okay," he said softly into the mouthpiece of the telephone "How did you manage to lose our two unidentified prisoners?" The sergeant watched quietly as the faceless voice on the other end of the line chattered away, this was not comfortable for

228

anyone, but losing two prisoners who were in custody on terrorism charges would not be fun. The inspector slammed down the phone and looked up at the sergeant who he waved to a seat in front of him. "They have already started an investigation as to how this happened. Apparently due to their being nameless they are difficult to control in the system. They got moved around about four prisons in two weeks then stayed in one place for about three weeks. They were going to some other evaluation place and the van just never arrived and on checking the evaluation centre didn't know they were even coming." The sergeant took a long look at his boss. "That either takes a lot of organising or they had internal help from high up." The inspector just nodded "That's what I was thinking, trouble is I now need to go and see Paul Gray and Mark Rae, let them know these guys are out. I don't think these guys are likely to come back here but you never know." He sighed and stood up to stretch his legs, he had been at the desk almost all the previous night and to get this information this late in the day did not help his mood at all. "I'm almost more worried what Mark Rae might do to them if they did come back." The sergeant looked puzzled "How come, he's just an average local guy, what's he going to do to them?" The inspector just looked at him before pushing the door closed "I never told you this but he's some form of ex military. I did a background search on him and got the blank history, red flag report and a phone call from the capital less than two minutes later asking what I was up to and, very subtly, warning me off" The sergeant sighed deeply and looked down before saying "Strange isn't it. Quiet, nice guy like that and he could probably snap your neck without blinking." The inspector nodded again "Don't speculate and keep that to yourself, he's on our side, let's keep him there." The sergeant shrugged, he didn't know who side Mark Rae was on and wasn't taking bets.

+

Marianne was tired and wanting to relax and just chill out in her flat with Mike. Mike on the other hand seemed to be hyper tonight, he couldn't sit down and was beginning to really annoy her as he bounced up and down and rushed off to answer his phone at least twice just after they had eaten. Right when she was trying to settle down. Marianne leant forward and looked back at him as he came back into the living room grinning from ear to ear "What is wrong with you tonight? Can't you just come over here and settle down for the night, please? I just want to relax." Mike hesitated, but came over and sat down on the edge of the seat next to her, obviously edgy and far from relaxed. Marianne sighed as she looked at him "What is wrong with you tonight?" Mike looked at her, startled "Who? Me? I'm fine as relaxed as I ever am. I'm in a good mood tonight." Marianne just sighed as he jumped up again and padded away quickly to the other room with his buzzing mobile phone in his hand. When he came back Marianne stood up and confronted him "I've had enough of this Mike, what is going on? You've been up and down like a cat on a hot tin roof with that bloody phone of yours acting like a cattle prod to you. Now tell me who is phoning you and about what? You're obviously excited about it and we're supposed to be a couple now in case you hadn't noticed so we're meant to share information, so tell me." He looked pained and shuffled from foot to foot as Marianne just stood there before crossing her arms and looking at him with an obvious temper building.

Mike sighed and his shoulders dropped as he glanced down at his phone again. "Okay, okay, okay. I guess I should have told you earlier. I've been offered a job, it's only a one year fixed term contract but its incredibly good money." She could see the gleam in his eyes as he began to speak about it, his excitement was almost contagious "It's a pilot for a long term project over in Denmark. They've got a very similar dune system over there but theirs is properly protected and it's impossible for anyone to do anything to it. I've been approached because of my involvement here to go over and set up the labs and offices, help get it kicked off and get my name put on it as the originating scientist." He looked at her as she sat down, feeling a little deflated and breathing deeply before she said "Denmark; and where do I fit into your plans?" Mike sat down slowly "Well I thought you would come with me, the deal includes an apartment and I'm earning a lot of money, come with me, please. We've got something good here between us, I don't want to risk that." Marianne just looked at him "You already have with what you've told me already." She sat forward and turned to look at him directly "Mike I have a good job, running a long term business and a fantastic salary. Does your new salary match what you and I are earning together now?" Mike shook his head as Marianne stared at him in disbelief as a thought began to worm its way into her head. "Who is offering you the job? Have you checked it out? Are you sure about this?" Mike shook his head. "This is my job, my life and I'm going. The company is Paradigm Environmental BV of Denmark. The contact has been with some guy at an agency over in the capital but come on we both know who owns the name Paradigm, so come on, I think its Mark giving me a leg up same as he did for you." Marianne shook her head "I don't believe that, I don't believe he would do that, it would mean destroying what he's doing here to send you over there knowing I won't leave my work here, its too important." She shook her head and shrugged his arm off her shoulders as she stood up and walked away across the room. The tears were running down her face as she turned back to him "If you take this job and go away now then it's the end of us." She paused as he just sat there and looked at her for a second

"Our friends here need us to continue this fight against the Silver Organisation." She was almost screaming as he replied "Rubbish, they've won. The planning permission was refused and all that's going to mean for me is looking after the same patch of ground for the rest of my life. This is an opportunity for me." Marianne was trying to look straight at him through the tears running down her face as she said "You told me that patch of ground was the most valuable one on the planet to you and you would do anything to protect it, so why abandon it along with everything else now?" He sighed and she saw him stand up "Silver is going to get a public inquiry, which they will win. It's all already agreed, that patch of land might actually be a horse paddock instead of a golf course but they're going to get their way; at least that's according to Paul Brown who is also acting for Paradigm Environmental BV. I've decided I'm going to be on the winning side for once." He sighed as he straightened up watching Marianne crying properly now. "I believe Mark is in on it as well, Brown hasn't said it in so many words but he has told me it's normal for them to have an opposition campaigner on their side, being paid quietly."

It was only a few minutes later Mike was standing on the doorstep in the drizzle. Turning up his collar against the cold night he stooped, picked up the bag he had packed earlier and walked away into the gloom.

13

Dr Jennifer James was sitting at her desk in the surgery when she got the phone call from Marianne. "Has Mark been setting up anything new, that you're aware of?" Jennifer was taken a back "Well good morning to you too, but no, not that I know of, why?" She could hear the strained breath on the other end of the line as Marianne struggled to breathe without crying. "Are you alright?" Marianne gulped a little and nodded before she spoke. "I am but Mike left me last night. He's gone to Denmark for a job setting up an environmental research project for some company called Paradigm Environmental BV." She drew breath but started to speak before Jennifer could "He also suggested that Mark had either set it up or at least was involved, but he was contradicting himself all the time. I don't think he knew what to think." She paused again "He's gone now anyway. Thanks and speak to you later" Before Jennifer could say anything the connection was broken.

Mark was sitting at his desk when the phone rang "I need to speak to you" was all Marianne said. Mark was surprised at the tone of voice but replied "Yeah, of course, do you want me to come to the office or do you want to come to the house?" Marianne swallowed "I'll come to the house if that's okay. I don't think I can face the office today." Mark was getting worried by her tone of voice "Yeah, just whenever. I'm not going out, I'll be here all day today." Marianne just nodded and hung up the phone.

+

Peter Barnard looked at his watch, he had to get back to the office but he really should wait here long enough to be sure that Mike had actually checked in for the flight to Denmark. He smiled to himself, he hadn't really thought it could ever be that easy, it would have been better if that other meddling bitch had gone as well, but they could deal with her some other time.

Mike looked back and waved as Peter Barnard raised a hand in recognition before stepping back and turning away. Mike smiled to himself, he had an advance of expenses in his pocket and the details of the local agent who he had to deal with to get things started once he was there. He was on his way, life would be good once he got settled. A pang of regret crossed his mind at the thought of Marianne crying as she had been when he left last night, but then again, he could get another woman easily enough. Weren't Scandinavian girls meant to be fun? His grin became even broader as he headed off down the tunnel to the departure lounge.

+

'Thug one' was looking forward to this, he had actually received the right type of orders for once, maybe a little more vague than he would really have liked and it could be argued by those with the fancy words that they never actually said kill someone but he knew that was what they meant.

He saw the car go cruising past the road end where he was sitting, waiting and carefully eased his way out onto the road. It was a powerful car and he would need to be careful. He would need to hurry as well it wasn't a long way to the turn off. He glanced in his mirror, there was no one else on the road as he pressed the accelerator to the floor. He knew the driver had seen him by the sudden blip in their speed on the road. At first glance the dark grey pick up could be mistaken for a police vehicle. He grinned when he saw the spot he had chosen earlier approaching. He tightened the straps on the four point harness he had fitted to the truck and pictured what was about to happen.

The car was just half way round the bend when the impact hit the driver's door. The first Jennifer knew of it was the sensation of being pushed across the road, followed by the sound of tinkling glass and rending metal. It seemed to be happening in slow motion as she watched the driver's door move in across the car and start to push her across the vehicle. The steering wheel changed shape and slid to her left before she noticed the other side of the car seemed to be coming towards her as well just as it struck the stone wall on the outside of the bend.

Jamie Forbes stopped the tractor and turned round, he was sure he had heard something and he reached up to turn off the radio that was playing in the cab to listen. Naturally he looked up the field he was working in towards the stone wall that bounded the road. It looked like a small wisp of steam was rising above the wall as he watched, but before he could do anything he heard a deep powerful engine, a diesel he was later to comment to the police, revving loudly before a screeching of metal reached him. There was a slow beat of the diesel as it reversed, then a loud revving followed by screech of tyres and the smashing sound of one vehicle into another. The stone wall he was looking at bulged and gave way as the crumpled and destroyed side of a powerful red sports car was pushed through. He grabbed his phone as he turned the tractor round to get up the

233

field. Pushing buttons he watched as the grey pick up reversed off the top of the car and drove away at high speed. Jamie stared in horror at the mess of the car when he got up close just as the voice on the other end of the line said "Emergency, which service do you require?"

+

Mark was surprised when he opened the door to see the police inspector standing there "Didn't expect to see you so soon, you'd better come in." he said stepping back but neither the inspector nor the female officer beside him moved "No, you'd better get your coat. Dr Jennifer James is in hospital and asking for you." A few seconds later they were in a marked police car and heading out the road. Mark watched as the female driver leant forward and pressed a switch on the dash, the sickly blue light that gave everything around them a grey cast and the speed they were travelling at told him it was bad. "What happened?" he asked. The inspector sighed "Hoped you wouldn't ask that, not yet anyway." He half turned in the passenger's seat to face Mark, "It was a car crash, but it was no accident. She was driven off the road then rammed by a grey pick up truck which then drove away." He paused and looked into Marks eyes for a second "Let us do our job, please don't get involved in this one, things seem to be getting more and more complex by the day." He had decided that just now was not the time to tell him that the two men who had tried to kill Paul Gray had escaped. Mark nodded "You have a week to find him. Then I start looking." The female officer glanced at the inspector who waved a hand to silence her as Mark continued. "Sounds like a planned job, so that will mean a special build. Won't be on the road for long, if they are really serious about what they do and who they are, then there will be a truck, a small box van probably with a ramp hidden inside. Your pick up will be driven into that and will disappear out of the area." The inspector nodded "Okay" and turned back to face the front before picking up the radio to put out a call.

When they got to the hospital Mark was taken straight through to a high dependency unit where Jennifer had just been assessed, he was able to spend ten minutes with her before they wheeled her off to the operating theatre.

Marianne turned up almost an hour later as Mark sat in the corridor outside, waiting for information. Not saying a word she sat down beside him and slipped an arm around his shoulders and gave him a squeeze. He turned and looked at her, distractedly, "Hi, glad you could come." He drew a deep shuddering breath before saying "What was it you wanted to see me about?" Marianne just shook her head, trying to get rid of the tears before he saw them. "Not important, we can deal with it after Jennifer is safe." He just nodded and turned back to look at the floor.

The female officer turned to face the inspector as he climbed back into the car after handing Mark over to the uniformed personnel on site who would take him to see Jennifer. "What did he mean by saying we have a week?" He sighed and looked at her for a second deciding she had to know something just not everything, yet. "He has connections, generally on our side. I've seen it once before when someone like him had a family member attacked by a gang. Two weeks later the gang were all dead." He sighed and looked into her eyes "Some people you push and get what you want. Some you should never push. He is somewhere in between, leave him alone and he won't bother you, threaten him and he'll ignore you. Hurt his friends you'd better run." He shifted and adjusted his jacket "I really didn't think he'd give us a week for this one. Not after Sharon Grant was shot in his arms." The officer looked out through the windscreen and said nothing.

+

'Thug one' smiled to himself, the local police would never understand what had happened, it would just be written off as a hit and run. The guy at the scrap yard smiled at him as he opened the back of the truck and he saw the pick up inside. He stood there looking at it for a moment or two "No plates and no log book I'll bet?" Thug one shrugged as the guy looked at him levelly "okay," he finally said "best I can do is two hundred euros and that's only because it looks fairly new." 'Thug one' shrugged again "That's what happens when you let a woman drive." The other guy laughed and waved at his colleague who drove over in the fork lift truck. With no further ado they fastened a rope onto the back of the pick up and pulled it straight out of the back of the truck. 'Thug one smiled and folded the cash in half before turning away to close the doors on the rental truck. He turned back and found the guy from the yard still looking at him, so he stepped forward and taking the cash out his pocket split it into two bundles, one went back into his pocket the other he held out to the guy and said "I would appreciate it if its broken for spares or crushed today; sooner the better. Don't want her coming back to try and buy it back off you." The guy shrugged and said "Sure" as he turned away, listening as 'Thug one' climbed in, slammed the door shut on the truck and drove it away. "Jonny" the guy shouted and the fork truck driver came running into the office "Don't touch that pick up at all and disappear for a while I'm about to call the police, you don't want them nosing into your benefit claim." Jonny nodded and disappeared away without saying a word.

Marianne had driven Mark home about two hours later some time after the surgeon had walked through the doors from the operating theatre, looked down at the two them and said "I'm so sorry…"

Mark had never even heard the rest of what he had said, he had switched off and Marianne was still worried about him as he lay on the settee in his own living room, looking at the ceiling. She stretched, she felt horrible on a physical level never mind the emotions running about in her head at the moment. She stepped closer and said "Would it be okay if I used the shower? I feel like I need one." Marks head swivelled towards her "Of course, help yourself, you know where everything is. Help your self to some of Jennifer's clothes as well if you want, she would not have minded." He smiled a weak smile but it was a smile none the less. Marianne nodded "Okay, I might just do that."

She had just stripped off and was standing outside the shower, letting the water run when she heard the phone ring and wondered if he would answer. It stopped after only a few rings so she sighed and stepped under the warm water, relishing the feel of it on her skin.

Downstairs Mark was sitting at his desk with the phone against his ear, it was Steve on the other end of the line. "I just heard, do you want me to come round?" Mark shook his head "No, Marianne's here already and to be honest I'd rather keep it as few people as possible for a day or so anyway." He drew breath and made a decision "The police as good as told me it was murder, add that to Sharon's murder and I'm fed up playing. Could you call the regiment for me please? I'm looking for a few private volunteers, you know the drill. Let's show these fuckers how it really works." Steve smiled to himself "I already did that, got hold of some new guy, I've never met before a 'Major Parker' he said you had already been flagged to them by something else that happened and he was going to be in the area soon with a stick or two. Official but quiet, so shouldn't cost you anything." Mark nodded "Good, if he makes contact ask him to come and see me, or arrange a meet at least." Steve nodded to himself "Will do. Before you hang up on me, I want to ask you something on a completely different matter." He paused and listened to his friends breathing on the other end of the phone line. "This might not be the right time but I have two questions to ask you." he paused and Mark said "Go ahead." Steve shifted in his seat before he asked "You ever hear of an organisation called Paradigm Environmental BV?" Mark thought for fractions of a second "All my business is through you. I've never heard of them." Steve made a note on the pad "Thought not. For information, Mike has left Marianne and gone to work for this lot

236

in Denmark, I'm about to do some digging to find out who owns them and what the story is. That is what Marianne came to see you about today; it just dropped on the priority list when she found out about Jennifer." Steve listened and could just make out that Mark was swearing under his breath that was not a good sign. He drew breath and spoke again. "Now, don't fuss about this, there is nothing anyone can do right now but if I don't tell you now you'll be annoyed at me later, but the Silver Organisation planning application has been called in." Mark sat silently for a second or two "What does that mean?" Steve shrugged "It means the Government Ministers have decided they need to deal with it rather than the local authority. They have something like three months to decide what to do with it and there are three options they can take. One is they decide about it behind closed doors. Second is arbitrated discussion between opponents and applicant and third is the Public Inquiry everyone has been pushing for." Mark sighed and sat back "Can we influence their decision?" Steve shook his head "Nothing we can do, it's all down to the decision of the relevant minister." Mark grunted before saying "Oh, well, I guess we have to wait and see what they decide to do. Meanwhile I am going to go and investigate the inside of a whisky bottle on my own and see what insights I can find. I'll speak to you in the morning, I'm going to switch off the phone." Steve just nodded to himself as he listened to the line go dead. He sighed as he set the phone in its cradle and sat there staring at the dead instrument wondering where all of this was going. He had hoped warfare was a long way behind them all. Now a few thugs and a couple of idiots seemed to bringing it back to the fore front again. He shook his head and picked up his jacket, whoever they were, they had better hope neither Mark nor the people coming to town tomorrow ever found them.

Upstairs Marianne had just dressed quickly in some of Jennifer's clothes and was combing her hair looking out of the window when she looked down the drive at the row of houses. She stopped and stared, trying to get a closer look. That had looked like Danielle going into Karl Benson's house; she hesitated as she thought about it. They worked together for the Silver organisation or at least that was what almost everyone believed so there was nothing to say they could not be friends as well. On the other hand to get to any of the other houses you had to go past the front of his place, so she could actually be going to see anyone. Marianne sighed and rocked back on her heels before turning away and padding downstairs barefoot, to see where Mark was.

+

Jenny and Andrea were sitting in the pub talking to Andy the barman "Is Mark not here tonight? I thought he might have been here after the news of the call in making the press." Andy shook his head "He won't be in tonight, might be a few weeks before he reappears." There was a laugh from along the bar and the three friends turned to see Peter Barnard standing there, he waited until they were all facing him before he said "Don't expect to see many applications for the post of girlfriend there in a hurry. That's the second one he's lost in a short time." Andy's face flushed with temper as he spoke "What do you want, you're not welcome here." Barnard shrugged just as 'thug one' and one of his accomplices came in through the door from outside "My friends and I only want a drink and a chance to set the record straight on a few points of misinformation that seem to be circulating" Andy shook his head "Well you can want. You're barred, now get out of my pub." Peter Barnard just smiled and laughed "Don't serve us and soon you won't be serving anyone, I can promise you that." The voice at the back cut through the heavy atmosphere "That sounds like a threat to me, and now as the publican has asked you to leave perhaps you should go. Or you can all accompany me to the station anytime you want." The police inspector stepped forward and laid his badge in the puddle of light on the bar. He noticed with interest as 'thug one' inched slightly towards the door before Peter Barnard just smiled "Next time." Was all he said before turning and leading his two associates out of the bar.

Andy had poured him a pint and set it on the counter in front of him by the time he turned round. "Thanks," said the quiet barman "On the house, and don't give me that bullshit about not drinking on duty." The inspector smiled as he lifted the glass "I'm not on duty." He said as he drank deeply from the glass. Magda poked her head around the door from the lounge area Andy," she called and he turned to her "That group that called in earlier, the," she paused and looked at a slip of paper before reading "the Stirling Lines outdoor pursuits club are here, do you want to check them in or will I?" Andy flipped the cloth he was polishing a glass with, over his shoulder and glanced at the spluttering and coughing inspector before he said "I'll do it, there's eight of them or so." He waited to be sure the guy was okay before he ducked under the door frame and Magda stepped through into the bar and went to speak to the two ladies further along the bar.

Jenny looked at Andrea, "What was that about Jennifer being dead that can't be true surely?" Andrea nodded at the inspector. "Maybe he can tell us." He turned and looked at the three women who were all looking at him and he could hear the silence amongst the few occupied tables behind him that meant everyone was listening. He sighed and set down his pint before

238

speaking "Dr Jennifer James was murdered today in a car crash that was no accident. Some one appears to be targeting Mark Rae's partners. We have a number of good leads and I believe I know who is responsible it's just going to be very difficult to gather enough evidence to make a conviction stick." He turned back and picked up his glass as the volume of conversation increased rapidly and he thought 'that was probably too much information'.

In a police garage over in the capital, just a few short kilometres from the scrap dealers yard the grey pick up was sitting under bright spotlights as a team of forensic specialists were taking it apart panel by panel.

+

Danielle had risen early in the morning and gone for a run, she had startled a few deer and a lot of ground nesting birds but what had startled her was the amount of foot prints she had seen all over the place. They were crisp and fresh and looked like boots prints to her, she was getting more worried as she thought she had overheard them say something about another squad coming into the area as well. She was shivering and it wasn't just the cold that was bothering her as she returned to Karl's place where she had stayed last night. He was waiting on her, sober and alert "Glad to see you back, feeling better this morning?" he asked as she closed the door behind her. She nodded "Yes thanks. Just a little wary about the amount of boot prints there are out there this morning." He hesitated, she knew she would struggle to get used to calling him anything other than Karl even though she now knew it wasn't his name. They had had a long chat the night before and he was quite sweet really. His eyes had narrowed slightly as he asked "Boot prints? What type of boots?" She shrugged. "Sharp edged, deep treads, hill walkers boots; that type of thing." He nodded slowly, he was trying not to scratch his balls with her here, normally the girls that stayed at his place overnight would have expected that from him. Danielle was different; for a start they had slept in separate beds.

He turned and looked at her "Don't mention anything about that when you go along to the office today." She looked at him, suddenly scared "They don't need to know about that stuff, it'll just make them more dangerous." He paused and looked at her, feeling himself soften "You can always come back here at any time you want and I want to see you back here tonight." He gave her a hug before pushing her away and saying "Now go and get dressed, you have to go to work today no matter what else has happened." She ran up the stairs and began to get dressed as she thought about what she was going to do.

+

Marianne was beginning to get worried about Mark she had risen at her usual time around six o'clock and rolled out of her lonely bed in the spare room before coming down stairs. It was now almost seven o'clock and that sounded like his feet on the stairs now. She relaxed as he appeared in the kitchen, looking tired but sober, she had expected him to go and try and empty a whisky bottle after what had happened yesterday, but he hadn't. He had obviously thought about it, the bottle was sitting where he had left it early yesterday evening and a clean glass was sitting beside it. She jumped up and gave him a cuddle, he kissed her forehead "Who's this for? You or me?" he sighed and before she answered he said "I think we can both benefit from it." she smiled at him through the tears in her eyes as he smiled at her "Thank you." was all she could say before she pulled him close again to hide the fact she was crying.

+

In the police garage the forensics superintendent was grinning as the inspector turned up "Got anything for me?" The superintendent shrugged, she liked the inspector he was smart and not completely impossible to deal with like so many others. "Well," she said "Both yes and no." He frowned as she continued "I have fingerprints for you that match the unknowns from the hanging case; dog hair as well, but no evidence of a dog in this truck. The dog has been somewhere else where this individual has been and fairly frequently at that as well." He smiled "I did not expect fingerprints, are they any good?" She shrugged "Well, sort of. They are a good match even though they are partials. We're busy running them through the system just now here and over the water but it's not like on television, it takes a long time to check fingerprints." The inspector shook his head "I know, it's a pity we're not all really that good isn't it?" She just nodded as he continued "What about the CCTV footage of the truck?" The superintendent shook her head "Cheap system, not good enough to enhance. All it tells us is the type of the truck and the colour. There's no way to get the number plate and there's no rental firms name on the side, so that looks like a dead end." He shrugged "You've given us more than I thought possible in the time. Keep looking for those prints or anything else please." "Sure" said the superintendent "What's the boyfriend like? I've seen him on TV and he looks quite nice." The inspector smiled "I never thought of you being desperate for a boyfriend." She coloured "I'm not, it's just that he looks like he might appreciate a cuddle." The inspector turned away and headed towards the door saying "He probably would but I think there's a queue for that position. Anyway this isn't finished by a long way and it might be a good idea to stay clear for a while at least." The superintendent shouted
240

after him "Sounds interesting, keep me informed please." The only reply she got was the click of the garage door as it shut behind the inspector as he walked away to ask someone else more questions.

+

The outdoor pursuits club that had checked in to the hotel the night before all met for breakfast, just as the kitchens opened early the next morning. They ate well but quietly, with not a lot of conversation amongst them, just some minor chatter, very general stuff with no details of their plans for the day ahead at all.

One of the men frowned at Magda "Weren't you on duty last night as well?" She nodded "I volunteered for the double shift. I am trying to earn money for my next year at University of Prague" He nodded "I guess as long as you volunteered that's all right then." she smiled and got on with bringing more tea to these guys. Parker looked around at the rest of the guys once the door had shut "Right boys, this place is almost perfect for us, so no funny business here. We want to keep the owner and staff on our side." They all nodded silently, no comment no dissention. He licked his lips, he'd been working with these guys for just over three years and he'd just gained his promotion just in time other wise he'd have been RTU'd and he did not want to do that. The silence did not bother him like it used to. He knew now that these guys listened to the orders and took them on board, but once they were out the door they would do anything they felt was necessary to get the job done. It was often simpler and better to tell these guys the end target and give them a list of what they were not allowed to do. They would listen to that and get the job done. Initially at least this was just an information gathering job. He doubted if that was where it would end.

+

It was four days after Jennifer's death that Marianne finally dressed in office clothes when she got out of the spare bed at Marks place and made as if to go into town. It was the first time she had been comfortable in herself to leave him alone and, if truth be told, to face the world alone herself. The telephones had never been switched back on and it felt strange kissing him good bye and stepping outside. She found herself being very conscious of every other vehicle on the road and every other person around her at all times. She realised she was scared.

He had watched her drive down the driveway, turn left along the back of the row of houses and vanish towards the main road with a strange hollowness inside. He shook his head, he had lived alone for almost ten years, and now after a few months, or maybe it was only weeks with some one in his house, and his arms he was missing the warmth of another person being around. He would almost have said he felt the house echo. He shook himself, he was being stupid. Turning he went back into the office and switched on the telephones again. He had to take hold of his life again and get on with it.

+

In his office on the fifty third floor Trente Silver sighed deeply again as his secretary stepped into the office "You okay?" she asked, it was a habitual pleasantry, she didn't really care and knew he would never tell her if he wasn't, that might be seen as weakness. He just looked at her for a second then shrugged, "It's just this annoyance," he waved at he computer screen in front of him, email was all he used it for and he wasn't even much good at that, she snapped her attention back to him, he was speaking again. "It appears that I have to go over to the," he paused and leant forward to read from the screen, "Public Local Inquiry into our development at the Doones estate. I don't want to waste that much time." He sighed again "That guy, the little fat man, President, or whatever they call him is saying that this is the best he can do for us, after all we've done for him. Once we take control we can replace him as well." She looked at him and said "All we're doing is a small housing development; he is the leader of the country, why would we want to replace him?" Silver grinned that deaths head grin of his and she shivered slightly, hoping he did not notice. "We have other plans for that little country, could be worth exploring, but we need to get in there first." He leant forward as she turned and left the office.

+

Marlene was sitting in the corner of the councillor's lounge with 'Xander's brother and they were talking softly between each other. Padruig walked in to the room and ordered himself a coffee, as he turned round to look at the room it was all he could do to stop himself laughing. It looked almost like a gentle take on some bad gangster movie as the two group leaders in the room were sitting in a far corner talking quietly but watching him closely. No one was sitting in the chairs nearest to the two of them and then each table in the next group of chairs and tables had two people at it, one from each party. Padruig shook his head and wandered off to the other corner where he sat down, alone, to drink his coffee and relax for a few minutes.

242

He sat there in the almost silence with just the murmur of two soft voices talking in the distance, wondering what made them try and hide the fact they were talking about something to do with this development or the upcoming PLI. He smiled to himself, he was wondering how they would try and get around the fact that the council's formal legal position was that of refusing the planning permission, somehow they would have to try and talk themselves into a position of supporting it, even if most of them didn't.

At the other side of the room, Marlene's eyes had widened slightly as she saw Padruig walk into the lounge. She was surprised at him, he was such a quiet man she had expected him to go into hiding, instead he was carrying on as normal, well as normally as he could anyway. If it hadn't been so much against her nature she would have had to admit some grudging admiration for the man. She turned back to the man sitting next to her and said "We need to get rid of him completely. I know he's off the ISC but he is on a number of other committees." The man with the slicked back hair nodded in his slow deliberate way, he knew he was operating at his limits here, he was beginning to realise his younger brother may actually be ahead of him in guile and deviousness because he could barely cope with what was going on around him just now, let alone what must happen around his brother. He forced his attention back to the present. "Well," he muttered "he's in your party, can you expel him or would that turn him into a martyr?" Marlene sighed softly "Hmmm," she said "I'd need to look closely at that, it might be possible, but it would need to be done with care. After all, technically, he's done nothing wrong." The man's head turned and he looked at her, she shivered with those cold blue eyes staring at her. "Don't say that too loudly, or in public." Was all he said before squirming in his seat. "Leave it with me," he continued "I'll see about the committees I'm on at the moment. Maybe we can do something to help out there. After all we need to pull together on this one or we're both in trouble." Marlene smiled "I don't think so, we're pretty well untouchable now the way this is going. Your brother is an obvious supporter and that makes it easier for us all. He just looked at her nodding slowly.

+

Peter Barnard walked out of the estate offices and turned left, away from the big house. It was only a minute or twos walk before he came to Ruriadh Cottage where old Arthur stayed. He stopped in the middle of the road and looked at the old and solid building. He had to admit it looked sound if a little shabby, but he could never say that out loud. His lip almost hurt with the permanent sneer he wore these days and he shook his head before actually opening his mouth to shout. "Better find someplace else to live old man. You'll be moving out soon, we own your house now and we're going to knock it down." he jumped as a quiet voice spoke close to him "Now that's not very friendly, is it Barnard? Or is it Brown today?" he spun around to find Mark Rae standing about ten feet away on the road setting down a shopping bag as he spoke. Barnard stared at him, he had never heard him arrive. "What the fuck are you doing here Rae?" he snarled "no one ever tell you, you're trespassing? Get the fuck off my land or I'll have you arrested." Mark began to laugh and Barnard took half a step back, this was not what was meant to happen. "First it's not your land, it may belong to the Silver Organisation but it's not yours. Second I own Ruriadh cottage through Paradigm Property so you will never be evicting Arthur and third and finally there is no law of criminal trespass in this country. Not even back where you come from so don't waste your breath on lies. I know it's second nature for you but you're going to have to stop it." Mark picked up his shopping back and took two steps forward as Barnard looked around him and took two steps back "Ruriadh cottage will be ours one way or another, even if you have to disappear off the scene like your girlfriends have done so far." Marks face twitched but he said nothing as he kept walking closer. Barnard kept walking backwards until he walked into a tree at the side of the driveway and Mark stepped up close until he was within touching distance. "If the police don't have their evidence and have you in court within a month you'd better run. Because then I will be coming after you for that, and I wont be so lenient." His voice was barely a whisper, but it carried with a depth and an authority Barnard had never heard before. He whimpered as Mark stepped back and let him turn and walk quickly away from the tree, back towards the estate offices.

Mark watched him go before turning back to Ruriadh cottage where Arthur opened the door for him, he had been watching through the window.

Ten feet away two members of the outdoor pursuits club grinned silently at one another in the middle of the rhododendron bush where they sat patiently.

+

The Police inspector was with his team in the hotel room where the two bodies had been found and he was reading the forensics report closely as he looked around the room, comparing the photographs to the actual room. There was something bothering him as he looked closely at some of the items in the room. The report had been read to him over the phone and he had wanted to come and see what they had found for himself before he

244

threw the switch and started serious work on the hotel. Knowing what else was happening locally and the fact the public local inquiry was due to start tomorrow he had to be sure or there would be pressure from above. Of that he was as sure as he could be.

He shook his head and pulled out his radio "Okay, let's roll, this is live and I want it closed down."

The receptionist turned to his assistant "You'd better go and get Mr Dull" was all he said as the door opened and a wave of police officers entered the building. The sergeant walked straight up to the desk and sat a sheet of paper on the desk "Search Warrant. I want all guests out of the building and all staff through here. Now." Dull appeared a few moments later looking as if he had just woken up and looked at the sergeant bemused as he read the warrant, suddenly the sergeant realised he had been expecting this and he was worried about what that might mean for his evidence. Dull just nodded "I need to phone my solicitor to ensure my interests are protected" the sergeant nodded "From the desk, here, and all other calls are stopped." Dull sighed and sat down behind the counter to make his call.

+

Away over in the capital at the other side of the country 'Xander felt like sliding under his desk as he looked at the TV screen which was showing a news broadcast and he was mentioned. Normally that was good news as far as he was concerned but this was not so good, not good at all in fact.

"It has come to light that the President actually visited the Silver Organisation at the hotel which they are using as a headquarters, the day before the planning application was called in to be considered at a Public Inquiry. This is the fist time, ever that a refused application has been called in, normally 'call ins' are reserved for applications that have been inappropriately approved. Allegations are also circulating about the President making a call to the chief planner on behalf of the Silver Organisation to initiate the call for a public inquiry. If this is correct it would be inappropriate behaviour and he would be subject to investigation by the ethics committee, but the fact is, the President is also the chair of the ethics committee." The news reader smiled at camera as she said "Watch this space, this one might run and run." Templeton had shut the door of his office and was laughing with glee as he watched the same broadcast just a few doors along the hallway. He stood up and began to pace around the office, with the inquiry due to start the next day there was very little they could do to postpone or stop it. It would have to go ahead as it was.

+

Andrew Crawford was furious when the police knocked on the door of their work room, then walked in without waiting to be invited. He stood there in the middle of the room "How dare you come in here uninvited. We are in the middle of preparing for an important inquiry which starts soon and you have no right to be in here, now get out." The officers turned round to the sergeant who lifted his radio and called on the inspector.

A few minutes later he appeared and Andrews shouted at him immediately "Are you in charge? I'll have you writing parking tickets by morning you pathetic little worm. This room is practically US soil, this could be viewed as a diplomatic incident. Now get out immediately." The inspector looked at him calmly "You have two minutes to do as you were told by this officer," he pointed at the sergeant, "and leave the room before we arrest you for obstruction of a murder investigation." Crawford looked at him "You wouldn't dare" The inspector shrugged and looked at his watch. He glanced at the sergeant before saying "Two minutes" the sergeant nodded and the inspector walked out of the room. Crawford stood still with his arms folded.

The sergeant looked at his watch and drew out his handcuffs, stepping forward as he did so. Andrew Crawford held up his hands and said "Alright, alright we're going." Looking around at the people in the room he said "Grab as much of our stuff as we can and let's go back to the estate" he turned back to the sergeant "You'll be hearing from my lawyer about this." The sergeant shrugged and muttered "You and everyone else here today."

+

The two watchers gasped and struggled for breath as they felt the weight of a fully grown adult each land on their backs and pin them to the ground. One made to shout and realised his face was getting pushed into the ground. As soon as he stopped trying to shout the man behind him let him breathe again. The plastic tie wraps bit into the skin on their wrists and one of the men began to whimper as a black cloth bag was pulled over their head and he was dragged to his feet. It was as much the metallic 'snick' of a gun being made safe that scared him as the hood. The two of them were bundled into the back of a vehicle and the cover was pulled down on top of them where they lay, still and scared.

246

They listened closely as they heard the vehicle driving through city streets, at least the ride was smoother than it had been in the country, wondering where they were being taken. Sooner than they may have imagined, they found out. The traffic thinned out and became heavier; more industrial than private before the vehicle turned off to one side, the sound of the indicator lamp clicking away seemed almost like a death knell as the vehicle came to a halt and the rattling noise of an industrial roller door came to the two men before the vehicle they were in drove inside a factory unit somewhere and stopped.

All they could hear was silence and the ticking sound of a cooling engine before the rear door was thrown open and the two men were hauled out onto smooth hard concrete floor. Forced to kneel, the two men were in fear of their lives as the bags were pulled from their head and they realised they were on a polythene sheet spread across the clean bright floor. They squinted up in the light at the men surrounding them. There were four of them, all holding automatic weapons, spread out in a semi circle around them, all dressed similarly with ski masks covering their faces. A fifth man was behind them, behind the lights, it was him that spoke. "Who are you why are you crawling around on the Doones estate? Identify yourself." One of the men looked into the light and managed to say "US Department of Justice special investigators. We're here to watch the Silver Organisation at work with a view to a number of prosecutions." The man behind the light was silent for a moment "ID?" he asked "Badge in my left rear pocket, my colleague will be the same." The other man on his knees nodded, saying nothing. The man behind the light waited where he was as one of his men handed his weapon across to a colleague before he walked around them to approach from behind. The silent man on his knees watched and thought 'Professionals, they don't get in each others way and only one of them talks. This may end well yet rather than a body bag' The man from the group took their ID's and returned the same way he had walked in, he was never between a gun barrel and the targets at anytime as he walked around and handed the badges to Parker who was standing where he had always been, behind the light.

Parker nodded as he looked at the badges, "Release them, they're on our side." The two men on their knees breathed a sigh of relief as the powerful lights were switched off and they were helped to their feet before their plastic cuffs were cut off. Parker smiled at the two of them "Come on guys, grab a seat, make yourselves comfortable." Turning he spoke to one of the other men "You're turn on the coffee I think." The guy nodded "Yeah it's my turn" he said casually as he slid the weapon over his shoulder before turning to the two men who so recently had been prisoners and peeling his mask off over his head "Sugar and milk?"

The silent prisoner finally asked "So who are you guys anyway? Parker smiled before saying "Outdoor pursuits club"

+

Back at the safe house the head of the watchers was beginning to worry about his two men. They had always known that if the Silver Organisations 'security' people caught them it could be terminal. He had just never actually considered it as being real, until now. They were almost an hour late in returning from the site and were also out of contact, not answering their phones or radios.

He was standing in the middle of what passed as a living room in the bland little house in the middle of the housing estate in Drimmie when a large, black, four by four pulled into the driveway in front. He watched wary and uncomfortable as three men climbed out of the back seat, two were his people and one was the federal agent they had as a contact. He did not know the driver or front seat passenger, both looked pretty unassuming guys, the type you'd pass in the street. He stood there and waited as the ones he recognised let themselves in to the house, and the vehicle reversed into the street and powered away. Something told him this was a completely different situation than what he had envisaged.

The federal agent was smiling, that was also a positive sign thought the team leader as he looked at his two men who flopped down in seats and looked up at him as the federal agent spoke. "Your guys are lucky this happened here. The men in the truck that just drove away are local special forces. Our people come here to get trained by them so don't think they are second best. They're anything but." He paused and looked at the two men slouching on the settee behind him, "These guys were captured watching the estate offices and were taken to be interrogated. When their IDs were checked as genuine I was called in to escort them back after I had vouched for them." He turned back to the team leader. "We've agreed a recognition code word and all of that so your people don't get hauled away again. It's likely they'll be being watched by the locals all of the time so I would suggest you view it as a safeguard for your personnel."

The team leader shook his head, he really was not sure what to make of this, but if it helped him do what he was here to do then he would not complain.

248

+

Steve was sitting at his desk preparing paperwork for the Public Inquiry, he was tight of time and wanted to get on with it when Parker arrived at the office and was ushered through to see him. Steve sighed but smiled as he stood up, before he could say anything Parker spoke "I don't want to take up too much of your time you'll be busy working for the inquiry, but I was wondering if you could tell me how our former colleague is getting on?" Steve sighed as he sat down "I've only spoken to him briefly since Jennifer was killed and he seemed okay when I spoke to him." He hesitated for a moment "If you don't mind speaking to someone else you might get more information from Marianne, it's her spare archive store that you guys are working out of. She's also staying at Mark's place at the moment." Parker nodded "Okay that might make sense. I don't need to tell her all the details of who we are at the moment either." Steve shook his head as he stood up from behind the desk and led Parker along to Marianne's office.

Steve knocked on the door and walked in as Marianne was shutting down her computer, she smiled at Steve and the unknown man behind him. "Marianne, this is Parker who is going to be looking after some of the details to do with the security and the like at the exhibition hall for the Public Inquiry. He's on our side and is not working for the hall or anyone else around here so you can trust him implicitly; I do. Could you maybe answer a few questions for him?" Marianne nodded as Steve turned to go but hesitated, he obviously thought about something for a moment or two before changing his mind and carrying on out of the office. Marianne pointed to a seat and said "Can I get you a coffee Mr Parker." He smiled at her "No thank you Miss and its just Parker, no Mister." She smiled "Okay then, Parker, but it's Marianne not Miss" he grinned "Touché, I accept your terms if you can accept mine." Marianne just nodded very slightly as he carried on talking "How is Mark Rae doing these days? It must have come as quite a blow to him to lose two girlfriends in such a short space of time." Marianne sighed and leant back "Well, yes it obviously did, but he is an incredibly strong individual and to be honest he and Sharon," Parker interrupted "The gunshot victim?" Marianne nodded "Yes, she was the one who was shot to death in his arms. Anyway, they were not really together and most people think the gunman actually missed and that he was really aiming at Mark, but to answer your question, he is doing amazingly well. The only slight worry I have is the he now worries about other people. I am currently staying at his house and if I'm not back when he expects me, he seems to worry, or at least wonder if I'm okay." She looked at Parker and noticed his really focused look as he listened to her speak, it was almost spooky "So in real terms he's come out of it unscathed." Parker nodded "Good thank you for your time, Miss." He paused "Marianne, I'm sorry," she smiled as he corrected himself "Thank you for your time and the information, it gives me a better idea what I am likely to be dealing with when we get to the exhibition hall." He stood up and started towards the door before stopping and turning back "It might be a good idea, not to tell him we had this conversation, at least not until I have met him face to face again." Marianne just nodded although that made her uncomfortable. Parker smiled again and stepped out of the door and away. As Marianne picked up her jacket and walked slowly out of the building towards her car she was running the conversation over and over in her head and the one word that kept coming back to her was 'again'.

+

Jenny and Andrea were talking in the pub one evening when Jenny turned to Andrea and said "Going to the Inquiry at all?" Andrea looked puzzled "Didn't think we were allowed to. The bit in the '*Evening*' the other day said that it would be a closed hearing" Jenny leant forward "That's not right, the very title of it tells you that it's a 'Public Inquiry' that means its open to the public. Certain bits of it might be closed due to the public but generally it's open. That is the whole idea." Andy the barman spoke up "That's right, it's a Public Inquiry so everyone can hear the details. All the '*Evening*' is trying to do is silence the public who otherwise would be there to voice their opinion and show how unpopular this thing actually is." He sighed and thought for a second "A lot of people are scared now as well, after two murders and the threats that were made to old Arthur who lives on the estate, some folk are scared to speak out." Jenny looked at Andrea before saying "Well I'm going and I'm going to tell the gymkhana society that it's public to try and get as many people there as possible." Andrea nodded "I'll do the same with the tennis association and we'll get a few more there anyway." Andy turned round as the door opened and someone walked in, set a bag down on the floor and looked at him. Andy turned slowly to look at the new arrival a slow grin spreading across his face. Paul Gray grinned back and said "Got a spare room for a few nights Andy?"

250

14

The hall was a strange building; it had started life as a war memorial at some point, but no one seemed to be able to tell which war, or when. Above the huge oak doors it had a large stone that proudly proclaimed it was the 'Memorial Hall' and it had bright, almost gaudy stained glass windows along either side that let strange patterns of multi coloured light into a vestibule like area that sported carved memorial tablets with the names of the dead from several wars chiselled into them, gold on black. They commemorated wars all the way back to the Crimean war in the eighteen hundreds but no one really believed the hall was that old.

Another tall set of dark oak doors led into a wooden floored hall that probably had been the extent of the original building being about twenty metres long by ten metres wide. The first thing that struck most people the second their footsteps echoed on that wooden floor was the large grey curtain that usually hung across the far end of the hall. Today that had been pulled aside and hung in swathes at either side to reveal the newer part of the building. It had been built about ten years ago by a local agricultural engineering company. A company that just so happened to be owned by the provost of the time; someone long since gone from the area, who had specialised in building tractor sheds. The building was steel framed and covered in profiled steel sheet or 'crinkle cut tin' as many people locally called it. The noise inside when it rained was horrific and almost reached the legal limit for 'noise at work'. This was the exhibition hall where the Public Inquiry was to be held.

The Reporter, who was to head the Inquiry, looked at it in horror as the team walked slowly in and looked at the set up. The three sets of tables were set up as they would expect with one set for them, one for the applicant and support, and one for the opposition. They looked at their notes and sighed, that explained a lot. The local authority had not yet announced which side they would be on, the formal legal position of objection or what a small minority of them wanted, which was to support the application. That was why there was a strange number of seats and one particular area was duplicated on both sides of the hall. The paperwork for both sides was starting to arrive in boxes and crates by the van load with a small bustle of incredibly busy looking people.

Steve watched as they walked around for a bit before he surveyed the area that was his domain, right down at the end of the line of objectors. The allocation of seats said a lot about who had made the allocation. He stood and stretched to ease his back and looked up the line of desks, at the very end, nearest the reporters was the space for the local authority if they chose to fill it, then 'Greensword' who should have had Mike on their team but he was in Denmark, working for the Silver Organisation. He paused, he had not had the heart to tell Marianne that was now a fact, not an opinion. Next to them was 'Bugs Around' the governments animal and wildlife welfare body; then it was the 'renegade councillors' followed by 'Architecture and Built Heritage' whose name told you what they did, the regional archaeological group, where Marianne would be sitting, and finally Steve's table representing the 'Green Wave' as the media seemed to be calling them. He turned and looked at the scaffold grandstand that rose to his right. The governments planning body and the town planners professional body had been refused permission to speak and would be sitting in the front row instead. There was actually a court case going on in the capital about that and whether it was legal or not but the Public Inquiry would be finished before that case would be over, so it was an interesting legal point but something of no relevance to the hearing.

He stretched again and looked across the hall, looking at the seats set out for the Silver Organisation, the local authority, if they did as they were told by their new paymasters, and the Chamber, who all seemed to believe they could make good money out of being here. Steve shook his head and carefully checked the boxes before leaving the hall with just the Reporters looking around; everyone else appeared to have disappeared while he was looking around.

The Inquiry was due to start at ten o'clock the next morning but a lot of people were already gathering by nine o'clock. The press were there and the international press were out in force because Trente Silver himself was supposed to be arriving. He had originally been supposed to arrive the night before but as the Wycliffe hotel was still closed by the police investigation and he did not believe that the big house on the estate was nearly good enough for him, no one really knew if he would turn up at all or if he would ignore the hearing. He had been called but as he was a foreign national and lived out of the country, he could not be forced to attend, unless he was already in the country. If he turned up in time, he would be the first witness on the stand.

+

Outside the hall, the few supporters that were local had arrived at seven o'clock to get the best spot and had stood there waiting on the press turning up. They were not so happy when the press filmed their support turning up in a bus from the capital complete with banners and placards supporting the Silver Organisation. They were even less impressed when the press filmed them asking for their money from the organiser and being paid in cash before they would unroll the banners and flags.

It was about fifteen minutes before the start time when 'Thug one and two' appeared and started to demand the attention of the camera crews before a borrowed limousine appeared round the corner and the camera crews surged forwards as the long car eased to a halt outside the front door. It was comical to see these two, big men, in cheap ill fitting suits rush to the boot of the car and drag out a rolled up red carpet. The crowd laughed out loud as they quickly rolled it out from the door of the hall to the car before brushing themselves down and standing back. 'thug one' called to the crowd "Okay, you can start filming now" The reporters grinned at each other, they were already filming. The door to the car was held open and Silver made to step out into daylight but his foot caught on the sill of the car door and he stumbled, he only stumbled and did not fall on his face, much to the disappointment of the majority of the crowd. They still redid it twice so the film cameras had a perfect shot of him leaving the car and walking up his own red carpet and into the front door of the hall. The problem with that was that everyone else was using the side or main door to access the exhibition hall and the second set of doors between the vestibule and the hall were shut and locked. He had to come back out and round the side of the hall to the main car park to get inside. He had hoped no one would notice.

+

Steve watched closely as people were filing into the hall, the space for the local authority on this side of the hall was empty but there were plenty of boxes sitting across at the other side of the room; it looked like the council had gone against the wishes of their constituents yet again.

Mark strode into the hall with Marianne close by his side, she kissed him on the cheek and smiled at Steve as she walked past to join her group at the table. The cameras flashed and lights flickered as that happened, but Mark seemed to ignore it as he joined Steve at the table nodding hello at his PA who sat on the opposite side of Steve and glancing at the empty seat to his right. Steve just smiled at that and could see in Marks eyes that he knew

253

something was up but obviously did not know what. It would surprise Steve if Mark actually asked who the seat was for.

It was almost exactly the official start time when the lead Reporter stood up and spoke. "Good morning Ladies and Gentlemen, in a few moments I will call the meeting to order but first I have to inform you that we have received a late request to be allowed to submit further information on behalf of the *'Green Wave'* group." She nodded in Steve's direction and a few cameras went click "My colleagues and I considered this very carefully and came to the conclusion that this should be permitted, even though some of the data is related to ongoing criminal investigations outwith this country." As she said this back room staff appeared and carried further boxes of documents into the room, one per group. Steve's side of the room merely grinned and looked on as the boxes were set down and the back room staff walked away. The supporters looked puzzled and confused as they swapped glances along the tables. Crawford Andrew stood up "Madam, I must protest at this late intervention and request time to consider this development. If this is permitted in this manner we may have to consider withdrawing from this hearing." The Reporter nodded "that is your choice as to whether or not you wish to withdraw. Be advised that this information is pertinent; it is being admitted and if you withdraw, this hearing will continue and it's findings will still be binding on you." she looked at him and looked at her watch. "I will give you ten minutes to decide whilst *'Green Wave'* make contact with their extra witness to advise him that the information has been deemed admissible. Steve slowly stood up and every eye in the hall turned to him as he said "Madam, if I may; that information has already been passed and the individual is on his way here now. In fact I think he may have arrived." At that Paul Gray walked into the hall down one of the side aisles flanked at a short distance by two members of the 'Stirling Lines outdoor pursuit club' as they were calling themselves, who seemed to melt into the walls at the bottom of the aisle while the murmur of recognition passed through the crowd.

+

Mike was sitting in a small hotel room in Denmark completely confused, he had been to the offices of the local environmental agency that he had been shown before, when he was over on a day trip with Paul Brown. He had gone to check that everything was okay with his permits and that they were ready to start studies. The floor of the office block he went to was empty, according to the doorman it had been empty for weeks, except for a couple of days where it had been hired for a film crew for something, he did not know what. Mike went back to the hotel via the office block he was

254

supposed to be using. It was real and they were expecting him so that was a bonus, it was even furnished and ready to go, but empty, no staff as he had been promised. It was one small office and an ante room in a block of serviced offices. The people at his apartment block, where he went next, apologised for it not being ready for him yet but the deposit had only just come through that morning so the apartment should be ready the next day. His advance of expenses was in the bank locally and he had been paid a portion of his salary as he had expected. He began to wonder if he had merely been removed from the scene back home.

Something just did not feel right, he was uncomfortable and lonely. He knew he had thrown away the chance of a lifetime because he had jumped at the chance of a lifetime, it had not been an easy choice, but he had made the wrong one. He went back to his small, cold and impersonal hotel room and cried.

+

Andy was polishing glasses in the bar while he prepared for opening time, it was a couple of hours or so away yet and he did not really think he would be that busy until lunch time when there may well be a lot of people looking for lunch. The exhibition hall was only about a hundred metres away after all. He had been pleased when Paul Gray turned up but he wasn't sure what he could do. Steve the lawyer had been even happier when he appeared, but the one thing Andy just could not figure out was the involvement of these guys from the 'outdoor pursuits club'. He shrugged and turned away as he heard the bell that told him the front door had opened.

The guy standing at reception looked like a reporter, probably a foreigner, there was something about the cut of his jacket and the way his hair was cut made Andy think he was not a local. The man turned round and looked at Andy levelly and with a coldness that made Andy uncomfortable "Hi," he drawled "place is kind of quiet." Andy still had a glass in his hand as he said "Yeah, just me here at the moment, everyone else is away at the meeting in the hall." The guy looked interested "Oh, important meeting?" Andy shrugged "To do with the Doones Estate thing." He suddenly did not want to tell this man much more as he leant in closer to the counter "You wouldn't do me a favour would you? I need to have a quick look around the room of one of your guests." His left hand appeared over the top of the counter with a fold of dollar bills in it and Andy glanced down just for a second "No chance pal and you'd better leave now." He had barely finished the phrase and he didn't even get a chance to say he would call the police when a gun appeared in the strangers right hand and came straight up so Andy was looking down the barrel. "Okay," said the stranger "Now we can forget the bullshit and you'll do as I tell you. Give me the key to Paul Gray's room." Andy smiled "You're too late he's already at the meeting." The stranger just pulled back the hammer on the gun and said "Now." Andy stepped back to look at the key board and see if he could do what he was told anyway, but suddenly a hand grabbed his belt and yanked him back hard through into the back corridor and out of the way. He was dropped to the floor and decided to just lie there silently hoping who ever this was, was on his side. He listened to the muffled sounds of a struggle which stopped suddenly. Carefully he looked round and could see no one as he rolled onto his knees and made to stand up one of his other guests appeared out of nowhere and offered him a hand up. He took it and looked around the edge of the door to see the stranger lying in the hotel hallway with a bag over his head and his hands tied behind him. Two men were standing over him with sub machine pistols pointed at him while the guy who had helped him up looked at and Andy and said "Mind if we use your back door to get his guy into the truck?" Andy just shook his head. "Help yourself guys" he said stepping back realising he still had a glass in one hand "I'm not even going to think about stopping you."

+

In the hall Trente Silver was looking annoyed as he studied the faces sitting across the hall at the end table, it was the first time in a lot of years that he had been so close to people that obviously did not understand the way the world was meant to work. These people were actually trying to stop him improving on the work of that amateur that called himself God. When he was finished the place would be unrecognisable and even more importantly it would have the 'Silver' brand stamped right across it and he might even be able to make some money on this one. He shifted uncomfortably in his chair as he waited for something to start happening, his eyes slithered across the crowd that had come to look at him, somewhere in that mass of adoring fans was his tame hit man. Silver grinned to himself, he knew Andrews would have made a mess of himself if he knew that man was here but he had felt it necessary to remove a problem he had been warned might be here. It looked like it was too late for today but it would be easier tomorrow when Paul Gray would be unable to attend the hearing, 'Yes' he thought 'death was a good excuse for non appearance'.

+

Marcus Dull was not enjoying his morning either. He had just finished breakfast, a meal he was not normally fit to eat because he woke feeling ill most mornings, however since his run in with the police in his car, he had been stopping drinking earlier in the evening and was beginning to rediscover what morning actually was. The problem was the dining room was empty, he had no guests. There was just the bare minimum of staff, a lot of police officers and him. He was supposed to be being interviewed this morning; he was not looking forward to that at all.

It was almost an hour later when he was realising just how bad his day was going to be. He had said to Andrew Crawford he should be able to be at the hall to support Peter Barnard and give him some back bone by now, he thought as he sneaked a look at his watch, realising, again, this was going to be a long day. The one bright spot was he had found why the police had shut him down completely rather than just closing off a few rooms. Unfortunately the down side of that was they had good reason to. They had found his cameras and the secret office he had been using to film the entire goings on. It did not look as if they were likely to believe him that he had not actually seen some of the recordings that had been taken. They had shown him some of the images. He hadn't known the human body could be so flexible and it looked like they had been enjoying themselves, so he really did not understand what had killed the two individuals, unless it had been overexertion.

He looked at his watch again, the inspector had left him alone half an hour ago and he would have thought he should be back by now. He was getting nervous, he knew a lot of things that the Silver Organisation had been up to, not everything and not as much as his films showed, that much he knew simply because he had not seen all the films, but he knew a lot and suddenly he shuddered, maybe he knew too much, he had heard the stories already.

The inspector was watching Dull with his own camera system and couldn't help wondering if he even remembered if this room was bugged or not. Dull had been making full use of the contents of his cellars for years and had probably been at least half drunk, continuously for almost ten years. So there was a good chance he really did not know what was on the discs they had recovered from the back room. There was a huge amount of data of all sorts, there was stuff that could be used for blackmail against a huge range of people and some seriously illegal behaviour, most of it would be inadmissible in court but a lot of investigations could be started because of it. He sighed and sat back looking at the monitor, Dull was scared and getting more scared as time went on, how long he would leave him before he went back in was a question he could not answer yet.

+

In the industrial unit the flood lights were switched on again and this time the figure on his knees in front of them was not shaking as much as the last two had been. He knelt there, listening to his captors breathe, this was not an unusual set up and it was pretty obvious, the way he had been taken down, these were professionals. He just didn't know who they were working for or what their instructions were. He didn't think it was kill on sight or he wouldn't be here, he was just hoping it was a case of hand over to the local police at some point. He could hide his identity and would get lost in the system. He understood that had already happened once, so if that was the case he'd be out in three weeks. He just didn't fancy torture if they wanted information, that idea did not appeal to him.

The bag was pulled off his head and he blinked in the sudden bright white light. A local voice called out to him "Well, well Danvers Redland, nice name to hang on yourself" he swallowed 'How had they got his name?' even the client didn't know who he really was, he had a work name that he used and had travelled under, the unseen speaker continued "Failed two attempts at Quantico, didn't get past the first week either time. One trip in Kosovo and two in Iraq as a bodyguard coupled with several years in the reserve in Iowa." He could hear the cover of the manila folder that he could only see in his imagination, being flipped shut as the local continued "Not really very good are you?" He didn't reply, they already had too much on him, he was not giving them his voice as well. "In our courts you would serve life for murder, maybe get out in ten years or so. Back home you will be tried for treason, that's life for you, guaranteed." Danvers looked up and laughed "Don't bet on it," he finally said "my client will look after me" He flinched when an American voice floated out of the darkness "It's you that shouldn't bet on that. I'm a federal agent and I'm taking you back with me to stand trial at one of our less public court rooms. You're going into a rendition program. You are just going to vanish; no one will know what happened to you." Danvers winced and just knelt there for a second until the local voice said "Stand up" He did as he was told; there was no point in resisting now, unless he got a chance to get away.

+

In the hall Trente Silver had just taken his seat as the first witness of the day and of the entire Inquiry. Andrew Crawford was nervous as the QC
258

leant across to him and whispered "What's wrong, don't you trust your boss?" Crawford muttered back "Actually no, I don't. He's liable to tell the truth at the wrong time and complete bullshit at any other time." He sighed and looked at the desk for a second as he saw the look of shock as his words registered with the QC before he continued "To be brutally honest with you, I actually think he is unhinged, literally insane in the truest meaning of the word. Once this project is over, I'm out of here. I don't know where yet but I am going to put as much distance between us as I can. Permanently"

The QC was nodding, he regretted his decision to take on this case, he hadn't really looked into it and had taken the Silver name at face value. In other words he had listened to what Silvers people had told him, his own research that he had started to last night showed a somewhat different story. He sighed, he just hoped it would work out alright; as he listened to the answers his client was giving to the Reporters he was beginning to have serious doubts about his ability to make this one right.

In the chair Silver was using his most winning of smiles, trying to make himself look human and approachable. His words were not helping the matter at all as he answered quite truthfully in response to some questions.

"So why don't you tell us in your own words, what it is you intend to do to the Site of Special Scientific Interest on the Doones estate that you recently applied for planning permission for?" the reporter asked. Silver grinned and leant back "Well, that's easy, I'm going to build the best golf course in the world based around those dunes up there." The Reporter leant forward and asked "Are you aware that within one hundred kilometres of here there are five courses that are officially ranked within the top ten in the world?" Silver just nodded as the reporter carried on "It is also a fact, is it not, that none of your five existing courses appear in the top one hundred in your own country let alone in the world?" Silver growled in his throat as he sat forward in his chair "No that is not true. That is a manipulated ranking system run by a magazine company who changed our ranking position when we stopped advertising with them. It was clearly a decision based on advertising income rather than the actual quality of the course." The Reporter frowned "As I understand it the ranking is decided by a poll of the entire membership of the International Professional Golf Association which is then independently verified before it is passed to the magazine; who is merely charged with publishing it. Are you seriously suggesting that the magazine in question changes the data so that those organisations who advertise with them gain a higher ranking?" Silver nodded "Of course, it's blatantly obvious, to anyone as intelligent as I am, that the published figures do not represent the facts. Everyone who has ever played my courses tells me personally that they are the best courses in the world." He paused and smiled for a second before continuing "That is why I am launching a new magazine myself which will base the rankings of golf courses on the comments I receive personally from my public. That way we will have a more accurate and fairer way of categorising golf courses around the world. We are already well advanced in negotiations with the International Professional Golf Association to take over the contract for publishing our results through their publications as well. On our own ranking system based on the data I personally receive from players; this course will be number one in the world by the end of next season." The reporter just looked at him "You mean the first season it's open for play surely?" Silver shook his head "No by the end of next season whether it's open or not." The QC was the only one who heard Crawford Andrews groan as he rested his head on his arms on the desk. The Reporter just sighed and leant back shuffling papers on the desk as Silver carried on talking. "I was over at Gleneagles in Scotland not long ago, now that is a wonderful links course, a very good copy of my own DaVarian course in New York State." The Reporter stopped and looked at him for a second before interrupting him "Excuse me, Mr Silver," Silver graciously nodded his head as the Reporter continued "but I was fortunate enough to be over in Scotland, myself, recently and I played the Gleneagles course. It is an inland course, not a links course and has been in existence for almost one hundred years, I'm not exactly sure of the age of the course but it has been around a lot longer than any of yours. In particular the DaVarian course, which I believe is built upon the old DaVarian estate, is that correct?" Silver nodded at him, obviously furious at being interrupted and carried on speaking. "Of course it's an inland course; but it's a links style course. That's what I meant. Yes, that's what I meant, any fool should have known that and it has been remodelled after the style of my DaVarian course. It obviously a poor copy and an easy play. I mean I made a round in forty nine shots but I am better than most professional golfers." The reporter shook his head and looked at Silver "Am I to assume that you are the best on the planet at absolutely everything you do?" Silver grinned and looked across the hall "Andrews, the man is beginning to understand, give him some shares." The female lead Reporter looked coldly at Crawford Andrews and made a note on her pad as Silver carried on speaking. The QC looked at Andrews sitting next to him and muttered softly "I see what you mean."

The next set of questions came from the new and very nervous 'Greensward' representative who hesitated for a second before gathering himself and picking up his notes before asking "In the Environmental

260

Impact Assessment submitted on your behalf it states that..." he never got to finish the sentence as Silver interrupted "Son, I don't do detail, so don't waste my time with page numbers and all that sort of crap." The young guy hesitated for a second before raising his head "Okay, sir, if you don't do detail than maybe I can suggest you look at the executive summary and on page..." Again Silver interrupted "Son, you're not listening to me. Executive Summary is a lot closer to where I work but you're still several levels below where I work. I might on a good day, look at the executive summary, as you call it, of the entire project." He paused and looked across at the ranks upon rank of incredulous faces in the public gallery, smiled at what he thought of as his audience and carried on "I don't look at individual documents. That's why I hire failures like Barnard and Andrews over there." Pater Barnard, jumped having just woken up at the sound of his name but managed to stay seated just in time as heard Silvers voice carrying on talking. "Truth is I don't care about how many blades of grass get crushed or bugs stamped on. This is all about profit. We use golf as a smokescreen, or any other sport you care to name build several hundred houses and a few thousand apartments then leave you to it once we've made our money." The '*Greensward*' rep just shook his head "No further questions" he said to the team of Reporters who were sitting shaking their heads behind the desk at the end of the hall.

It was all that most of the audience could do not to burst out laughing as the evidence carried on in a similar vein for the whole morning, it passed very slowly.

At the lunch break there was small press conference held in one of the side rooms of the hall, it was one of the few that could be accessed from the outside as well as the inside of the building. It had a small table at the back of the room with a single chair behind it and room for about thirty journalists standing in front of the table. He was sitting there grinning his idiot smile with his hands clasped and fingers interlocked on top of the desk in front of him. If the truth was known he was scared of crowds and hated being in public like this, but he did not have the courage to deal with it properly so he pretended it was not an issue and dared anyone to challenge him. No one did.

One of the journalists decided to start the session by asking "Mr Silver, how did you feel your time on the stand went? Did you feel you got the points across that you needed to?" Silver nodded "Yes I feel that went very well, I had no problem with any questions that were presented to me and so far the opposition have failed to give a good account of themselves at all." The journalist was a little surprised at this "But, Mr Silver, you've been on the stand all morning. No one else has given any evidence and none of the opposition have given any evidence as of yet." Silver looked puzzled for a second "Then who's the guy asking the questions?" There was a snigger that ran around the room before the journalist replied "That's the Reporter, she's in charge of proceedings." Silver laughed "Well then this should be even easier than I thought, he's not doing a good job at all is he?" No one said anything as they all just looked at him wondering if he realised what he had just said.

When the afternoon session started Silver was sitting in the middle of the front row of seats with thug one and two either side of him to fend off his adoring public. What he didn't realise was the man sitting directly behind him, one row back was a member of the 'Stirling Lines Outdoor Pursuits Group' who just sat and watched, and listened.

Silver was sitting sprawled out with his arms across the back of the chairs either side of him and had actually pushed his guards further out to give him room to do this so that other people had to move to make room for him, he liked displacing people with his thugs.

He was looking straight at his new architect, the best golf course architect in the world. It would almost have been a believable boast if it wasn't for the fact that he was the second person to have that title handed to him by Silver on this one particular project. The man hated speaking in public, he was a shy self effacing type of individual who liked nothing better than to spend the morning out on the land wandering around to form an idea of the landscape before spending the afternoon at the drawing board drawing something that might fit within the area of land he had available to play with.

The new representative of 'Greensward' was asking questions, but this time he was getting answers, not answers he liked, but at least they were answers. "So tell me sir, at what point do you look for any environmental concerns that you might need to take into consideration in your design?" The man looked at him hesitantly before replying "There is nothing of an environmental nature that I need to take into consideration in my designs. The wildlife will move on to find a better location for itself and the landscape will always be immeasurably improved by what I do for it. So in essence, it's not a case of taking it into consideration. It's a case of making it fit with my design. We have occasionally had to have the laws changed to be more appropriate to our designs." The young man stared at him as the architect had spoken softly and he could not believe his ears at what he was hearing. He tried again "Let me try and understand your answer. I don't

262

want to go away with a misunderstanding of your position." Suddenly from the public benches Trente Silver spoke out "He already answered you. This is a waste of my time." He stood up and pointed at the lead Reporter where she sat "Get this finished up today and I want the permission on my desk tomorrow morning at the latest. I'm fed up with this rubbish." He turned and looked across at where his team sat watching proceedings before bellowing "Crawford, fix this." Trente Silver then turned around and walked up the side aisle out of the hall as the crowd sat there laughing at him. The lead Reporter banged her gavel on the desk to bring the meeting to order and looked at the man sitting on the stand "You can conclude your answer then we will take a fifteen minute recess." She looked at the young man from '*Greensward*' "Please continue, you were asking a question." He swallowed and looked down at his notes "Yes, I was. I was asking do you never worry about things like Sites of Special Scientific Interest or similar rare and irreplaceable sites?" The architect just shook his head "They are irrelevant if you have enough money. If we need to, we just buy another one, especially with the Silver Organisation as my client." The young man sat back and sighed "No further questions ma'am" he said to the Reporter who smiled "Okay," she said "We will now have a fifteen minute recess while we consider how to take this forward from here."

The scrape of chairs and the sudden sound of voices raised in laughter and discussion filled the hall as Mark sat there thinking about what had just happened for a second or two. He turned and looked at Paul Gray sitting by his side "Good to see you back here but I thought that was not allowed under the terms of your deal with them." He jerked his thumb in the direction of the other side of the hall. Paul grinned and shook his head "It's not, but I've got evidence which shows the deal was fraudulent to begin with so I should be able to get my estate back and maybe even keep some of the cash they paid me as compensation." Mark smiled and was about to start laughing as Andrew Crawford strode up to the desk. Pointing at Paul he said "You obviously didn't read the penalty clauses in your contract very well you little prick. I'm going to have every penny we paid you back and we'll keep the estate as well." Paul just shook his head "Do us all a favour, go away. You're already losing this case easily and you're going to lose a lot more, believe me." Crawford scowled and stood there threateningly for a while as he tried to scare these two men who were laughing at him. Eventually he turned and stomped away, back towards his desk with his QC.

The QC looked at him and studied the notes he had written on his pad before he slid it across the desk to Andrews who looked down at it, puzzled before saying. "What's this?" The QC smiled at him "My bill for today's

263

services. I will not be representing you tomorrow. I make it a policy not to represent those who are clearly clinically insane." Andrews just looked at him and slowly smiled "Thank you, you may have just bought us some more time. If you pull out now they will have to postpone the rest of the Inquiry. Surely they cannot let it proceed if we are not formally represented." The QC shook his head "Don't bet on it. I think something else is about to happen." Andrews shook his head and sat back laughing as it became obvious the QC was not going to say any more.

The fifteen minutes of the planned recess came and went and it was almost half an hour later that the team of three Reporters re entered the hall and sat down at the top table. The clerk stood up and spoke "Will we be continuing with the last witness on the stand or do you wish to move on to the next witness Ma'am?" The lead Reporter stood up and the clerk sat down hurriedly, this was different. The lead Reporter smiled at the audience and wet her lips delicately before speaking "My colleagues and I have discussed this matter at length and have come to the conclusion that this Inquiry cannot proceed at this time. It is our belief, due to the attitude of Mr Silver and his team that they are unwilling to recognise the authority of this Inquiry or the process it represents. It is with this in mind that we have now decided to review the plans submitted one more time, in private, and we will consider these along with the attitude of the applicant towards the landscape and the final product as well as the methodology and practice of the application process employed by the local authority in this instance. We will be making our findings public in due course." She paused and looked around the hall, "That means, these proceedings are concluded here today and a final decision will be forthcoming in due course. Probably about a month" Confusion reigned as almost everyone stood up and some people cheered while others jeered. It seemed as though no one wanted to leave, maybe because they were not sure the meeting was actually over.

+

It was late afternoon, maybe early evening and almost the whole crowd of locals were sitting in the bar at the local hotel as Andy worked at serving them as quickly as he could. Paul Gray turned and looked at Mark and said "Can the Reporter do that? I mean, can she just decide she'd heard enough and call proceedings to a halt?" Mark shrugged and turned to look at Steve who was sitting at the other side of the table. Steve shrugged "To be honest, I don't know. I've never heard of it happening before, but then I've never heard of an application being called in after it's been refused either and that's happened here." Marianne just sat there and nodded as she tried to cuddle closer to Mark. He shrugged and almost spilt his beer as he saw

264

Jenny and Andrea weaving their way through the crowd. "I'm not sure what happens next" he said "It could be a good thing for us, I mean Silver made a complete arse of himself in there today. Or it could be that they have instructions from the Capital and we've lost." Andrea just leant across the table and kissed Paul Gray. Mark laughed as he saw a couple of the 'outdoor pursuits club' twitch that was a form of attack they had not expected. They winced even more when Jenny dropped herself into Paul's lap. "You don't mind do you?" she asked him "There's no more seats left anyway." Paul just laughed and slipped an arm around her as Mark saw Parker in the far corner of the bar shaking his head. It was more than another hour later that two of the 'club' gave Mark and Marianne a lift back to Marks place.

+

In the wine bar at the other end of town a similar story was being played out Marlene was sitting next to 'Xander's brother with his slicked back hair and worried expression. It was an uncomfortable group as people who had been political enemies for a long time sat beside one another and bought each other drinks. Eventually Marlene turned to him and asked "What do you think will be the outcome of this?" He shrugged and caught himself quickly but several people had seen that instinctive move, before he said "It'll be passed of course. 'Xander has it all under control. This whole exercise was a smoke screen from day one. The approval of this development was signed and sealed a long time ago. Silvers reactions in there were the perfectly justifiable actions of a busy man who hates having his time wasted by a bunch of meek, lily livered environmentalist wasters." He didn't notice at least two of his team shake their heads and slide off into the evening away from the group of self congratulating politicians.

Marlene sat there nodding slowly as she thought about all the excitement that had gone on lately, she would maybe need to consider her future career path now she had succeeded in getting this through the council. Maybe President would be a good job for a woman.

+

Down at the big house on the Doones Estate Crawford Andrews was actually indulging in a third glass of wine. He knew he was out of control and he had not had this much to drink in one session since he was a student. He smiled to himself, he was entitled to it. It wasn't every day that you closed a five hundred million Euro deal like this one. He smiled and sipped at his wine again and smiled around the room. Barnard, Benson, Danielle and a few other administrative staff were here, pity that was all. Once he got home he would slip away for a week at one of his hidden haunts and be his true self for a while and no one would know. If it went the other way and they lost he just would not come back as he had hinted to the QC.

Barnard was thinking something the same, he had hoped he might get some time with Grayson but that turned not to be possible unfortunately, he might have some strange tastes but a dead man was just a stretch too far, even for him. Never mind he could take a quick trip over to Rotterdam from here and spend some time with his boyfriend once all of this was dealt with in another day or two.

Andrew Crawford was shaken awake by Peter Barnard as he dozed in front of the fireplace. He was annoyed, not just by being shaken awake from a deep sleep but by the fact that the television was on. He hated the television in this room for casual viewing, he scowled at Barnard as his foggy and still half asleep brain tried to make sense of what the television was saying. Then he froze, this was not what he had approved as a press release.

The clip had obviously been filmed at the hall as Trente Silver had arrived right at the start of the proceedings. It showed him stumbling out of his car and walking down the red carpet and into the hall, then a few seconds later reappearing only to, literally, tip toe his way round to the main entrance before striding into the hall once more as if nothing had happened. The voice over was also less than favourable "Today at the memorial hall in Drimmie the Public Inquiry into the proposed housing and golf development planned by Trente Silver got underway 'the great man' as he likes to call himself made a fool of himself on arrival by having his own red carpet rolled out to the wrong door of the hall and then continued in the same vein, even after he gained access to the building." Andrews had tuned out at that point and grabbed the remote control from Barnard before starting to flick channels. This was terrible and could not be right at all. The press coverage was all negative. He began to get annoyed as he watched this, glancing at his watch he knew it was too late to affect the local papers, they would already be out to print and out of reach. He would see what they said in the morning. Now he had to phone home and see if he could influence the press in the States.

+

The lead reporter was sitting in a private dining room with her two colleagues in a hotel that had often been described as the second best in town. That might be changing. She was sitting with her mobile phone
266

pressed to her ear watching her dinner cool as she said "Yes Mr Templeton, it's a perfectly proper process. I checked with the chief planner on a 'what if' basis before we left just to be sure that if the situation arose I was comfortable that I knew how to deal with it." She paused and cut another mouthful of steak, listening all the time "Yes, all our meetings are noted and all the data is properly recorded so it will stand up to full scrutiny. Yes sir, Good night sir." She broke the connection and switched her phone off before dropping it on the table beside her as her colleague spoke "You know what's going to happen don't you?" Without waiting for an answer he continued "Whatever we decide, whatever result we put out, we will be wrong." The lead reporter just nodded as she chewed on her steak before replying "Yes, but that was always going to be the case anyway: So nothing new there anyway." She paused and looked at him "Have you got an idea what way you're going to vote on this one?" He nodded slowly but said nothing.

+

Dull was looking at the outside world and found it looked strange, the thick glass blocks that made up what passed for a window in the cell at the local police station distorted everything and he found the view fascinating. It was also strange having to try and sleep without the assistance of alcohol, that was why he was still awake at three in the morning.

The inspector was sitting at his desk with a mountain of paperwork in front of him and the sergeant falling asleep opposite. He leant forward and gave the sergeant a shove to wake him. "Go home, get some sleep. I don't think we can keep Dull." The sergeant was rubbing his eyes trying to wake up. "Why not?" The inspector shook his head "Oh, don't get me wrong. He's done plenty wrong and will probably end up with time, or someone less prominent in the business world would anyway, he might get probation. I just don't think we can keep him here, apart from anything else we need the space." The sergeant shrugged "Do you think he might get community service?" The two men laughed "There's always a first time, an opportunity for him to put something back rather than take."

+

It was mid morning that Steve phoned Mark at home "Sorry to bother you after the excitement of yesterday but I have to speak to you, here at my office. Soon would be good." Mark leant forward on the table, the tone of his friends voce told him this was important and Marianne stopped what she was doing as he moved, he didn't say much most of the time and he didn't normally give much away by his movements, so when he did something this definite and different from normal she noticed. "Important?" was Marks only question. Steve barely drew breath "Very. I have the club members here at the moment and I'm going to be giving them some data to take care of for us as a back up." Mark nodded, that said it all.

He put the phone down as he stood up and looked across at Marianne who was watching him closely "Coming?" Her face changed to a cold frown for a second or two "You going to try and stop me?" he shook his head and smiled as she said "Give me five minutes to change." He nodded, he needed at least a clean tee shirt as well, the one he had been wearing to cut the grass earlier was probably not appropriate for a visit to the lawyers office.

It was almost an hour later that Mark and Marianne were sitting in Steve's office along with Steve's PA, there was a 'temp' at the reception desk and two of the 'club' members were sitting in reception while two more were in the kitchen drinking coffee. Mark had been surprised at the show of strength but now as he looked at the documents Steve was showing him he was beginning to understand why. Marianne was silent as she had been reading over his shoulder and slowly sat back looking at him wide eyed "That is illegal, surely?" Steve nodded "Very much so, but it's the type of thing that is very difficult to publicise due to the political sensitivity of it. There is a perception that you can't accuse the head of a government, or anyone at that type of level, of corruption whilst they are in government as it may destabilise the whole government." Marianne interrupted "but surely someone that corrupt and that blatantly corrupt shouldn't be in that position in the first place." Steve nodded "I agree completely but there are enough government bodies out there that will block anything they see as a destabilising influence," he paused and licked his lips "under, of course, instructions from their political masters." Marianne nodded her understanding as she sat back. Mark spoke "So, are you saying that while this is public information, available to anyone with sufficient skill," he nodded at the PA "and provable by the fact that it exists in the first place. There is actually nothing we can do with it?" Steve was shaking his head "No, that's what a lot of people want you to believe. It just means we have to do things differently. Remember the comment from before, Mark? If they slam both front and back doors in your face, then you can always go in through the window, or if necessary the wall." Mark smiled at the comment as the two women just shook their heads. Sometimes they just did not understand what these guys were talking about.

+

268

It was the first time for a long time that all of the watchers team were sitting together in their safe house in the middle of the housing estate in Drimmie and the leader was speaking ".... So that just about wraps it up. We've got some good information and enough hard evidence to make it all stick so it should be fun when we get back. I would like to try and get this situation ..." He never got to finish his sentence as the front door crashed in under the impact of a sledge hammer swung by a large well muscled thug in camouflage gear, wearing a ski mask over his face. The thug and two friends came charging in through the splintered remains of door and frame, straight through the flush panel door from the hallway to the living room, which was closed at the time, and confronted the group at the dining table. At the same time another two man team used the same type of 'universal key' to smash in the back door and come in that way. The noise and confusion was incredible as the mass of bodies all rushed into the one room. The watchers mainly sat where they were, like startled rabbits in the headlights as these men crashed in and grabbed them all one by one and threw them to the floor. The last man in through the front door was grabbing all the files and discs off the table and was busy pushing them into a sack when suddenly he stopped and held up an arm "Quiet." He screamed over the noise as he tried to hear something he could not quite make out. He shook his head and waved an arm "Carry on, hurry. Something's not right" less than five minutes later the five man team walked quickly out through the remains of the front door and went back to the two cars that were parked next to one another, three or maybe four doors down the street, the witness who was interviewed later could not remember exactly. The leader watched impassively as his team threw the bags into the back of the cars and climbed in. He looked around, he had that prickle between his shoulder blades again that told him something was wrong but they were in the cars and moving, so he began to relax. He was a little premature.

The two cars had just reached the end of the cul-de-sac and slowed to turn onto the main road when all hell broke loose. Back at the house a few seconds earlier the watchers team had heard the sound of a powerful engine revving loudly as it seemed to power past the house. What had happened was the first of two large black four by four vehicles that had been waiting in the street behind theirs had started up and raced across the open grass area immediately behind the house. The two metre high wooden fence had been no match for two tonnes of steel driven forward by almost six hundred horsepower of engine aimed straight at it. The posts and boards bent and splintered as the 'bull bars' on the front of the vehicle hit and passed on through. The first vehicle went straight down the drive way and onto the street in front, the tyres screeching as they hit tarmac and the vehicle heeled over at an alarming angle as the driver pulled hard on the steering wheel turning it to the left as the four by four powered down the road after the departing cars.

As the two thugs cars slowed at the junction another four by four exactly the same as the one chasing them down the road, was accelerating towards them from their left hand side on the main road. It was only at the last minute it braked very slightly as the driver corrected his aim and turned the wheel to run the two tonne vehicle straight into the front of the escaping thugs stolen family saloon. The first saloon stopped immediately and was suddenly at least a foot shorter than it had been. The second car ran into the back of it as the chasing four by four pushed the two cars together. The thugs slowly shook their heads and looked out and around them. The majority of their field of view was small black and circular as they looked into the gun barrels of further representatives of the 'Stirling lines outdoor pursuits club'. Back at the house the watchers were slowly picking themselves up off the floor as a group of four men dressed all in black this time came charging into the house and pushed their faces back down into the carpets. The ambulance crew who had followed them sat in their vehicle on the grass looking at the black four by four parked in someone's back garden, engine idling with bits of fence scattered everywhere. The driver turned to his partner and said "I never saw anything happen that fast." his partner looked back and said "I never even saw it." they swapped glances and the driver said "Why don't we just wait here until they actually ask for us?" His partner just nodded.

The police inspector sighed as he looked round behind him at the crowds starting to form beyond the barriers. He paused and frowned as a man in a suit walked up to him and flashed a badge. He frowned a little deeper as the suit from the capital smiled a strange cold smile. "We will separate the vehicles now, we've got all the weapons and the data these guys were after is safely in our custody. We will send you a report in due course but I would look closely at one of these guys who are now in your custody, for at least one murder you've had here about recently" The inspector nodded, he wouldn't bother asking questions, he knew enough to know he would get whatever information he would be given. He sighed and nodded as the suit turned away and climbed into a black mini van. Inside he turned to the man in jeans and said "Will you be withdrawing your teams now?" The man in jeans shook his head "Not just yet. There might be more fun to be had here." The suit sighed, that was why he wore a suit, he was happier behind a desk.

270

The federal agent jumped when the telephone on his desk rang, it was a rare occurrence, very few people had his number and the last time it had rang was some one who he had not given the number to. He hesitated and finally decided to lift the receiver, it was the same man. Parker spoke "Ahhh, at last. I was beginning to wonder if you were ever going to answer the phone." The agent shook his head "I might not have been here and how did you get this number anyway?" Parker laughed "I wouldn't have called if I hadn't known you were in the office. Anyway, that rendition flight you have arranged, are there any spare seats on it?" The agent hesitated as his mobile phone began to vibrate in his inside pocket he looked at the number and made a decision "Something's come up I'll need to call you back." He hung up on Parker as he pressed the button on his mobile and lifted it to his ear. Parker laughed as he dropped the handset into the cradle, he could almost imagine the sound of the agent groaning as he listened to the story from the watchers team who had just called him; Parker walked through to the other room and looked at the screens as the man in a wheelchair sat there listening to telephone calls and recording every single one of the international diplomatic calls that came and went from the country.

15

Marianne ran her fingers through Marks hair as they sat there watching television. It had been a couple of days since the inquiry and it had been both mad and magnificent. The press coverage of the actual inquiry and the actions of Trente Silver had been fantastic. One of the channels had even had a fully qualified therapist on the show, doing an assessment of the man based upon the statements of some of the audience and the reporters hand written notes from the day as well. She had decided he was unhinged and whilst unlikely to do anyone else any harm, might be better restrained for his own safety. Mark was grinning at that when a separate news item made him stop and listen. Marianne stopped what she was doing to watch and listen as well. It seemed like five men had been arrested the day after the Inquiry in a housing estate in Drimmie in connection with an ongoing murder trial. 'Information had only just been released due to international involvement and potential conflicts with other matters still ongoing' Mark sighed as he heard the phrases that he remembered from a long time ago. That meant it had been a military operation to tidy something up. He wondered if Parker had been involved. Sighing he sat back and looked at Marianne sitting next to him on the sofa. "Thank you" he said as she looked at him, puzzled. "For being here, for coming to my rescue when I needed company, for putting up with me being an idiot and everything else I can't think of right at this moment." She shook her head and hugged him tightly, pushing her face into his chest as she said "I think it works both ways. You've put up with me being under your roof and hanging on to your arm at all sorts of places and times when I am sure you would far rather have been alone. Then you go and hug me when I need and hold me close as well. I don't think you need to thank me for anything." She was pushing her face hard against him and he knew better then to try and look her in the face as he hugged her tight against him.

+

Andrews was inside the big house trying to hide from the press and make plans to get out of the country and back to the states. The more he looked back at the inquiry the more obvious it was that his boss had blown it completely. Obviously he did not admit that in public, as far as the story to the press went it was simple. The delays in the bureaucratic system in this country had merely been too much for a busy and important man Like Trente Silver to put up with and he had returned to the States to look into

272

other options as to where he could site the 'best golf course in the world'. He sighed to himself, surely even these locals in the council and the government in this barely civilised backwater would recognise such a basic threat as what it was. It had worked in other places but some of them were even getting wise to it. He shook his head and ignored the doorbell as it rang again.

He was standing looking at the wood panelling above the fireplace when he heard Barnard screaming for him from the front door "Andrews, come quickly, please." He sighed and walked through the house. Outside the front door stood Paul Gray along with two men in black suits, and two reporters from the local papers, he looked at the shocked look on Barnards face as he turned towards him and decided to bluff it out. "What are you doing here? You know the penalty clauses in your contract of sale preclude you from coming back into the area." The cameraman at the back was recording everything as it happened and the two newspaper reporters were making notes as fast as they could. Instead of wincing as he had expected him to do. Paul Gray smiled at him. "Yes that was one of the terms of the original contract," Andrews interrupted "Well then, go away right now and I'll consider not applying the other terms and penalties that now apply." Paul Gray grinned even wider, if that was possible before continuing speaking "As I was saying before I was so rudely interrupted. That contract has been voided by the courts here in the country where it was written and executed due to its being fraudulent." He paused and looked at the two men standing in front of him for a second or two "As such the court decreed that ownership of my property be returned to me immediately and all funds, related to this contract, paid by me to other parties are forfeit and have to be returned to me immediately as well." He paused again "That means you are standing on my doorstep in front of my house and the money I paid to my wife will also be coming back to me due to your collusion with her in order to fraudulently obtain my house and property." He paused for another second "Oh don't worry, I have already raised writs against her in the States for the return of my money; I'm not chasing you for it, yet. What I am here to say however, is that while the court order says immediate return of my property. I am going to give you twenty four hours to get out." he stopped and looked at his watch "Okay maybe slightly less. It is now two o'clock in the afternoon, I will be back tomorrow at twelve noon and if you haven't already left I will be evicting you from my house and retaking possession." Andrews face was bright red as he stood there furious once more. He turned and pushed Barnard back inside the door before the fool could open his mouth to say the wrong thing and said "We'll see about that, I intend to enforce our original deal and we will retain this structure as the clubhouse for the 'best golf course in the world'. You will never get this place back." He stepped back as he heard Paul Gray say, "Make sure and pack all your belongings, anything left will be disposed of." The door slammed hard as Paul turned to face the press that was still standing there watching the proceedings. "As I said to you all earlier, I have here a formal writ giving me the legal right of repossession of my property, which just so happens to be my home. I believe I have been more than fair in giving the current, illegal, occupants twenty four hours to vacate the site. I will be taking back control of my home at twelve noon tomorrow." One of the reporters called out "Does that include the land and if so will you continue with the resort development?" Paul Gray hesitated and spoke more slowly than normal as he thought out the answer while he spoke. "Yes it does include the land, all of the land that forms the estate. As for the resort that is something that will require to be considered carefully. All I can say with certainty is that the plans as currently submitted will not be constructed if I have anything to do with it."

Inside Andrews picked up the phone and got through to the QC who had represented them at the Public Inquiry. "I need you to arrange the application and activation of the penalty clauses in the contract with Paul Gray." The QC sighed on the other end of the line. "Then why are you calling me?" he finally said. Andrew's was lost for words for a moment, "Because I need it done legally" finally exploded from his mouth as he almost swore at the phone. The QC sighed again "You really do not understand the legal structure in this country do you? You need a lawyer for that, not a QC. I would suggest the one that drew up the agreement for you in the first place. That is of course if they are prepared to work for you." Andrews spluttered again "What do you mean if they're prepared to work for us? What reason would they have to not want to work for us?" The QC laughed "Simple they haven't been paid either so there is a very good chance they won't work for you until you pay their outstanding bill plus a contingency for the work in the future. It's exactly the same way as I work. You haven't paid me so I will do no more work for you until you do and this phone call will be charged at my normal rate." He could hear Andrews draw breath before asking "How much is your normal rate?" The QC shrugged, silently "For you, I can do a special rate due to your previous non payment and international reputation of non payment of one thousand Euros an hour, minimum charge of one hour." He just smiled as Andrews hung up the phone without another comment. Leaning forward he pressed the intercom and spoke to his secretary "Amelia, please add another thousand Euros to the Silver account for telephone calls please." "Yes Sir", she replied and hesitated before saying "do you think you're likely to get paid at all from them Sir?" His reply was honest and short "Not really, but it all adds to the compensation claim for the administrator when they go

274

into liquidation." He broke the connection and leant back shaking his head thinking 'What a fool I was, rushing to accept a deal based upon what they said. I should have checked the facts first' sighing he leant forward and continued with his preparation for the next case.

+

Paul Clancy was sitting at his desk shaking his head. 'If only that man had been able to keep it together for a few days more they might have gotten away with it. Okay the result was not in yet, but after the performance by Silver in the hall he could see no way any reasonable person could grant permission based on what had been said. Even if they could ignore some of the more ridiculous statements he had made.' He sighed and leant back in his chair. Now was the time to resign, get out of the line of fire and quickly, he had his cut and it was enough to make his retirement comfortable if he did it carefully. He picked up the phone thinking he would call Dull and tell him to start making his play for the job. After a few minutes he hung up, a puzzled look on his face. There was no reply at the hotel.

+

The Chief Executive of the local authority was almost unnaturally still as he also sat behind his desk, thinking deeply about the situation he had landed himself in. The letter was written as a draft and only as hard copy and it now sat on his desk waiting to be signed and copied if he decided that was what he wanted to do. He was far from certain about what he wanted to do. It had seemed so simple and so obvious at the beginning, now he had more information he was far from happy about the whole thing. What had confused matters even more was the head of planning had gone and bought himself a new car, nothing too special in that, but the fact that the car cost more than a years salary made a few people look again. The fact that the fool had done it less than a month after the planner on the case had been found dead was extremely insensitive and would most definitely call his judgement into question. He shuddered as he thought about the report that he had seen on the computer screen of the man in question and shuddered again. Leaning forward he picked up the old steel nib pen and lifted it cleanly out of the ink well that sat on his desk and scratched his name in that beautiful flowing copperplate handwriting he was famous for. He sighed again as he looked at what was effectively the end of a happy career, the blotter rolled over the handwriting and made it secure before he folded the sheet and slid it into the envelope which, in turn, vanished into the inside pocket of his jacket.

Mark was watching the television again, he had seen more television in the last week than at any time in his life up to that point. It was yet another assessment of the development that he was watching but this one was looking at the environmental costs ranked against the financial benefits the project might bring to the region and the country. He watched as the television presenter danced about on an electronic map of the estate describing what each area would be if the development went ahead. Mark was totally engrossed as he watched it closely wondering just how accurate the data was when he heard the doorbell ringing, he sighed as he remembered he was recording the programme anyway so he left it running while he went to the door. He frowned a little as he looked through the glass at the shapes on the other side and sighed to himself he knew who this was before he even opened the door. Reluctantly he swung the door open and looked at Peter Barnard and Andrew Crawford standing there, not looking happy at all. Barnard almost literally growled at him as he opened the door and stood there silently waiting on them saying something. Crawford waited a few seconds and then said "Not inviting us in then?" Mark shook his head "Sorry, I have absolutely no wish to have you in my house so the answer is no." Barnard growled again and started to speak before Crawford shut him up "The thing is Mark, we need your house to make this place the best resort in the world, the best it is possible for it to be, so, we have already asked you nicely to buy it from you so take this as one last chance to be nice." Mark snorted "You guys don't know what nice is and right now you are wasting my time, so go away." He stepped back and made to shut the door but Barnard stuck his foot in the way as Crawford spoke again. "As you wish Mark but you have to realise we are in the habit of getting what we want, and we will here too. It is easier for you as well if you sell it to us willingly. That way we don't need to use," he paused and licked his lips as he chose his words carefully "other measures." Mark shook his head "Don't threaten me. I'm sick of your innuendo and lies in the press and now you threaten me on my own doorstep. Go away, now." Barnard did not move as Andrews spoke again "We have a right of pre emption on your house. A legally formatted document which you signed in order to get more land at some point, obviously not realising that it means we can buy your house out from under when we see fit." He smiled as Mark began to laugh at him "If you don't accept the price we have already offered you, we will force a purchase and throw you out." Mark just shook his head as he leant forward "You need to get yourself a local lawyer who knows what the words and the legal terms actually mean in that document, because you obviously don't." he straightened slightly "Now, get your tame half – wits foot out of my door
276

before I am forced to call the police." Barnard looked offended and stepped back before Mark slammed the door and locked it behind him. He watched from the end window as they both climbed into the silver four by four and drove off down his driveway as Marianne stepped up behind him "Can they really do that? Throw you out I mean." He shook his head "No, what they have is a pre emption which means if ever I choose to sell the place they can step in and buy it at a price equivalent to the best offer on the table. What they think they have is an option to buy, a completely different thing." He sighed and turned away from the window "I'll call Steve in the morning and make sure that is the case, but I have no doubts." He glanced at the TV screen where the programme had changed to something else. "How did the show end?" Marianne laughed "I'm not telling you, you'll just need to watch the recording." He shook his head and sat down to watch whatever was on, he'd watch the recording later.

In the morning Mark was just reaching for the phone when it rang. It was Steve "You'd better sit down, before you fall over laughing." Was the opening line before Mark could say anything "Okay," he said "I'm sitting. I was just about to call you anyway." Steve grunted on the other end of the line "I guess you had a visit last night going by this letter I have in my hands here." Mark didn't say a word as Steve carried on talking "Well, they've obviously not got a clue about our local laws and have probably got it mixed up with their own laws back home. They have however made an offer to purchase your house at what they call 'market value'." He paused before he said "Do you want to know how much they have offered?" Mark sighed "Yeah, go on give me a laugh, if nothing else." Steve laughed out loud "Sorry, I already did that when I opened the letter and basically fell off my chair. Well I'm not going to give you a number but it's basically enough to buy your garage and no more, even if you were in a good mood." Mark grinned to himself "Well tell them, write them a letter that is, with a two word answer from me." Steve sighed, knowing exactly what his friend meant "Sorry Mark, I can't do that and continue practising as a lawyer, no matter how much I want to." He moved in his seat "What I will do is write back to them that their offer is simply not acceptable as the property is not for sale and that they need to hire someone who knows at least a rudimentary amount of local legislation." Mark just grinned to himself before saying "So I'm right about the difference between a pre emption and an option. There is nothing they can do at the moment?" Steve grinned broadly "Exactly, there is nothing they can do to throw you out of your own home." Mark grinned "Thanks Steve that was exactly what I hoped you would say."

+

Andrews was sitting in the office looking at Barnard when he suddenly realised that Danielle wasn't there. He turned and looked back at Barnard "Where's Danielle? Isn't she meant to be here to be here by now?" Barnard frowned and looked at his watch "Well she moved out of the flat upstairs and is living with Benson now, but I would have thought she'd have been here by now." Andrews looked at him coldly "She moved in with Benson? Are you sure about that?" Barnard nodded "That's what she said anyway and he's been dropping her off and picking her up or walking her over most days. What's wrong with that? I thought you might have approved actually." Andrews was slowly shaking his head before standing up "Come on and let's go and have a look at the house. This is not meant to happen." Barnard trailed him out to the vehicle wondering what all the fuss was about.

Bensons house at the end of the row looked empty. It had that vacant, almost abandoned look that empty houses have even when the furniture and other odds and ends still occupy the spaces. Barnard waited outside by the vehicle where it had stopped and they had just gotten out. Andrews was standing in the hallway on the ground floor looking around himself carefully. He had heard of Benson a few times before he met him, but of course he had never been called Benson before. The hallway told him nothing and he was very wary of going too far into the house, amongst those people that knew him Benson had a nasty reputation. He pushed the door to the living room open with a knuckle and stood there looking in. On the coffee table was an envelope with his name on it, he looked carefully at the floor, but it was hard wood and bare so there shouldn't be anything set there, the table was glass and the envelope was the only thing on it so there shouldn't be a problem there either. He stepped in and picked up the envelope, it was nothing more than an envelope with a single sheet of paper inside. He opened it out and read the note. *'Andrews, I'm assuming it's you that will come and see what has happened, your local stooge Barnard isn't smart enough to realise anything is not as normal. The simple fact is I have left, Danielle has come with me and neither of us is intending coming back. Don't look for me.'* The note was signed *'Benson'* and Andrews sighed as he looked around before turning on his heel and walking out of the house again, pulling the door shut behind him.

Outside he looked at Barnard and thought about what the note said, silently he agreed with Benson but had to deal with what he had available for a little bit longer. "Come on," he said as he walked around the vehicle "we'll get someone in to clear it later. Meanwhile let's get back to the office." Old Jock stood where he was behind the wall as the vehicle drove away, up the

278

road in a cloud of dust. He was worried, the way this was shaping up he would not be getting his big bonus from these people as they had promised, because they would not have the money. He walked back inside, slowly, and switched on the television to watch the news.

+

Jenny and Andrea were being interviewed by the local TV station and they were both quite excited about it as the sat in the lounge of the hotel drinking coffee. Jenny was speaking "Of course the area needs development, this region has been starved of income and development funds for many years with the Capital taking all of the money that was available, including disproportionate amounts of tax money from the oil industry, basically stripping this region bare." The reporter leant forward "So you are a supporter of the proposals put forward by Trente Silver and his team?" Jenny flinched "Under no circumstances. I maybe was a supporter of what was originally offered but that was not what they intended. They lied to the locals to gain support and then used large volumes of misinformation and just general lies to try and give the impression of unanimous local support which has never existed." The reporter twitched and turned to Andrea "Do you agree with that comment. It has always been fairly clear to us that support locally was pretty nearly unanimous." Andrea laughed before she replied "The only place there has ever been unanimous support is in the press releases issued by the Silver Organisation, other wise the opposition has been strong and unified. Unfortunately also fairly quiet, hence the silent majority position that we have held since the beginning of this destructive and damaging development campaign is still very much the case with however a change in the attitude now in as much as the silence is being broken and the facts are becoming public knowledge so that more people are beginning to speak publicly about the fact that they do not support this destructive eyesore." The reporter looked puzzled "You have both used the word destructive, could you explain that to me please? What is there to be destroyed?" They looked at each other and it was Andrea that spoke "Well, the most obvious element is the Site of Special Scientific Interest that would have to destroyed and stabilised to make the back half of the golf course. That mobile dune system is unique in this country and one of only three in the world. It has been in existence for almost four thousand years and is of vital importance to climatologists to study the effect of earth movements on magnetic fields and tidal effects on land structures." The reporter interrupted "We have been advised that is incorrect, that the whole thing is only about one hundred years old." Jenny laughed and took over the conversation "That has obviously come from the Silver Organisation,

279

peddling their lies again. Each individual dune may only be one hundred years old but the system of which they are a part is over five thousand years old. If you don't believe us try the geology and geomorphology specialists at the local University, they will tell you." The reporter nodded and decided to try another tack "We have also been advised that the claims of significant archaeological finds have been grossly exaggerated and that what has been found is nothing more than the remains of a gypsy encampment of about fifty years ago. How would you respond to that?" Jenny leant forward "I would suggest you speak to Dr Marianne Presley who is currently living close to the site and is responsible for the excavations. However I will say that who ever told you that has no concept of what they are talking about. The site is actually a Neolithic right through bronze age long term encampment that gives a picture of human development during that time period that has never been found anywhere in the world. That makes it invaluable and an essential addition to the repository of human knowledge. Destruction of it would be unconscionable and should never be considered let alone allowed to happen." The reporter stopped recording and began to put away her equipment obviously thinking about what had just been said "I obviously have to verify your comments before I broadcast anything but it sounds like I need to check where my researcher was getting her information." She pursed her lips and turned to her cameraman, "You got all of that okay?" he nodded "Every word" he muttered as she turned back to the two women "Where do I find this Dr Marianne Presley?"

+

The TV crew knew where to find 'Old Jock' , they had been there a few times doing supportive pieces for a documentary that was being planned for later once the whole scheme had played out and the resort was either built or cancelled, they had been advised it would be after construction. The reporter was now having doubts. They were set up in his garden which was looking good at this time of year, other than the bit around the central heating boiler which was scorched. The reporter turned to him and said "Jock, we've spoken a few times now and you've always been a resolute supporter of the project. I would take it that is still the case." Jock surprised her by shaking his head "It hurts to say this but I was wrong. I've been badly misled by people who know how to twist other people Karl, the guy that used to live next door for a wee while filled me in on a few facts. He worked for them as a mole and has left them and the area. They're a right twisted bunch and now looking back on it, it was obvious." He swallowed and the reporter could see tears in his eyes "I'd like to apologise to my neighbours and all the other locals I have probably helped mislead since

280

this whole thing started. I'm sorry, I'm an old fool and I was taken advantage of and used to take advantage of others." He looked down for a moment before he looked up at the reporter again "I'm sorry, I can't do any more. Please don't come back to me again."

The cameraman filmed the empty house through the glass before they packed up and moved south up Marks driveway to speak to Marianne.

She was startled that it was her they wanted to speak to and not Mark, but pleased that the archaeology could be valuable to the area. They had been speaking on camera for almost an hour about the general site when the reporter asked "Is there any way this site and the finds you are producing could benefit the area with a view to tourism and the like?" Marianne hesitated before saying "Why yes of course. The significance of this site should never be underestimated and I am sure that a museum on the site exhibiting some of the artefacts from the dig could form part of a greater tourist attraction. It would have to be a sustainable attraction obviously." The reporter smiled and sat back, this story was changing quite dramatically as the facts came out rather than the polished hype that had been all that was available until recently.

+

A week later the watching team finally arrived back at their headquarters in New York. Tired, worn and slightly confused after their long and undefined journey. To be honest they had travelled in some comfort compared to the passengers in the rear compartment of the plane. They had been on seven different planes and had passed through something like nine different countries. They weren't sure, no one would tell them and after a short while they stopped asking. The day they arrived they were put into secure accommodation which was basically an armoured five star hotel in the middle of Manhattan and were whisked off to meet their boss the next morning after a decent nights sleep, a shower and a good breakfast. The leader was taken off to one side to speak to his boss while the rest of the team were ushered into de briefing sessions. He had never been in this office before and he hesitated as he was shown in and the door closed behind him. He looked around slowly, a large office with glass on two sides with a beautiful real wood desk with an empty large leather chair sitting behind it. He paused and looked around again wondering when his boss would appear, instead another door opened and the head of the Department of Justice walked into the room. The team leader just stared at him in shock, this man normally kept his distance from field ops but he walked straight over that deep carpet, making clear footprints but no sound until he shook the team leaders hand and without letting him go dragged him around behind the desk and pushed him into the chair "Like the seat?" were the first words he used The team leader nodded without saying a word as the man continued "Well it's yours if you want it." he stared as the other man walked around the desk and sat down opposite "You see it's like this" He adjusted the way he was sitting and continued "Your boss, had other allegiances that were not helping either your career or your operations. I think the people where you just came from figured this out amongst other things. So when they sent your files back here," He held out a hand to slow down the team leader who was half out of his seat at the mention of his files. "Copies I'm afraid not the originals. We've been promised they will send them on as well once they have concluded what they need them for." The team leader sat down again and listened as his boss continued. "Anyway when they sent the files back here they sent them to my office instead of here, so we reviewed them first, because those people don't usually make mistakes. It turned out to be a good move. He wasn't named but the details of certain bank accounts tallied with others we have been watching for some time." He paused and looked more closely at the team leader as he said "He's been taking from Silver and his team for many years in many different ways. The result is he's sitting in a room along at the hotel you guys came from this morning. His room doesn't have a handle on the inside of the door, or a window with a view of the street." He watched as the team leader nodded slowly taking in the information. Your debrief will begin in about two hours time. You have just returned from the last field trip you will ever go on and you have secured the right result." He leant forward to make sure the other man was looking at him. "I want you to take on this job, you will work for and report directly to me and your first general briefing will be in two hours so get yourself together and get ready to listen. Your secretary has a sealed envelope out there with your terms and conditions and all that stuff, bring it along, signed, to my office in two hours. I'll see you then." The man stood up and the two of them shook hands before the boss walked out of the room leaving the door open. The smartly dressed woman who had shown him in, walked back into the room with a large sealed envelope in one hand. "Here you are sir. The departments tailor will be here in fifteen minutes, it's normally part of your package," she tapped the envelope he now held with one elegantly painted finger nail "Page twelve I think, and my name is Vera." He smiled and spoke for the first time "Thank you, Vera. I will no doubt need your guidance occasionally, but right now that will be all thank you." She smiled and turned round, walking out as he sat down and tore open the envelope.

+

282

It was the hammering on the door that had first made Arthur jump, he had become used to that with Silvers people always trying to throw him out of his home, but the last day or so it had gone quiet, almost as if they weren't there. He hadn't seen Mark for a day or two either, but this didn't sound like his knock and he would normally shout as well so that Arthur knew who it was. Carefully the old man moved to the door and shouted "Who's there?" Surprised he stepped back when he got a reply, a woman's voice "TV news, can we speak to you for a minute please?" Arthur hesitated but thought it might be worth a look, he hadn't spoken to anyone for days. Slowly he lifted the bar and turned the key before swinging the door open to find a young woman standing there with a bloke behind her, he was carrying a camera which was turned off and pointed at the ground. He stood there blinking in the sunlight as she looked at him, puzzled for a moment, before she shook her head and carried on talking. "We actually came here to talk to the Silver Organisation about the threat that's been made to evict them from the site by Paul Gray the previous owner, but it almost looks like they have already gone. Have you seen any of them around?" Arthur shook his head, looking at her with a puzzled look on his face. Stepping back he said "Want to come in? I was just about to put the kettle on." She smiled and the two strangers stepped into his house.

+

Paul Gray was ready for battle as he walked up the last bit of the driveway to what he still thought of as his home. He had left his vehicle at the side of the driveway so he could get out and look at it from a distance but instinct had taken over and he had walked away from the vehicle and up to the door. He stopped at the bottom of the steps and looked up at the name stone inset above the door "What the f..." was his reaction as he looked up. Instead of reading 'Doones House' as it had done when he lived there and for at least four hundred years before that, it now read 'Silver Mansion' The camera crew were filming him as he growled "That won't last"; they were the reason he had stopped mid sentence earlier. Turning he nodded at the two bailiffs who were with him, for legal reasons, and looking beyond then was large black four by four of the 'outdoor pursuits club' who were with him just because they could be. He nodded and walked up the steps stopping at the top as he noticed the key was in the door. He reached forwards and stopped as the crunch of gravel under tyres came to him. Looking round, he decided to wait until the police inspector got out of his car and he could find out what it was he wanted. The inspector smiled at him and stopped at the bottom of the steps "Please, carry on," he said "I'm merely here to make sure this goes legally and in an acceptable manner." Paul nodded and turning round, walked into the house. It was empty.

Paul walked through the house followed by an attentive camera crew and the police inspector who said nothing. It looked like the previous occupants had left quickly. The office still had a few papers lying around on the floor but most of the place had been stripped of furniture and belongings. Paul sighed as he looked around at the décor. "Well," he finally said out loud "At least they seem to have left most of the bits that I had to leave when I moved out, so there is still some character to the place." He sighed and looked down at the purple and yellow tartan carpet before adding "Even if I will need to change some of the colour schemes. The latest version of the 'tarts boudoir style' does not sit comfortably with me." They finally went back to the office and Paul was startled to find the police inspector still in there looking at some of the paperwork that was lying on the floor, he looked up as they entered "Paul can I ask you to voluntarily allow me to take this paperwork away with me, it may help in some of the other elements of a case we are building." He paused and looked at the camera crew "I'd also like a copy of your tape and ," he turned and pointed to a corner of the room where there was a small black box sitting on a table with a blinking red light on it. "I'd like the tape from this machine, if you don't mind, but I'd really like to listen to it first, again, if you don't mind" Paul shrugged "As far as I am concerned anything they left will be getting thrown out anyway, so if it's of use to you, please take it." The inspector hit the play button and the four people listened to the message without a word until, when it stopped and the machine clicked the inspector pushed a button and flicked the tape out and into a paper tissue which he folded around it before putting it in his pocket. He straightened and looked at Paul for a moment "If you don't mind I'll have scene of crimes send a van over and we can clear the office block as well. I'm sure immigration will be interested if no one else is." Paul shrugged "Help yourself, as far as I am concerned it's rubbish anyway."

+

The producer of the TV station called the inspector just as he sat down at his desk to ask him a favour "Our people filmed a scene with you and Paul Gray at Doones House earlier today and I was hoping to use it as part of our show tonight. That wouldn't be a problem would it?" The inspector hesitated for a minute as he thought about what had been filmed before he replied. "I have no objection to the visuals being used but I would request that the audio track from that section not be used in your film. That may actually be evidence in an immigration case that is still very much live." He could hear the producer thinking as he spoke slowly "Okay, if that is the situation could you let me know as soon as possible when it becomes viable

284

for us to use it without prejudicing your case?" the inspector nodded to himself "Yes, that shouldn't be a problem, we can let you know, it may actually help your show as well." The two men agreed and broke the connection.

The inspector sat back in his seat and thought about that tape, it was interesting to say the least but was it relevant? He sighed, it almost certainly wasn't relevant to him but the immigration boys would love it. Leaning forward he began rifling through the papers stacked on his desk. He smiled and pulled a large sheet of paper out of the stack and smiling leant back. He opened the sheet out and spread it over the top of the desk and everything else. He was still looking at it when the sergeant walked in. "What's that you're looking at? I didn't think you were into pretty pictures." The inspector shook his head "It's one of the drawings from the Doones estate, a general layout drawing. See," he pointed at the sheet "That's the golf course, there's the housing estate." His finger was over the top of the drawing indicating different coloured blocks as he spoke but the sergeant interrupted him "Look, sorry, but you're wasting your time. I can't see that." The inspector looked at him, puzzled as the sergeant walked across the office and sat down at his own desk "You see, it's simple I just can't interpret that drawing it makes no sense to me. Building plans, layout drawing all that type of thing is just a pretty picture to me, it makes no sense. I've spoken to a lot of others who have the same problem as well. These types of things make absolutely no sense to us. We're probably in the majority." He turned and picking up his cup stood up to head back out to the coffee machine in the hall before he said "What was it you were going to point out to me anyway?" The inspector smiled "I knew your curiosity would get the better of you sooner or later." He leant forward and jabbed his finger at the drawing on his desk. "It was this, it's been a point of contention with the objectors since day one. The hole in his argument about local staff being imperative to make the place work has been the inclusion of this 'six hundred unit' accommodation block' right here on the site." The sergeant set down his cup and stepped closer "I don't remember hearing anything about that in the public statements." He said as he squinted at the pink rectangle on the drawing with the words 'six hundred unit accommodation block' printed across it. The sergeant looked at him again "How does that affect us?" His boss smiled at him "Go get your coffee and I'll let you listen to a tape that will answer your question when you come back." The sergeant frowned and walked out of the office.

+

Jenny was sitting in the café in the middle of Drimmie when Alison walked in, ordered a coffee and walked over to her table "I know I've made a fool of myself but can I sit down please? I really don't want to sit alone." Jenny looked at her over the top of the paper "Yes, of course, please sit down. We've been friends for some time; one mistake shouldn't poison that for the rest of our lives." She paused and looked at the other woman "Are you alright? You don't look your normal self." Alison just shook her head "I'm not feeling too good. I've just been at he doctors and he's sending me for some tests, just to get a few things checked out." Jenny just sat there watching as a tear trickled down her friends face as she sniffed softly and continued speaking. "I made a fool of myself with Peter Brown and now I think he's infected me with something." She looked up suddenly at her friend across the table. "Nothing too serious I don't think, just unpleasant." Jenny nodded as she struggled for something to say, she knew that almost any comment right now would be a mistake and do more harm to the woman sitting opposite. As she folded the paper Alison leant forward and looked at the front page as it lay there on the table "What is that about?" she asked, her finger pointing at the headline article. Jenny carefully picked up the paper again and open out the front page so it could be read. "It says that some news crew was up at Doones House when Paul Gray retook possession and there were some documents that confirm the six hundred unit accommodation block was for the use of immigrants from eastern Europe who had been lined up to come over and start work. A contract has been found that shows the agency would be paid the national minimum wage for each person they provided. The wages would be paid less the cost of uniforms and protective equipment where appropriate, the cost of accommodation would also be deducted before the money was paid to the agency who were going to be taking a management fee before passing on the remainder to the staff who would in some case be left with as little as one Euro an hour." Jenny stopped reading and looked up at her friend who was sitting silently opposite her. "Are you okay?" she asked again as Alison shook her head "No, I'm not. That just proves he lied to me again on more than one occasion. He made a point of saying that the rumours of foreign staff were lies. They could never do that here, the accommodation block, which I thought was three hundred staff by the way, was so they could house the unemployed from the capital if it was needed." Slowly Alison stood up and smiled at her friend "Thank you, for speaking to me. I have to go now, but I'll see you around?" Jenny nodded and smiled as her friend left the café, slowly, head down obviously unhappy about the situation she had landed herself in.

The waitress leant forward and asked "What papers that in? I don't see it in the 'Daily'." Jenny smiled at her "No you won't, they only print stories in support of it. It's in the '*National Independent*' here; have mine. I've finished with it." She said as she stood up and handed over her copy of the news paper.

+

Steve was sitting looking at the computer screen in his office once again, checking and double checking that the data he was looking at did actually say what he thought it did. It showed a huge reason for bias and improper behaviour at a very high level. He was nervous, he had been in some strange situations before and seen some obviously corrupt people get away with things they should never have been allowed to get away with. This could be another one of the same, if it was handled badly, the problem was he just wasn't sure how to get the information out there into the public domain without putting his life on the line. He looked out through the open door at his PA who was sitting out in the reception area, it was her who had uncovered the information in the first place, looking in places a lot of people never thought to look, for details that people never thought to look for. This was a major finding and could cause serious problems for a lot of people, turning he picked up the phone and dialled slowly.

It did not ring more than twice before a deep brusque voice at the other end of the line said "Serious Fraud Office, how can I help you?"

+

Arthur was sitting at his kitchen table looking at some old photos when there was knock at the door. Carefully he got to his feet and shuffled to the door, he smiled quickly and easily when he saw who it was standing outside in the light but persistent drizzle.

The door opened and the young reporter smiled almost as broadly as he did as she stepped past him into the warm dry interior of the little cottage. She stopped as she looked at the pictures spread out on the table, the smile on her face getting even broader as she looked down the mixture of pictures. Some were faded and torn, some were creased, a few were perfect. Slowly she picked up one from the middle of a group of photos on the table. It showed a couple with two little boys at their feet, maybe taken in the nineteen fifties or so, Arthur was smiling and shaking his head at the same time. "That was me and the wife when the boys were small. They were good boys and that was a good time." She was shaking as she asked him "Do you ever see your boys?" Arthur just shook his head "John, went away to Canada a couple of years ago. I went with him, but came back, I just

287

couldn't settle, and now they tell me he's dead. Andy on the other hand left home almost thirty years ago and I've never seen him since." The young woman noticed he had tears in his eyes, which was just as well as she had tears in her own eyes as she asked "Why did Andy leave home?" Arthur shook his head as he looked down at the photo that was sitting on the table. "Never did find out, he just left us a note saying he had done something that would shame us, so he would leave before it did us any harm. I wish I knew if he was okay." The young woman turned slightly and taking the large cotton bag from over her shoulder pulled out a large photo album. Arthur stared as she laid it on the table before opening it near the front. Gently she reached out and took the photo from Arthur's hands and compared it to an almost identical copy that was in the front pages of the album. Arthur stared down at it as he tried to see any differences. The girl spoke as she looked at him. "This is a picture of my father, one Andrew McIntyre with his brother, and his parents when he was quite small." She stopped and looked at him "I think you are my Grandfather and I am the reason Andy McIntyre left home, all those years ago."

+

Jackson was sitting in his office with the company lawyer, discussing what was next as far as they were concerned, the lawyer was talking "….basically the *Evening* is damaged goods and is a huge liability to the group. This latest cost of damages and compensation to Mark Rae is only really the tip of the iceberg, there has been a steady drain on the group finances for some years now and it doesn't really look like going away. From my viewpoint, as your legal adviser, I would strongly suggest you unload the '*Evening*' one way or another. It is no longer an asset." Jackson nodded as he was listening to the other man talk. "In some ways Grayson's death has simplified things. I have also told the new guy at the '*Daily*' not to print any fancy stories about it, which I know he finds galling because the more we find out about what he was up to the more juicy the story looks to be." He paused and sipped from a cup of rapidly cooling tea "However, he was one of ours and we need to do the best by his widow that we can." He sighed deeply and looked into midair past the lawyers head, who knew him well enough to let him think and not to interrupt at this point. "Meanwhile," he continued "The '*Evening*' is starting to lose readers; it looks like more and more people are realising it really is not a good paper at all and they don't believe what it prints; for a local paper that is not a good position to be in." He turned and looked over his shoulder as if expecting some one to walk in and listen to the conversation. Turning back to the lawyer he sighed deeply and continued talking. "I don't know what to do about Jamieson. Since we moved him over to the '*Evening*' he's improved the paper a lot, it has become better. To be honest I did not realise just how bad it was with Grayson in charge but now the paper looks like its about to fail completely I feel like I should pull him back into the fold, but If I don't hurry up, the paper will be past saving and he'll go down with it. I really don't want that to happen." The lawyer looked at him thoughtfully for a moment. "What about pulling him over to the corporate side and selling off the '*Evening*' as a going concern if you can. That way he gets the period where it's for sale to consider his options in the corporate group. Might be worth it, if you really think he's worth saving." Jackson scowled for a moment and sipped at his tea, not committing himself to an answer either way.

16

Steve was looking at the computer screen again and he knew his friend Mark would be getting annoyed at him if he could see him right now. This had always been one of his problems, if he once allowed a seed of doubt into his mind about some of these things, he became almost paralysed by it on that subject and would struggle to complete what he had to do, unless he found a way round it. Right now, he knew what he had found should be publicised but he had already given the data to the Serious Fraud Office and so should leave it alone, let them do their job. He sighed and turned away to look at the other figures that had been coming his way, they looked suspicious to say the least, but the trouble was he was not sure anything would happen about it in time to have any effect. In other words the man might be caught but the damage would be done, and it would be irreparable. Suddenly it struck him he had something else that was worth looking at, he pulled open his desk drawer and pulled out the padded envelope with the memory stick in it, he turned it over in his hands before finally dropping it on his desk and picking up the telephone.

It was almost four hours later that the police officer left Steve's office with the padded envelope and the memory stick in his hand, both in clear plastic bags. His other hand held a fingerprint sheet with Steve's prints on it so they could be excluded. The inspector was shaking his head while Steve was smiling and nodding into the phone. He was speaking to one of the newspapers about the stuff on the stick, the policeman had told him that it may be important before it was sent to a solicitor but it just looked like some kind of report to him; so Steve had immediately phoned the paper, the sooner this got into the public domain the better, before someone stuck a writ on him.

+

Jonathon Diarmond sat back in his office at the '*National Central*' he was slightly puzzled as he looked at the press coverage from the Drimmie area and the majority of the broadsheets. He looked back up, through the glass wall of his office, at the TV screens that were at the far side of the news room and realised the story had gone already, there was just a ticker line at the bottom the screen repeating what he had seen on the main screen. He tapped into the international news feeds on his computer and looked up the story, it was there and in more detail. He began to look more closely, this could be interesting.

It seemed to relate to a court case that hadn't been publicised over in Europe, 'yet' he thought. Slowly he dug through the information, file, after file, after file. Hours later he sat back and suddenly realised the office was quiet and more than half in darkness, he had missed lunch and even the normal train he took home, he would just need to catch a later one. Glancing at his watch he realised that if he didn't leave now, he would miss that one as well. Slowly he wandered down the stairs in the building, it was dimly lit and quiet but he was used to that. The offices may not be ancient but they were not the newest in the country either so the staircase that spanned the four floors from the newsroom down to the ground was a little grubby but almost always silent. Suddenly a door banged further up in the stairwell and he froze. There shouldn't be anyone up there at this time. Shaking his head he carried on down and out of the building, probably just some one else, like him, lost track of the time or just trying to catch up on something else.

The early evening air in the Capital was warm and grimy as it always was, laden with the scent of fumes from all the vehicles that crowded into the city every day. The pavement was wide, but still half full of people as he said good night to the security guard and headed towards the tube station. He turned his head to check the road was clear as he came to the first side street and he stopped dead in his tracks as he saw the fire door at the bottom of the stairs he had come down swing shut. Two people who had been walking behind him walked into him, not realising in time that he had stopped. "Hey, wha' cha' doin?" was the startled comment from one of them as he regained his balance quickly and hurried on to wherever he was going. Jonathon stood there and looked around the crowd of people swarming over the pavement around and towards him, for a moment there was a touch of panic as he stood there scanning the crowds for a familiar face. If they had come out of the building he should know them, especially at this time of night, he checked his watch again in a reflex action and looked away again just as quickly, still not knowing the time. As he thought about it he became more and more uncomfortable, there was no reason for anyone to use the fire exit. If they were in the building, they should sign out at the front desk, as he had done. Anyone who didn't want to sign out, shouldn't have been in the building to begin with. He shook his head and turning walked back to the front desk where Steven the security guard looked up at him, startled as he asked. "Did you just get an alarm on the side fire door?" Steven nodded "Yeah, we did that. Andy's just away to check it out, should be back in a minute, why?" Jonathon shrugged "Just thought I heard some one in the stairwell when I came down. I ignored it, thought it would just be someone else working late but when I went onto the side street I thought I saw the fire door swinging shut. Didn't see anyone, just the door swinging." He looked thoughtful as he reached out and turned the building register round to look at it. Andy the security guard came back at the same time and looked at his colleague, with a puzzled look on his face. "There's been some one in alright. The catch was wedged back with a match in the mechanism so the door wouldn't latch but I just don't know how they opened the door in the first place." He looked at Jonathon scanning the register and continued "According to the book, you were the last one in this part of the building. Production through the back is fully staffed but all the link doors are locked at the moment so no one can get through from the presses to the offices." Jonathon nodded "As I just told Steve here," he nodded at the guard behind the desk "I heard someone on the stair as I came down and then I saw the fire exit door swing as I went onto the side street." He paused and looked at the two guards "Looks like we had an unofficial visitor who was upstairs, came down the stairs at he same time as me and went out the side door. Andy was nodding as Steve said "Yeah, but how did he get in, in the first place." Jonathon just shrugged as he turned and waved over his shoulder "Maybe you'll have it figured out by morning, meanwhile good night, again." The two guards just grunted as he walked out the door and left them to it. One turned to the other "So what do we do about it?" Andy looked down at his young colleague "Simple, we log it. Then I go and do a full sweep of the building starting at the top until I get back down here." Steve nodded "Checking in regularly I guess." The other man nodded before pushing himself upright off the wall he had been leaning back against "Sooner I get started, the sooner I get finished." He grunted as he turned and walked away towards the lifts.

Jonathon stopped just before he passed through the glass doors at the front of the building and looked out on the street and the crowds that flowed past. Many different faces in a stream, each indistinguishable from the next, he shuddered slightly as he realised he did not know who he was looking for and would never be able to pick anyone out in a mass of people like the one he was looking at. He sighed deeply and stepping forward pushed the revolving door in front of him and walked out into the early evening air for a second time.

It seemed a far longer walk than usual to the tube station and the half empty platform where he stood and waited, he stood a long way back from the edge, and waited, and waited. The platform seemed threatening and unfriendly. Even the crowd of students, all laughing and giggling, as they

292

headed back out of town to somewhere else, was a threat. He looked at them closely and he wondered if he was really scared, or just panicking. He finally relaxed when the door to his flat clicked solidly shut behind him. He had written about this type of thing often but had never experienced that uncertainty that caused his stomach to tremble and every flicker of movement in the shadows caused his head to turn and see what it was. He resolved a good nights sleep would help and he could get back to it in the morning.

+

Andrew Crawford was sitting at his desk in an almost empty building listening to the silence, the only sounds he could hear were those of his secretary starting to clear her desk. Her shape moved as a shadow on the frosted glass of the wall panel between his office and her working area and he watched distractedly as she moved around collecting together the few personal belongings he had allowed her to gather together in her workspace. He was sitting there, not doing much of anything, thinking about his own life and how empty it actually was. For the last few years he had been working with Silver he had had no real friends or relationships of any kind. He had been kept busy running around the world looking after failing plan after failing plan. Now it looked like this one in Europe was the final straw and the house of cards, as he thought of it, was about to come crashing down around them all unless they got out and away in time. He sighed and looked at the calendar that hung on his wall, the right time for him had probably been last year when the first offer of the Bermuda job had come in. Now he would always have the taint of the Silver Organisation on him.

His thoughts turned back to his visit up to his bosses office earlier that day. It had been frightening. Trente Silver was still sitting at his desk and had been talking on the telephone when Crawford's had walked in. That hadn't been a bad thing until Crawford's had realised that the telephone cord did not reach the wall and it was God he was talking to, giving instructions to, he corrected himself. The man had ignored him as he walked around the office just the eyes had followed his every step through that deep pile carpet until he had walked out into the reception area of his bosses office, closing the door behind him and met his wife. Number three as everyone called her; they could not pronounce her Eastern European name, so they just did not try. She had the wide flat stare of the dispossessed that he had seen on television so many times. He had never expected to see this expression face to face and definitely not in his own office building. She scared him as she turned and regarded him with disdain and disgust "One

293

of his flunkeys" she said, her accent all but gone after the time she had spent in the US but the sneer in her tone evident "Are you here, like a vulture, to pick over the remains?" he did not answer and made to walk past her but she moved and stood in his path, forcing him to look at her. "I was," that made him stop "I married him for money, and did okay for a while. Now I realise too late he has no money. Has not had for several years but no one had the courage to say so. Now there is no hiding, people will crawl out from under the floorboards to get what they are owed," she paused and turned away before continuing to speak "and there is not enough for everyone. He will not know" she pointed at the closed door at his back "He does not see anything any more, he does not understand that he is not himself any more let alone anything else. He cannot help you." she stepped closer again and looked him in the face "If I were you I would take what you can, what you are owed, and leave." He looked at her as she turned and walked away towards the private internal staircase that led to their apartment on the floors above but stopped and looked back at him "Why are you still here?" he asked her. "Because I may still stay with him. There is still a little honour in me, not much, but some and he is still my husband." Without another word she turned away once more and climbed those marble spiral stairs up out of his sight as he just stood there and watched her vanish upwards.

Back in his office he was still sitting there, confused and unsure what to do. He would have packed his desk when he came back down if he had not met her upstairs and now as he sat there he realised even his own apartment in the other block across town at the side of the plaza was not his. It came with the job and so as soon as he was fired or quit his post he was meant to vacate it. Without a word he stood up and walked out past his secretary who smiled at him uncertainly as she sat down quickly unsure if she was allowed to be preparing to leave. Crawford just smiled back and kept walking, they were the only two on this floor as he found out in a matter of seconds, even the office where Matt had been packing boxes when he first arrived back, was empty and looked like it had been cleared in a hurry. The lift took him down to next floor and it was completely empty, there was no one there. As he went further down the building he gradually found more and more people until he found the bottom ten floors were fully staffed. He smiled and nodded to himself, 'that was about normal. The further down the ladder a person was the less information they had available to them.' He paused and looked around and down from the glass fronted balcony he was standing on at the fourth floor, looking down into the reception hall and the bustle and noise of people moving round. It seemed a little quieter than normal but that might just be his imagination.

Slowly he walked across to the lift and pushed the button, His floor was silent as he came out of the lift and turned towards his own area, his secretary was sitting there reading a newspaper on the internet, looking efficient and ready to do work. Trouble was there was nothing to do. He sighed and looked at her "Go home" he said as she looked up at him startled "I'm sorry sir," she asked her voice wavering slightly. He smiled before he repeated "Go home, if you want to. I would suggest you begin looking for another job. Tell as few people as you can please, and if you want to still come in here and use the internet and stationary until you get another position please do; but if you want to just go home. Then go home." She smiled at him and he was surprised at just how pretty she actually was "What if," she started "I keep coming in here and do my job search from here, that way I can also do any secretarial work you need doing as well, better for me, better for you." he nodded "Good idea, just please tell me when you get another position and I'll make sure you keep getting paid as long as its possible." She smiled and turned back to her screen as he just walked past her into his office, but this time he left the door open.

+

Steve hadn't actually been talking to a news reporter as he had made out to the police officer, it was an investigating officer of the audit commission who was most interested in seeing a copy of the report with the changes marked. Steve had emailed it to him and it was now the next morning, almost ten o'clock when the phone rang in Steve's office. It was a bad connection from a mobile phone as the voice on the other end said "Good morning sir, we spoke yesterday. I'm from the audit commission." Steve grinned "Yes, I recall the conversation, how can I help you?" "Well," said the voice "would you be able to meet this morning?" Steve looked at his clock "Yes I could but will you be able to make it here in that time?" The voice on the other end of the line laughed "Oh, yes, we're just coming into the outskirts of Drimmie now and should be at your office in less than half an hour." Steve grinned to himself "Come on up, you will be made welcome. I take you don't want too much fuss about this?" He could hear the smile in the voice as it said "You take it correctly. I will see you soon. Thank you."

So it was less than half an hour later his PA buzzed through to Steve and introduced his visitor. He was pleased with the no nonsense attitude of the visitor who took notes and discussed the contents closely with Steve while his driver sat in reception and waited. Eventually the man sat back and said "Looks to me like a flagrant breach of rules and alteration of a formal document by an individual who is not qualified to do so. I am glad you passed this on to the police because I have my own suspicions as to why this was sent to you." He stood up and the two men shook hands before parting. The official looked back at Steve and said "My next stop is the police station then I will be going to the council buildings with at least two police officers in tow as well as my own body guard. In the mean time, and this is in confidence, there are a small number of forensic accountants working in the background to sort out some of the issues that we suspect are the drivers for this behaviour." He turned towards the door but stopped and turned back "I will keep you informed as far as I can, but if there are legal proceedings..." he didn't finish the sentence but Steve nodded "As a member of the legal profession my self I understand fully. Any information you can share with me would be welcome." Steve stood there and watched as his visitors driver stood up and walked out of the door first. That was when the words his visitor had used came back to him and he smiled, not just a driver then. That meant the relevant authorities were taking this whole thing seriously.

+

Marianne had been surfing the web when she found the first hints of something not right in the Silver Organisations rosy world. It was a small article from a small town paper in Ohio where there was apparently a development under construction, or at least that was what the investors had thought. It now appeared that the investors had been told by someone who was just locking the door of the site hut as they ran away from the place, that there was no money left and all that had been built was all that would be built. The picture showed a hole in the ground. She sat back and looked at it on the screen. She was still crying when Mark found her in the office almost an hour later as he returned from the shops.

It was not a screaming sobbing fit, just a continuous slow trickle of tears down her face as he looked at her and immediately slipped his arms around her and held her close. "I'm sorry" she muttered "What's wrong?" was his reply She shook her head trying to clear her eyes as she pushed him away and waved at the computer screen which had gone black as it waited on her to do something. "That is what they want to do here." He looked at it as the screen slowly came back to life and the picture showed itself. He stared and sat down on the arm of the chair to read the article. It was only a few minutes later his head came up and he looked out the window, seeing nothing as he thought it through. "They, that's the Silver Organisation, say that it was a franchise deal and they have no responsibility for anything on the site other than some advertising." He looked at Marianne before saying

296

"How do we know that isn't the case here?" She shook her head "We don't." was all she said as he sat back staring at the picture on the screen "Shit" was all he said.

+

It was the same word used by the Chief Executives secretary when she saw the ID card being held out to her by the visitor who had arrived in her office unannounced. She had enough self control not to say it out loud but it was the first word to cross her mind as she looked at the closed door. She stammered "I'm sorry but he's not in at the moment and as such his office is off limits to everyone." The visitor shook his head "Sorry that is not the case. I will be using the office and I will be examining all available files." She looked at him blankly for a second "I'm sorry I cannot permit you to do that..." She did not get to finish the sentence as he interrupted "This," He said brandishing his ID again and another sheet of paper "gives me absolute authority in this building to go where I like, look at what I like and speak to who ever I see fit. This," he lifted the paper "is a warrant drawn under the authority of the Advocate General that gives me access to every document, computer file and person in this building. That is in addition to the access rights granted to me by my office which is shown by this." He held up his ID card again and she let her eyes slide past him to the two police officers who were standing behind him looking very formal and official. She sighed and opening her desk drawer slid a key across the desk. He smiled at her and said "Thank you, now I suppose a cup of tea wouldn't be impossible to arrange would it?" She smiled and stood up as he turned towards the heavy wooden door that stood in front of him.

He froze immediately he opened the door and stepped back signalling to the two police officers "I think you need to be first in here" The two officers looked at one another and stepped forward. The only odd thing about the desk was the simple white envelope that was lying on the leather pad in the middle of the desktop but the chair behind the desk was still occupied. The Chief Executive was still at his desk and had been sitting there for at least one day; he had not gone home last night and never would do so again, a fatal stroke, brought on by stress as the coroner would later say, had made sure of that.

He finally got a desk and computer access just down the hallway, his driver was sitting on a chair in the actual hallway watching people who scurried past pretending not to see him or know why he was there. The bodyguard smiled he was used to spending time people watching. It was one of his core skills now and one that was essential to the successful performance of his job. So when he saw the same man pass the end of the corridor for a fourth time, each time looking more nervous than the last, he began to look more closely and watch for him coming back. When he didn't reappear the bodyguard shrugged and went back to boredom, until he went to the kitchen to make a coffee, it just so happened that the kitchen had a window that looked down into the staff car park and his eye was drawn to a particular vehicle. He whistled softly, that was special and not too flash but just something that was worth taking a better look at. He pulled a lens from his pocket and took note of the registration number before heading back to check on his boss. He glanced in and saw he was still working away, calmly tidying up his notes after the last interviewee had left. He nodded as the bodyguard caught his eye and vanished again. The man behind the desk smiled, the bodyguard put up with a lot of insults from people who did not understand his value, but as far as he was concerned the man was a valuable addition to the team. He had sharp eyes and something had obviously attracted his attention, he carried on with what he was doing until a soft cough made him look up as the bodyguard slid the sheet of paper across the desk to him. "There is a fifty thousand Euro car, in the staff car park, less than a month old, its registered to this individual who is on a thirty five thousand a year salary grade." The visitor pulled the sheet towards him as the bodyguard continued "He just so happens to be head of planning who until a month ago drove a ten year old pile of scrap. Comment and description is from the maintenance people who he warned recently to stay a minimum of three metres away from his car. They don't like him." The visitor smiled, his bodyguard had proven his worth again.

+

Andrew Crawford was standing at the window in his office; the whole of this part of the building was almost silent. His secretary was sitting out in front wearing jeans surfing a few job sites looking for work. He was just staring out as the rain slithered down the glass. This high up in New York the rain had an almost grey look to it, grimy and gritty as it washed the dirt and dust out of the air of the dirty city and left it on the glass, stone and steel of the buildings. One floor below there was a terrace where a lot of the smokers went to indulge their habit, there was even a few of them out there just now. He shook his head, he could not understand the habit at all, add the rain and it just became ridiculous. He leant his head on the cool glass and closed his eyes, he had seen the figures earlier in the day and no matter what he tried to do he could not get the pictures of the balance sheet out of his head. It was worse to him than a horror movie would be to some people. There was no money left and he was the only person left in the organisation that could be called to answer for the situation. Everyone else had vanished

298

into thin air and his boss was sitting upstairs talking to God on a telephone that wasn't plugged in. Crawford was still fielding calls and making it sound as if all the projects would be going ahead, the organisation had one or two minor difficulties, nothing they couldn't handle but he knew that as time went on he was becoming less and less believable simply because he was believing it less and less himself. Suddenly he stepped back from the glass as a cold shiver ran up his spine, just for a second he had imagined himself falling and could put himself in the position of the tycoons from the thirties when it had all gone wrong. He knew he would be left with nothing, nothing at all to show for his years working with Silver but worse, he was actually starting to feel guilty about the damage he had done to the planet in the course of making money; money that no longer existed. He shivered and stared at the glass again before turning away and sitting down quickly facing the other direction, looking straight at the computer screen in front of him.

Eventually it filtered through to him that the screen was showing a moving image rather than the usual still one showing figures or projections or graphs. He must have been looking at the news channels before he went to the window. Leaning forward he began to read the article, it was about one of the other projects, he had not been involved in it at all but it still carried the Silver name. He groaned as he read it. It was a golf resort in Patagonia, he turned and looked at the map on the wall but couldn't find it, and he could look properly later. The IPGA were looking into the recent opening golf tournament that had been held there. They had been caught off guard when almost one hundred thousand spectators had turned up to watch and indulge in the hospitality. What had surprised the IPGA was the fact that they normally could predict visitor numbers fairly well and they had predicted only just over forty thousand spectators. The spokesperson for the organisation was quoted as saying they were investigating the claim that the Silver Organisation had issued a large number of direct invites to specific people from around the world. In other words they had flooded the event with their own direct invitees without official clearance. Andrews groaned and laid his head on his arms, he could actually remember seeing the invites going out to some very specific people. This was not good, the IPGA were not people you wanted to upset; no one in their right mind would upset the governing body that had the final say on whether or not your product was good enough to be used for their competitions.

+

Templeton was also watching the TV although it was late evening where he was, at home. His constituency was on the South eastern corner, down

299

toward the point of the peninsula and close enough to the Western Ocean to know what it was and sometimes feel the serious storms but also protected by being on the other side of the land mass. It was a small stone cottage, traditional in this part of the world but massively modernised. Inside he was warm and comfortable as he sat there listening to the wind moaning behind the sound from the television, he cradled a rare glass of malt Scotch whisky. It was expensive to get it imported due to his own people's taxes but it was just so much smoother than the local stuff it was worth it occasionally. He lifted the glass and let the light amber coloured fluid swirl in the bottom of the glass as he watched the documentary on the television. It all sounded depressingly familiar and this was national television so everyone would see this and be aware of it. That could make things more interesting as the journalists began to draw comparisons, he could feel his stomach start to sink as he realised it would only take one to start asking questions and the rest of them would pick up on the fact very quickly.

He knew the right place to take the small black plastic box that nestled in his briefcase was the ethics committee; the problem with that was 'Xander was the chair of the ethics committee. Anything brought up to them when he was in the seat would almost certainly vanish; he was turning things over in his head when suddenly it struck him. He knew how he would be able to do this. It would not be straightforward but it might actually be simpler than it looked and he was sure he could do this without too much real hassle. He raised the glass in mock salute to the TV and sipped the strong smooth liquor with a smile on his face, he was happy again, happy that his life was coming back under his control for the first time since he had made the mistake that allowed 'Xander to push him around so easily; but not for much longer.

+

Jonathon Diarmond of the 'National Central' picked up the phone on his desk and was surprised to hear from a former colleague of his, it was Jamieson from the 'Evening' whose opening line was "Any jobs going with you lot?" Jonathon sat back silent for a moment. "Why are you looking for work? Thought you were settled over there at the 'Daily' Jamieson laughed before replying 'I was, but a few things have happened here, some of which you'll have heard about I don't doubt. Bottom line is I'm now at the 'Evening' which is failing and I expect it to be shut down in a month or two at the most even though it is getting better." Jonathon sat back properly and made himself comfortable as his former colleague began to talk freely, apparently not caring about the tape recorder that he knew his friend used on all phone calls to his office number.

The two men spoke for a while, more than half an hour, before Jonathon finally said "What about a guest editorship in the group? It might mean you moving around a few different papers for a while until we find out which is a mutual 'best fit' for you. Would you be interested in that?" The pause was distinct as Jamieson thought about what he had just been offered but it was Jonathon that spoke first again. "Tell you what, think about it for a day or two and you can call me sometime before the weekend with a decision one way or the other." Jamieson nodded and said very little as the two men exchanged the usual pleasantries before breaking the connection.

Jonathon sat there wondering about the call, he could do what he had suggested, it should be fairly easy for him to get him a guest slot for a month or two, anything longer than that would depend on how he did in that time. More interesting was what he would be writing about, it seemed he had a whole raft of information from 'behind the scenes' of the Silver affair that almost looked to have run its course but this could just kick it up into the public eye again and make it more of a story. This could be elevated to a very high level and could bring down some very important people. He smiled and sat back this could be a very interesting time to be a reporter.

Over in his office in Drimmie, Jamieson was sitting quiet and still at his desk. He was amazingly calm as he sat there thinking about what had just been said on the 'phone and what it actually meant. He had just taken the decision to leave the company who had been his employers for the last thirteen years and it didn't bother him in the least. Jackson the new guy might actually be a good boss, he seemed okay and he seemed to be honest, Grayson's death was in many ways a relief. He had been getting more and more out of control as time went on and now he was gone things were heading back towards normality, if a newspaper could ever be called normal. He was sleepy and it was warm in the office where he sat, the sun was streaming in the window and gradually heating up the whole office despite the air conditioning unit that sat under the window behind him. He sat back in his chair and closed his eyes for a minute.

It was late afternoon that they found him. Debs the office junior had been putting off going to see him as it looked like he was asleep. Head back, eyes closed, the glass panel in his door told you a lot, but now she had to speak to him as her bus left in twenty minutes. She clutched her assessment sheets in her hands and was almost physically shaking as she knocked on his office door, he didn't even flinch, which surprised her. She had expected him to jump and growl at her that was why she had been putting this off all afternoon. She looked through the glass panel and yes he was still there. She opened the door and stepped inside, leaving the door open. Opening her mouth to speak she drew breath and suddenly her head swam. The clatter as she fell to the floor made everyone else in the office look round. Johnny the cub reporter ran over and stepped into the office to see if he could help. It was his collapsing beside her that made Shivaar, the compositor, look round again and suddenly he realised something was wrong here. Running over he grabbed something used as a paperweight from a desk as he passed and threw it straight through Jamieson's window before reaching round the man who still sat lifeless in his chair and switching off the air conditioning unit. Turning round he was still holding his breath as he grabbed Debs and Johnny by the ankles and dragged them into the main office slamming the door to the office shut behind him. He fell to the floor and dragged air into his lungs before shouting to the gathering crowd "Call an ambulance, no make that the police, let them bring an ambulance. These two," he pointed at the two figures starting to stir on the floor beside him "need help, while he is dead." He pointed over his shoulder at the closed door as he said this. Slowly he pushed himself to his feet and made sure the other two were starting to come round before he sat back down to wait on the emergency services arriving.

The police inspector stood in the middle of the, now cleared, news room as the figure in the big yellow suit opened the door from the other side and waddled out into the open space before unzipping the plastic bag that was actually a hazmat suit and smiling at the inspector "Conclusive," he said "Atmosphere in that room is over 80% pure carbon monoxide" The inspector looked at him "Exhaust fumes? How did he get a lungful of exhaust fumes all the way up here? I mean we're on the fifth floor or so aren't we?" The scenes of crime officer shook his head "No not car exhaust, pure Carbon Monoxide, no soot, no nitrous compounds none of that type of thing. This is scientific maybe even medical grade, that's if you can get medical grade Carbon Monoxide that is. Some one went to considerable lengths to make sure it was introduced here. I'm not sure yet, but I have my suspicions, either way this looks like a very definite case of murder." The inspector shook his head "I know a lot of people who may have wanted to kill a newspaper reporter at some time but to have two editors die gives me a headache." He stepped back and went to speak to Shivaar who was sitting at the far end of the news room sipping on coffee from the vending machine on the landing. The inspector sat down and looked at this man who had just saved two lives "How did you know what to do?" Shivaar shrugged and hesitated for a moment as he could see a rebuke building in the inspector's eyes. "Not sure really," he started "I used to work offshore on the rigs, and I seem to remember hearing stories of

302

people falling down in confined spaces. One falls down then another and another, apparently there was a case in Venezuela in the early 2000's somewhere when up to twenty people died in that type of situation." He nodded towards the door to Jamieson's office which was now standing wide open "That looked just like that same situation. Debs opened the door after Jamieson didn't answer her knock and I heard her fall down and looked over. Johnny was already on his way over and from here, this is my desk, I could see Jamieson sitting there. There was just something about his colour that bothered me and I remembered what it was just as Johnny collapsed as well, so I did something." He paused and a wry smile crossed his face as the inspector watched him. Shivaar shook his head "Sorry, was just thinking I'll need to see about replacing Pauline's prized piece of the Berlin wall. That was what I grabbed and threw out the window, there's not usually many lumps of concrete in a journalists office." The inspector nodded as one of the sergeants walked up with a lump of concrete in a plastic bag, Shivaar's eyes fastened on it as the inspector grinned and the sergeant spoke. "Is this relevant? I took it off a guy across the street who is jumping up and down and wondering who is going to pay for the replacement sunroof on his BMW." The inspector grinned even wider as Shivaar lowered his head "I'll take that, it's evidence in this case and your BMW owner will just need to file a claim with his insurance company and the criminal injuries board. This lump of concrete just saved two lives." The sergeant nodded and wandered off as another officer appeared "Inspector, just to let you know, the two who were carted off by the ambulance are awake and will be okay; going to be kept in overnight for observation though." The inspector nodded and looked back at Shivaar "Looks like that's two of your colleagues who owe you some gratitude." Shivaar just smiled, nodded and sipped at his coffee.

It was almost another two hours later that the inspector got a call from the Scene of Crimes Superintendent again, and he relaxed as he heard her voice on the phone, she usually called with answers. "I've just finished taking apart the Air con unit our guys brought back from the newspaper offices, it's a work of art. Do you want to come and see it?" he sighed and rolled forward in his seat "I would love to but I'm kind of busy here right now." She smiled down the phone and he could almost hear it on the other end of the line as she spoke "Okay then, some other time. Anyway the system was both simple and complex. Two different systems actually, both operated by remote control. The first one shut the vent so stopping the extract side of the system, meaning nothing was drawn out of that room. The other opened the valve on the bottle of Carbon Monoxide that was fixed to the bracket underneath the unit. It's been painted the same colour as the bottles of refrigerant are so anyone who knew what they were looking at would probably assume it was there for a reason. The bottles also have a serial number on them and this one was stolen from an industrial gas supplier at the other side of town less than a week ago. So the question is, have they had any work done on their AC system in the last week?" The inspector nodded slowly to himself. "Thanks a lot that is all good info. Let me start asking the right questions rather than just the usual general stuff and we'll maybe get an answer to this one soon." Suddenly he stopped "Before you go, the radio controlled servo's you found, what sort of range would they have? "The superintendent thought for a second or two "No more than half a mile" He grinned "Okay, thanks a lot."

+

Templeton stretched as he looked at the small memory stick, he was amazed at the amount of data you could get on one of these. He turned it over and looked at the number marked on it in black marker pen, it was a number seven he noted and grinned to himself as he wiped it down with a cloth before dropping it into the small padded bag. He was happy that the rough finish of the paper the bag was made from would make it impossible for it to hold a fingerprint, the flap was a 'peel and seal' type and the stamp was self adhesive as well so there should be no DNA evidence available to anyone. He sighed, was he being paranoid? Probably, was the only answer he could come up with, he shrugged to himself and carried on with what he was doing. Some of it would come back to him, that much he was sure, but he would deal with that when it happened. Now he at least felt better, his conscience was better already and he might be able to sleep at nights again.

+

Mark was re reading the screen that Marianne had been crying about the previous week when he saw the news 'ticker' across the bottom of the screen change to highlight a difference in topic. It was the leaking of a private report to an international news agency that had held onto the report for at least two weeks whilst attempting to get a reply to their queries from the Silver Organisation. Mark looked closer and followed the links to read the full story.

He couldn't quite make out what the court case had been about but it appeared that Trente Silver had been in court somewhere else and had made a complete idiot of himself in a very similar manner to what he had done at the public inquiry down in Drimmie fairly recently. Mark read on, as a result of the court case a private internal report that showed the actual net worth of the Silver Organisation had been prepared by one of the major

304

international banks. The news agency had seen a copy of one of the summary pages and it was damming. No figures were mentioned in the article Mark was reading and that was what he was looking for, but it finally concluded that the Silver Organisation was actually worth about ten percent of what its boss claimed it was. Mark sat back as the phone began to ring, casually he reached out, lifted the receiver and listened to silence for a second or two before he heard a voice on the other end of the line. It was quite a polite, well educated sounding voice but it quickly became clear that it was not a fan of his "Mr Rae?" queried the voice as Mark wondered who this was "Yes," was all he said as he waited to see who was calling him "You don't know me, but I am one of the people you and your pathetic little band of soap dodging half wits have just cost a considerable sum of money." Mark sat forward and listened a little more closely as the voice carried on "If you and your friends had not started to argue about the benefits of the Silver development to your pathetic little country it would have been more than half built by now, if that had been the case our funds would have been safe and clean. Now it looks as though the Federal government is taking an interest in those funds and we will have to disengage from them to keep ourselves safe." Mark was listening intently and wondering what this actually meant to him as the voice carried on in its soft monotone "This means that some of my associates would dearly like to kill you, but mostly they are too stupid to know how to as long as you stay at home. So I would suggest you stay on your annoyingly influential little island, do not visit the States for a holiday or any other purpose for the rest of your life and stay out of any negotiations that follow on from here." The voice drew breath and paused before continuing "Take this is a subtle hint, Mr Rae. If you get in the way again we will kill you and do not even consider coming to our country, some of my associates will take great pleasure in eradicating you. It is only by my own good graces that you are still alive so far. Do not try and report this call either, it will have a similar effect." Mark just sat there silently as the caller hung up the phone and the flat 'Brrrrr' of a disconnected line was all he could hear for a few seconds before there were two very distinct clicks and another voice came on the line "Mark you still there?" he just grunted "Yeah sorry about that. It's Parker here we've been expecting something like that for a few days now so, sorry, but we took the liberty of tapping into your line for just that purpose. Our 'cousins' gave us the heads up that some of these people might be involved and that his was likely to happen soon. Now that they have made the play we have notified those that matter over there and they will be picked up in a matter of minutes. At least that is what I've been told" Mark could hear the smile in his voice as the doubt was obvious to both of them. "if you want some special protection we can arrange that for you and your lady friend" Mark sighed "No, I don't think that's a good idea, we have too much to do around here still and I'm not prepared to go into hiding which is probably what some of the suits would want. No," Parker could hear him shift in his seat as he thought about what was needed "what about maybe a couple of the 'club members' staying around for a while. Nothing serious, just to be local so there's back up if needed" Parker just nodded to himself "I'm sure we can arrange that, Mark. Take care now and we'll see you soon." Mark just grinned as the receiver went silent in his hand before he dropped it in the cradle and looked out the window wondering how long it would be before some of the club members miraculously appeared in the area. He doubted they had all left when they supposed to, they just didn't do things like that.

+

Andy was looking at the TV that was on in the bar as the programme changed to a news flash "It has been claimed in the US that Trente Silver the international property developer and entrepreneur is suffering health problems. He apparently has not been seen since his return from an appearance at a disastrous Public Local Inquiry in this country where he appeared in support of what he was calling the best resort in the world, a phrase he has used on every single development he has been involved in. Mr Silver apparently retired to his office suite on the fifty third floor of the 'Silver Needle' as his office block is called and has not been seen since. There is apparently concern building over the financial arrangements of his organisation and its ability to pay its way without the famous figure at the helm of the organisation." She paused and looked at her script "Now in other news...." Andy turned away from the screen smiling to himself as the door opened and in walked Peter Barnard with a small holdall in one hand. Andy looked at him coldly as he spoke "Any rooms available for tonight?" Andy shook his head "You stand no chance. This place could be empty and there still would be no rooms here for the likes of you." He reached round behind him to the side of the till and pulled out an envelope that was sitting there "This is yours" he said handing it over "Barnard looked surprised but took it from him as Andy carried on talking "It's your bill from last time. Now pay it before we have to file a writ." Barnard laughed at him "Don't waste your time. You'll be bankrupt long before it gets to court, just add it to the rest of the Silver accounts." He turned and looked around at the empty bar "Yes, this place could be quite acceptable once we run you out of here and take over. We'll have to clear the village as well of course. We can fill it with our eastern Europeans who do twice the work of you lot for half the money and some of the girls are very accommodating if you know what I mean." He sneered at Andy with a wink. Magda who had been coming in through the other door stared at him with disgust. "How dare

306

you insult my people as if you are a god." She screamed at him as she stood still rooted to the spot. Before she could do anything the door opened and in walked two local police officers. Barnard pulled himself up to his full height as he looked at the two of them and said "Good timing officers. I want to file a complaint against this woman, you didn't happen to hear what she just threatened me with did you?" the two officers looked at each other and one said "You are Peter Barnard?" he nodded as the two officers stepped closer, as they reached out and took him by the arms one said "You are under arrest for the murder of Jim Jamieson, a newspaper editor of this town and immigration want to discuss your involvement in a conspiracy to conduct people trafficking operations." Barnard fell silent and did not say anything as he was led away while Magda and Andy both just stood there looking at each other as this little drama played out in the empty bar.

+

Steve was sitting there as Marianne knocked on the door frame and stood there until he looked up "Hiya," he smiled "Sorry I haven't been able to get to see you today, just been far too busy with everything that's going on." Marianne shook her head and smiled back at him "No worries, just thought I'd say hi before I disappear out the door for tonight. I need to get back to Marks place. I'm still staying there and I like to be home reasonably early." Steve smiled as he sat back in the chair looking at this smart and pretty woman who stood in front of him. "I'm sure Mark looks forward to you getting home. Don't believe all his stories about liking his own company. He may survive well enough but I know he likes intelligent woman like you being around him when he gets the chance." Marianne wondered about the comment and decided she wouldn't be likely to get much more information out of him just now. "Anyway," she said "I was wondering if you had heard the news about this banking report that says Silver is only actually worth about ten percent of what he claims." Steve looked at her puzzled "It's been on all the news channels since about lunch time." She looked at his face before adding "I guess when you say you've been busy working, you mean you've been busy working." He just nodded as he opened up the internet browser on his computer and began to look for it. It didn't take long to find, it was the first story on most of the news channels. He raised his head to thank her and found she had already gone, leaving just a hint of perfume in the air behind her as she left.

The article was just a written equivalent of what Andy had seen on the TV in the pub but Steve read it with interest and the little grin was all the way across his face by the time he got to the end of the article. He pulled out a drawer and opened a small black business card wallet that he kept in there.

Slowly he turned pages until he found the one he was looking for and then checked the time before he began to dial the number on the card. He might just be able to get some more information on this report from the source rather than the media.

17

The article had been seen by a large number of the locals all of whom were in the pub that night and Andy was run off his feet trying to serve bar and tend to the hotel with just Magda to help out. Meanwhile Mark and Marianne were at home and had eaten their meal and were sitting in front of the television when the news came on. The Silver Organisations financial situation was again the lead item, Marianne leant against his arm and said softly "Do you think if they actually go bust they might just go away and leave us alone here?" Mark looked at her as he let his arm slip around her shoulders and pulled her in close "It's always possible but I am just wary of this being a Mark Twain moment." Marianne looked at him puzzled until he made to answer "Mark Twain was an American author who actually used what they call a '*nom de plume*' or a pen name as we would call it. Offhand I don't remember his real name but once when he had retired from writing but was very much alive there was an article appeared in one of the main newspapers of the day claiming that he had passed away. So he wrote to the paper, in his own name stating something along the lines of "Contrary to popular misconceptions I feel I must make it known that reports of my death are a little premature" That was the meaning of it anyway and as such I am wary that these buggers have a habit of rising from the flames. All they do is draw in money that they shouldn't have, money that they've had stashed out of the tax authorities reach, and re invent themselves." He sighed as Marianne spoke "Or they go to some of their more gullible investors and get them to hand over more money for more failing and impossible schemes and the whole thing goes around again." Mark nodded and hugged her close to him as he watched the item on the TV.

+

The account manager from the Euro bank was waiting to see his manager and he was nervous. He was grateful that he had called his boss and asked for this meeting before his boss had called and asked him for a meeting. It would have been better still had it been a week earlier. It was almost fifteen minutes after the allocated time that he was called into his boss's office by his PA. The door shut silently behind him as he strode the few paces across that deep soft carpet that looked like it had only been laid the night before. The soft leather chair in front of the desk sighed gently as it welcomed him into its embrace and he felt fairly secure as he looked across

309

at his boss who looked up from the file and regarded him levelly. "I take it this is to do with the news items that started to break last night?" The account manager nodded "Yes it is, although we have actually started legal proceedings in Denmark and the Netherlands as well as being one day away from serving writs in the UK and Patagonia as well" His boss nodded "Is it possible that our legal actions are what caused the news items." The account manager shrugged and his boss watched as the silk suit settled smoothly down again before the man spoke "It is possible, but it may be that they are also being pursued by the Norgan Bank and International Funding. I found out yesterday that these two bodies are also looking for repossession of the Denmark site as well as the UK one." His boss sat back "How is that possible? We normally only lend on an exclusive basis and I would suspect the others are the same." The account manager nodded "I believe that is the case and I haven't found out how it's possible, yet. However I have found that they used different legal representatives for each bank deal so it looks like it is a deliberate fraud. As such I would like to fly out to Denmark and New York to discuss with the bodies what has happened with a view to making it a combined action against the Silver Organisation." His boss looked at him for a second and nodded a single curt nod to signify his agreement. "Speak to Lucy, get her to arrange the jet, take number two, and you arrange the appointments. If the other banks agree we'll file a combined action and shut him down permanently. He's causing too much damage worldwide to be allowed to continue." The account manager nodded and stood up, he knew he had been dismissed from his boss's presence just by the way he spoke.

Outside he turned to the PA who smiled at him and said "It is now two o'clock, by the time we get the pilots ready and the flight plans filed etc it will be six o'clock at the earliest before you can fly. I will arrange that if you want to make sure you have the appointments arranged and go and pack your bag." He smiled back at her "I cheated, I brought a bag with me, it's in the car downstairs ready to go."

+

The police inspector was looking at Peter Barnard through the one way glass of the interview room where he sat looking calm but unhappy. He had his arms folded and was trying to pretend to be asleep. Finally the inspector just shook his head and went round the corner and into the room. Barnard sat bolt upright and made to stand up but stopped at the last minute. Instead he forced himself to sit down and lean back, trying to make himself look as if he was in control before he spoke. "I demand you let me go, this is a waste of my time and simple interference with my business." The inspector said nothing as he sat down opposite Barnard and opened the brown folder on the desk in front of him. The first sheet was actually a photograph of Jim Jamieson as he had been found, sitting in his chair apparently asleep, just the strange cherry red hue of his face showing something was wrong. The inspector said nothing as Barnard looked down at the photograph for a second or two then shouted "I want my lawyer, now. I'm not saying another word until he gets here." The inspector sighed and closed the folder and stood up "First there will be no lawyer for you at this time. You have been arrested under the special provisions of the terrorism acts and as such I can hold you here for six months without telling anyone. Second, that time can be extended by a further eighteen months if there is concrete evidence of a serious crime having been committed. As we have your credit card shown as being used to buy electronic components used in the murder of a newspaper editor, that ticks both boxes, serious crime and terrorism, so it could be two years before we even have to tell anyone you're here. Then we take you to a closed trial and you'll get at least ten years for your part in all of this." Without saying another word he stood up and taking the file with him, left the room. The sergeant met him just around the corner by the two way mirror. "That was a bit harsh wasn't it?" The inspector shook his head "Not really, you see his credit card, which incidentally is a corporate card drawn on the Silver Organisation was used to buy the remote control elements they used to poison the newspaper guy. It was also used to draw cash from an ATM outside the filling station where the petrol and clocks etc were bought that were used in the attempt to kill Paul Gray a few months back. It's my bet that if we dig just a little further we'll be able to tie him to the murder of the planner as well." The sergeant looked at him puzzled "I thought one of the guys picked up by the club the other week was in the frame for that one; DNA and everything." The inspector nodded "I don't doubt he actually did it, but I think Barnard was the guy at the back of it and I am sure that we can prove it with just a little more digging." He paused and chewed on his lip for a moment or two "I also want the guys who tried to kill Paul Gray back in custody and I think he can tell us where they are." The sergeant was nodding "You think he bought the stuff and they actually did the job, on the newspaper guy as well?" The inspector nodded "Yeah that seems most likely to me at the moment. We'll see, I have no doubt it'll all become clear in time." With that the two men turned and walked away along the corridor.

+

Andrew Crawford was standing in his office looking out the window again, this time his secretary was standing in the, now permanently, open doorway of his office. They were having a disjointed but serious conversation about the company and where it had been, let alone where it was going. She looked at his back and said "You know, this is going to sound terrible, but a few weeks ago. I'd have been standing here willing you to jump out of that window. Now, I don't want you to do that." He didn't reply immediately to what some people would have called an offensive comment and just those same few weeks ago what she had just mentioned would have cost her, her job. He sighed and leant away from the glass as she said. "You've changed, for the better" he grinned at his reflection in the glass "Thank you," was his first comment "I've noticed that myself." He turned and sat down at the desk. "But I don't know what it is that has changed." She smiled and without asking stepped further into the room and leant against the wall "Part of it was the influence of your boss. Now he is not having any input you seem to have settled down a bit. You don't have the same ups and downs that you did, you're not nearly as aggressive, or threatening." He sat there nodding, he knew she was right and that now he seemed to be happy to take that type of criticism "I never thought of myself as threatening" it wasn't an argument just an observation. She smiled at him and left the office without saying a word. A couple of minutes later she returned carrying two mugs of coffee, he just grinned at her as she sat down in the chair on the opposite side of the desk after passing him a mug. She shrugged "Not much else to do is there?" he sighed "I'm not sure, to be honest." He paused and looked at this woman who had worked for him for several years but he had never even really noticed before and said "I feel someone needs to be here. Just to fend off the press if nothing else although it seems like the PR department are doing a good enough job of that." She smiled at him wondering what had changed him. He sat back and began to talk "It was only a few days ago, I went up to see if I could speak to Silver directly but he was on the phone talking to god." The secretary giggled until she saw him look at her levelly as he continued and she realised he was being absolutely serious "The problem was the phone was not even plugged in, so it was bound to be a pretty one sided conversation. When I left the office I was intending coming down here and picking up my briefcase on the way out the door." he sipped from his mug as she sat there watching him, listening intently to every word he had to say. "On my way out of the office I met number three. Who is still with him and said she intends to stay." He paused and looked away to try and hide the almost tear that had appeared out of nowhere before he continued. "She accused me of being a vulture and being here merely to pick over the remains. She was right but what she said made me think and that is why I am still here. I am trying to make some amends for what we have done worldwide, but I don't know where to start." They sat there for a long time, just looking across the desk at each other, neither of them having anything to say but plenty to think about.

312

The team leader was sitting at his desk, still getting used to the idea that it was his desk when his PA called through to him. "I have a gentleman on the phone from one of our bigger financial institutions, 'International Funding'. He's wondering about filing a formal complaint against the Silver Organisation, would you care to speak to him?" The team leader smiled to himself as he said "Just put him through, please. Anything about Silver I want to be kept informed as soon as possible."

There wasn't a lot of pleasantries before they starting talking business, the team leader listened as he heard what the other man had to say before he responded "Okay, from you've said that all sounds very clear cut. If you want to forward on as much of that data as you can I will have a look at it and we can maybe arrange a meeting to confirm what I get out of the documents. Now you mentioned other banks also being involved, who exactly were they?" The conversation began to get detailed and legally specific about who had known what and when and actually dragged on for almost an hour and a half before the team leader finally hung up the phone and sat back as his PA came into the room and looked at him "I know its none of my business but you have a team available to do that you know. You are only meant to guide and control them, not actually get involved in the cases yourself." He nodded and looked sheepish "I was wondering about that as the conversation went on. I will pass it on to some of the other guys. I will have them sit in on the meeting and carry it forwards from there themselves" He glanced up at her from his desk and she grinned before turning and walking away.

+

The account manager from Euro bank was smiling to himself, he was standing on the steps of the offices of the Norgan bank in Stavanger having just had a very productive meeting with their account manager who had been dealing with the Silver Organisation on an exclusive basis, or so he had thought until a few days previously. The two men had agreed to meet again formally, at a mutual location along with representatives of International Funding, the third bank, and their legal representatives to agree a common approach to situation that would mean that all three of them should get something out of it. Rather than being left empty handed completely, he smiled to himself, he knew he was lucky, if he had missed this by a day he would have been looking for another job, not standing here looking at a night in a good hotel at the banks expense. He turned and walked along the pavement, it was not far to walk and the place was clean and fresh. Suddenly he wondered what assets Silver had in Norway.

He pulled out his mobile phone and called his boss, as he had suspected his boss had already had discussions with the regulators and moves were under way to obtain warrants to seize any and all property within the region they had access to. Things were apparently really stacking up against Silver now and it was unlikely they would be able to get away from this one.

The newspaper that he picked up on the counter at his hotel confirmed this view of the world. The headline of the business section was about Silvers apparent ill health and how he had not been seen since the Public Inquiry back at home. He read it with interest as he made his way to the room and prepared for dinner with the representative of the Norgan Bank who was joining him shortly.

+

'Xander was getting more and more worried as he read the third news paper of the day, all of them had the same lead story in the business section and in the '*Daily*' it was the lead story on the front page. In some ways it was good that this was all they had to throw at him. In other ways it was worrying because it meant they could actually start looking at him directly very soon. The main headline was saying that his pet project had probably fallen at the first hurdle as the developer had turned out to be insolvent. 'Xander grinned to himself, they would regret saying that once Trente Silver got back from wherever he was actually hiding at the moment. He was renowned for going to lawyers as a first line of attack when anything that was said could be viewed as slanderous or defamatory in anyway. Even if it was almost slanderous or almost defamatory he went to lawyers. 'Xander just shook his head, he could not see where his one was going to end up, but it didn't look like it would be good for him.

He sat there and pondered the words of his father all those years ago when he had first suggested going into politics might be the career for him. His father had been a simple and honest man with a black and white view of the world it had been something like "You'll be alone there son. Politicians are all either liars, frauds or thieves." He shook his head to himself as he recalled that day, he had fought to do what he wanted to do and he thought his father had actually, eventually come to respect him and what he did for a living. Now he was realising that he had let his father down. Instead of changing the system, breaking the mould, he had just fitted right on in there with the worst of them. He was all of the above he admitted to himself, a liar, a fraud and a thief. He had stolen the election by a bit of judicious dealing behind closed doors and had landed the top job, but was it worth it now? He did not have an answer to his own question. Worst of all was his wife had been telling him all of this routinely for a few years and he had ignored it. That was one of the reasons she stayed so firmly out of the public eye, she really did not want to be associated with his public persona. He was convinced that she still loved him and he had absolutely no reason to doubt her on that subject at all. It was just that she might leave him out of shame at all he had done. The paper rustled slightly in a breeze coming in the window as it sat slightly open to let some fresh air. To him it sounded almost like a death knell. This could be the end of him and would almost certainly cost him his career no matter what happened. He sighed as he felt the soft prick behind the eyes that meant tears were close. Everything he had ever done. All the good for the country would be wiped away in one fell swoop, everything that had actually been worth doing was now gong to be called into question, nothing that he had done that was good would be remembered well, it would all be tainted with the touch of this organisation that had promised so much and delivered so little. He shook his head again, laughing this time, they almost sounded like a political party when you described them that way. He turned away from the table and opened his briefcase where it lay on the seat next to the table. Pausing just for a second he pulled out the share certificate he had been given, well it was only a photocopy with most of the details blacked out. The real one was in his vault overseas as part of his retirement fund, along with the annual dividends that would probably never come now. He sighed as he looked at it; it had been his vanity that had caused him to accept it, amongst other things, greed being one of them he finally admitted to himself.

This had been safer than cash, no hard trail to follow, getting shares in a company that had shares in a company that had shares in a company etc. etc. etc. made it very difficult for people, like forensic accountants to track exactly where the end beneficiaries were or who they were, or at least that was what he'd been told but now he knew too many other people knew so the word would be out soon and he would be finished. He had to figure out how to get out quietly without causing too much trouble to his family and his wife, he wanted to keep her with him if he could but if that was not going to be possible he had to distance her from all of this and he did not see how that could be done at all. He finally realised that his personal greed had just about destroyed several people, not just himself.

+

It was a day or so later that Jonathon Diarmond was sitting at his desk again, turning the memory stick over in his hands, he was a little uncomfortable about it as he really did not know what was on it. The large number one that had been written on in black marker pen intrigued him, it hinted that there was at least a number two somewhere, question was, would it cost him to get it? He shrugged he didn't know, slowly he stood up and walked through the main news office to the corner where the stand alone PC stood. They had this particular computer installed which was not connected to the office network or the internet, that way if there was a virus on anything that was sent in to them it was contained and did not do their main systems any harm. At least that had been the idea, some of the stuff the other reporters ran through their machines made the IT guys tear their hair out by the roots. He pushed the stick into the slot on the front of the machine and watched as the automatic scan ran its course and showed up clean, the stick was safe to use. He sighed and laughed at his paranoia as he clicked on the icon and the file opened up. He frowned, this was not what he had expected, but then he did not know what it was he had expected. His eyes opened a fraction wider as a name he recognised crossed the screen, then another and another. Quickly he shut the program down before pulling the stick from the machine. He would do this in his own office where he knew no one was looking over his shoulder.

He sat back and rubbed his eyes with both fingers, he was tired and stunned at what he had been reading. If even half of it was true there were several careers sitting here, ready to be shredded if he wanted to print this, even more if it turned out to be genuine. He sighed and looked up at the clock on the wall he had been at this for hours, slowly he stood up and looked out into the dark newsroom main office, he had to stop doing this, he was last out of the building again. Sighing once more he made his way to the stairwell and begin what felt like a long slow climb down the four flights to the ground floor. He was on the last flight when he heard the clatter of a door slamming shut somewhere above him followed by the sound of feet running down the stairs. He stopped and listened for a second before the knowing panic started in his belly as he remembered the last time this had happened and he almost leapt the last flight of steps in one go as he was aware of rattling, clattering sound that made him think of a can of beans thrown in the rubbish and a small green cylinder about the size of a can of beans funnily enough bounced off his shoulder and landed on the floor below him before suddenly, with a bang, it started spraying out a white cloud that bit into his eyes and the back of his throat. He had tasted CS gas once before so knew what it was he was breathing great lungfuls of as he stumbled, blindly, through the door into the foyer, startling the two guards who were sitting at their desk watching the monitors. The older one was on

316

his feet in a flash and stepped round him where he lay retching on the floor. The other man was already on the phone to the police as the other slammed the door to the stairwell quickly and shouted across "Gas, we're under a gas attack" The younger one repeated this into the phone as he pulled Jonathon across the smooth polished stone floor away from the stairwell, before all three of them cowered behind the large reception counter that had been previously laughed at as looking too much like a left over from a public bar. Now they were glad of the high solid wooden frontage and sides. They sat there, the three of them cowering on the floor as they heard the door to the stair well screech open and bang shut again as what sounded like steel shod heels stalked across the polished stone floor accompanied by the sinister Darth Vader like breathing of someone in a gas mask before the almost silent swish of the front door swinging open and shut as the steel shod feet stalked out onto the pavement outside.

The younger of the two guards was up onto his knees immediately and was working the CCTV camera to get a good shot of the man leaving the building. He had just left the range of the camera when the first wail of sirens could be heard in the distance.

+

The Police Forensics Superintendent was not happy, she had been called in to help the Eastern Region forensics team in an emergency situation. In a country as small as this there really weren't that many people with her level of skill and experience so when one went off ill they had to cover for one another. She had sighed deeply and cursed under her breath when she saw the body the first time, she knew the face as did most everyone in the country one way or the other. "When did they realise he was missing?" The local policeman shrugged "Maybe an hour or two at most." She looked at him carefully, that had not answered the question she had asked and it showed that the local boys were worried about something, was that why she had been called in? Had the local man decided he did not want to have anything to do with this one? She shook her head as she looked down at the cold, slightly blue tinged corpse on the table in front of her. He had been brought in before she had been called for and so she had not seen the scene in anyway shape or form. He was still dressed she noted, that was always something, even if the seawater was trickling onto the table and into the drains as she stood there looking at him. Quickly she reached down and closed the valve under the table before straightening up and walking away to get changed.

When she returned she carefully but quickly stripped the man and sorted out his clothes. Nothing really unusual there, the one thing that made her stop for a second was the memory stick in his left hand; it was a high capacity stick with a number twenty seven written on the side in black felt marker pen. Carefully, she set it aside, it was about his only personal possession, the scan that had been taken of the body had shown nothing inside him, but they knew who he was. After all that was why the police were so quiet, he had a twenty four hour permanent police guard, there was an officer in hospital because of this. It didn't matter if he had done his job perfectly or not his career was now over. He would always be remembered for this incident, any single item of good work he had done before would now be forgotten. Shaking her head she turned back to the man on the table who would still be waiting on her no matter how long she took. She had to be sure and get this one right. There was no room for error.

It was late the next morning when 'Xander received the first draft of the post mortem report. He looked at it in shock "Is she sure?" was all he could say as he read the first page. The senior Forensics officer looked at him from inside the door "She is the best we have, she has been on loan to the UK for a while as well as undertaking teaching trips to the US to bring their people up to our standards." He waited until 'Xander looked up at him again before he completed the sentence "She's sure." The little fat man behind the desk nodded slowly as he read and leant back slowly once he had finished the four pages of closely printed text. He had not really read all of it, only the executive summary, the rest of it was almost certainly too technical for him. He had only just understood the executive summary, so the technical parts were going to be well above him. The facts were clear however, Templeton had been murdered.

+

The doctor was sitting very still listening to every word Trente Silver muttered, it was illuminating and interesting. The man had opinions and beliefs on almost every subject under the sun and a few more beyond that. He sat here silently in the corner of the room watching the needle on the dial of his digital recorder flicker as it recorded every word the man uttered. He had barely even looked at the doctor as he set up the microphone right in front of him. The monotone voice droning on and on into the mouthpiece of the telephone that wasn't plugged in to the wall. Number three had asked him in about, to try and understand what was wrong with him and see if he could be healed. It was looking more and more certain that he was permanently broken now, probably been badly damaged for a long time, it was just that no one had noticed how badly damaged he had been. It seemed to be expected that these types of people had some form of problem or just a strange behaviour pattern, so no one had been too worried when the arrogance had increased and the willingness to compromise had slowly vanished a little bit at a time until there was nothing left. He was suspicious as to what the problem was, it would be difficult to prove but would probably be worth it just for the reputational factor alone. He was tired, he had been sitting there quietly all day long just listening to a very long monologue that basically meant nothing. It sounded as if the man behind the desk was on his third repetition of the same words. There was a pattern to what he was saying but it really was generally rubbish, biased, arrogant and racist rubbish. The doctor sighed and sat back looking at the man who was not looking at him. He knew he would have to listen to these recordings several times over again to make sure of his diagnosis and to be sure that when he wrote the paper on this mans mental failure he would be tripped up on some minor technicality. He was shaking his head as he thought about that but there was still a slight smile on his face. He was confident that he had found the first recordable case of Narcissistic Personality Disorder or NPD as most professionals called it. It was an illness that had been around for a long time but never really proven, until now. It sometimes been called megalomania but in reality it was much, much more than that, it was when a person truly believed he was better than everyone else and all laws and rules should be changed to suit his will and his bidding. He smiled to himself as he looked across the room at the man who was busy giving orders to God on a telephone that wasn't plugged in, yes, it fitted perfectly.

+

'Xander looked at the report again and he knew he was totally and completely finished no matter what else happened now, his own career had ended. He had no doubt he would soon be a suspect in this matter, the fact he had nothing to do with it and absolutely no knowledge of anything to do with it was beside the point, he was finished. He re read the page of the document and sat back again, staring into space, where was the memory stick that Templeton had in his hand when he was drowned, and what was on it? Maybe almost as important was what was on the other twenty six memory sticks? Templeton was no idiot and if he numbered a stick twenty seven that meant there were twenty six others out there and the sinking feeling in the pit of his stomach told 'Xander, he had a fair idea of what that might be. He looked down at the drawer of his desk and shuddered, the portable hard drive was a liability and he should really leave it in the safe at home. The question was, was it any more secure there than it was here? He shook his head he didn't have an answer and it might be too late anyway judging by what had happened and what he was guessing was on the stick.

+

Jonathon Diarmond was sitting in the office with his editor having just handed over a copy of the memory stick he had received in the mail the day before when the whispers started to fly around the office about the murder of Templeton, the government minister. The editor looked at Jonathon and said "Right, run with it. Make sure you have multiple copies of this so we can be sure of having the information even if the police confiscate the original and the packaging for forensics but I want this out on the streets from us as soon as possible. I want us to be first." Jonathon smiled, he already had copies stashed around the building, just in case this was his bosses decision. "I can leave you to deal with the police and we can state that we are speculating that it's the same as the one he was found with in his hand." He turned to leave his bosses office but stopped before he reached the door "My main question with all of this is what happened to the other twenty five memory sticks and what is on them?" His boss smiled back "That's why you're the reporter, go find out, and hope its as good as what you've got on this one. If it's anything like it the 'Xander is history." The two men smiled as Jonathon turned to walk out of the office and get on with his job."

+

In the small rented flat the two men were sitting discussing the state of their work at the moment. "I'm getting sick of this. We haven't had our next lot of expenses yet and the cash is running low. Okay they got us out of prison and that had to be good but we've done everything they asked of us and a bit more. Now they go and drop out of sight." The other man nodded, he had been thinking along the same lines but was not so good with words "Yeah," he said "now Barnard has vanished and is not answering our calls I think we should just take the last of the cash and get out of here." He pointed at the battered television set that was perched on top of a chest of drawers in the corner of the room. "That news piece last night said Silver is out of the game, he's off his head. Barnard worked for him and he's vanished into thin air. No one seems to have heard of him for a week or so now, it's time to save our own skins and go home." The other man nodded and leant forward slowly letting his head sink into his hands as he thought this through before finally nodding again a little more animated this time. "Okay, lets go today. We'll take the car up to the ferry port and get across to the UK. Once over there we've got a safety deposit box with new

320

passports and some cash, we can get a flight out from London and vanish back home, let them sort it out themselves." He shook his head as he stood up "This job is a good example as to why you should always take half the cash up front. At least that way you get something out of it if all goes bad." The second man nodded, he had made that mistake once before and had never repeated it since.

In a bunker far away the man sitting watching the computer screens smiled and leant forward before thumbing the intercom. "Parker, you'd better come and listen to this. I think we've found our two missing thugs." The intercom cracked twice in replay and a few seconds later Parker appeared with the suit in tow. Neither of them said a word as the man at the desk pushed a few buttons to allow the audio that had just been recorded to play out of the speakers in his armoured little hide.

As it ended Parker leant forward and hit a button on the pre programmed telephone that sat on end of the desk. "Roll the club, we have two potential targets on the road to the ferry terminal. Details following by burst." The voice on the other end grunted and hung up, as the phone was hurtling towards the cradle Parker thought he heard the strident blasts of an alert siren sounding in the background and just for a second he could see, in his minds eye, the practiced, orderly rush to the two black four by fours that sat permanently fuelled and armed, ready to roll just inside the garage doors at the base. He shook himself slightly as he could feel the adrenaline beginning to kick in, as if he was there himself, rather than stuck in the bunker.

The suit looked past him at the older man sitting at he desk "How did you pick up on that? Surely you don't monitor all of the channels all of the time." The old man grinned and shook his head "No you're right there lad." The suit ignored the familiarity, he had never understood these people and the way they worked. He stopped worrying about the way they had done it and began to listen to what was being said. "You know how a mobile phone is never actually off? That's how the alarm still goes off at the time you set it even though the phone is switched off. Add to that the fact that they routinely check in with the nearest mast for a location signal and any updates so the system basically knows where any mobile phone that has its battery installed in it is at any time of day or night, give or take three metres." The suit was surprised but he knew to show it would be taken as a sign of weakness by this man so he stayed quiet as the old man continued to talk. "In the old days it used to be possible to set a pencil across the cradle of a phone so that the microphone was still live and that way you could listen to what was happening in another room just by picking up the

321

phone elsewhere in the building." He paused and looked at the suit, the look of interest on his face was a surprise but meant they might be able to teach this youngster something yet. He carried on "Well, basically this is a high tech way of doing the same thing. All we do is locate the phone and boost the power to the mast and put in a small piece of code into the phone company's mast control programme and it sets up a watching brief for us." The suit shook his head "I'm sorry I don't understand that." Parker grinned, his colleague was a wiser man than he had given his credit for. The old man at the desk grinned as well and leant forward "Well, what happened is this, we picked all the regular numbers out of Barnards phone and put priority on the unlisted pay as you go ones that called him regularly or he called them." The suit nodded as the man continued "Then we do a search and locate the phones, insert our code and the masts increase the signal power to those phones, just enough to activate the microphone. That way they are carrying our listening devices into the room where we need to know what's going on. The system then listens to the phone and some really fancy software identifies when certain words or names are used and alerts me here." He smiled and leant back as the suit shook his head before speaking "So all you need is a mobile phone number to locate me, then listen in to what is being said, certain words trigger the system and you then call in the hounds." The man at the desk looked at Parker who was smiling "Yeah, that about it. Saves a lot of problems and means we can close these things down with a lot less collateral damage to the public." The suit wasn't quite happy "Don't we need a warrant for this type of thing?" It was Parker who replied "Normally that would be a yes, but as Barnard was picked up on a terrorism warrant, this whole thing comes under the terrorism acts so we don't need any more warrants. There is a blank general one outstanding for things like this; add our own operating protocols and rules of engagement and we are good to go." The suit smiled, he had never actually heard anyone use that phrase before.

+

The wind tugged at the jackets of the two men as they walked across the tarmac of Newark International Airport where jet two had touched down. The men were tired after their journey but determined in what they were here to do. Both of their institutions had suffered at the hands of the Silver Organisation and they wanted to make sure it didn't happen to anyone else at some point in the future. The wind was bitter as winter started to set in here a month or so before it did in Europe but the representative of 'International Funding' was waiting for them with a limousine, ready to whisk them away to their hotel and to brief them on the meeting she had arranged for the next day. They did not have the details yet but they knew

322

that they would be meeting with a government representative who had an interest in the case. She smiled as they slid into the limousine and just waited for a minute or two until their luggage was loaded into the boot of the vehicle. She glanced sideways and realised the car was moving and the two men sitting opposite her were starting to relax,

"Well guys," she started to speak as their eyes swivelled to regard her evenly "I have a meeting tomorrow with the new head of Department of Justice. This guy used to be a field agent and if my sources are accurate had just returned from a trip observing Silvers European Operation which appears to be going down the toilet as we speak. Any way he got his post because it appears his boss was in Silvers pocket for a lot of years. He's now in a silent prison apparently awaiting a hearing, but he will be interrogated long before then." She paused and looked at her audience, the two men were listening but obviously tired and she smiled "Why don't I just drop you guys at the hotel and let you rest tonight? We can catch up in the morning with a breakfast meeting maybe?" The two men nodded and settled back in the soft leather seats to watch the city streets slide past in the late afternoon gloom of smog and people.

+

Barnard was not enjoying this prison at all. He had never been locked up in his life and this was an eye opening experience to him. He was locked in a small cell three metres long by two metres wide, it had a bunk a desk and a toilet and wash basin which were at the back behind a small wall. That was the only privacy there was as the whole of the front wall was open grillwork. Not even bars like in the movies, this was the type of grating you used for walkways on offshore oil platforms and the like. It meant nothing could be passed from cell to cell and you only got out of your cell at meal times or for interrogation. He had been here something like three weeks as closely as he could guess and had been interrogated at least twice a day, every day but no one had asked him a single question. He was taken out of his cell along the corridor under that flat fluorescent lighting, through a large exercise hall that was illuminated by orange sodium lights so that everyone in the hall looked sick, it was usually empty, before ending up in the 'I' block as it was called. He shrugged to himself; he guessed the I stood for interrogation. It was there they would push him into another small room about the size of his cell but this time it was solid walls all the way round if you ignored the two mirrored windows that were in the wall opposite the door he entered by and the door that shared the same wall with them. In the room was a nasty plastic topped table and two plastic chairs either side of the table. The process was the same every time they took him there. He would be released from his handcuffs in the corridor and pushed into the room, where he would sit down at the side nearest the door and he would sit there for a period of time, maybe two hours, he thought, before they would come back for him and take him to back to the bare cell. If he was lucky they would stop in the refectory and allow him to get a meal before they returned him to his cell, most of the time he was just taken back and had to eat what was supplied later in the day. No one had ever come into the room and no one had ever spoken to him, not even the guards. He was scared; the inspector had told him he could be here two years before they even had to admit he existed let alone anything else.

The inspector watched from the other side of the glass in the small observation cubby hole that sat alongside the access door into the interrogation room. He turned and spoke softly to the man in uniform sitting next to him, watching Barnard closely through the one way glass. "How long does he think he's been here now?" The man grinned before replying "You don't need to whisper in here sir, it's totally soundproof." He stopped and drew breath "To answer your question, he thinks he's been here three weeks instead of the four days anyone else's calendar would show. We accelerate the days by means of controlled lights and ventilation, no external sounds and no communication with anyone, no news, no TV, no radio or anything of that sort. He's completely isolated from the outside world so we can control all he sees and hears for as long as we have him." The man smiled he was obviously proud of this facility built deep under the streets of the capital. The inspector did not comment, he just turned back to look at Barnard through the glass and wondered how much he really knew about the death of Templeton and the rest of what had been going on.

+

Mark was standing looking out of the window at the dunes as they drifted slowly and spectacularly in the breeze that was coming in off the sea. Almost lost in a dream world of his own he did not notice when Marianne arrived home and kicking off her shoes at the door padded softly across the floor to stand behind him for a moment. He jumped as she slid her arms around his waist and cuddled in closely behind him, looking past his shoulder at the spectacular view. "What were you thinking about?" She asked quietly. He shrugged and remained silent for a moment before softly he said "I was just wondering what greed would drive people to. I mean this place is absolutely beautiful, it's unique and can never be replaced if it is allowed to go ahead." He paused and licked his lips as Marianne hugged him a little tighter and listened to him breathe, knowing he had just paused and wanting to hear what else he had to say. He continued "It's all about

324

money for an immoral organisation that would appear to stop at nothing. There have been at least two murders that we know of, directly related to this so called project, here locally and very personal to me." She heard the catch in his voice and hugged him a little tighter as she felt him almost sag at the thought of the two women who had died, one literally in his arms. "I just hope there can be some good come out of this, no matter what finally happens." Marianne said nothing as she stood behind him hoping he would not feel the dampness of her tears through the back of his shirt as they stood there, together each lost in their own thoughts.

+

Arthur was sitting at the table in his house listening attentively to the reporter girl who had just proven to him that she was his granddaughter. A granddaughter he had never known he had and who was beautiful and smart, he knew in a younger man it would have been infatuation, but in him it was just incredible pride and relief that his son had survived and done well enough to be able to do a good job of raising this young woman to be a strong and confidant individual. The whole thing was just tinged with a touch of sadness that neither of his sons was here, and this girls father he had not seen for almost thirty years. Suddenly she stopped talking and looked him in the face. "I'd like you to meet someone, now. Sorry I've dropped this on you but I really want you two to meet each other." Without waiting for a reply she pushed her chair back from the table and stood up as Arthur spoke "He'll need to be a strong bloke to be your boyfriend for any length of time." Her laughter was something he loved to hear as she stepped back and opened the door before waving at someone outside who stepped forward and in through the door. "He's not my boyfriend." She said as Arthur sat back down in his chair "He's my father."

In the bushes further up the drive the man in camouflage gear lowered his binoculars and wiped his eyes. This was a development he had not expected, he had never planned for this and it should not be a problem but it could distract him from what he was trying to do, thankfully the game was almost played out, at least he hoped it was, and this new element should have little effect on his plans. He shrugged and put the glasses away before turning and vanishing noiselessly into the undergrowth.

+

Jonathon Diarmond sat quietly at his desk in the quiet office. There was no one else around, he knew this for a fact this time as the security guard who had been here less than ten minutes ago had told him that as he completed his rounds. They had agreed that if people were in the building the guards kept up a continual patrol now and kept in continuous contact with their partner at the front desk. Jonathon was nervous as he sat there in the gloom of the late evening and suddenly his waiting was worth it. The faint rumble that was below the threshold of human hearing was there, he could feel it through the soles of his feet as he sat there at his desk, feet flat on the concrete floor below him. The vibration began to be irritating as the noise increased to the point where he could actually hear it before the vibration passed beyond the itching and uncomfortable stage to a dull beat. He knew that if he stood up and walked out of the main news room into the corridor, turned left and unlocked the sound proof door at the end of the corridor, he would find himself in the print control office looking down on the presses as they thundered on through the night. The large metal slug lay across the building as he thought of it with the web of newsprint blurring past so fast it almost looked stationery with a noise and a vibration that would almost deafen you in minutes, or at least make your ears ring for hours afterward. The smell of the web presses was unique, a mixture of oil and chemicals that was somehow obviously artificial and yet not offensive, sweet but sharp at the same time. He grinned to himself, there was no longer the hot smell of the lead compositor as it had been when he first started that was all done by computers now. Computers, he thought bitterly as he turned the little memory stick over in his hand; that was where it had started. He didn't think it would be where it would finish. He pushed the stick into the steel box that was bolted into the bottom of his desk drawer and locked it before standing up and slipping on his jacket. The butterflies in his stomach were actually a good sign he thought. They normally arrived just as something big broke for him, he had them now as he walked down the stairs to the ground floor and out into the reception area all the while listening to the presses thundering away into the night printing his exclusive story that would destroy a President and a Government.

326

18

Andrew Crawford was literally sitting with his head in his hands as he looked at the computer screen. It was a financial projection of the current month that was what was horrifying him at the moment. The spreadsheet showed existing financial reserves versus projected outgoing costs, it looked like they would run out of money before the month end in three weeks time. He raised his head and looked again, there was no 'looked like it might happen', the facts were clear the company would not have funds to pay their staff, or anyone else, in just a fraction over two weeks time. They were bankrupt, again.

His secretary was looking in the door "Is it really that bad?" her voice was barely a whisper as she stood there looking at him fearfully. He amazed himself by raising his head and looking at her levelly and honestly, he was even more surprised when he responded honestly by saying "Yes, it's that bad. The organisation will be completely bankrupt in just over two weeks time." He hesitated and licked his lips "We can pay this round of wages but not the next." He pushed himself out of the chair and turned to look out of the window and smiled at her weak attempt at humour when she said "Don't go thinking about jumping now." He shook his head "Didn't cross my mind this time, but thank you for that." She smiled at his back and said "There was a time you'd have fired me for that comment." He nodded and spoke slowly "Very true, but that time is not now." He stepped back from the window and turned towards her saying "I have to go and speak to number three, see if there is anything we can do to protect her and Silver." His secretary just looked at him "Why them? They did nothing for you and would drop you as soon as look at you." He nodded as he stopped in front of her and reaching out took hold of her shoulders before saying "That may be true, it is true, I'm not going to argue with you about that, but if we can protect them and so protect the name of the Organisation it may help our own positions as well, make it easier to get another post somewhere else." She nodded as she let him move her to one side and walk past into the front office.

Number three just looked at him as she opened the door to the apartment on the top three floors of the building "You, I am surprised, and impressed, that you are still here. I thought you would have cut and run long ago." He shook his head and closed the door behind him as they walked across the marble floor of the apartment. "No," he said "but I am here to suggest you do just that very thing." She turned and looked at him "The end is near then I take it?" He hesitated until he was sure he understood the language being used, then nodded "Very near indeed. In a little over two weeks this entire organisation runs out of money world wide. We have spent years chasing money around the globe and now it is catching itself up. We have effectively 'maxed out' our credit cards borrowing on one to pay off another." She looked at him smiling, she knew that analogy only too well. Slowly she hesitated as she handed him a mug of coffee, it was a reflex action that he took it and the act surprised them both as neither of them had even thought about it at all. "So," she said "Why are you telling me this? I know most of you all hate me, so why do you tell me this and what do you expect me to do about it?" he shook his head as he sipped at the steaming black liquid. "To be honest I don't know why, but I thought it would only be fair to warn you it was heading your way." He sighed and studied the woman who stood opposite him. "You were honest with me when we spoke a few days ago and in this industry and with your husband that is an extremely rare thing so I thought it would be good to return the favour, as far as I can and at least give you some warning to get what assets you can to somewhere safe." He paused and looked into the mug "This will not be Chapter eleven, bankruptcy protection; the Organisation is too far gone for that. We will become bankrupt in a little over two weeks." She looked at him and he was sure he saw tears in her eyes as she said "Thank you, you have grown a little I think since the last time we spoke. You now have a heart and understand what it's for." He looked down embarrassed but pleased: quietly he set down the mug and walked out of the apartment. That was the last time he ever saw number three. On the way down the stairs he stopped outside the closed double doors to Silvers own office and he thought he could just barely hear the soft continuous murmurings of the man behind the desk talking into a disconnected telephone. He closed his eyes and saw again the mad staring eyes that followed him around the room. Shaking himself gently he walked away back down the stairs, trying to forget that image, instead, trying to remember the man as he had been before, strong powerful and capable. It didn't work, in Crawford's memory Trente Silver would now always be the broken rambling individual that he had been the last time he had seen him in the office.

+

Jackson was reading the 'National Central' almost the minute it hit his desk and he did not set it down as he reached for the phone, he wanted to get a syndication on this immediately so he could have it running in the 'Daily' the next day. To miss this article to the extent that another paper

328

could run it first was bad but to miss getting it a day behind was completely unthinkable.

A few minutes later he hung up the phone, not quite panic stricken but definitely horrified. The editor on the other end of the line had almost literally told him to fuck off and hung up the phone. It hadn't been quite that blunt but very nearly. It was a long time since Jackson had been spoken to like that by some one he considered an equal. It did not feel good.

He sat back and looked around the large and empty office space that he sat in. It was a waste of space, he knew that but there had been a day when these offices had been full of noise and people and bustle and work. Now the paper ran on less than half the staff it used to. It was going to be even less shortly if he shut down the *'Evening'* as he currently planned to do. He shrugged, the quality of the paper was nothing like it had been. When he had first been hired, almost a year ago, these two papers had already been in decline for over ten years. They had lost the respect of the local people and most of those who bought it did so simply because there was nothing else local to buy. 'Some people would buy anything' was his own thought on that matter and it shocked him that he had thought it without considering what that meant to him, or maybe that should be what it said about his leadership. He sighed as he finally put the paper down and began to switch on the television sets in the room. He knew what he was going to see, screen after screen of the story he could not print. He had been warned in no uncertain terms that if he did, what was actually quite normal, and just copied the story the *'National Central'* would prosecute not just the Newspaper group but him personally for allowing it to happen.

+

In the capital 'Xander was sitting in his office, the door open. No one came to see him but he could hear the hushed whispers in the corridor outside as they all discussed the latest news item which involved him directly. He had thought today would be a bad day but that most of the media coverage would be about the sudden death of Templeton. Slowly he looked at the two sheets of paper in his hands and tore them across. It had probably been several hours work from one of the party's spin doctors and a few minutes of a typists but somehow he knew from what he had read earlier that if the press came to see him today it would, initially at least, not be about the sad 'accidental death' of Templeton. 'Xander looked across at the newspaper, lying on the bench seat by the window where he had dropped it after reading the headline article. His own face looked back at him, a lot younger

329

but still very recognisable, the way the paper had crumpled as it had fallen you did not see the other man in the picture. The man who had given him his first 'bung' as he had called it; the newspaper had found him after getting access to some of his own computer files. 'Xander had no doubt someone would be in trouble for that at some time, but it would be long after he was out of office. He had been in a UK nursing home, or hospice was more accurate, dying of cancer so he had nothing to fear. He told them everything that the files hadn't told them. For an old and dying man he had a phenomenal memory, he had told them how the money had been transferred and where it had gone. He shook his head, all for one hundred thousand Euros he thought. I'm a lot more expensive now and I wonder if they have the more current figures as well. He glanced back at the paper and wondered about the last paragraph of the article. It said there was more to come in later editions. It could be just journalists whipping up a news story, but he doubted it, after all he knew there was more to come.

+

Jenny had read the paper with mixed emotions, horror that someone in public office could be so corrupt and also a sense of almost relief as it became clear that the paper was heading towards more current revelations. She set it down and looked across the table at her husband sitting there reading another paper, he looked up at her surprised at the way she was staring at him, looking for a reaction. "Well?" she finally asked as he set the paper down slowly not understanding what it was she was asking. "What do you think of the news about 'Xander then?" He looked just as puzzled as before replying "There's nothing in this paper about 'Xander" Jenny froze for a second before turning and switching on the radio. The presenter's voice was loud and clear as she read out the article from the 'National Central'. Word for word she read it out as Jenny's husband sat there his brow furrowed as he listened closely. Eventually as the news ended and the presenter moved onto general discussion of the topic, he sat back and regarded her with a thoughtful look "Okay," he finally said "do you want me to start making inquiries locally to see if the people who have been affected can make a claim against him and the government. See if we can get compensation out of them for the damage that's been done, not to mention the people that have been killed." Jenny smiled at him "That would be great, but lets just make sure the bastard doesn't get away with this one." He nodded as he stood up and putting on his jacket headed out to the car. It would be a long day in the legal office of the Prosecution Service.

+

330

In Andrea's house it was her father in law who was smiling most at the table that morning. He had a plane to catch later that day but would be going home happy. He hugged his daughter and said "Wait until I tell Jimmy about this, he will be so happy to hear that Silver has messed up finally and may be getting what's due to him yet. Might not get him his business back but sure will make him feel a whole lot better about where he's at now though." Andrea just shook her head, it was good news whatever you took out of it.

+

Mark was outside giving the grass it's last cut of the year when Pete came charging in about waving a newspaper at him, he had barely stopped running and thrust the paper into Marks hands when a shiny new silver four by four came across the field on the inland side of the building. He watched it carefully as it drew up alongside and to his surprise Paul Gray stepped out of the leather and walnut lined interior. "Nice truck," he said "Didn't think that was really your style." Paul laughed at him before replying "It isn't, but as Silvers mob left it in the garage and I sold mine when I left I thought I might borrow it for a while." He stopped and waved a hand in Marks direction and more accurately at the news paper in his hand "I see you've got the news, think it is of any relevance?" Mark pointed at the still panting Pete who for some reason had run the one hundred metres from his house up to Marks place "I don't know, I haven't had a chance to read it yet. Pete just brought it in about." Turning round he flicked open the news paper as he said "Come on inside, I'll put the kettle on and we can discuss it." The other two followed him in the door, slowly, Pete was still panting as they all sat down in the kitchen.

It was fifteen minutes later that Mark raised his head and looked around realising that Pete had finally recovered his breath and Paul Gray had made the coffee and dished out the mugs while he sat here and read. He sighed as he looked at his two friends "All very interesting" he started but Pete interrupted "Interesting, it proves the little bastard is a liar and I'll bet he's done the same here; lined his own pockets at the expense of the locals and the people of the country." Mark smiled as Paul jumped into the discussion "That is almost certain, and probably for bigger amounts than mentioned in here," he flicked the paper in Marks hand with his fingers "trouble is, this isn't current and we don't know if the paper has any more current stuff or is the latest stuff they've got?" he paused and looked at the other two for effect before continuing "Another thing to consider is how long will it take for them to do anything about it? Even if they have evidence it will be difficult to do anything because it would have to go to the ethics committee and he is the chair of the ethics committee. That could be a problem in getting a fair and realistic answer in a fair and realistic time frame. This thing," he flicked the paper again "could carry on long enough to let his pals get started on the job and destroy this place before anyone can do anything about it." he stopped there and looked at his two friends, Mark was looking at him obviously thinking about the options and what effect they would have on the area while Pete looked deflated. He was a great guy but very black and white, if his plans did not work out the way he wanted the first time round they were usually just dumped and left to be forgotten. Paul lifted his mug and sipped the hot black liquid as he thought about the situation.

+

'Xander had called a surprise press conference and even his closest advisers had no idea what he was going to be talking about. They had been barred from his office all day and he had closed the door and stayed inside; the only visitors he had seen were a couple of guys in grey suits who had appeared out of nowhere and had gone into his office without being asked. The building security had brought them in and taken them out again, but it had looked more like a courtesy escort than a security or controlling escort. The two men in grey suits had been in control that much had been obvious, 'Xander had risen from behind his desk to shut the office door behind them when they left, he had spoken to no one and did not even answer the phone.

Now he stood on the dais in the main public chamber of the parliament building, the usual place for press conferences, and looked out at the sea of faces, lights and cameras. The front edge of the lectern was covered in microphones and others were sitting as close as it was possible to get them to the dais without actually throwing them at him. He stood there and looked around for a few seconds, knowing this would probably not be his last time no matter how much he wanted that to be the case. His mouth was dry and he could feel beads of sweat on his forehead just starting to appear as well as that slight stickiness under his arms that betrayed a nervousness that he thought he had conquered so many years ago.

"I have a prepared statement which I am going to read and copies will be made available after the press conference. No questions will be taken." The media people all looked around at each other in surprise, this was not his style. He usually just gave them a small element of information and let them ask to draw out the real news afterwards. Giving them a single statement with no questions made it quite clear that whatever it was he was

332

about say was of significance, to him at least. This was the sort of thing a politician could only ever get away with once.

He cleared his throat and began to speak, even as some of the reporters scrambled to get their equipment ready to record every word he spoke. "It is with sadness that I have to announce my immediate resignation from the post of President. The sudden and unexpected death of Templeton, a close friend of many years, brought home to me the frailty of life and how much living I still have to do, as well as how much I have been missing out on whilst trying to fulfil my obligations as a politician and trying to lead a normal family life at the same time. The recent upsetting and scurrilous allegations that appeared in the press have also factored into my decision in as much as I wish to take time to clear my name properly, fully and completely. This would not be possible whilst fulfilling my duties here in the role of President, as such at close of business today I will leave this building for the last time." He stopped and looked at his watch "It is now half past three, so I do not have much time and I have a lot of people I need to see and say goodbye to." He looked out at the crowd of lenses and microphones, seeing only a means of communicating to the public and not the people behind them that operated all of the equipment. "With that I will bid you farewell and thank you for your patience with me over the years that we have had meetings like this." He stepped back down off the dais and turned away, walking quickly down the corridor ignoring the shouts and calls for answers to the many questions they all had. All he could actually hear was the sound of the man in a grey suit's voice as he had said "We will give you one chance to resign. It has to be done before the end of this week or we will publicly prosecute you to the full extent of the law. That will damage the government and this country to an incredible extent but sometimes such sacrifices will be made. Resign and you may get away without doing any prison time at all. I cannot promise that, but I can say it is a possibility." That was when he had stood up and walked out of his office leaving the door open behind him. 'Xander was crying when he got back to his office and shut the door behind him again, for the very last time.

+

Jonathon Diarmond was sitting in his office watching the live feed from the Parliament building on the other side of the capital. He had sent one of the staffers over rather than go himself as he was busy dealing with a memory stick that had turned up in today's post. This one had a number two written on the side of it and had some very interesting information on it. He was not really surprised at the resignation of 'Xander, but the timing of it had caught him completely unawares. Jonathon had expected it to take several weeks before the man either resigned or at least launched a legal attack. His editor had thought the same and so had the legal team. This was a major boost to his personal ego that the man had decided not to fight it publicly at the moment, he would need to be careful in case 'Xander decided to take that route at a later date; but he would worry about that later.

+

The police inspector was sitting at his desk in the now suspiciously quiet town of Drimmie when Parker walked in with a man in a grey suit behind him. The two men exchanged very guarded pleasantries, the Inspector did not like people in his district who he could not touch when he knew what they were doing must break some rules somewhere but he had to let that go. His eyes slid to the man in the grey suit who had not been introduced and the man smiled before he spoke but the smile never reached his eyes. "I am pleased to meet you at last" he said in a very careful voice, no accent and no emotion as he continued "You handled what could have been a very delicate situation well and tactfully. I can now tell you that the two men who attacked Paul Grey have been re apprehended at the airport and one of them has admitted a 'fear' campaign as he called it against a journalist over in the capital as well." The inspector interrupted "Jonathon Diarmond by any chance." The man hesitated and his eyebrows nodded as he continued "Indeed, however, they will not be returning for trial I am afraid." He paused almost as if he expected a challenge at this point, it never came. "The two men will instead be held under anti terrorism rules, without trial, until we get some of their sources and other information from them that might be useful in our fight against these types of people." He smiled again and held out his hand "As I said, it has been a pleasure meeting you and I will be in touch at some point in the future. Thank you again." without further ado the man turned away and walked out of the office. Parker looked at the inspector shrugged and said "See you later." Before turning and walking after the unidentified individual.

+

Marlene was sitting on her sofa at home watching the television news, she was crying and wringing her hands as she watched the resignation of 'Xander. It wasn't that she was fond of him in anyway shape or form, she had for long enough hated everything he stood for but it was the fact he was effectively being forced out of office because he had made a few mistakes. She hugged herself tightly as she thought about it; the problem was it could be any of them, everyone took a little something to ease the wheels a bit every now and again. That was one of the main reasons people

334

went into politics wasn't it? She had been asking herself this question time after time all morning and had so far not come up with a good answer, not once.

She was looking at the screen again and had been half listening for a few minutes before she began to realise this was different. They were talking about something else, it was related to 'Xander's resignation but that was not the actual topic. She turned up the volume to listen more closely.

In another house not far away 'Xander's brother was also sitting watching the television feeling lost and alone. He knew that if they could get to someone like his brother he himself was easy pickings. He had been trying to get hold of his brother all day since he had first heard the news but his personal mobile was not taking any calls, neither were any of his other phones or emails. He sat there and waited for the knock on the door. It was about three o'clock in the afternoon before it finally came. When he opened the door and saw two police officers standing there it was almost relief he felt as the inspector spoke to him and 'invited' him to come down to the station with him for a 'little chat'.

+

Andrew Crawford was sitting at his desk when his secretary walked in with two men in suits behind her, they looked official. "Andrew," she stammered "These men are from the fraud squad and the Department of Justice." He held up his hand to stop her "That's alright, I think I know what this is about so its okay. Could you maybe get these gentle men some coffee." He let his voice just tail off as the two men nodded before she turned and left the office. Andrews sighed as he turned to the two men and waving them to seats said "How can I help you gentlemen today?" They smiled and began to talk.

They had consumed two cups of coffee and had taken possession of several computer disks of data before they left the office in the early evening. Other operatives of the two agencies were working throughout the 'Silver Needle' and they were still working as Crawford's stepped out of his office. He was surprised to see his secretary still there, sitting looking at a blank computer screen, all the staff had been told to switch off their equipment and to go home if they wanted to. They were not allowed to be working in the network at all while the investigation was ongoing. He looked down at her and said "Come on, let's get something to eat. I'm buying" She grinned at him, unsure what else to do and let herself be led from the building and out through the basement car park to avoid the throngs of reporters there were surrounding the front door of the building. It also meant they would avoid the lower floors of the building where there were still some confused and disoriented staff wandering around trying to salvage some of their days work.

They didn't realise they had nothing to fear from the boss, he wasn't even in the building any more.

+

Back at the estate a very nervous individual drove slowly down the main drive, past the big house and past the stable block that was now offices and on wards the few metres until he saw Arthur's cottage on his left. He stopped the car and leant on the steering wheel for a few seconds before gathering his thought and reversing the car back to the offices where he parked and got out. Stretching as if he had been driving for hours, he looked around at the greenery and the silence, broken only by the rustle of trees in the wind and the recurring high pitched call of the buzzards circling above the beach just a few hundred metres away. He shook his head and drew breath before walking slowly down to the cottage again. He paused again, looking around and finally he spied the reporters car where she had said she would leave it, pulled off the drive and along side the stone dyke that marked the edge of old Arthur's garden. He stood there for a second or two with one hand on the latch off the rickety wooden gate, before finally he pushed it open and walked quickly the three paces to the door and knocked sharply, three times. He smiled as the reporter opened the door and stepped back, smiling but not saying a word while he stooped instinctively to step inside the small cottage. Arthur was looking at him in amazement as he said "Hello Dad, long time no see."

+

The man with the slicked back hair was sitting in the interrogation room waiting on the Inspector. He knew his brother couldn't help him now, He was on his own as he sat there slowly sinking into misery and despair with his head in his hands. The inspector watched through the one way glass and decided when the time was right to go in and speak to this man, who he was confident would fold and admit most everything quite quickly.

His head came up as he leant back and folded his arms trying to out stare the police officer who smiled as he sat down opposite him, dropping the beige cardboard file on the desk between them. The officer said nothing as he looked at a the few pages that lay between those thin cardboard covers

336

as the man opposite sweated, but did not say anything. "Now," the police man started "because of the nature of this case I've managed to get copies of your bank statements quite quickly. They are quite interesting. Do you want to comment?" the face opposite just stared back balefully from under that dark slicked back hair as he shook his head slowly from side to side. The inspector shrugged "Okay, no problem, let me tell you what we have seen here and what conclusions I have drawn and you can contradict me at any time." He paused and pointed to the recorder that sat on the desk between the two men and said "As you will no doubt have noticed this interview is being recorded for records purposes and there is another officer in the room for witness purposes." The man opposite nodded, still saying nothing as the inspector continued. "Okay, no problem. Let's start at the beginning will we. I see a cash deposit of twenty thousand Euros, do you want to explain that to me?" the man shook his head while the inspector pursed his lips and shrugged "Okay, well that wasn't very smart putting it in the bank like that. You see the banks have a legal obligation to notify the police of any deposit of over five thousand in cash, ten thousand if in cheque or a bankers draft. So you were under the spotlight from then on and quite cheap too I would say. Some of your colleagues had sums of up to fifty thousand Euros deposited." He paused as the man opposite seemed to swallow before he groaned out loud but made no move to speak, The inspector smiled "Feeling a little sick I would expect now aren't you?" The man stared at him, still saying nothing. The inspector then looked down at his notes "You had quite a lot of work done to your house this summer I believe. Strange, I don't see any payments to the building companies in here." He looked up at the man opposite and thought he could detect an extra pallor on that craggy face, an unhealthy grey tinge to his skin as he looked even more uncomfortable. The inspector looked back at the file "I have already drawn copies of the accounts from 'Drimmbuild & Co.' and it shows quite clearly that they did work at your home that was paid for by a third party." He paused at looked levelly at the man opposite "I know who that third party was and Drimmbuild & Co. are amazed that they have actually been paid. The third party in question has a nasty reputation of not paying bills of small companies who do work for them, they rather force them out of business and asset strip them where they can, so they are unusually honoured to be paid in this instance. But then they didn't ask too many questions when asked to do work on a number of councillors homes and bill this particular third party." The man opposite licked his lips and just for a second the inspector thought he was going to speak. He didn't, shaking his head the inspector looked down at the folder in front of him "Then there this charity you do work for, and" he looked at the folder in front of him again as his eyebrows rose in surprise "it would appear that you get well paid for the hours you don't put in for them." He smiled as he raised his eyes to meet those of the man opposite. "You see I've checked your official diary against the hours you are being paid for here and you are a remarkable man. I don't know any one else who has developed the ability to bi-locate, or in more common terms be in two places at one time. Care to tell me how you do that?" The man opposite folded "Get my lawyer and I'll tell you what you need. I know I'm in trouble here and so will a few others be by the time I'm finished." The inspector smiled at him "Wise man, want to tell me more first?" the man shook his head "No. call me a lawyer, I don't have a criminal practice lawyer so anyone will do and let me speak to them first, then I'll tell you what I can." The inspector smiled and stood up, taking the folder with him, he left the room.

Outside the door he leant back against the wall and the Superintendent of Forensics stuck her head round the corner from the cubby hole they laughingly called the observation suite and smiled at him "Well done. That was quite impressive to watch, did you expect him to be so easy?" he shook his head as he smiled at his friend, whose presence had taken him by surprise, he had thought she was still working over at the Capital rather than here in Drimmie. "Both yes and no," he replied before explaining "I thought he would probably be the easiest of the lot, but was far from sure he would be easy as such. After all he knows the game." She nodded as they turned towards the canteen to get a coffee. "Didn't he ask for a lawyer?" she asked as he nodded "Yeah, but he can sit there and think for a while yet. I'll get him a lawyer before the end of today, meanwhile you can tell me all about your trip to the east and what wonderous things you did find." She laughed, as much at his stupid expression as his words, as the two friends headed off down the corridor.

+

Mark was still sitting drinking coffee with two of his friends when the door bell rang. He hesitated before going to the door to find one of the local reporters standing there. He smiled up at Mark as he surveyed the driveway over the top of his head and leant against the door post making it quite clear the reporter wasn't getting into the house. He grinned lopsidedly as he made the cigarette between his lips dance a little while he moved it to the side so he could speak with it still in place. "Hi Mark," the little man started while Mark said nothing and just looked at him "Was wondering if you could shed any light on what's happening with the councillors and the like today?" Mark frowned and thought for a moment before replying "I'm sorry I don't know what you're talking about. What's happening?" The reporter grinned at him "Thought some of the local police or that, might have kept you in the loop." He grinned up at Mark as he put away his

338

pocket recorder while he continued to talk "looks like a few of the obvious councillors have been picked up by the police and are being interviewed down at the station." He glanced sideways up at Mark as he spoke and just before he turned away he said "I've been told the police have also drawn their bank statements and the accounts from a local builder and a certain charity organisation. The implications obvious to me, they've been on the take and have been caught. See you later." With a cheery wave he turned and walked off down the driveway leaving Mark standing in the doorway amazed and shocked that such news could be passed on so casually. Slowly he turned round and walked back into the house to tell Paul and Peter who were both still sitting at his table.

+

Steve knocked on the open door to Marianne's office and she smiled as she looked up at him. He was grinning from ear to ear as stepped into the office and pushed the door almost closed behind him "You need to know this, Mark will almost certainly know by the time you get home tonight so you need to know as well just in case he doesn't." Marianne was puzzled at the smile on his face, Steve didn't normally let himself be affected so easily by news of any kind, but something was making him smile. She leant back as he sat down in the chair in front of her desk. "One of my contacts at the police station along the road here tells me seven of the local councillors have been arrested for fraud and are currently being interrogated with a view to formal prosecution. It appears it all started out here when Silvers people hired Drimmbuild & Co. to do some work during the summer holidays on some of the councillors homes and send the bill to them, the Silver Organisation." Marianne leant forward shaking her head "So Silvers people obviously didn't know that John, Drimms cousin or whatever he was, was ripped off by Silver a few years back." Steve smiled "You got it they hired the relative of a previous victim of theirs to do some dodgy work on their behalf. So he just waited until he got paid, and yes he did actually get paid which is a miracle in itself, then he went along to the police and told them what he knew." Marianne began to laugh as Steve carried on with his tale. "It now appears that at least three of them also had 'consultancy' positions with a charity run by Peter Barnard, you know Silvers token local, for which they were well paid, all undeclared on the register of interests. Apparently some of them even had cash payments right at the beginning as well. Talk about blatant, they deserve everything that's coming to them." Marianne had finally managed to stop laughing "I'm sorry. I just had this picture in my head of Marlene's face as she realised she would never make President now." She sighed and gathered her breath as she smiled across the desk at Steve who was still grinning from ear to ear. Slowly the smile vanished from Marianne's face as she looked at her friend "So," she almost whispered "what happens now?" Steve looked at her puzzled. "Well there has been an application to the local authority for planning permission for the estate and it was passed up to a public local inquiry. I seem to remember hearing somewhere that once an application had been made there was a duty on the local authority to consider it. As far as I recall there has been no determination of that application yet. So does that mean it still has to be decided, or if not what happens to it now?" Steve looked at her, puzzled, for a second before he replied "Well, I would think the reporters will still need to issue a decision but I don't know who to. I mean the Silver Organisation appears to have withdrawn from the area completely and Paul Gray has taken over the estate again. As far as that goes, even if the planning permission was approved I don't see the development of tower blocks and such going ahead. Even if Paul wanted to I'm sure Mark would be able to talk him out of it." Marianne just grinned and went a little pink as she said "Yeah, Mark can talk people out of many things." Steve didn't ask what she was talking about as he stood up and went back to his own office.

+

Mary eventually came up to Marks place looking for Pete and found the three men sitting in the living room watching the early evening news as the story about the arrest of the councillors broke. Marianne arrived home at about the same time and the two women sat down beside the men to watch the news and see what they knew that the television wouldn't say. It was actually the other channel that led with the raid on the offices of the Silver Organisation in the US. The details were sketchy but it became obvious the organisation was in disarray as there was no spokesman available. "Rats from a sinking ship" was the only comment passed by Paul Gray as they watched the story unfold on the screen in front of them. It was worse than they had thought at first. It now looked like there were developments across the world coming to a grinding halt. There were news items from reporters in Patagonia, Saudi Arabia, Mexico, Dubai and several others not forgetting, of course, the Doones estate. Marianne giggled as she watched the screen before jumping up and running to the window. "There" she shouted pointing across towards the coastal dune line where, just inside of the dunes sat a large van with a satellite dish on the roof. As she pointed it out the camera panned across and the TV screen showed an image of Marks house from the dune line, they laughed amongst themselves as the bright yellow of Marianne's blouse showed up on the TV screen at the other side of the room.

340

Mark turned and looked at Paul who was obviously thinking. "Penny for your thoughts" he said as he looked at his friend who shook his head "I was just wondering what happens next." Peter laughed "Well that is up to you, you own the place again don't you?" Paul nodded as he replied "Yes I do, but I was getting ready for a battle with Silver and his people. Now I would almost be surprised if I don't have to fight a battle with some of his creditors. Some one somewhere will claim that my retaking ownership of the estate is unlawful and that Silver still owns it. That way it would become an asset of the Organisation and be available for sale to recover some funds of theirs." He went silent as Mark thought about this as well. "Well, I can see the argument coming about, but the situation was quite clear as far as I recall." He paused and looked at his friend "I would bet that your solicitor will be on top of that situation and if not, I'm sure Steve would be willing to help out if you need him to." Paul nodded slowly, obviously thinking about getting a second opinion before he really needed it.

+

Marlene sat in her prison cell looking at the graffiti scratched into the paint on the inside of the steel door. She was only in the local police station but she had been 'asked' to stay here until they found a lawyer for her. That had been two hours ago and she knew there would be several who would not want to have anything to do with this case in any way, shape, or form. The graffiti went all the way from a name, or nickname even, and a date, to something that looked like it could be a poem. She couldn't read it, someone had tried to clean it off and had succeeded in making it illegible, but what it did tell her was the amount of time some people spent in places like this. She realised suddenly she did not have that amount of patience or the ingenuity to get anything you could scratch a message with, into the cell in the first place. She shuddered at the thought of spending a long time locked up in one of these places. It was not her idea of fun or a good career move. She was intensely grateful when she heard keys in the door and she saw a dark suit standing in the corridor when the door swung aside on heavy steel hinges. She sighed and slid herself off the bench she had been sitting on and walked out to meet her lawyer.

Once back in the interview room they were left alone and the recording equipment was switched off. The lawyer smiled his encouragement at her as she glanced at the one way mirror before he spoke "Relax, I've been here before and know how these people operate. They are basically trustworthy and I have been assured that all recording and listening devices have been switched off." He paused "Add to that they are audited regularly and if it was found that they recorded, or listened in to, the conversation between a solicitor and their client it would be a disciplinary offence for the officers involved and would cast doubt on any case they were involved in." Marlene shook her head as this smug man smiled at her again "I don't care about all of that. I've made a bad mistake and I want to confess to it so we can leave all of this behind us and try to correct the situation." He looked at her knowing there was something else in her eyes "Are you sure that all you want from this?" That was when he saw the fear in her eyes "I don't want to go to prison." She looked at him as he realised she was shaking "I don't think I could handle it at all. I just don't want to go to prison, do you think if I confess fully to everything I've done I might get away with that." He shrugged "I don't know, this is a high profile case, If you confess it will be easier for you, yes, but I can't promise you wont go to jail. As long as you cooperate fully it is unlikely that you will end up in high security or anything like that, add to that the fact that all the prisons are nearly full and I doubt that a criminal like you will get sent to jail. At the worst you might get a suspended sentence or an open prison; maybe some community service." She laughed a high and false sound that made him wince "Community service, me? That's what I thought I was doing all the time I was leading the council. I doubt they will let me near planning matters ever again." The lawyer did not respond, they both knew she was right.

+

'Xander had been driven home, to his own home over in his constituency, not his official residence in the capital or any of his other official homes that he had instituted as essential to the office of President. Sitting on the seat beside him was the half empty cardboard box of personal effects he had taken with him. He had not had the energy to clear his office, he had asked his aide to do it for him and send the boxes on. From what he had heard on the radio someone else might be doing it for him. His aide had also been on the Drimmie local council and if he had been doing as he had told his brother to do, would have his own problems to deal with before too long.

The house was empty and quiet as he walked in through the door and he was scared. His wife had always stayed out of the public eye and hated the fact that he was corrupt, she had known not long after they had been married and she had been at him for years to stop taking and start doing what he should be doing. He had never been sure what she had meant but had been too proud to admit it and ask her. Now he was terrified she would leave him. He knew he had been wrong and he had promised himself every time that it would be the last time, now the last time was past and he may

342

have just lost everything he had ever gathered over the years. If they did come and take it away from him he would be just like any other pensioner, he opened the folder that had been given to him on leaving the building and looked at the numbers on the printed sheet inside. Okay so he wouldn't be just like any other pensioner, he was going to be okay even if they did take it all away from him.

He was leaning on the worktop a little while later, waiting on the kettle to boil when the door opened and his wife came into the room. She dropped her handbag on the table and wrapped her arms around his neck "I'm proud of you." She whispered as she kissed him, his confusion showed as he said "Proud of me? I thought you be ashamed of me." She pushed him away "I'm ashamed of what you did to get yourself in this position but proud of the way you got out of it, or at least dealt with it so far. I don't think you are out of it yet." She grinned at him and hugged him again "Anyway," she continued "I love you and nothing can change that." He was crying as he realised just how lucky a man he was.

+

Andy McIntyre sat down at the table between his daughter the reporter and his father and said "Can you forgive me?" Arthur nodded slowly "Of course I can son. I would have forgiven you all those years ago as well, as would your mother. I might have been bloody mad at you for what you did but I can't stay mad all my life now, can I?" He glanced at the young woman sitting opposite him "Anyway how can I be mad at you after you giving me a granddaughter as good looking as this one." Father and daughter smiled at one another as Arthur carried on speaking "I just wish your brother had come back to me before he died." He wiped a tear from the corner of his eye as Andy sat back "Well, Dad," he looked down at the table and looked up again "I may be able to help there a little bit. You see John isn't dead." Arthur stared at his son as he continued to speak but it soon became clear it really was too much for the old man and he wasn't following the tale. The three of them relaxed as Andy said "Well never mind. I'm sure you'll get the details soon, maybe from him directly if needs be. I think he's in London right now and he will be flying into the country in the next day or two and then he's coming here to see you and us," he squeezed his daughter's hand "and some guy called Mark Rae who lives around here somewhere; any idea where?" His daughter grinned and Arthur smiled broadly "Wait around, he'll be here sometime soon. He usually drops in past at least every second day, if not him then Paul Gray is in past at some point as well. They've looked after me well have the locals." Andy just nodded slowly, he was sure the story would be interesting once it all came out. If it ever all came out, he actually doubted all the details would ever be known.

+

Somewhere in the basement of an anonymous grey building in the capital a lowly security clerk slid a computer disk into the binder as he had been instructed and fastened the twine across the opening. Slowly he picked up the stick of wax and held it in the flame of a pocket disposable lighter, he laughed to himself that in this age of thirty two bit encryption and special algorithm encoding the best security they could get for a physical file was a hard wax seal locking the threads together. Carefully he pressed the date stamp into the hot wax and blew on it to be sure it was cool before taking the file into the depths of the archive and sliding it onto a shelf at the back in the 'release in fifty years section'.

19

Marianne was laughing as she stood on the side of the trench, happy and comfortable again in jeans and boots even if it was cold standing outside in the breeze. She looked up at the top of the bank wondering if she would catch sight of Mark, her lover as he was now, while he watched what was going on around the area as he had done for some time. She knew there was still a lot to be sorted out but things were going the right way and as far as she was concerned, she thought turning to look down into the maze of trenches that lay open before her, the archaeology was safe and they would get to finish their work here.

She stepped down into the trench and looked at where one of the students was working, slowly exhuming another set of skeletal remains from the Bronze Age. She was amazed at the new energy on the site, the almost palpable excitement that flowed from almost everyone that was around the area. The offers from universities around the world were still flooding in at an almost alarming rate, and she was still turning them down as fast as they arrived. The last few had been more interesting and she was still looking at them. Instead of trying to lure her away to work at their facilities they were now asking if they could send people to work at the site and assist in the excavations. Mark even had an architect looking at building a shelter for the site to protect the dig and give them on site offices and labs for some of the really unusual stuff with a view to adding a visitor centre at a slightly later date. This was true sustainable development; for a minute she wondered what had happened to Mike, he had been a great guy who had meant a lot to her at the time, he had just made a wrong choice. The new representative of 'Greensward' still had a lot to learn, she was good but all of her knowledge was from a book; that would change. She was already becoming more relaxed around the site and learning more by looking first and checking the books later.

+

Paul Gray was sitting in the office of the big house, looking at the computer screen but not really seeing anything he was lost in thought about his options here. He had originally sold the estate because his wife had conned him out of it and almost everyone in the area knew that now. That would make it uncomfortable for him to continue to live here, add to that he was getting headaches with the colour schemes that had been chosen for the place and why anyone had chosen the same carpet as on the floor of the pub down in Granitburgh he would never know, it was hideous and an insult to this country. He shook himself, he was letting himself get sidetracked in meaningless detail.

He sighed and turned to look out of the window, he loved this place both the house, even in its currently disfigured form, and the estate, let alone the country, but he really did not want the work of looking after the estate any more, he was tired of it all but did not know the way out from all of this. His lawyer had been on the phone again, early, apologising for even speaking to Silvers people let alone anything else. Paul didn't know what anything else was, but he had a fair idea; however the thing that mattered was he had kept to his obligations to his client when it mattered. Paul might just give him another chance.

He turned back to the newspaper, it was the 'National Central' he didn't buy the 'Daily' any more than he absolutely had to, and it was speculating about what was going to happen to the estate. Apparently, as he had expected, there was a creditor of the Silver Organisation who was claiming that the estate was still an asset of the organisation and so should be resold to return some cash to the organisation. Paul just shrugged, he had taken very good legal advice and the land was his and would remain his at all costs, anything else was just press speculation. But what would he do now? In many ways he wanted to stay here but in others it was a problem, he wanted to move on in his life and the estate would forever be tainted with the name of the Silver Organisation and their stench of corruption would linger for a long time. He leant back and wondered, would anyone else want to buy the land with its reputation? He didn't know was the only honest answer he could give himself.

+

Andy McIntyre woke up in the hotel room he had hired for the night and looked up at the ceiling. He was warm comfortable and happy, his daughter was in the room next door and his father was warm safe and alive in his house not far away. Yes the house needed improvement but it was secure and he had friends round about who looked in on him every day. He was pleased he had been able to get together with him before it was too late, but he missed his brother deeply. All the way from childhood up to eighteen when he had left home they had been really close. It struck him that had been twenty five years ago, it was his daughters birthday in a weeks time and at least now she would have a grandfather to celebrate it with.

346

He looked at his own rough hands, he was a builder to trade so he could do the work on his fathers house that he felt needed doing if he could find out who the owner of the place actually was. Suddenly he felt a dread in his stomach, he hated dealing with people who were better than him he always felt so inadequate.

In the room next door his daughter rolled out of bed, she was so happy it almost hurt, to get her father together with his father for the first time in her life was a major success, she just didn't know where it would lead. Suddenly for a second a shadow crossed her happiness as she thought about the uncle she had never met who was now gone as well, she brightened almost as quickly again as she thought about her grandfather. A man she had heard so much about, now to have met him and to have him in her life was incredible, she was frightened she was going to start crying before she got as far as the shower this morning.

+

Mark was sitting in his office working out some figures and wondering what he could do with what he had. Of course it all depended on the response and attitude of his friend and the actual owner of the property he might just tell Mark to 'go away' or words to that effect. The last thing Mark wanted to do at the moment was to offend Paul, he was only too grateful that his arrival back in the area had made it impossible for the Silver Organisation to do what they had wanted to do. He paused and looked out of the window inland over the fence and into the field that was adjacent to his house, past the wild bit that had never been properly farmed for several years and onto the golden grain crop that was almost ready to be harvested, before you came to the farm road that led to his place and the row of cottages. He stopped and looked again, there was a black saloon car stopped on the road, just at the head of the bank, just where the full grandeur of the place became apparent. Mark watched as the car moved slowly forward, coming closer all the time but so incredibly slowly that you had to watch it to be sure it was moving. Mark stopped what he was doing and picked up the telescope to have a better look. He stared and dropped the lens for a second before bringing it back up to his eye once more just as the car changed direction slightly and the glare on the windscreen made it impossible to see the driver. Mark set the telescope down and went to put on the kettle. If it was who he thought it was, then he'd be in need of a coffee as a minimum and something stronger would almost certainly be welcome. Mark waited impatiently and a few minutes later heard the car stop at the end of his house, he waited again and listened closely to the footsteps as they came up the path to the front door before the doorbell rang. Mark slowly, walked through the hallway and opened the door before smiling at his long lost friend who just turned and smiled back at him a little uncertainly before Mark said "Well, well, John McIntyre, so it is a Mark Twain moment. I did wonder you know." Stepping back he turned away and called over his shoulder "Are you coming in or are you going to stand on the doorstep all day?"

It was early afternoon when Mark drove the old Land Rover round the estate road to the side of the offices that had once been a stable block and stopped close to Arthur's little house, drawing breath he walked up the path and knocked the door before calling out "Arthur, it's just me, Mark." He paused as he pushed open the door and saw other people there "Oh I'm sorry Arthur I didn't realise you had visitors." Before he could move Arthur called to him from the kitchen table where he was sitting "I hope you brought more milk, I want you to meet these two." Mark laughed and hefted the carrier bag he had in one hand "I did that Arthur, I thought you might need it." The reporter took the bag from Marks hand and glanced inside "And another bottle of whisky I see, you've been well looked after." She smiled at Mark and a frown caught her face as she looked past him, where he still stood in the doorway as Arthur carried on speaking "I want you to meet my son Andy and his daughter, my granddaughter, the pretty young lady standing in front of you." Mark smiled at the two new faces and relaxed before stepping to one side "Well then, I can let my passenger in to see you as well. I'm sure you'll recognise him." John McIntyre stepped round his friend and looked at his father who was staring at him as if he'd seen a ghost while Andy, his brother, stood up so fast the chair he had been sitting on clattered to the floor behind him. Mark watched from the doorway for a moment or two as the four family members all greeted and hugged one another. Quietly he stepped back and shut the door behind him before climbing back into the Land Rover and heading off to the big house. He had to speak to Paul about what was going to happen to the estate.

+

Mike was settling in well to his new life in Denmark, his command of the language was a little shaky but improving as each day went past. Marika, his new local girlfriend helped a lot with that and his job here had changed. Once they had realised that all communication with the Silver Organisation had stopped they had found him a job doing very much what he had been doing back home. He still had trouble with the forms and it wasn't just because he couldn't read them all of the time. He smiled to himself as he picked up his bag and headed for the door to get out on site; they had a far stricter system of regulation here and that made his job a lot easier. It

348

would have made it impossible for Silver to do here what they had tried to do at home. That was something he did not need to worry about any more, he had a new life here and he was happy, suddenly a cloud crossed his thoughts as he thought about Marianne, they had been good together, but his desperation to get himself ahead had caused that to fail, dramatically, he hoped she was okay, she had deserved better.

The sky was clear and the sun was out, even this late in the year, this far north it was warm and comfortable outside, even if it was a cool breeze blowing from the Western Ocean on to his face, he breathed in the salt and relaxed once more. Life was good, he felt he had been forgiven and he hoped he had not hurt the others too much when he had run away. That was his shame and he would have to live with it for the rest of his life.

+

Padruig McCarthy was sitting in front of the new leader of his political party who was looking at him with a mixture of distaste and fear. Marlene was indisposed and would not be available for some considerable time was the way it was being put as nothing had been formally admitted or stated. It was almost as if the matter had never happened and as Padruig looked at the younger man obviously uncomfortable in front of him, he realised why the man was so uncomfortable. He had to admit that Padruig had actually been right, they could dress it up any way they chose but the facts were still the same. Padruig had taken the only decision that was actually open to him by the rules and processes of the council. Now the man had to find some reason to keep Padruig in what they called censure which was like a political limbo, they didn't want to throw him out of the party that could cause them all sorts of trouble, in significant votes and he might even gain more sympathy from the public than he already had. Most people knew the facts and understood that it was wrong what they were trying to do to him. He smiled and leant back watching the young man squirm even more as he began to speak. "You may have lost the chairmanship of several committees but as you know we cannot throw you off the actual committees without a unanimous vote from all the other members of the committee and we don't want to do that for a number of reasons." He looked up only to find Padruig was still smiling at him so he looked away hurriedly and pretended to read from the almost blank page in front of him. "However it may be possible to have you reinstated to full membership of the party if you renounce your position and admit that you made a mistake. The whole development should have gone ahead at the first time of trying and that you now support the concept. Would you be prepared to do that?" He finally raised his head and looked Padruig in the face for the first time just as he realised Padruig was laughing at him.

It was a few moments before Padruig was able to stop laughing "What you mean is you want me to call myself a liar, discard my principles just so you cal reallocate the whip to me so you can be sure of an extra vote in the chamber when you feel the need." The young man was shaking his head "You know there is no whip in local politics, it's not allowed by the code of conduct." He never got to finish the sentence as Padruig interrupted him "And we all know how well adhered to that has been locally, hence why you are here and Marlene is probably in a cell as we speak, along with fourteen of our other colleagues." He paused for breath and the young man saw the temper in his eyes and knew that to argue was a waste of time. Padruig continued "I may never be the chair of another committee but very few of you have the courage to vote me off the committees I sit on, and as long as I can still provide value I will continue to sit on the committee where I can. As for regaining your whip you can shove that sideways. I'm resigning from the party because I know I was right and will be proven right yet and probably sooner than you think." With that and not another word Padruig stood up and walked out of the office and along to the canteen for a coffee with the other councillors who were present.

Back behind the desk the young man put his face in his hands, he knew his party was now in trouble. They had needed Padruig to confirm a majority that they now didn't have for a vote of no confidence that was rumoured to be upcoming at the next full meeting. He didn't know what to do next.

+

The woman was quite elegant as she took her seat at the table on the slightly raised dais and looked out at the mass of cameras and microphones all pointed at her, waiting on her to speak. She glanced to her right where assistants were wheeling in box after box of copies of the report and stacking them against the wall behind another table that ran the full length of the room. Some one moved close by and she turned to nod at the police inspector from the fraud squad as he took his seat next to her on the platform. She could hear the stir in the press as many of them recognised the police officer. They knew this meant something significant was about to be made public. The man to her left nodded, she glanced at her watch and looked to her right again before picking up the sheet of paper that lay on the desk in front of her and prepared to speak.

As the chief reporter opened her mouth the room fell into an almost unnatural silence as all the press stopped to listen closely to what she had to say. "After suitable deliberation and consideration I have to announce that
350

the decision relating to the application on behalf of the Silver Organisation for a leisure resort and hotel complex has been refused." She paused as some of the press left the room rushing away to send in immediate copy leaving others behind to capture the details and the explanation. She continued "My colleagues and myself came to the conclusion that these proposals were inappropriate for the location and this country. The concept was flawed from the start with the attempt to impose ill fitting and badly conceived designs on a natural landscape that has protected status and will continue to have protected status. It was argued that the departures from the local and national plan were mitigated by the incredible revenue that would be forthcoming from this development. However the only figures that were available for review were those of the applicant themselves and no alternate financial projections were available. On review of these projections it soon became apparent that they bore more resemblance to the profit projections of a couple of the large US financial institutions that were issued the week before they collapsed so publicly, than any semblance of reality or believability. It was therefore concluded that the environmental damage to an irreplaceable and totally unique site far outweighed any possible financial benefit that may have come from this project going ahead." She paused and licked her lips glancing at the officer to her left who nodded and just smiled a fraction before she continued "In addition, and not directly related to the fact of the planning matter before the inquiry were a number of other elements that have led to criminal proceedings being taken against specific individuals who were involved in this matter. I will leave this gentleman to explain those elements of the case." She waved a hand in the direction of the police officer to her left who moved slightly to sit a little more upright before he began to speak.

He let the reporters fester a little and waited until he saw them start to become uncomfortable before he opened his mouth to speak, he hated reporters. They were often the ones who initiated the crimes he investigated, but he couldn't say that here. "Good morning ladies and gentlemen," he began " It is very disappointing to me that I have to state that due to this planning application a few issues came to light that required further investigation by my department. Not just investigations of Granitburgh local authority but up into the lower levels of government itself." A few of the reporters nodded to themselves, they had thought as much when 'Xander had announced his resignation so hurriedly, but they also knew corruption at that level would never be publicly admitted. The inspector continued "As a result of these investigations a total of fifteen councillors are facing prosecution for crimes of dishonesty. A number of local authority employees, about twenty two I think, are also facing charges of a similar nature. While a small number of professional criminals are facing charges relating to crimes of violence. I cannot expand on those cases as some of the individuals involved are also being charged under anti terrorism legislation for unrelated happenings." The room fell silent as he stopped speaking, but only for a second or two as a sudden barrage of noise erupted from the press as they all asked different questions at the same time. The chief reporter was taken aback; she had never understood what one of her colleagues had said about the press being like a baying mob at times. Now she understood.

+

Paul Gray turned away from the TV set and looked across the desk at his neighbour and friend, the man who had saved his life and asked. "Okay Mark, now that the threat of a hotel on your doorstep is over and done with, what do you intend doing with my estate?" Mark laughed before he spoke "Well, that is up to you as you are well aware. I would like to do a lot with this place, but first you still own it, no matter what some half witted lawyer in Alabama says. Second I don't have enough money to buy the place and do what I want to do with it. Three you might have a better offer already in your hand or on its way for all I know." He stopped and looked up at Paul before saying "And finally I don't know what you want to with it. The final call is yours; the future of this whole place is up to you so I will ask you, what do you want to do with it?" Paul Gray smiled and sat back "That's what I like about you Mark, you're honest to a fault." He sighed and spoke slowly "I've had my lawyer on the phone this morning asking something very similar, he is in possession of two offers for the estate as it is, planning situation unknown. They may of course both be withdrawn now that we see planning permission has not been granted. However as both of them included the house I am not inclined to accept them." He sighed again as he gathered his thoughts before continuing "I actually want to continue living here. It's a fantastic house, even if it does need redecorating" he glanced over his shoulder at the tartan carpet that could be seen in the hallway through the open doorway from his office. "Anyway," he continued "I would consider selling off most of the estate to someone like yourself if I could get a guarantee of some degree of control in what you did with the place and I was left to my own devices here on something like maybe forty acres or so." he paused and looked at his friend "Remember it would just be agricultural land with a limited value now that the planning permission has been refused, that might make it more affordable for you as well. Do you think you could do something there and keep me in the loop, let me both stay here and be useful for something at long last." Mark smiled at his old friend as he stood up "Of course I'm interested. I just need to go and adjust my figures now and see what I can do. Don't go away now, I'll be

352

back shortly with a revised plan and maybe a different way of doing things. Would you be prepared to consider something unconventional?" Peter just grinned "I will consider almost anything as long as I get to live here without having to look after the estate. I am just getting too lazy these days to worry about that sort of thing" Mark nodded and walked slowly out of the building, confident once more that they could do something here with long term value. Paul's support had been the missing piece of the puzzle and his wanting to keep the house made things a lot easier financially as well. He smiled as he climbed into the Land Rover and drove away, tyres crunching loudly on the gravel of the driveway.

+

He hadn't been back at his house for long when Marianne came in the door laughing and smiling at him. She always brightened his spirits these days, since she had gone from being a lodger and had become his partner she had a very different effect on him. Today was no different she was bubbling over with enthusiasm for the dig and what it might mean for not just her career but the area and her students as well. The fact it was on private land and under her sole control made it a lot easier for her and he was just wary that might be the reason she was with him. He doubted it but she had been the one who wanted to end it the last time they had split up so many years before.

He relaxed a bit as he thought about the last time Mike had stayed here as well. That was probably what was bothering him more than anything else, he was worried that Mike might come back and whisk this beautiful creature away from him without warning, after all they didn't know what had happened to Mike, he had just disappeared when the Silver Organisation had stopped paying its bills.

He looked at her bright smiling face and relaxed, she wasn't being smart, he was confident she was in love, as was he. They kissed and she stepped back quickly as the door bell went, she blushed and shook her head at her own embarrassment as he turned and went to the door. She watched him walk away a little scared at that feeling of dependence she couldn't shake but knowing it was too late, she was hooked.

The sound of voices and laughter came through to her from the front door as it sounded like Mark had invited a party of people into the house and taken them straight into the living room. She put the kettle on and went to see who all was there.

353

She stopped in the doorway there were only four people, and Mark, in the living room but hey all seemed to be talking at once and they were all happy about something. Mark stood up and turned round "Marianne, come on in here and meet some friends, some old friends and some new ones as well." He waved his hand at the old man who sat in a chair already while the rest of them stood around him. "This is Arthur an old friend of mine who lives in Ruriadh Cottage along by the big house stables." Mark stepped back and waved at the other two men "these are his sons Andy, who I had never met until today and John who is looking pretty good for a dead guy. While this," he paused and waved at the reporter who now sat on the settee. "Is Abby, Andys daughter who has been around the area for a while following the story but only realised there was a link recently." He paused as Abby shook hands with Marianne "I'll let her tell you the story, she knows it better than I do anyway." They all laughed and before Mark could say anything Marianne looked at the group and said "Tea or coffee? The kettles on already," And pushed Mark into a seat before taking her requests and disappearing through the doorway with Abby.

+

Down in the pub in Drimmie Magda looked around the quiet bar and sighed to herself just as Andy walked in from the hotel side. "That was a serious sigh Magda, what's the problem?" She smiled at him a weak but genuine smile, "Well," she said "While I never thought the Silver development along the road was a good idea it might have made things busier here for a while. This is your quiet season now and it looks like you will not have enough work here for me so I may have to back home to Poland. I wanted to stay here. I like it here. I like being here with you" He smiled at her over the bar counter as the door opened and a face poked in around the door.
"Sorry to bother you but do you do rooms? We haven't got a booking but our nature club was desperate to come up here after hearing Silver has lost the fight for their planning application. We don't know who might be coming in next to destroy the place." Andy smiled at the young woman looking around the door "How many rooms do you need?" he asked "Five" was the reply as he smiled again "Then come on in, we can manage all of you and food as well if you want." The woman hesitated and turned back to them "Do you have a vegetarian option?" Andy hesitated as Magda spoke up "Of course we have a vegetarian option, it might take a little longer as it will need to be made specially but we can do that for you." The woman smiled and shouted "back in a minute" as she vanished out the door they could hear her call "Come on girls, they have rooms available and can do a vegetarian option for food as well." Andy smiled and turned to Magda only

354

to find she was not there. She had already gone to the kitchen to find out what was available.

+

Andrew Crawford was standing on the balcony of his thirty second floor apartment looking across the plaza at the silver needle where he used to work. He hadn't started to look for work yet, knowing that a lot of people would never touch him because of what had happened with the Silver Organisation. Jennilee, who had been his secretary walked out of the spare room where she was staying and walked over to stand beside him. He had become used to her being around and yet a few short weeks ago he had not even known her name. They had agreed that she could stay at his apartment until such time as they were thrown out by the repossession people who were bound to be coming around soon. Then they would move to her place, he wasn't sure what would happen then, he was fairly sure she didn't have a spare room like he did, he would worry about that later. She had wanted to see what these apartments were like inside so he had agreed to let her stay here, he was glad he had done that.

He had to admit he had become used to having her around and it was easier than being alone, she was easy on the eye and friendly as well. He just didn't know what she wanted from him, he had been a New Yorker too long he laughed at himself, not everyone wanted something from you. He froze as he thought that and in that instant he knew where that thought had come from. His time in Europe had changed him in ways he could not imagine. Jennilee smiled at him as she stepped in close and without thinking he slid an arm around her. The smile broadened as she hugged him back. Now all they had to do was wait on the bailiffs.

+

Number three looked back and waved as the old man in the wheelchair was taken inside the nursing home, slowly she turned away and walked down the path and out the gate to the red Cadillac that sat at the kerb. She slid in behind the steering wheel and eased the big car along the road the few miles to where she turned off and through the high steel gates that swung shut silently behind the car as it passed through. She was nearly impossible to recognise as the pneumatic blonde in the designer clothes that she had been. Now she was dark haired, having let her blonde grow out, and was dressed in jeans and a tee shirt, designer jeans but still just jeans. She sighed to herself as she watched the gates close tightly behind her. She had had this planned for years, had actually owned the house in her own name for almost three years and had been siphoning money off through several companies for a long, long time. She just had never figured on taking Silver with her. The nursing home was the best going and it had been easy to get him in under the guise of being her partner. No one asked too many questions of a crazy man who was able to pay for the services they provided.

She knew that if ever the money ran out, he would be homeless, she would worry about that when it happened. As she thought about the safe downstairs in the basement she locked the car and tossed her hair feeling good about herself, she realised it was unlikely the offshore account that paid for his medical bills would run out in his lifetime. It was also untraceable.

+

Jonathon Diarmond sat at his desk as before, but this time it was a new desk several floors higher up in the building. The memory sticks just seemed to keep on coming, with no identifiers on the envelopes it was impossible to tell where they were coming from and as far as he knew no one had tried to find out. The information was incredible and sold a huge amount of news papers, but there was so much information they could not print it all in the paper. That was why he was still here at this time of night, writing his book. It looked like it could be the first of a few if the memory sticks kept on coming as they were. The 'National Central' had a deal with a publisher who had taken him on easily and quickly, advance sales of the book were already good and he just had to keep working to get it out on time.

A buzzer sounded and he glanced at the small screen on the side of his desk, it was just the security guard doing his rounds, making sure everything was all right. Jonathon gave him the thumbs up and let him get on with his rounds while Jonathon kept hammering at the keyboard wondering what would happen when the memory sticks stopped coming.

He shrugged and looked across at his notes, there was already enough material here to publish another two books let alone news paper articles. He should worry about the supply drying up later he thought as he turned the stick over on the desk where it lay. The number, handwritten in black marker pen looked up at him, it was a number four.

+

356

Peter Barnard sat there knees pulled up to his chest looking out through the grating at the dimly lit landing outside his cell, he knew he could scream and shout all he liked, there was no one else there, this wing was empty and even the guards did not come around all that often. The barriers at regular intervals across the walkways made sure of that, even if he could get out of the cell he had no chance of getting out of the prison.

What he didn't know was that those other empty cells did not actually exist. What he was looking at outside the bars was in fact a large flat screen which showed an image about two metres from the bars he clung to so often. It was the same sideways, the barriers on the walkways were to stop him getting too close and finding out he was not in nearly as big a building as he thought he was.

In a room not far away one of the guards turned round and asked "Has he slept yet?" The other guard just shook his head "No, he's too scared, So far he's only slept when we've given him something otherwise he just keeps going." He looked back at the screen and said "Wonder if he realises he's going to be lost in the system forever, once we wipe his records and take away his nationality no one will ever be able to find him again shortly" the other guard shrugged "Who cares, once he leaves here he's not my problem anymore."

+

Parker so happened to be listening in the underground room not far away. He turned to the old man sitting next to him who had to turn round a long way to see him as he only had one eye. "How is it this rumour of the 'vanishing place' seems to have taken root so quickly and easily" the old man laughed, a single deep snort before he replied "People will always believe in evil. If someone once tells them about these things, the more you deny it the more they will believe it and when he goes and vanishes as I think he probably will do they will believe they had just had confirmation." He stopped talking and turned to fix his one good eye on Parker "You are going to vanish him aren't you?" Parker nodded "Yeah, too sensitive politically to have the man who successfully bribed the President in a conventional prison, so we'll be moving him to one of our European allies. We have an agreement with them whereby he will end up in a mental hospital for asylum seekers. One of those places where he will never be believed and will never come out of again. A few years in there and he will be as mad as they will say he is." The other man nodded "Hide in plain sight" Parker did not comment. Slowly he stood up and before he left pulled a plain brown padded envelope form his jacket pocket and dropped

357

it on the desk next to the old man "Do me a favour, post that on your way out when you leave please. The mail box at the end of the street will do." The old man just nodded and flipped the envelope over, it was stamped and the address was typed onto a label on the front of the envelope. The first line was 'Jonathon Diarmond' the old man just grunted and not reading any further swept it off the desk and into a drawer before turning back to his screens. Parker grinned to himself as he closed that heavy steel door behind him and headed up the stairs to the street, he had no doubt that the old man had noticed there was no return address on the envelope either.

+

Mark sighed as the house returned to an almost silent state again, the stereo was playing something classical, more Marianne's taste than his but not offensive as it played low in the background. The only accompaniment was the faint crackle of the logs burning in the stove and in the distance the sound of bare feet on the floor as Marianne came back up the hallway to the living room carrying two glasses and a wine bottle. He smiled at her, she was truly beautiful and she was happy as well after today's discussion, it looked like the world was a good place to be again, for a while at least.

He turned back to the window and looked out at the moonlight as it fell on the ocean in the fading blue light of evening. He could almost hear the sound of the few waves breaking on the beach and smell the salt that he knew was in the air outside, a deer suddenly moved out on the darkness, its white rump sharp and distinct against the ever growing darkness. It was a reminder that life still existed even where it was not obvious and that it would always survive somehow. He sighed once more before pulling the curtains closed and turning back to the warmth inside the room. Yes, life was good he decided.

20

Paul Barnard vanished without trace and was never heard of again, as did Number Three and Trente Silver himself; although the National Enquirer tried to do an article about some crazy old man in a home somewhere who claimed to be Trente Silver trapped and being held against his will. When they arrived all they found was some dull eyed old man in a wheelchair, suffering from Alzheimer's and under heavy medication. He had a telephone handset clutched in one hand that he would not let go of. When asked about it he said he was waiting on a call from one of his staff.

Andrew Crawford and Jennilee ended up running a 'dude ranch' in Montana. 'As far away from normal people as you can get' was the phrase they still use today to advertise themselves and their business, quietly to a very select and unpretentious clientele; in other words no one that might have known them in their previous life.

The Leyfield Environmental Centre now operates on land that used to be the Doones estate. The three directors of the company are Paul Gray, John McIntyre and Mark Rae. The 'Andy Mac' Construction Company are their preferred contractor for all work around the estate and in the local town as well. 'Leyfield', as its known, does a steady trade in environmental research trips to the area as well as developing renewable and sustainable energy sources which are slowly taking over the areas business stream and turning the area around Granitburgh into the 'Energy Capital of Europe.'

Ruriadh Cottage still exists but is a lot larger than it ever was before and has space for a live in carer. There isn't a live in carer at the moment as Arthur is fitter and more able than he has been for years, it seems as though having his family around him has almost reversed the aging process.

Andy and Magda still run the Drimmie Inn together and have a strong healthy pair of twins to help them. The twins are bilingual, Andy isn't. They also run photography tours and holidays for environmentalists on the local estate with the full support and cooperation of the owners.

Abby McIntyre works as a freelance writer and journalist from a small apartment tucked away above the offices in what used to be the stable block, just across the track from her grandfathers cottage.

Jonathon Diarmond is also a professional freelance writer and author, he still occasionally does specials for the *'National Central'* and the memory sticks keep dropping through his own letter box, not that of the newspaper, at regular intervals.

Parker is rumoured to have been seen buying a grey suit.

About the author

This is David's second book, his first, "Blinded by the Bling" (ISBN 978-0-9559269-0-7) was published by MilHouse Publishing in 2008 and is a small factual book about the Donald Trump development at Menie in Aberdeenshire.

David is currently working on a variety of other projects; but he has a question for the reader; what do you see on the front cover of this book?

www.itsonlysand.com

Lightning Source UK Ltd.
Milton Keynes UK
05 June 2010

155150UK00001B/46/P

9 780955 926914